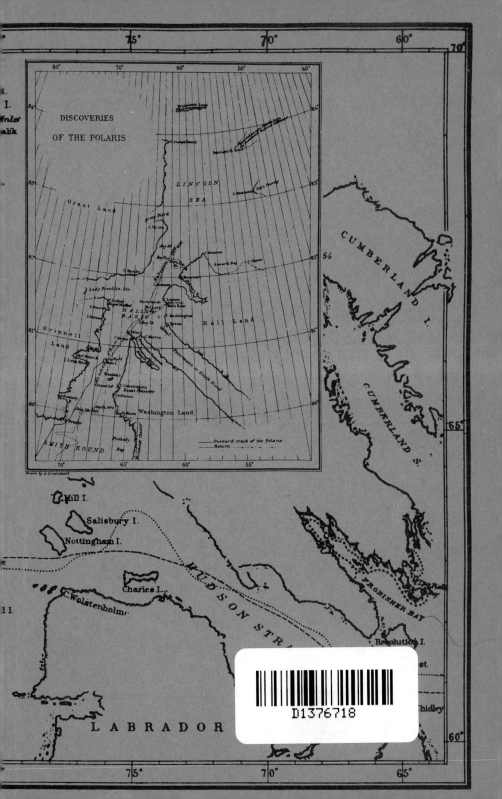

CALL OF THE ARCTIC

CALL OF

Robert Steelman

THE ARCTIC

Coward-McCann, Inc. *New York*

THE FIRST VOYAGE

1860–1862

Chapter 1

THE first time I saw Mr. Charles Francis Hall, he did not look to me like an Arctic explorer. Wretched to the soles of his boots, he hung over the rail of the *George Henry* whaler, giving up his recent supper to the North Atlantic cod. A merest greenie myself, it seemed some comfort to find someone sicker than I. Misery being relative, I felt better for the sight of him, and did not suspect how our lives were to be knotted together during the next ten years.

But how can I tell you about Mr. Hall if I do not first tell you something about myself, Adam Burritt? Well, I was born in Cincinnati, where my father was a shoemaker. He wanted his son to have a good education, and managed to send me to Harvard College for a year. In studies that I was interested in, such as languages and philosophy, I did well, but after a year my father's funds ran out. Being nineteen, and thoughtless and adventuresome into the bargain, I fell in with a student of like tendencies. Josiah Clegg was nephew to a man connected with

Williams and Haven, the New London whaling firm, and wealthy. Both of us had tired of the classroom, and we considered enlisting in the army. A war seemed to be brewing; the President had just declared a blockade of Southern ports, and some of the states talked of seceding from the Union. But finally, through Josiah's uncle, we shipped instead on the *George Henry* for the Arctic whaling. When it came time to sail, Josiah Clegg backed out. Now here was I, Adam Burritt, friendless and frightened, sailing down the channel toward the Race, and regretting my rashness. Making shoes in Cincinnati, it seemed to me then, might have been a better idea.

Captain Budington of the *George Henry* was a severe man, but just. A small, compact Presbyterian with a fringe of pepper-and-salt chin whiskers, he wore a flat-brimmed felt hat winter and summer, and was reputed to wear it in bed. Twice a week he conducted prayer meetings for the ship's company, and he must have been very familiar with the Lord and the various Apostles, because he brought them frequently into his conversation.

The crew was a varied lot: raw landsmen, a few old Arctic hands like Coleman and Shipway and Vess and Sterry, a sprinkle of Innuit natives, and the passenger named Hall, a would-be Arctic explorer. Coleman, who had been told by the captain to keep an eye on Hall's deckload of supplies, told me the story. Charles Hall was from Cincinnati, too; a big brown-bearded man with deep-set eyes, who had talked the whaling company into delivering him and his traps to Cumberland Sound. On his own, the ex-engraver and newspaperman had gotten together funds to investigate the fate of the lost Franklin expedition of 1847, some thirteen years earlier. Now, a complete amateur, Hall had a longboat, a sledge, several hundred pounds of pemmican, and a few scientific instruments under a canvas on deck. "Jesus!" growled Coleman, and spat to leeward. "Why did old Bud wish him on me?" He shook his head, tightening down the lashings on the longboat. "The ice country ain't no

[8

place for fools! It'll throw him up and spit him out, soon enough!"

I looked over my shoulder at New London, disappearing behind us in a haze of fog. A whaler leaving that town was of no more consequence than another pot of beans fresh-baked in Boston, or a gross of copper-toed boots shipped from Lynn. The docks were filled with whalers fitting out for the coming season, and no one noticed our departure. No bands played, no speeches were made; it was a business, no different from baking beans or making boots. I felt a clammy hand at my heart, and wanted suddenly to run and jump over the side; anything to get out of the foolish project I had entered on. But the *George Henry* kept on her silent way, slipping down toward the Race, and I stood there and did nothing, watching our companion, the schooner *Amoret,* on our quarter.

"Sick?" Coleman snickered, and hitched up his pants. "We ain't out of the channel yet!"

I shook my head. "I'm all right."

If I felt tolerable, in spite of my sadness at seeing land slip away over our stern rail, there were others who made no bones about their queasiness. Mr. Hall, the explorer, stood for a while on the quarter-deck with Captain Budington, and seemed to be enjoying himself. After a while, though, he went below to his cabin, and was sick for three days. Since I was not yet good for much else, Mr. Rogers, our first officer, kept me busy picking oakum and helping the cook. I might have been sick, but I was too busy. And after a while, I began to enjoy the roll and pitch of the *George Henry.* When you are nineteen, there are no problems in life except love, and I had nearly forgot the black-eyed New Haven miss who had given me a lock of her hair in a little enamel box.

The forecastle of the *George Henry* was a rough-and-ready place, and I had my share of jokes played on me. Some of them were merely the good-natured horseplay that I already knew from my Harvard College dormitory, but others were mean and spiteful. Coleman, a misanthrope and braggart, delighted in ragging me. Others grew to be my friends, teaching me the names of the sails and the yards, and showing me the stars by night, and imparting a smattering of navigation. Sterry, the blacksmith and cooper, was a roistering rascal who could eat more pork and beans and drink more whisky out of a quart pantry pitcher than any three men aboard. I tended his forge and worked the bellows, listening to him talk.

"Now there's the porpoise." He drank a tin cupful of whisky, and spat part of it on the harpoon blade he was mending. "A curious fish, Adam. Look now, are you in love? You must be, of course; a handsome young lad like you, with blue eyes and ginger hair."

"I was, I guess."

"Well, I'll tell you what to do. It's not generally known, but the porpoise is a sentimental fish. Some night try this. Go up in the chains and whistle for a porpoise."

"Whistle?"

"Aye." He nodded, serious. "They like musical sounds, you see. Just whistle, very soft and low, and they'll come under the bow and listen to you. Then all you have to do is whisper a message to 'em—any old thing at all, like how you're pining for your sweet gal. And do you know what?"

"What?"

"Why, they'll see the message gets to her, that's what! She'll know. I've never seen it fail."

I dumped another bucket of coal into the forge. "How's a porpoise to get all the way up to New Haven? That's where she lives."

Sterry grinned. "That's not my problem, nor either yours. Leave that to the porpoises."

Kudlago was another who befriended me. He was an Innuit, as they called the Esquimaux of Greenland and that vicinity, a stocky little brown man who was perpetually smiling. Dressed in an old stocking cap and sealskin jacket, he was the best of the topside sailors, more at home on the highest yard than on the firm planks of the deck. Captain Budington had brought him to New London on a previous voyage, and now Kudlago was anxious to get back to his wife and child. In the forecastle he had nailed a wooden shelf above his bunk, and placed on it a small carved ivory idol—his *an-ge-ko,* he called it—that he prayed to every night and morning. There was bad blood between Kudlago and Coleman; one night the insufferable Coleman had taken up the idol to examine it, and Kudlago knocked him down and threatened him with a knife.

Mr. Hall had paid a sum of money to Kudlago to act as his hunter and guide on his proposed expedition, and when Mr. Hall was free of his *mal de mer* they frequently got together to discuss plans. The Innuits were born topographers and map makers, and Kudlago drew maps from his memory of the coast of Greenland and Baffin Island, maps which to Mr. Hall's delight checked closely with Mr. Hall's own, obtained from the American Geographical Society.

"Here," Kudlago would say, pointing with a stubby finger, "is where Kudlago born. Long time ago, in great storm."

"Yes," Mr. Hall would say eagerly, "and here, near the mouth of Lancaster Sound, is where the *Erebus* and *Terror* were last seen. Over here, near what Kudlago indicates as Point Victory, is where McClintock of the *Fox* found the note that indicated Franklin himself had died, and Crozier had abandoned the ships to start with the survivors on a march to Great Fish River. Over a hundred men! Where are they now, eh?"

We were far out on the North Atlantic, well on our way to Holsteinsborg, in Greenland (where we were to stop for coal and supplies) before Mr. Hall seemed to find his sea legs. The *George Henry* was a steam whaler, having a small engine below decks, but she depended for the most part on sail. Now the patched canvas bellied and snapped, and every few seconds a generous dollop of green water roared over our bows and flooded the foredeck. It was a fine day, and perhaps the fresh bracing air at last cured Mr. Hall's seasickness for good. He came up beside me at the rail, winding a plaid muffler about his neck, and pointed to a ruffle of foam snaking along our quarter.

"*Balaena physalis,*" he said. "The sulphur-bottom whale."

I had thought it was only an extra-large porpoise, but I did not let on.

"Not much good for either blubber or bone," he said. "The whalers will not take them unless there is nothing else."

He did not sound like such an amateur as I had been led to believe. "I'm Adam Burritt," I said and held out my hand. "And you're Mr. Hall, the one that's going north to look for the Franklin people."

He took my hand in a quick powerful grip and leaned on the rail beside me. "I hope to find them," he said. "I will find them, if they are living. If not, I will find out what their fate was, and carry back such relics as there may be for proof."

"How did you know that was a sulphur-bottom whale?"

He laughed and turned toward me. I was impressed by the way his deep-set eyes glowed with an inner light; no, not light, but rather a heat that seemed to warm and excite.

"Adam, I have read every book on the Arctic and the northern oceans that has ever been written. Every tract, every pamphlet and monograph, every diary, every scientific journal—I have read them all."

"But—reading—"

"Is a fact any the less true because one man read it in a book, while another knows it from experience? No, my friend—that is *Balaena physalis,* you may depend on that."

When he learned that I, too, was from Cincinnati, he was very pleased. "I live on Celestial Street," he said. "Do you know where that is? My wife and children are there now." He went on to tell me how the sad fate of the Franklin people had moved him, how he had poured his own savings and the small amount subscribed by friends into his "expedition." He spoke

with the eagerness of one who suddenly finds a willing audience. "Twelve hundred dollars, and now it's all gone, and some
I borrowed besides." He nodded toward the canvas-shrouded
bulk of his supplies. "But I've got what I need. My boat, the
sledge I had made, a thousand pounds of pemmican and meat
biscuit, my nautical instruments and thermometers. And I engaged Kudlago to travel with me, and be my guide and hunter.
That was a stroke of good luck."

Sterry called me away then to pump his damned bellows, and
I left Mr. Hall standing at the rail, face wet with spray, his
brown beard flying in the wind and a look of fierce enjoyment
on his face. A remarkable man, I thought. A fool? Perhaps. But
there was something solid you felt in speaking to him; a kind of
rocklike quality, that might embark on a fool's errand, but
would never give it up.

Coleman, as I have said, had been told to keep an eye on Mr.
Hall's supplies. No one else was allowed to come near them,
and Coleman shirked his other work considerably on the pre-
text that it was time to check the lashings on the load. It was a
problem, of course; with the *George Henry* reeling about in
heavy seas, two or three tons of deckload come adrift would be
dangerous. That was exactly what happened one afternoon. A
pass of a rope around a bitt came off, and the upside-down longboat began to swing to and fro under the canvas, scraping and
bashing, one end of it thudding into the boxes that held Mr.
Hall's scientific instruments. The canvas tore down the middle
and the loose ends flapped and popped in the wind. Mr. Rogers
whistled us all out, and we had the devil's own time, one man
getting a mashed foot when the swinging longboat caught him
against the rail. Coleman was nowhere around; only when the
load had been lashed down again and a fresh canvas pulled
over it, did he appear.

"Now where in the name of Judas Priest were ye, eh?" old
Bud shouted. "Coleman, ye scut, I told ye to keep an eye on Mr.
Hall's outfit!"

Coleman was an old-timer, and knew just how far he could press the captain.

"In the galley, having a cup of coffee. I ain't supposed to sit here all day and night, am I, and watch the precious stuff?"

Mr. Hall was angry, too, and shaken. "I told you those lines weren't tight enough!" He advanced on Coleman, eyes wild and fists clenched. I think he would have beaten him if Captain Budington had not stepped between them. Old Bud knew as well as I did that Coleman carried a Malay knife in a sheath up his sleeve, ready to hand. "If anything had happened—"

"Easy now," old Bud said. "I'll take care of this, Mr. Hall."

Coleman stood his ground, eying Mr. Hall for a moment. But there was such a terrible anger in Mr. Hall that Coleman suddenly licked his lips uncertainly and dropped his eyes. He squirmed like a bug dropped on red coals; in Mr. Hall's gaze he seemed to shrivel and die. Mr. Hall's wrath was majestic, like a thunderstorm at sea; impersonal and awful.

"I'm sorry," Coleman whined at last. "I didn't mean to do no harm, Captain. Can't a man make a little mistake?"

Mr. Hall trembled, so filled with wrath that its earthly container was about to burst. I was glad that I had not been the one to tamper, accidentally or otherwise, with his traps. His mission was to him, at least, almost holy. Interfering with it amounted to profaning an altar.

Captain Budington looked Coleman in the eye. "It won't go so easy with you next time. When I give a man a job, I expect it to be done proper. If that load should come adrift again, I'll string ye up and give ye a dose of the cat."

Mr. Hall turned abruptly on his heel and stalked off to his cabin.

"All right," said old Bud. "Back to your work, all."

That was the end of it, for a while.

Every ship has its cliques. Sometimes they are so strong in their organization that they will not work properly together, even when the ship is in danger. The test of a good captain is whether he can take all these separate groups and fit them together in a way that lets the work of the ship get on as it should. Old Bud was a good captain, one of the best. The Budingtons of New London were known from the Sandwich Islands to Disko. And so the *George Henry* plowed on toward Holsteinsborg. Whaling gear was got ready; the ship's longboats were newly calked and painted; lines were examined inch by inch, and coiled into tubs. The aggrieved Coleman had his adherents, who were of the opinion that he had been badly treated by the captain, although their principal grievance was against the landsman Hall. Kudlago was the champion of the other group, who had oftener than not suffered at Coleman's hands. This latter group did not generally subscribe to the belief that Mr. Hall would be successful in his search. Instead, they championed Hall only out of dislike for Patrick Coleman. In addition to these principal groups, there were subgroups, common to both parties, who were Douglas men, Lincoln men; believers in a flannel rag around the neck for a colic, and scoffers at the remedy; men who had signed the pledge and men who drank a quart of whisky at a sitting; men who were Baptists, Presbyterians, and Holy Rollers; men who knew certain intimate biological facts about Esquimaux women, and men who denied their knowledge. I was fast becoming educated in a way my father, or Harvard College either, had never intended.

A snowbird came and settled on our rigging, which Sterry told me meant good luck. We passed through a fleet of Newfoundland cod fishers bobbing about in their tiny sloops, far out on the banks. One hailed us, and the captain sold them a keg of rum, which they were out of. And we came into the latitudes of the northern lights. The days had by now lengthened greatly, so that it was light until far into the evening. After I had peeled a half bushel of potatoes for the morning mess, Cookie turned me loose and I was free to go abovedecks for a while. I stood in the bows watching the dying light, only to be aware that as the sun slipped over the edge of the world, a new and growing light waxed in the north. Vertical red and gold rays shimmered and moved like silken draperies. Along the base of the curtain, from end to end, ran a continuous stream of prismatic fires, and golden rays of light jetted upward and raced back and forth. For a long time I watched, fascinated, and when I looked around, the ghostly glow cast a pale radiance on the faces of the crew—and on the face of Charles Hall, who stood by my side. His eyes shone back the glow, and his face was turned up as if to catch the full impact of the light.

I spoke to him and he did not seem to hear me.

"Isn't it wonderful?" I asked again.

He looked at me, seeming to ponder, and then turned back to watch the scene. Although no more than a pistol shot away, the lights fled as fast as the *George Henry* and the *Amoret* came up on them. After a long time, wherein everyone was silent and there was no sound but the licking of the water at the hull, the creak of timbers, and the muffled beat of the whaler's engine, the lights disappeared from the sky, one by one, fading mutely away until it was full dark.

"You may think it very queer of me, Adam," Mr. Hall said, his voice low and grave, "but I must tell you something. I, who have never been there, love the snows and ice of the North. I love the circling sun, the long day, the Arctic night."

"I don't find it queer," I said.

"Then you are different from most of the others." He sighed. "I do not mean to ask for sympathy from any man; I am strong in that respect, and will continue so. But it is a fact that I have taken abuse from scientific men who discount my theory that I may yet find the lost Franklin men living as natives in the Far North. I gave a lecture once, to raise funds, and was hooted from the stage. I have given up my newspaper, my family, all my hopes of material gain in this life, only to go on a mission of love, for that is what I call it. I feel to be in the performance of duty I owe mankind—myself—God Himself!"

He was so strong in his feelings that his voice quivered.

"I know it may sound foolish to those people who are experts in the field, but I believe that the fate of the Franklin people is too important, too pressing, to be left to the experts. They have decided that nothing can be done; very well! That is their privilege. I have decided that something *can* be done, and I will do it."

He was eloquent, and there was a roughhewn sincerity to him that moved me. "I believe you," I said warmly. "And if there is anything that I can do to help, Mr. Hall, just you let me know, sir. I am your man."

For a long moment he looked at me, his face in shadow, but a feeling of great emotion seeming to emanate from him and link us. Finally he thrust out one big hand and took mine in it, wringing it until I almost cried out with pain.

"Thank you for that, Adam." He gave my hand another squeeze and hurried away.

On the Fourth of July we were still at sea, almost becalmed, running too low on coal for our engine to proceed under steam. Becalmed or not, it was a holiday. Cookie made a duff from sea biscuit and dried apples, moistened with rum and baked in the oven. There was firing of pistols and much yelling from the crew when old Bud ran up the national colors and announced an extra whisky ration to all hands. The extra whisky was, I think, what led to the trouble that came next.

Mr. Hall had been making a dictionary of the Innuit language to guide him in his proposed explorations. Each day he and Kudlago would get together in a protected angle of the deckhouse, and when the Innuit pronounced the words Mr. Hall would write them phonetically in the big ledger he carried. I, too, was interested in Innuit; I had always had a flair for languages, and when Mr. Hall mentioned that Innuit had no letter "c," and only twenty-four letters in all, that was enough to whet my curiosity.

"*Muk-tuk*," Hall repeated, writing the word in his ledger.

Kudlago roared with laughter at his queer way of saying the word. "*Muk-tuk*," he said again, trying to correct Mr. Hall. "That word mean 'whale.' That very important word. You better learn right, sir."

"*Muk-tuk*," said Mr. Hall again, very patiently.

Some of the crew members not on watch, enjoying the good-natured wrangling, gathered around in the thin sunlight, laughing and eying Kudlago and Mr. Hall. They had recently watched Mr. Hall measure the temperature of the sea water with his patent thermometer, and there was much speculation about his prediction that we were near icebergs, on account of the water being only at 34° on the Fahrenheit scale. Old Bud stoutly denied it, claiming that he had never encountered bergs so far south at this time of year.

"*Tupik*," Kudlago said. "That small skin tent my people make to live in. *Tupik*." His face became sad, and his eyes were moist. "My woman, my little baby—they live in *tupik* right now. I make *tupik*—very good."

When the session was finished I went below to my bunk. The extra whisky, in which I did not join, had had its effect on the rest of the crew, and there was much singing and scuffling and carousing. I was half-asleep, pondering on the singular lack of the letter "c" in Innuit, when I heard the sounds of a fight going on topside; loud shouts, the stamp of boots, cheers and curses. I came awake in a spatter of reality, like a soap bubble bursting in my face, and sat up half-dazed. Then I got into my boots and jacket, and hurried on deck.

Kudlago and Patrick Coleman were fighting. In the lee of Mr. Hall's canvas-wrapped longboat they pummeled and beat each other, rolling fiercely about. Captain Budington was bawling from the quarter-deck through his speaking trumpet, and I saw the mate, Mr. Rogers, hurrying toward them. Coleman was a good head taller than the stocky Innuit, and was having the better of it. He had Kudlago in a bear hug, his head under Kudlago's chin, pushing hard and forcing the Innuit's head back at an angle sufficient to snap a man's neck. But Kudlago was wily. A few seasons in the whalers had taught him the tricks of rough-and-tumble fighting. As I watched, he got a knee into Coleman's belly and drove it home, hard. Coleman yelled in pain, and relaxed his grip.

"Here, now!" Mr. Rogers yelled, trying to pull them apart. "What's this all about?" He grabbed Coleman, and Mr. Hall, who had just come on deck, pinioned Kudlago's arms. "Stop it now!" Mr. Rogers shouted. "Stop it before I take a fist to the both of you!"

Old Bud bellowed through his speaking trumpet. "What's the matter, Mr. Rogers? What's going on down there? By the Prophets, sir, speak up!"

Kudlago motioned at Coleman. "Him thief."

"Dirty heathen!" Coleman panted. "Call me names, will he?"

Kudlago gestured at the canvas-wrapped supplies. "Him try to get in there. Steal."

With a sudden twist, Coleman broke away from the mate's grasp and seized a belaying pin from the rack at the rail. With an oath, he brought it down on Kudlago's head. The Innuit slumped in Mr. Hall's arms, blood running from a cut over his ear.

Old Bud himself broke through the grinning crowd, and although several inches shorter than Coleman, he took a handful of the seaman's jacket and shook him. "By every Apostle, I'll put the both of ye in irons! Now what's the truth of this?"

"I wasn't doing nothing!" Coleman protested. "I was just tightening the lashings, like I was told! This drunken heathen rushed at me from behind, he did, and like to choked me to death before I could defend myself proper."

Mr. Hall had Kudlago's head on his knee and was trying to

stanch the flow of blood. "Ah, Kudlago! There's a good fellow; try to sit up. Maybe it will stop the bleeding."

"He's all right," old Bud said. "They've got heads like oak, all of them. Is it true, Mr. Hall? Was anything taken?"

Mr. Hall examined his traps. There was no evidence of tampering, but perhaps Coleman had been surprised by Kudlago before he had broken into anything. "No," he said. "Nothing's been taken. There is a valuable sextant in there, and a nautical chronometer. I should have been very angry if they had been taken, or damaged in any way."

Coleman said, "I didn't do nothing, I tell you. He's a damned liar."

Captain Budington was angry, but uncertain. He looked from Kudlago to Coleman, and then back again. "A sextant would be worth quite a bit of money on the beach," he said. "Low in funds, were ye, Coleman?"

Kudlago tried feebly to get at Coleman again but Mr. Hall restrained him, and finally old Bud said, "Well, there's no way to get at the truth of it, Mr. Hall. It's one saying he did, and the other saying he didn't." He dropped his grasp of Coleman's jacket and motioned the sailors to get back to their duties. "Take him to the galley, please, Mr. Hall, and have Cookie rub some butter on his head and tie a rag around it. And hear this!" He raised a knobby fist, and his gray whiskers stood out as if there were electric fluid in them. "The *George Henry* is a good ship, and there's no room aboard for trouble-makers of any color! That goes for you, Patrick Coleman, and for you, Kudlago, and for anyone else that needs the advice! The next time there'll be a dozen lashes for all parties concerned."

Calms and head winds made our passage unbearably slow. For days the ship's log showed nothing but tack, tack, tack, with the wind dead ahead. We were already forty days out on a passage that should not take more than thirty at the most. The

Amoret, being faster into the wind than the *George Henry,* was often forced to lay to so as to keep our company, and the slow progress told on the ship's company. Tempers flared, stomachs rebelled at the endless diet of salt junk and ship's biscuit, we having some time ago run out of all fresh stuff. Mr. Hall, however, put his time to good use. He was endlessly eager for knowledge, and when the talk turned on scurvy he caused both old Bud and Mr. Rogers, the mate, to tell him their experiences.

"On the old *Georgiana,* in fifty-five," said old Bud, "I lost thirteen men by scurvy, but by our Lord Jesus Christ I am not afraid of losing any more the same route. Whenever there are appearances of it aboard, I will have every pork and beef barrel—salt provision of every kind—boarded up at once. Every man shall live on bread and such fresh provision as the good God grants."

Mr. Rogers agreed, and I saw Mr. Hall copying into his ledger what the mate said.

"In the South Seas, nine of the men of the *Henry Terry* got sick from the scurvy, and one died. But the queer thing about it was this: those who had it seemed *determined* to die, for against all reasoning and advice, they would have salt pork in preference to the fresh stuff which was in abundance."

Mr. Hall would have worked also on his Innuit dictionary, but for Kudlago feeling ill and complaining of headaches. The native was excused by the captain from his duties and went to sit on a box in the sun, his back leaning against the deckhouse. I went to take him a cup of soup from the galley one day, but he suddenly leaned against me, deathly pale.

"What is it?" I asked.

For reply, a needlelike stream of blood shot from his ear, driven with tremendous force like a jet of steam. It splattered my shirt and hands, and I dropped the cup and tried to help him, calling at the same time for Mr. Hall. Kudlago was insensible, and between us we dragged him to the forecastle and put him into his bunk. Outside, in the companionway, the sailors gathered to offer advice.

"Something he ate," Sterry said. "Them Esquimaux, they'll eat anything! The worse a piece of meat stinks, the better they like it."

"Rub camphor oil on his chest."

"It's colic. Give him turpentine."

I tried to wipe the blood off my hands with a rag, and felt myself getting sick.

"You had better go outside, Adam," Mr. Hall said. He and the captain rummaged through the medicine chest, looking for something to bring him around.

Mr. Hall shook his head. "A brain fever of some kind, I think."

"Got calomel and spirits of niter and such as that in here. What do ye think?"

Mr. Hall knelt beside Kudlago looking at the ashen face, listening to the labored breathing. "I will stay with him for a while. Maybe some sign will show itself—a rash or a griping. Then we can know better what to do."

The rest of that day, and all of the night, Kudlago lay senseless in his bunk, Mr. Hall tending his wants and being as gentle with him as a woman. The cook brought broth from the galley, and the captain got out a bottle of Scotch whisky and heated some in a tin cup. The liquor only rolled out of the unconscious man's jaws. Mr. Hall knelt beside him, talking in soothing tones.

"You'll be all right. You've got to be all right, Kudlago. I depend on you! I need you to be my guide and hunter when we get to Cumberland Sound."

Later—much later—Kudlago woke from his daze. He seemed not to know Mr. Hall or me, but he clutched Mr. Hall's hand and muttered thickly.

"Eh?" Mr. Hall put his ear close to the Innuit's lips. "What was that?"

"*An-ge-ko*," I said. "That's what it sounded like."

"Of course." Mr. Hall went to the shelf above the bunk and brought down the carved ivory figure. "That's what he wants." He put it into Kudlago's hand. "There, old fellow. There's your *an-ge-ko*, or medicine man, or whatever you call him."

After that, Kudlago seemed to rally. His ear no longer bled, and he lay quietly in his bunk, staring at the ivory idol with a kind of contentment. Occasionally he would rouse himself and speak to Mr. Hall in Innuit.

"*Teik-ko-seko?*" he would ask, over and over. "*Teik-ko-seko?*"

I asked Mr. Hall what it meant.

"He's asking 'Is there ice?'" Mr. Hall was gaunt and hollow-eyed from his unending attentions to Kudlago these past days, with very little sleep, and he reeled when he straightened up from his accustomed kneeling position. "Ice means home to Kudlago. He wants to be home again, among the ice floes." He wrung out a cloth that he had dipped in cold water, and put it on Kudlago's brow. "Yes," he said. "We are coming into the ice now. This morning I measured the temperature of the water again, and it is only a degree or two above freezing."

The next morning Kudlago died, slipping away very quietly. They wrapped him in his blanket and buried him at sea, Mr. Hall reading a service over him from the Masonic Manual. Afterward Mr. Hall stood for a long time at the rail, looking at the gray waters that had closed over his good friend. Captain Budington came up and stood beside him, trying to cheer him a little. "He wasn't a Christian," old Bud said, "but the good Lord's bound to look out for him wherever he's gone."

"I'm sure he will," said Mr. Hall quietly.

"He was all right. He was a good man. Always pulled his weight, and never asked for favors."

"That is true." Mr. Hall went into his cabin.

Feeling sorry for him at the death of his friend, I followed him to his cabin hoping to cheer him. At my first knock, no one answered. I knocked again; no response. Finally, screwing up my courage, I opened the door and went in.

I will not soon forget Mr. Hall's appearance. Disheveled and distraught as he was by his constant attendance on the sick Kudlago, the death and burial of the Innuit had put him in an almost maniacal state. Before others he preserved an outward calm, but in the solitude of his cabin he gave full rein to bitterness and anger long kept down.

"Coleman!" He gnawed at his knuckles, scarcely seeing me. "That devil! It is queer I had not thought of it before." His deepset eyes burned. "Of course! The blow on the head, while I held poor Kudlago's arms behind him. Adam, what a part I have played in this sorry business!"

He rose and rushed toward the door. Fearing he would do himself harm, or harm others in his rashness, I caught his arm. It was like trying to stop a charging bull, and the force of the encounter spun me around and drove me into the bulkhead. But I cried out after him, and at the door he stopped, breathing heavily and staring at me with eyes like two hard and polished agates.

"Where are you going?"

"To settle accounts with the rascal."

"Wait a while. Let me talk to you, first." As he paused, uncertain, I pressed on. "You have no proof it was so. Innuits are apt to die suddenly and strangely, with no apparent cause. Sterry said it was so. He's known it to happen."

"No," said Mr. Hall. "I won't let you talk me out of it. This is something I am bound to do. The man must be punished."

Seeing this tack was getting nowhere, I tried another.

"Trouble of this sort will not do your expedition any good. You have made extensive plans; I should hate to see you in chains because of a thoughtless action."

His eyes widened as if a strange thought had come on him. The heat went out of his gaze and his bearded chin fell on his chest. His hand dropped from the doorknob and he seemed to slump, becoming inches shorter and pounds lighter. "True," he muttered. "Ah, Adam, you have hit me for fair!"

Going to the small table and chair that were the only furniture of his tiny cabin, he sat down, head in his hands. For a long time he didn't speak, nor did I. The only sound was the creaking of timbers and the slatting of the sails as the *George Henry* wallowed on.

"Hit you?" I stammered. "I—I don't understand."

"I—I hope you will not think ill of me, Adam. But I must confess that your words struck home, in a way that I must make clear. I was very fond of Kudlago, that is true. But in my anger at Patrick Coleman, I now see that I was not thinking of poor Kudlago. I was only desperate because my own plans had been so upset. It was selfish of me and your words have brought me to my senses." He shook his massive head in a regretful way. "If you, or the others, only knew what I have gone through to get this far—"

I would never think, nor would anyone, of calling him anything but Mr. Hall. But I did touch him on the sleeve timidly and say, "You will succeed, sir. People will hear of you."

He looked at me with pathetic gratitude. "There are precious few who believe in me, Adam."

I went out on deck and closed the door after me. Standing at the rail to clear my head and let my pulse subside, I looked aft. There, over Kudlago's watery grave, was an immense iceberg, the first I had ever seen. We had come into the ice Mr. Hall had predicted.

Chapter 2

AT LAST we put into the harbor of Holsteinsborg, on the west coast of Greenland. It was late in July, and old Bud was grumpy because the whaling season was rapidly passing; as yet we had nothing to show for it. We were still a long way from the whaling grounds off Baffin Island, but we were out of coal and fresh provision, and there was no choice but to take on these things at Holsteinsborg. Mr. Hall was pleased to make that port, also, since the mate had told him of Lars Kleijt, a famous Esquimaux ice pilot who might be induced to go along as guide and hunter in his projected trip.

I got a good look at Holsteinsborg and didn't think much of it. There was every opportunity of inspection, since the sun now hardly set at all, only dipping under the horizon and then coming up again to start the day over again. The harbor was good and landlocked, and there were many buildings of wood and rock, including the governor's house, a church and schoolhouse, and others to the number of thirty or so. Although the principal city of Greenland and the seat of the Danish colony, it looked to me like a small country hamlet in Ohio except for the towering snow-capped mountains that reared up back of the town.

After two months at sea, everyone was anxious to get ashore. Being such a landsman, and not yet good for much but cleaning bilges and polishing brasswork, I had little hope of getting ashore, at least not for some time. But Mr. Hall put in a word for me, and I was allowed to pull an oar in the longboat that went in with Captain Budington and the officers to pay their respects to Governor Elberg.

"See there!" Mr. Hall called out, pointing to the native boats all around us. "Adam, those are called *ki-as,* those small one-man boats. And the larger ones with the women in them are called *oo-mi-en.*" He had quite recovered from his depression, and was jolly and eager. "Did anyone ever see such a land?" He spread his arms wide and inhaled the cold clear air. "A great land, a big land, an important land!"

"Whales is what I'm after," old Bud said. "If we don't get whales, you can have this icebox, Mr. Hall, and welcome to it!"

Coming in to the dock, we shipped our oars, and immediately ran into hordes of mosquitoes. They hung about us in smokelike swarms, whining and singing, pausing only to tattoo us with red-hot stingers. I had seen mosquitoes around the Ohio River before but these were a new and deadly brand, three times the size and with audacity unmatched by a catamount. Before we got ashore, we were all of us lumpy and blotched.

The governor met us at the dock. He was a plump and cheerful Dane, speaking excellent English, and quite immune to the mosquitoes. Wearing a gold chain of office about his neck and sealskin boots of spotted fur, he welcomed us in the name of the King of Denmark. Whalers were the chief diversion of this lonely port, and when we reached the governor's house, only a short walk away, it was evident that preparations had been made for the *George Henry*. A table was laid with duck, salmon, trout, butter, American cheese, and white-flour bread. Flanking this spread were a dozen or two bottles of a Danish strong drink they called *akvavit*. But these refreshments were for the officers of the *George Henry* and *Amoret,* and Mr. Hall. The sailors, including me, were put to work loading coal into tow sacks and dragging them down to our boats.

I had never worked so hard in my life as I did the next three days. But there was a good feeling about it that can only come to a healthy young man, long penned in the classroom and suddenly called upon to use the muscle and sinew that are his birthright. I was black and sooty as a chimney sweep. At night I ached and smarted in every square inch of my body, but I was proud to find that I could keep up with Sterry and Keeney and Stokes and the rest. Besides, labor was somehow different—transformed and exotic—in this remote Greenland harbor, smelling of fish and tar and seaweed. The gulls squawked and wheeled, grinning Innuit children surrounded us begging for pennies, tobacco, sugar—it was all new and wonderful, and here was I, Adam Burritt, in the midst of it!

Hard labor is the lot of the sailor, and the sailors from the *George Henry* worked willingly, not imagining that anything less was expected of them. All of them, that is, but Patrick Coleman. Every ship's crew has its shirker, its professional gossip and talebearer, its sea lawyer. Where these men get their information is unknown; there is some kind of an electric telegraph in them connected like a spider's web with the sources of ship secrets.

"I hear," said Coleman, "that our fine Mr. Hall is not getting on too well with Governor Elberg."

It was the third day of coaling and we were all glad of a rest. Usually we let Coleman talk, and paid little attention. But tired as we were, and all of us interested in Mr. Hall, we laid down our shovels and listened.

"It is about Lars Kleijt, the pilot," Coleman said. "Mr. Hall wants him to come along to Cumberland Sound and be his guide."

Sterry took out a dirty kerchief and wiped his mouth, leaving a whitened ring like the end man in a "Bones" show. "You're a nosy one," he observed. "Better keep your tongue secured, or old Bud will tie a knot in it."

Coleman grinned, unperturbed. "Kleijt doesn't want to come," he said. "Mr. Hall asked the governor to persuade him, but Elberg won't have nothing to do with it. He says it's a decision for Kleijt to make. They say Mr. Hall spoke very sharply to the governor about it, claiming it's his duty to aid and assist him; he's got a letter of some kind from the governor of Ohio calling on all men to help him. But Governor Elberg never heard of Ohio; he thinks it is in the Sandwich Islands someplace."

"Talk!" scoffed Keeney. "If you carried coal the way you flap your mouth, we'd be done with this here coaling, and off to Cape True!"

"What else do you know?" someone asked.

Coleman looked important.

"If you don't believe what I have to say——"

Sterry grinned. "Ah, we believe you, Coleman. You're a monument to truth, a whited sepulcher!"

"All right, then," said Coleman. "There's to be a dance when we finish coaling. On Sunday, that is, after church, in the government dance house."

"A dance?" I asked. "Whom do we dance with? There aren't but a couple white ladies in Holsteinsborg; Mrs. Kjer and Miss Bulou."

Sterry roared with laughter. "Why, Adam, you dance with the Innuit ladies! Mrs. Kjer and Miss Bulou is for the officers' entertainment, not for the likes of us common seamen!" He took a swig of whisky from the stone bottle he always carried with him, and drove the cork back in with a blow of his hand. "What do you think they let us load all this coal for, man? Why, it's to get us in shape for dancing with Esquimaux women! It takes a strong back and great endurance! Aye, they'll swing you off your feet and out the window if you don't grapple with 'em, and stand your ground. And smell!" He raised his eyes heavenward and groaned. "Some say it's the rotten fish they eat. Whatever it is, it hangs about them like a fog, and it takes a strong man to strike out through it and find the woman beneath!"

Someone whistled a warning through his teeth. "Here comes old Bud!"

We went back to our work. A moment later Captain Budington and Mr. Hall came down the path, Mr. Hall with his Greenland dog on a leash. Barbekark, he was called, and Mr. Hall had bought five others too, and paid ten Danish dollars for the lot, along with several bushels of dried fish for their feed while on the *George Henry*. They had been conferring with Governor Elberg, and from the look on old Bud's face, the talk had not gone well. Mr. Hall was frowning also, and biting his lip. As he passed I spoke to him but he did not appear to hear me.

"Now ain't *he* got a bug up his bum!" Sterry said.

"Who?" I asked.

"Mr. Hall."

"He was thinking," I said, and a moment later I was surprised to find I thought it necessary to defend him. "He often gets into deep thoughts, and isn't aware that someone has spoken to him."

Sterry grinned and clapped me on the back, a sly look in his eye. "If you say so, Adam."

When we were not busy loading supplies (which was not often) I had a chance to roam about Holsteinsborg. I did not know either Innuit or Danish, but that was little bar to my enjoyment. A smile, even a friendly word in an unknown tongue, was sufficient to satisfy the Esquimaux that I meant well. They were the most cheerful people I had ever seen,

always on the grin. They grinned at me and my knickknacks—
my pocket compass and comb and case knife. They grinned at
my furrowed brow and halting speech when I tried to make
myself understood. They grinned here and there, at this spot
and that, at night and in the morning and during the day. Many
times they grinned at nothing at all, apparently on the theory
they might have missed a previous occasion and were determined to make it up.

"Slice an Innuit through the middle," explained Sterry, "and
he's made up like a roly-poly pudding. Seal on the outside, for
that is what they dress in; Innuit in the middle; and inside the
Innuit, more seal, because that is what they are full of—seal
meat."

For a plug of tobacco they would put on a show for me in
their *ki-as,* or canoes. Wearing a sealskin jacket which extended
from the shoulders down over the round hole in which the boat-
man sat, they would turn somersets in the water, spinning over
and over till I was dizzy watching them. Because of the tight fit
of the jacket, never did water enter the canoe, and the boat-
man would finally bob upright, grinning, only his hands and
face wet. Another trick they were fond of performing was to
paddle hard and to drive one *ki-a* completely over the top of
another, nearly amidships.

Harvard College, I thought. What a dull place it had been
compared to this strange land!

Patrick Coleman, I found, was correct in at least some of his
gossip. The Esquimaux Sabbath ended in the afternoon on Sunday, and a ball was planned for us by the governor, to start on
the stroke of four. We finished loading our coal and dried fish
and other supplies at noon, and spent the rest of the day cleaning up for the event. The forecastle was filled with soapy splut-
terings; hair pomade was put on, celluloid collars shined, and
boots were blacked. Promptly at four, all except the mate and
a small deck watch went over the side, and pulled away to the
accompaniment of singing and good spirits.

"Now you watch that *akvavit*," Sterry said, putting a hand on my shoulder. "Adam, it's a treacherous drink, and takes care and skill. Most other liquors will give you a warning first; the dry heaves, or a list to port. But *akvavit* is different. All of a sudden everything goes black, and it takes three days to revive you."

"Don't worry about me," I said. "I don't drink—just a little port now and then, and the wine at Communion, of course."

Stokes, paring blue-black nails with his sheath knife, gave me his opinion on Esquimaux women, going into great anatomical detail. "But mind this!" he said in conclusion, peering down his long nose at me. "They're mostly someone's wife, so make sure first before you take one outside for a walk."

"You don't need to worry about me," I said and think I blushed, because they all roared with laughter except Coleman, who only looked at me with a faint smile.

The dance was a huge success. An old Innuit sailor named Iron-Face played his fiddle, keeping time by stamping on the floor with his heel. The governor was there, sitting on a kind of dais with Mrs. Kjer, the wife of the minister, and Miss Bulou, who was the attractive daughter of the governor of the district of Godhaab. Mr. Hall also sat there, with Captain Budington, and both seemed to enjoy themselves although neither danced. They were not missed, however; never have I seen such whole-hearted and spirited caperings. The Esquimaux women and girls were not bashful—instead, at the first strains of the fiddle they charged across the floor and collared the partner of their choice, dragging him bodily out on the floor. A short woman in a calico dress and boots of sea-leopard fur took my hand and pulled me after her, laughing and chattering as if she had a prize catch. I was not a good dancer but it seemed to make little difference. Being spun wildly by this lady in a kind of "lancer's quadrille," I looked around just in time to see Sterry carom by, his arms around *three* ladies, and all of them shrieking with joy and excitement. Sterry had the most capital faculty for gaining the affections of the fair sex, and proved himself excellent on the variations.

A buffet had been set by the governor, and Miss Feoken Bulou and Mrs. Kjer had outdone themselves to decorate the dance house with streamers of dried seaweed, festoons of fishing nets, and piles of varicolored rocks. Panting for breath and perspiring, I excused myself from my lady companion and sat down in a chair by the fiddler, hoping soon to get my second wind.

A kind of a berry punch was in a bowl on the table and I took a dipperful of it from time to time, being thirsty from the dancing. Although I am not particularly musical, I noticed that after a while I began to tap my feet, and to clap my hands also. It was not very good music, but it was loud, and it moved me in a peculiar way. Sterry lurched over and shouted in my ear, but I could not make out what he said. Finally he gave it up and poured a bottle of *akvavit* in the punch, tossing the empty bottle through a window someone had opened to cool off.

I screwed up my courage and asked Miss Bulou to dance with me. The fiddler, Iron-Face, played a waltz at my request, and we dipped and glided gracefully about the floor. Miss Bulou sometimes winced as I stepped on her foot, but she was otherwise gracious. "You *do* waltz remarkably," she whispered in my ear, and smiled at me as she hurried back to the dais.

I went back to the punch bowl and had a dipperful. Sterry was emptying another bottle of *akvavit* into it, but the liquor did not affect the fruity tang of the berries. Remarkable berries, they were; probably some native shrub that grew at Holsteinsborg. It was about this time I began to notice the strange behavior of my pocket watch. No matter what I did, it seemed to remain obstinately at about seven in the evening. I danced with all the ladies, I drank more dippers of excellent punch, I took the fiddle away from Iron-Face and played a difficult solo, although I am not musical, as I have said. It was still only a few minutes after seven. Sterry wrung my hand and congratulated me, and put two bottles of *akvavit* into the punch; it was still only a few minutes after seven. I held the watch to my ear and listened to it. The steady ticking puzzled me. I seemed to be suspended in time—happy, gay, a devil of a fellow—kissing all the ladies, shaking hands with Captain Budington, proposing toasts to the King of Denmark, and eating dried fish with the heads and tails on, which I would not ordinarily do. In a final display of talent, I ordered Sterry to clear the dance floor and performed a Russian *kazatsky,* arms folded and legs kicking in and out with the precision of steam pistons. The *kazatsky* was the last thing I had any remembrance of.

When I awoke (if that is the word for swimming out of a limitless black nothingness) I was in my bunk on the *George Henry.* We were at sea, I could tell. A head sea slapped hard into her planking, and the creak of timbers made my head ache. It seemed as if the top of my skull was made of India rubber, and expanded and contracted with each beat of my pulse. My mouth was dry and feathery-tasting, and there were evidences I had been sick. I lay there for a long time, wondering if I had caught some Innuit disease. I tried to get out of my bunk, but found that someone had tied me in with a length of line, and I lay back again, trying to get my thoughts in order.

It was a remarkable thing that next happened. As I lay there, sick and dizzy, a scene played itself out in my mind—precise, ordered, the voices of the actors crisp and clear. I could recall every detail, although it seemed that I myself was not concerned, being only a spectator sitting in an orchestra seat. There was Adam Burritt, the principal actor, standing in a snowbank outside the government dance house, feeling very peculiar. I saw myself hold my pocket watch up to my ear and shake it vexedly. Over my shoulder, at stage-right, was a small lighted window, and through it came voices—Mr. Hall's and that of Governor Elberg, with occasionally a word from Captain Budington. They were in a small room that opened off the dais, and I stood there, cold and shivering, winding the watch.

"I cannot help it," said Governor Elberg. "I have no control over Lars Kleijt. If he will not go with you, Mr. Hall, that is his privilege!"

"You have influence with them!" protested Mr. Hall.

"I will not influence a man to go on a trip he does not want to take."

"Sir, this means everything to me! My life is dedicated to this journey. I must have a guide—a reliable man, a hunter, an ice pilot! Can you not—"

"This is enough!" broke in Captain Budington. "Mr. Hall, the governor has been very patient. Now I must ask you—"

"But why?" Mr. Hall demanded. "I have offered him a good wage. Why will he not go with me to King William Land?"

The governor's voice was angry. "Why? Need you ask me why? Lars Kleijt has no confidence in you, Mr. Hall. He would not guide you for any amount of money, poor as he is. A trip to King William Land with a man who has never been in the Arctic before! I wonder you are rash enough to attempt it yourself, without asking others to join you in such a scheme! This is not Cincinnati, Mr. Hall, or Chicago, or wherever it is you come from! This is the Arctic, and danger is on every hand. Myself, I do not blame Lars Kleijt. I am sorry to say it, but it is true."

There was a long silence, and I remember trembling in the cold. My face was hot and flushed when I put my hand there, and over my head was the late Arctic twilight, the first wink of stars, and the cry of a bird somewhere along the shore. Then the whole scene faded away, and nothing I could do would bring it back, or tell me what happened after. But I knew it had all happened and I had been there, standing in the snow outside the window.

About noon, I think it was, Sterry came in. He looked fresh and vigorous, and gave me a hand when I tried to stand up. I reeled and would have fallen had it not been for Sterry. I thought I was dying, and sat down again.

35]

"You'll get over it," grinned Sterry. "Another week or two and you'll be able to take solid food."

I groaned and put my head in my hands, which only made it worse. Sterry handed me my pocket watch, the one my father had given me when I went away to college. "You better take it back."

"Where did you get it?"

"You gave it to me last night at the dance. Told me to take it to a jeweler and have it fixed. Said it was slow."

I groaned again, remembering the remarkable behavior of the watch. My own behavior, it appeared, had been at least as remarkable.

"You look kind of peaked," observed Sterry, "but you better go below and lay aft to the galley. Cookie is mad because you wasn't around to lend him a hand." He stuffed shag tobacco into his pipe, looking thoughtful. "Matter of fact, that's the general state of mind on the *George Henry* this morning. Ain't no one on good terms with anyone else. Old Bud is cross as two sticks. Him and Mr. Hall been yelling at each other all morning. Something happened last night, I guess. Dunno what."

I could guess, but I did not broach the subject. Instead, I thanked Sterry for his care of me and dragged myself to the galley, where Cookie gave me the sharp edge of his tongue for an hour running, not using the same obscenity more than once. I sat on a stool next to the coal range and peeled potatoes for two hours, my eyes almost closed, because even the dim light of the galley hurt them. *Never again,* I told myself. I was not cut out for a life of sin and carousing.

Early in August we saw the west coast of Davis Strait, having made heavy weather in the crossing. Snow in August was new to me, yet my first sight of Baffin Island came through whirling clouds of snowflakes, each seeming as big as a baby's fist. The sun was gone, and heavy lead-colored clouds lay all about us; the waters of Davis Strait were gray and cold. The *George Henry* pitched and bucked in the chop, and the wind was obstinate and changeable. Without our small steam engine, depending on sail alone, it would have been dangerous to come so close to a lee shore. But Captain Budington was anxious to locate a bay called by the Innuits Ookoolear, which we were to use as a base for our whaling operations and into which we would be frozen for the coming winter. The *George Henry* clawed her way along the rocky shore, old Bud on the quarterdeck with his brass spyglass to his eye, calling out orders to the helmsman. There was still great coolness between him and Mr. Hall, and the latter stayed very private in the bows, staring over the rail at the land, wrapped in a blanket against the wind.

For three days we beat up and down while the weather worsened. It was dangerous to attempt to enter Ookoolear, and we were about to leave for God knows where when two Innuit fishermen in an old and leaky longboat rowed out to us from a village on the shore. One of these was a plump, jolly man named John Bull who was known to Captain Budington from a previous voyage. The other was called Ebierbing, but answered to the name of Joe. He was a handsome man, tall for an Innuit, and of a proud bearing. Through them Captain Budington learned that many whalers were now anchored in a nearby bay called Kowtukjua.

"Good anchorage," said Joe. "*Black Eagle* there, *Georgiana*, and *True Love*. You go there?"

"All right," said the captain.

"We take you for two plugs tobacco," said John Bull. He pointed to Joe. "One him—one me."

In several hours we made Kowtukjua, the Esquimaux Joe giving steering directions to the helmsman. It was a fine sheet of water, over sixty miles long, Joe said, and six wide. As we went in, our steam engine failed us and Sterry went to work to fix it. In the meantime, several boats from the *Black Eagle* and the *True Love* came out to tow us. I wished for a sketch pad and a pencil and some talent to draw the scene. Seven boats in line pulling the *George Henry* onward, merry voices singing and brawny arms pulling in uniform strokes, and all about us the still waters of the great bay, the sheer rocks hemming in the channel, and in the distance the snowy peaks reaching up to the sky.

We had no sooner come anchor than Mr. Hall and the captain got into an argument. I was standing near them, having been put on the anchor watch, and heard their every word.

"You cannot stop me," said Mr. Hall. "This is why I have come north. I will ask you again, Captain, to put my boat and supplies over the side."

Old Bud was vexed and angry. "Look at the weather, Mr. Hall! There's a gale making up. How in the name of Peter and Paul do ye expect to handle a boat in these strange waters, all by yourself, with dirty weather to boot?"

Mr. Hall was very determined. "I have offered John Bull and Ebierbing—the one they call Joe—money to go with me to the nearest village. They will help me handle the boat."

The wind was whistling now through our bare poles and rigging, and the force of the blow caused the *George Henry* to strain against her anchor cable. Whitecaps, looking unnaturally foamy and white in the dull light, dashed against her sides, and a spatter of snowflakes drove by.

"You are against me," Mr. Hall said. "You are all against me. Everyone is against me. But I have come here with one purpose in mind; to find the Franklin people. Now we are here, I intend to go!"

Old Bud's flat-crowned hat started to blow away, and he pulled it down hard over his ears. "All right, then. Go, God help you!" He bawled out an order for Mr. Rogers to swing Mr. Hall's longboat on the davits and let it down over the side. "But don't be a damned fool, sir! Leave your sledge and your supplies here for now. The weight will swamp your longboat. Take only what ye need for a few days. Look around, visit, pick up what news ye can about the Franklin men, and then come back to us. We'll be here."

[38

Mr. Hall toyed with his plaid muffler, thinking. A scowl was on his face, and a magnificent scowl he could make, too, with his heavy brows and deep-set eyes. "I won't inconvenience you," he muttered. "Williams and Haven Company have been good enough to bring me this far, as they promised. From here on in I am on my own. That was the agreement."

"Blast the agreement!" old Bud snapped. "I did not bring ye all the way to Baffin Island just to get ye drowned! Good Lord, Mr. Hall, don't be an ass! We may not see eye to eye about this fool's errand of yours, but ye are a human being, or I took ye for one, and so am I, I hope." Taking Mr. Hall by the shoulder he shook him, half angry and half beseeching. "Go—take your damned little boat and John Bull and Joe, if they will go with ye, as ye say. Leave your supplies here—they'll be safe. Stay on the windward side of the bay, and God be with ye, as he is with all sailors."

"Yes, sir," I said.

Almost reluctantly Mr. Hall agreed to this plan. He and John Bull and Joe got into their longboat and Mr. Rogers gave the order to put it into the water. The weather was still making up, and more snow fell. In the lee of the *George Henry* was a slick of fairly smooth water, and into it went Mr. Hall and his longboat. Joe and John Bull kept her away from our vessel with their oars while Mr. Hall put up his tiny sail. A moment later the wind caught them and they drove away on our quarter, past the *Black Eagle* and the *True Love*. As they drifted away Mr. Hall raised his hat to us in a grave and ceremonial gesture, and then they vanished into the snowflakes. I felt we would never see him again.

Captain Budington paced the deck for a while, pausing only to squint his weathered face into the wind for a sight of the longboat. Once, sometime after, I thought I saw the white of their sail against the dark rocks a few points off our bow, but I was not sure.

"The damned fool," old Bud said, coming up to me with

hands locked behind his back. He stamped back and forth, occasionally peering to windward. Finally he gave it up, and sighed. "Lord, what a man! He's a lunatic, that's what he is! A raving lunatic!"

He seemed genuinely moved, for he was a good man and a decent one. "Can't talk sense to him, Adam. Don't understand sense. All he knows bangs head on, all sail filled and drawing." He sighed. "Ah, well. There's an end to it, I fear." He looked around at the canvas-shrouded bulk of Mr. Hall's supplies, the pemmican and the rest of it. "Guess we can use the stuff when grub gets short this winter."

That night the storm became worse—much worse.

Chapter 3

WHAT could be done with a man like that? Nothing, I suppose. He was going to King William Land, one way or another, and had not even said good-by to me, whom he might have supposed to be his friend. Even the weather that was making up was of no concern to him. For all my ignorance otherwise, I recognized the dirty weather that was coming and said a quick prayer for Mr. Hall and his two Esquimaux companions.

I stood my watch, and at six in the evening Sterry relieved me. The wind had by now increased to a gale, a perfect hurricane, with thick snow. The noise was such that he had to put his mouth to my ear to make himself heard.

"Perfect summer weather, ain't it?" he howled.

The evening sky was filled with sulphurous yellow light. On the horizon was a slash of red, a brilliant carmine band that was strangely out of place. Above and all round us were fleeting clouds of almost jet black, torn into strange and fantastic shapes by the wind. Fascinated by this weird display, I stayed by Sterry's side instead of going below.

During Sterry's watch the *Amoret*, anchored some fifty fathoms distant from us, began to drag her anchor and slide toward us stern on. "Call the captain!" Sterry told me. I turned to go, but old Bud was already beside us, equipped with the sixth sense that tells whaling skippers when trouble is at hand. He was watching the *Amoret* too, the way she bore down on us stern first, her running lights winking cheerfully.

"She'll miss us," said Sterry. "See, they've put out another cable." They had indeed, and this anchor got some purchase in the rocky bottom. The *Amoret* sloughed round, coming up hard on her anchor chain so that it tightened like a fiddlestring. But no sooner had this menace been removed than the *Georgiana* dragged her anchor also and came rapidly downwind toward us. Seeing her come at us, pitching and surging, I was frightened and wondered why the captain did not call for the engine to be started up so as to take us out of harm's way. Then I remembered; the engine had broken down while we were standing off Kowtukjua Bay, and we had to be towed in. Sterry was probably still working on it.

Fortunately she passed well on our beam. I could see dimly through the snow that her men were on deck trying to put a boat over the side, although what good that would have done in this howling sea I do not know. But having passed us, she was caught in a sudden eddy of gigantic proportions and spun end for end. A moment later she struck head on against a small rocky island near the mouth of the bay.

"God help 'em!" the captain cried.

For a moment the *Georgiana* hung irresolute, a ghost ship, her bare poles black and burned-looking against the yellow sky. Then a freak gust of wind caught her and she was thrown high on the rocks, caught for good, masts and rigging slanted at an extreme angle. Men went over her lee rail like ants over an upturned bowl, dropping into the foaming surf and struggling to safety on the island.

We could do nothing for them. It did not seem possible that our own anchors could hold. Wind and storm and a raging sea had conspired against the whaling fleet in the bay called Kow-tukjua. At sea, we could have run for it. Here, in this sheltered bay, we were in peril, with no sea room. The *George Henry* first threw her bows low down, taking the briny sea, and then surged high up, springing on her anchor chain. In spite of the protection offered belowdecks, all our crew were on deck, huddled wetly in whatever shelter they could find. Vessels had been known to capsize in such fearful weather.

"We'll make it now," Captain Budington said. Dried salt crusted his cheeks, and droplets of sea water sparkled in his chin whiskers. "Thanks to our good Lord who walked on the waters, we'll make it."

Perhaps we would, but in the pale light of dawn we saw that the *Amoret* also had been driven aground. For a moment, I could not make out the strange dark bulk on the shore of the bay. Then I realized it was the *Amoret*, and that she no longer bore any resemblance to a ship. Her masts and rigging were gone, snapped off and broken by the force of her striking on the rocks. They lay on her decks in a gigantic tangle, and each successive wave bore her heavily up and then dropped her again on the cruel rocks. But there was a fire on the beach near her, and apparently some of the men had been saved.

About noon the storm abated further and the snow ceased. A fearful sea still ran, but the motion of the *George Henry* was less violent. A low rack of cloud scudded across the horizon, but from time to time the sun shone through, lighting the scene of devastation with an unreal and cheerful radiance.

"She'll do," said Sterry.

"What'll do?"

He clapped a hand on the rail. "Why, the *George Henry*, of

course! Never had a doubt, I did. Beelzebub himself couldn't lay a hand on her. No, not even the Prince of Darkness!"

I had not been so sure myself.

The great gale of latter August damaged much of the Arctic whaling fleet. At Cape True, the whaling station some five miles south of us, the *Samuel Hardy* and the *Rose of Sharon* were driven aground, and three men drowned. Another lost a hand when it was mashed between a swinging boat and the rail. The sailor died soon after, a surgeon not being available. In Kowtukjua Bay, two men drowned when the *Georgiana* went on the beach, and a sailor off the *True Love* died later of injuries. Of Mr. Hall and his small boat there was no trace. Captain Budington sent Mr. Rogers several miles up and down the bay on a fruitless search for news of him. But in a body of water six miles by sixty, and edged by so many rocky coves and hidden inlets, it was not surprising that no trace of Mr. Hall could be found. Accordingly he was listed in the ship's log as drowned, and Captain Budington held a service for him. But hard lines were expected in this business. A man did not come to Davis Strait on the whalers without expecting to take chances. And so, after cleaning up the wreckage, parceling out the wrecked sailors among the other vessels, and burying the dead, the work of whaling went on. A sailor's "lay," or share of the profits, could with luck amount to a thousand dollars, and everyone turned to with a will, forgetting his late hardship.

Mr. Rogers' boat took our first whale. All sail set and the men pulling at the oars, they towed the beast in through the channel. Behind them lolled the great bulk of the whale, the first I had ever seen, glistening black where it broke the surface of the water. The blue of the bay was stained with crimson, a bloody track that stretched behind the boat like a tail, curving in a graceful sweep till it disappeared behind the headlands at the mouth of the bay. Someone breathed heavily at my elbow, and I saw it was Patrick Coleman. Running a tongue over his thin lips in the way he had, he said in a husky voice, "Aye, it's a fine one, ain't it? Just look at that, now!" He did not seem to be talking to me, or even to notice me.

When they chained the carcass alongside, Coleman and Vess and Keeney and the rest swarmed out on the cutting stage, their blubber spades flashing in the sun. Like a monkey, Coleman went down a line and dropped on the whale's broad back. He raised the spade high and brought it down like an ax to a tree. Blood gushed, spattering him from head to foot, and he hacked away in the dreadful shower like a farmer long denied rain. The flesh of the whale gaped wide and white and the immense body rolled and quivered, resenting this last indignity.

The flesh came off in blanketlike pieces, hauled up over the side with a chain fall. Sterry had set up the try-pots just forward of the main hatch, and it was my job to tend the fires under them. Coal started the flames, but soon the boiled-out pieces from the try-pots took over the job, and the fire roared and crackled. From a distance the *George Henry* might have been taken for a steamship under way, so high and wide went the smoke. The decks ran with blood and oil and bits of flesh, the slippery mush the whalers called "gurry." The smell was horrendous. A week-dead goat might approach it but could never come up to it. Everything was drenched with oil washing about ankle-deep, and a layer of greasy soot lay over all. I began to damn the day I first saw a whale.

Fortunately, to everything there is an end. The clacking of the mincing machine stopped some sixty hours after we first brought the monster alongside. The last of the oil drained from the cooling tanks into Sterry's casks. All the bone was scraped and bundled; the tools were cleaned and stowed away, the decks and upper works washed down and then mopped and scrubbed with lye, the carcass of the whale turned loose to drift away.

"Over a hundred barrel of oil," old Bud crowed. "And the bone runs more than a ton. Lads, it was a fine day's work, and never doubt it!"

A day's work! I thought. Another day of such work would kill me. Going below, I fell into my bunk just as I was; stinking, greasy, bone-tired. I think I died, then, but my shade got no rest. In an instant, it seemed, Keeney was shaking me.

"Mr. Jessup's boat just came alongside. Got a big one, lad! Shake a leg."

I would, I knew, never make a whaler.

The days swung by, and I lost track of their count in the endless labor. I became impregnated with soot and grease, like most whalemen; I developed a set of muscles I was vain about; I grew salty in my language, to old Bud's dismay, and raised a sandy beard. True, it was not much of a beard compared, for instance, to Keeney's red brush. But it was a beard, the first I ever had, and I was proud of it.

I thought often of poor Mr. Hall and the tragedy of his passing. He had been a rash and thoughtless man, and what had happened was his own fault, surely. But I could not help but feel that the rashness had not been that of the fool, but only the audacity of a man in a dreadful hurry, reaching for a goal, impatient of obstacle. When I got back to Cincinnati, I would make a point of going to the house on Celestial Street to tell them how he died. In the meantime, I missed him very much. Sterry and Vess and Keeney and the rest were good men, by and large, and meant well; I enjoyed their horseplay and rough jokes, but at times I yearned for a different kind of talk, something with substance in it. Mr. Hall and I had talked, during the voyage north, of many things; of Aristotle and Plato and Socrates, of Mr. Darwin and his theories, of the classifications of birds and trees and animals and fishes and shells, of books and philosophers and military men and long-dead cities. I missed all this, and the strange new sights and sounds and smells of this Arctic world were not enough to make up for it.

Well, there was no cure for it but hard work, and there was plenty of that. Now that the whaling was over, we hurried on against the day when the *George Henry* and the *True Love* and the *Black Eagle* would be frozen into Kowtukjua Bay for the winter, and the boats could no longer put out to sea to seek the whale. The season wheeled, the sun dipped low over the edge of the world, great blizzards came almost daily, whirling in on us like mad dogs, slashing and biting and moving on to give way to another. During the night an inch or so of ice would form on the bay, only to break up and melt again next morning. But finally, late in September, the ice stayed through the day, becoming thicker. We were frozen in.

As soon as the thickness of the ice permitted, work parties went out and started their labors. Snow was banked up around the *George Henry*, almost even with the rail. Split and useless sails were spread over her upper works and snow banked over that also, to bury all but masts and spars in a huge mound of snow and ice. A hole was cut in the bay ice directly beside the ship, to get at water in case of fire. Fire was not too improbable, with the forecastle stove roaring day and night, red-hot. Once caught, the oil-soaked vessel would go up like a Fourth of July rocket. Mr. Rogers found a fresh-water pond ashore, and it was my job to cut up the ice with a long ice saw, hauling it back to the ship on a sledge for later melting and drinking. For this I used Mr. Hall's sledge and his Greenland dogs. Barbekark, Mr. Hall's favorite, had the roam of the ship. He often came to rest among Mr. Hall's boxes and bales and crates, head between his paws, as if waiting for Mr. Hall to return. When I whistled he would come to me, very grave and dignified, to accept a bit of ship's biscuit or to lick molasses from my fingers.

"Good old boy," I would say. "Where is your master?"

His ears would prick up, and he would look at me expectantly. But that was all. He would blink once or twice, lick his chops, and return to his vigil beside the supplies. Barbekark was an unusual dog, not at all like the rest Mr. Hall had bought, who were vicious and fought constantly among themselves.

I had known cold before, of course. In Cincinnati the temperature frequently went to zero, and once to eighteen below. But that was nothing beside the cold of Baffin Island. This new cold was a great sucking cold that drew the warmth from a man as a magnet draws iron. The fires roared on the *George Henry*, but at best they could raise the temperature only to about freezing. Molasses in barrels became so hard it was necessary to knock the staves away and chop up the molasses with an ax. If left outside an iron pot would split into fragments with a noise like a pistol shot. The bay ice thickened to two feet and then four and eight and ten, so that each morning it was necessary to dig deeper to get to water. The wind blew and blew, never silent, never still.

Now that we were frozen in, the Innuit natives visited us, begging for molasses (which they loved), wanting to trade for combs and needles and thread and looking glasses. They were the same as the natives of Greenland I had met at Holsteinsborg; always happy and grinning, friendly, ready to lend a hand or share whatever they had with you. Many small villages of them lay about us, the people having abandoned their summer *tupiks* to live now in the icehouses they had built.

To pass the time, I took walks when the weather was fair, going to the neighboring ships for a gam or visiting the igloos at the Innuit villages, carrying with me a gallon tin of molasses or a plug of tobacco to make friends. I did not speak the lingo as many of the other sailors did, but most of the Innuits knew some English from the whalers, and with gestures and smiles I got along pretty well. Old George was a favorite of mine; blind George, or Paulooyer, they called him, who lived in a village about a mile from where the *George Henry* was fast in the ice.

One day in October I left the ship early in the morning, intending to visit George and his family in their igloo. The day was still, the wind having dropped, and the Fahrenheit thermometer stood at some twenty degrees below zero. In the distance the peaks glowed near their tops with the glow from the hidden sun, soon to rise above the horizon for its brief daily visit. When I arrived at George's house, the sun had just topped the peaks and long shadow-splashed rays lay across the snow as I walked. George was sitting, as usual, before his igloo, sightless face turned up. Unable to see, the warmth of the sun on his face let him know the direction of the sun, and on a good day he would sit thus for hours, puffing on his pipe and calling out to passers-by.

As I came closer, I saw George had visitors. A sledge and dogs were at his door, and from a lance driven into the snow beside the sledge fluttered the hard-frozen bladder of a polar bear —*ninoo*, the Innuits called him—which the owner of the sledge had recently killed, it being the custom to fly this flag for three days after. George was in conversation with a strange Innuit, a roly-poly little man wearing an old uniform coat with brass buttons over his sealskin *koo-lee-tang*.

I knew about six words of Esquimaux, and as I approached I called out *"As-shu-e-tid-ley?"* meaning "Are you well?"

The behavior of the man in the uniform coat was strange. Seeing me, he became frightened and pulled the hood of his *koo-lee-tang* over his face and turned away. He seized his lance, snapped the whip over the dog team, and away they went, the man running beside them. Knowing the Esquimaux are usually very courteous, I was puzzled. They enjoy meeting others, especially the *kod-lu-na,* or white man. I turned to George in mystification and asked, "Who was that? Why did he hurry away so?"

As I asked the question I knew the answer. At least, I suddenly remembered where I had seen the visitor before, if I still did not know why he fled in such haste. It was the Innuit called John Bull, the one who had boarded the *George Henry* off Ookoolear Bay, and for a plug of tobacco for himself and his friend Joe offered to pilot the ship to Kowtukjua. John Bull and Joe had sailed away with Mr. Hall in his cockleshell of a boat on that stormy day in August last, and had never been seen again. Yet here was John Bull, alive and well, if unfriendly. Then Mr. Hall might also live! But my inquiries of George got little information.

"John Bull," he finally admitted, shrugging.

"But he's the man who went away with Mr. Hall in his little boat last August! He and the one called Ebierbing—Joe, he was called too—and Mr. Hall. We thought they were all lost in the great storm."

George was embarrassed. He knew something and wanted to tell me, but apparently dared not. His features, normally pleasant and composed, took on a woebegone look. "Maybe," he said. "I dunno. George dunno, sir. No, by goddam, George dunno at all. No, sir."

"You *do* know!"

He shook his head and refused to say more.

I was at a loss. Something queer was going on, and I felt I must get to the bottom of it. Rummaging in my pockets, I found my case knife, a good one with several folding blades and an auger. George had admired it before.

"Here!" I pressed it into his hand. "I'll give you my knife. It's the one you liked." I guided his hand to it and watched as his fingers touched the carved bone handle. A light came into his sightless face. "No one else has got a knife like that, George. It's all yours, George. Just tell me what John Bull told you. What did he say? Did he mention Mr. Hall?"

Desire and loyalty clashed on George's open features. He screwed his face up into the most horrendous grimaces and wagged his head in perplexity. I had put him a nice question in morality, but it was in a good cause. If Mr. Hall was alive, he must be found.

"Mr. Hall is my friend!" I insisted. "If he is alive, he may need help. If you were in trouble, I would want to help you, George."

His fingers caressed the handle, softly, lovingly.

"When a friend is in trouble, you must help that friend," I said. "Isn't that so, George?"

Taking a deep breath, he turned his sightless gaze on me. *"Ee-uk!"* It was the Innuit word for regret, or sadness, or disappointment. *"Ee-ee-uk!* John Bull no like me!"

"That isn't what counts," I said firmly. "What counts is helping your friend."

"John Bull tell me no say, but I tell. Hall your friend. All right, I tell." Turning away from the sun, he pointed north, toward the rim of mountains that hemmed in Kowtukjua Bay. "Hall, he there. Sick, John Bull say. But don't want John Bull tell anyone. Don't want anyone know." He wagged his head, face averted from me in shame. "John Bull mad at me now. *Ee-uk!*"

Mr. Hall was alive, somewhere up there to the north! I felt my heart beat faster. "Where is he? How far? You say he is sick? But why doesn't he want anyone to know that he needs help?"

George tried to hand the knife back to me, but I pushed it aside. "You keep it, George. It's yours. But tell me where Mr. Hall is!"

He waved his hand northward again. "Day. Two day. John Bull very tired. Village at Oolootong. Very far. Hard to get to."

Oolootong! I didn't know where it was, but surely Captain Budington or Sterry or someone on board the *George Henry* would know.

"Is he very sick? Is he dying, George? Why doesn't he want help?"

Apparently thinking he had already said too much, George became sullen and would not say more.

"All right," I said. "Thank you, George."

I turned and ran back toward the ship. On an icy hummock a

good quarter of a mile away I stopped to catch my breath. Blind George stood there, face to the sun, and I think the knife was still in his hand. It had been a good knife and I was sorry to lose it, but it was a fair trade.

To see old Bud under ordinary circumstances, one would not have thought him the person he was. In his long wool coat and flat-brimmed hat he looked like the Dunkard farmers who came to Cincinnati of a Saturday morning, bringing chickens and cheeses and vegetables to market. The curl of beard around his plain face, the wrinkles at the corner of his blue eyes, set him off as a mild, uneventful man, living a placid life, unaccustomed to decision. It was the way with most whaling skippers; they all looked like farmers. But there was a difference when action and great decision were called for, and I would sooner trust my life to old Bud than to any of the brass-button spit-and-polish man-of-war types.

"What's this ye're telling me?" he demanded.

Strugging for breath, I repeated my story.

"Oolootong." He nodded. "A good sixty mile. Clear at the end of the bay. Must have been blown there, and piled up on the rocks. Hurt, ye say?"

"Or sick. George wasn't too clear."

"Why don't he want help?"

"I don't know that either. It sounds very strange."

While I was wheezing out my story old Bud motioned Mr. Rogers close. The mate had sailed with Captain Budington on many voyages, far and near, and there was a great understanding between them. In response to old Bud's gesture, the mate was already uncovering Mr. Hall's supplies and getting together rations for a rescue trip.

"Round up the dogs," the captain instructed Sterry. "Put that brindle one—"

"Barbekark," I said.

[52

"Aye, Barby what's-his-name—put him out front. He'll lead, or I miss my guess." Sterry brought the captain a *koo-lee-tang* and a pair of skin trousers, along with Innuit boots. My face must have reflected surprise, because the captain glowered at me and said, "By Judas Priest, boy! Ye think I'm too old and decrepit for a little trip to Oolootong village?"

"No, sir," I said untruthfully.

Sterry and Vess and Mr. Rogers were busy stowing supplies on the sledge and lashing it down—cans of Mr. Hall's meat biscuit, powder and ball, a musket, a tin of tea, the captain's little chest of medical supplies.

"Sir," I said.

"Eh?"

"I want to go with you."

"And so ye shall."

"I may?"

"Why, I *order* ye to go! Adam Burritt seems the only man in the Arctic on good terms with Hall. I have no intention of sledging to Oolootong village just to lose an argument with the obstinate fool. I want ye along to give him the smooth side of your tongue if need be, Adam. Hike, now; get busy!"

The captain left instructions with Mr. Rogers for the conduct of the vessel while we were gone, and we started off in late afternoon, me in Esquimaux clothing I had borrowed from Mr. Rogers. The moon had risen from her sea bed, and as she sailed higher in the sky the scene was almost as light as day. From time to time the dogs would get the scent of some wild thing and veer from the track with an excited yipping.

"Seal, probably," said old Bud, and lashed them back into line.

We might have been the crew of a seagoing vessel, beating to windward on the watery wastes of the South Atlantic. The feeling was the same; a vast ocean of snow with no landmark, no human habitation, no animal or vegetable life apparent, with the exception of us and our frail vessel. On, on, we sped, pausing only for the captain to look at his pocket compass and correct our course.

Once, passing through a shallow basin filled with snow and water, a strange phosphorescence occurred. When the dogs put their feet into the mixture, it was like stepping into molten gold. The precious stuff flew high and far, drenching us in a golden rain. At the touch, the water seemed to harden and freeze at once, so that when we had crossed the basin, we were lightly clad with ice and had to stop to beat it loose, and also to pick ice from between the toes of the dogs. This last, I was to find, was an onerous and frequent duty. Hardy as they were, the dogs would still pull up lame if regular stops were not made to relieve them.

On, on we went, flying through the Arctic night. In waning light of the moon, the country ahead looked no different to me than the country we had passed. I was winded, and every muscle in my body ached with its own separate and identifiable pain; my booted feet seemed made of lead. But the spry captain, some forty years older than I, jogged untiringly behind the sledge, even finding time to sing Presbyterian hymns.

"Tired, boy?" He halted the team and peered at me. A rime of frost was on his beard and eyebrows. "Let's stop for a breather."

"I'm not tired."

"Ride on the sledge for a while."

"I'm damned if I will."

"No need to be profane," he grinned. "All right, then; whatever ye say."

"How far have we gone?"

"Twenty mile. Maybe twenty-five."

Not halfway to Oolootong village! Well, there was no cure for it. I had wanted to come, and here I was. I fell in behind old Bud and away we jogged again.

All that night we traveled, and the next day, pausing only to boil tea and eat some ship's biscuit and pemmican. I slept for a little while in the lee of the sledge, while the captain sipped his tea. After a while, he shook me and stood up. "Time to go again."

Stiff and sore, I reeled to my feet. The snowy wastes shimmered in a weird half-light. The sun in its limited arc was gone again, and a great red moon rose in the east.

"I'm ready," I croaked.

In the later stages of our journey a wind of gale force sprung up, of such viciousness and strength that we had to walk leaning at an acute angle. The dogs had constantly to be whipped into a quartering course, preferring instead to run with the wind, letting it come at them from the back. In such circumstances, even the most commonplace of functions had to be gone at in a special way. For instance, elimination was a problem. Old Bud showed me how, by digging a hole in the snow and throwing up a low windbreak, it could be accomplished without frostbite of the important organs. Because of the force of the gale, speech was almost impossible and signs had to be resorted to. In the whirling snow it was necessary to cling together, and to the sledge; death from freezing lay only a few feet away. Frostbite of the face also was a hazard, and every few minutes we would stop and examine each other for the telltale whitening and numbness of the cheeks and forehead, for all the world like two furry monkeys searching each other for fleas.

Finally, when it seemed human endurance could do no more, the wind suddenly dropped. The stars came out twinkling and dancing, and old Bud pointed to a low double-humped hill that lay ahead of us.

"The camel!" His voice was hoarse, and unnaturally loud in the new silence. "Right on course, lad! Another hour and we'll be at Oolootong village!"

The sudden relief from peril made me giddy. My face was

stiff with ice, and I winked and grimaced to break it loose, combing it from my beard, staring up at the Arctic night, so beautiful after the howling gale.

The scene was dreamland, painted in all the delicate tints of the imagination. The night sky was an enormous cupola, blue at the zenith, shading down into green, then lilac and violet at the edges. The stars seemed great and brilliant, bluish in tint, hanging in the sky like the diamonds of some great mogul. The aurora borealis shook out its veil, and curtains of shimmering light waved in the vault of heaven, shot with red and yellow, silver and gold.

I began to understand a little of what Mr. Hall had meant when he spoke of loving the Arctic so. Half-drunk with the beauty of it all, I staggered on behind old Bud, feeling almost as if I had again drunk too much *akvavit*. Reins in one hand, whip in the other, old Bud trotted briskly ahead singing "Rock of Ages" at the top of his voice. This land would, it seemed, touch even a Presbyterian. I was a Baptist, but I joined in on the chorus. That was the way we came to Oolootong village, singing so, and hoping to find the lost Mr. Charles Francis Hall.

Chapter 4

I HAD not realized before how life is bound to go on in an Esquimaux village in the absence of the sun. As we came to Oolootong village after a sledge journey of some thirty hours, what I saw at first seemed queer. In white man's time it was about ten in the evening, but in the light of the moon Oolootong village was wide awake and busy. A dozen igloos glistened in the night, reflecting the moon's rays as if dusted with diamonds. Each of them had one or more windows of fresh-water ice, and through these lenses danced the warm glow of the lamps within. Through a hole in the ice of the bay a group of women gathered kelp for food, and a small party of seal hunters dragged their prize over the snow, singing and laughing. In the cold air their voices were distinct, although they must have been a quarter of a mile distant.

In response to our hail, a face popped out of a subterranean passage.

"*Kod-lu-na*," old Bud said. "Where *kod-lu-na?*"

The startled Innuit stared at us as though we were beings from another planet. Oolootong village was a long way from the area where the whalers operated. Finally, accepting some rock candy from the captain, he grunted in what seemed a friendly manner and pointed to an icehouse a little distant from the others, and considerably larger.

"*Kod-lu-na*," he said.

We tied the dogs before the grand igloo and scuttled through the long tunnel on hands and knees.

"Anyone to home?" the captain demanded.

As we straightened up, a woman's voice met us—a most remarkable voice; cultivated, delicate in British accent and inflection.

"Good evening, sir."

In the flickering light of the oil lamp, I was astounded to see a graceful and modest Esquimaux woman, wearing a crinoline dress with flounces over her furs.

"*Ki-ete*," she said, motioning. "Come in."

In proper dress she would have been recognized as a lady in any social gathering, whether in Cincinnati or Rome or Paris. Behind her, as my eyes grew accustomed to the rich yellow light, was an Innuit man, fine in appearance, intelligent-looking.

"I am called Tookoolito," the woman said. "Some call me Hannah. And this is my husband Ebierbing."

I recognized the man as the Innuit Joe who had left with Mr. Hall and John Bull on their ill-fated trip in the whaleboat.

"Ma'am," said Captain Budington, "we are looking for Mr. Hall, an American we heard was living here, in Oolootong village."

The woman smiled. "Come. I will take you to him." Obviously long pregnant, she bent over with some effort and motioned us to follow her through a passageway to another icy apartment within the igloo. Here, lying on a low ice shelf strewn with furs, we found the object of our search.

[58

"Adam!" Mr. Hall struggled up on one elbow, holding out a hand to me. "What are you doing here? And Captain Budington!"

I was overcome at seeing him again, raised from the dead, though ill and haggard in appearance. His hair and beard were long and uncut, and he was dressed in Innuit furs, the only remnant of his shipside clothing being the threadbare plaid muffler about his throat. His eyes seemed deep caverns under the jutting brows, and there was about him such an atmosphere of physical decay that I almost cried out.

"We are here to save you," I said, dropping on one knee beside him and taking his hand in mine. "Captain Budington and I have come all the way from the *George Henry*."

"Aye," said old Bud. "We've sledged all the way from the mouth of Kowtukjua Bay to take you back with us!"

Mr. Hall sank back on his couch and his brows knit together in a scowl. "How came you to find me?"

Old Bud gestured to me. "Adam here ran into John Bull. The lad figured there was something queer going on. Paulooyer —him they call Blind George—finally 'fessed up. Said you was up here holed in—didn't want no one to come near ye, either."

"I didn't want help!" Mr. Hall burst out. "I didn't need any help. When John Bull said he was going back, I expressly forbade him to speak to anyone about me." In the violence of his anger, the *koo-lee-tang* he wore slipped down and I saw the reason for his infirmity. A huge abscess, the size of a saucer, covered most of his right shoulder. Inflamed, rimmed with a coarse crust, it was vile in appearance and suppurated.

"What is this?" cried the captain. "Man, what have ye done to yourself?"

Hannah slipped forward, a dish of some queer salve in her hand, and pushed Mr. Hall gently back on his pillow. "He has hurt himself in the wreck of his boat, sir. He has been very sick. But he will get better. God will see to it, gentlemen."

Mr. Hall closed his eyes and groaned. "It is all my own fault.

My insufferable pride! That's why I didn't want anyone to know I was here."

"Your boat?" I asked. "Wrecked?"

He nodded and opened his eyes to stare at me; very feverish, very bright. "Nothing left but the sternpost and a few inches of hawser. The storm drove us for twenty-four hours or more, and we didn't know where we were. Finally we came to Oolootong village, but we lost our sail and oars, and were driven high on the rocks. That is where I hurt my shoulder. Joe and John Bull were more fortunate."

"But why didn't you send to us for help? We thought you were dead."

A bitter smile twisted his lips. "Ask for help? After I had parted with the *George Henry* under such conditions, against all good advice? No, I thank you, Adam. Not I."

"Well," said Captain Budington, "all's well that ends well. We've come to take ye back."

Old Bud meant well; he was a religious man and good-intentioned. But he and Mr. Hall generated sparks when they were together. Each was stubborn and uncompromising, and I could see a well-remembered thundercloud spreading across Mr. Hall's pale features. "Take me back? Who are you, Captain, to speak of taking me back as if I were a sack of grain, to be delivered sound and full-weight to Williams and Haven?"

Ebierbing—the one called Joe—came into the room, undoubtedly attracted by the loud voices, and the look on his face and the skinning knife in his hand left no doubt of his loyalty to Mr. Hall. Hannah, too, pressed close to Mr. Hall, and took his hand in hers. "I do not think you ought to talk to Father Hall so much," she said. "He is not well."

Father Hall was what these Innuits called him, with love and devotion in their eyes. Deciding that we were getting no place, I spoke to Captain Budington. "Sir, if you will go away for a little while and let me talk to him—"

[60

Old Bud shrugged, and chewed at the corners of his beard. "What's the matter with the man? I intended no harm!"

"I know," I said.

When he had gone grumbling into the outer room, I squatted beside Mr. Hall and said, "Now tell me your plans, sir. What do you intend to do?"

He stared at me with the same anger in his face, and then he suddenly lay back on the couch again, smiling. "Adam, I am glad you came. It has been a long time, not seeing a white man's face, although these are good people and I owe much to them."

It was cold in the igloo. A film of wet ice covered the bowl-like interior, and the flickering seal-oil lamp did little to take off the chill. I must have shivered in my furs, not being used to such frigid quarters, because suddenly, almost before I knew it, Hannah had slipped off my boots. Very gently but firmly she pushed me down beside the couch and drew my feet into her *koo-lee-tang*, holding them against her naked breast to warm them.

"Here, now!" I protested. "What's this?"

Mr. Hall laughed and patted me on the shoulder. "Hannah likes you, Adam. This is a rare courtesy, reserved for those they love and respect. Don't blush so, lad! It's a custom of the country."

"Well—"

"There, now," said Hannah in her precise and well-modulated voice. "Sir, is that not better?"

I had never been in such a situation before, but I determined to make the best of it.

"Yes," I said. "Thank you very much, Hannah."

"Adam, I've come into the most remarkable piece of luck here." Mr. Hall spoke softly, almost secretively, as if afraid he would be overheard. "You know my desire to search for the survivors of the Franklin expedition?"

"I do, indeed."

"I had thought to look for them in King William Land, because that is where all reports last placed them." He shook his head in an expression of regret. "Poor men—even now eking out an existence in some far-off Arctic village, waiting for rescue, while I lie here with a weevily shoulder! But no mind; I will find them soon, because I have found out something from Hannah and Joe and Joe's grandmother, Ookijoxy-Ninoo!" Excited, he clutched me by the sleeve. "Adam, somewhere up there—" He pointed north. "Somewhere up there is what these people call the Dreaded Land. It's a land they can't be induced to visit, because one time a hunting party from the village went there, and the ground shook under their feet, and they were afraid and came running back. The hair of the hunters turned white overnight, Ookijoxy-Ninoo said. It was an earthquake, don't you see? That's why they call it the Dreaded Land. But Ookijoxy-Ninoo told me something else. There was iron there, she said. 'Big iron, can't move him.' She drew a picture for me, and guess what it was!"

"I don't know," I said.

"An anvil, Adam! A white man's anvil! There was coal, too, she said, and a ruined hut, and some buttons and bits of cloth. I believe the Franklin men were there! Perhaps, after their ships were destroyed in the ice pack, they brought supplies ashore and lived there. Maybe there are records there, notes left to guide me, some clue to their present whereabouts!"

Hannah motioned to Joe, and he brought me a tin cup full of meat stew, and a chunk of walrus fat, white and frozen hard. The stew, I suspected, was seal cooked in its own blood, but I was famished and drank it down, burning my lips and tongue. After that, I chewed on the walrus fat, finding it delicious. From time to time I wiped my greasy fingers on my *koo-lee-tang*, and wondered what my New Haven sweetheart would think of me.

"Perhaps," I said. "But you are certainly in no condition to make such a trip."

[62

He stared at the dripping roof, following the course of a tiny water droplet that eventually halted and froze. "Just so am I," he said, pointing. "Stuck fast here with this illness! But if I were completely well, there would be another great and insurmountable problem. I don't know exactly where this Dreaded Land is, or where in it these bits of evidence are to be found. Not one of these people—not even Joe and Hannah, who are my friends—will guide me. Adam, you cannot realize the terror that strikes these simple people when the Dreaded Land is mentioned." He nodded at Hannah. "Even this fine lady, who has lived twenty months in England and spoken with the Queen, shares the superstition!"

Hannah smiled. "Sir, there are many things not known to the *kod-lu-na*. In this land we know these things, and are afraid."

"You see?" Mr. Hall shrugged. "What can I do?"

"You can do this; come back to the ship with us, where you will have proper care."

"I have the best of care here. An *an-ge-ko*—a kind of medicine man—comes here three times a day and casts spells for my benefit." Mr. Hall, I knew, had absolutely no sense of humor, being too serious in his purpose, and I wondered whether he said this to pull my leg. But there was no twinkle in his eye; only a great resolution. "Besides, to go to the ship would be to turn back. The Dreaded Land is north of here, farther yet from the *George Henry*."

I could understand why he grated so on Captain Budington. Old Bud was used to commanding, and Mr. Hall was a stubborn and intractable man who could be commanded to do nothing. He might, however, be talked into things if properly approached.

"That is true," I said, "but there are other things to consider. First of all, the rest of your supplies—your scientific instruments, your meat biscuit, your books and journals—are still on the *George Henry*. You will need them. Second, you have said that none of these people will guide you to the Dreaded Land.

But on the *George Henry*, or in the villages nearby, there may be someone who will risk it."

He pulled at his beard, thoughtful.

"I do not bring this up lightly," I went on, "because I have only the greatest respect for you and for your purpose. But it is true that you left the *George Henry* too hastily, and by so doing lost your boat and were badly injured. Is it not better to go back to the vessel now, to take your time, to plan a little better and act less rashly?"

"So you are against me too!" He threw himself back on the couch, exhausted, and Hannah crept close to him, a look of concern on her face. "To get thus far, and then—"

I had said all I could, and did not see how further argument could but add to his anger. Water dripped again from the roof and I heard the distant howl of some kind of an animal, probably a wolf. The yellow light from the lamp painted shadows on the wall and Hannah squatted silently near Mr. Hall's feet, waiting. For the first time I noticed the pattern of tattoo marks on her cheeks. In spite of her residence in England and her meeting the Queen, there was something old and timeless and exotic in her face that made me feel uncomfortable, and wonder how did I come here? What on earth was I, Adam Burritt, doing in this igloo, squatting here filled with seal meat and blubber, some sixty-five degrees north in latitude?

"Adam," said Mr. Hall after a while, "it is very hard to be no longer young. You will not understand that; the young never do. Someday you will realize that you are mortal. It came to me a dozen years ago, when I was thirty, and I saw I had done nothing with my life, and was apt to do nothing in Cincinnati. That is when I decided my life must take on meaning. I was a vain man and proud, and could not accept a life that meant only existence, guttering out like a spent candle. That is when I became interested in the Franklin people and made a vow to go to their rescue. If the rest of the world gave them up, this was all the better!"

[64

"You must not talk so much," I said. "You tire yourself."

He raised a hand impatiently. "I have never spoken like this to any man, and you must hear me out, Adam. It is important, because I begin to see that you might help me, if you understood. It is important that you know what it is that drives me." He half-rose on his elbow. "I am a vain and proud man, Adam. I know I am going to die soon. I have a feeling of having ascended some mathematical curve and now to be on the downward slope of it, rushing headlong on a steeper and steeper course, at the end of which is only blackness, nothingness. I do not mind that; it comes to all men in one form or another. But I am too vain to go down into that blackness without being remembered. That is why I am driven so. That is why I must find the Franklin people, or perish in so doing." He looked steadily at me. "If you know all this, you begin to know Charles Hall. And I want you to know him, Adam. He—he is really not such a bad fellow."

"Sir," I said, "I think I know the gentleman well—very well, indeed. And will he now take the advice of his good friend and come back to the *George Henry*, there to make further plans for going somehow to the Dreaded Land?"

For a moment he looked at me, eyes in shadow so that I could not tell what he was thinking. Then he got painfully up from the couch, knotting the plaid muffler about his neck. "I think it is a good idea," he said.

Our winter wore on. The days began to lengthen, although the *George Henry* was still locked in the bay ice. Nightly the world was on fire with the aurora, and the temperature hovered at thirty and forty degrees below zero. The bay ice "sang" from the commotion of stormy waters below it, and the improvident Innuits, finding it now too cold and unpleasant to hunt, came daily to the *George Henry* to beg for food. Mr. Hall, beginning to recover from his abscess (although still thin and gaunt), talked to them in their Innuit tongue, asking about the

Dreaded Land, begging one and another to lead him there. They all knew of the Dreaded Land; it was as I, from Cincinnati, might mention Columbus or Cleveland, not very far away. But when he asked them to go they were terror-struck. Even gifts of needles and cloth and mirrors could not move them. That was a bad place, they said. Yes, they had heard of the big iron there, and the coal, and the ruined dwelling and bits of cloth and buttons. But go there? *Argi! Argi!* No! No!

As the winter wore itself out Mr. Hall was like a wild man. Feeling better, the abscess almost healed, he became again a problem to Captain Budington. He had no boat and old Bud refused to give him one. The time was rapidly passing when a sledge journey could be made to the Dreaded Land. He drove his sledge to the native villages, arguing endlessly with them, cajoling, begging, coaxing. But no one would listen. They were even reluctant to speak of the Dreaded Land, fearing retaliation from evil spirits that dwelled there, who might be listening to them from afar.

"I don't know what I will do," he said to me, sitting in his cabin and fondling Barbekark's ears. "Adam, it is a dreadful thing to be thus blocked, thus frustrated, with the key to the whole Franklin business in my hand!"

"No man could do more than you have tried to do, sir."

"But he could!" Mr. Hall's face became very grim. "And I will, very soon. If no one will help me, I will go entirely on my own. I will buy a native boat—an *oo-mi-en*—and go north alone!"

I said no more, fearing to discuss the prospect lest it cause him to think more seriously of it, and perhaps do what he threatened.

When the weather improved, I left the ship and went out with Blind George's friends hunting seals to provide fresh meat for the ship. Koojesse, Koodloo and his wife Jennie (who weighed two hundred pounds and more), Jack, Suzhi, little Annawha—they became my good friends, in spite of their unpredictable ways. An *an-ge-ko,* or shaman, was always one of the party. It might be old Peong, with his wispy beard and crossed eyes, or again it would be Kargtoon, a greasy young man who was always hungry and operated only upon receipt of gifts of food from his clients. But the *an-ge-ko* was with them, wherever they went. When a seal was killed, the *an-ge-ko* would sprinkle the carcass with water before anyone was allowed to touch it, and sing for a while over the dead body. Afterward he got the seal's eyes as recognition of his status, and the people brought him hot blood to drink. While the skull of a walrus was like seasoned oak, that of the seal was paper-thin, and it was Kargtoon's delight to crack the skull and eat the warm brains with his fingers. But there was, I began to believe, something to these *an-ge-kos.* They had a great hold on their own people, at least. Occasionally, on our sledge journeys in search of meat, Kargtoon or Peong would suddenly caper about, rolling in the snow, twitching and trembling and shouting at the top of his voice. No matter what was in prospect, no matter the storm or game ahead or imminent peril from a crevasse, they would all come to a halt and gather around the medicine man. They would sing and clap their hands and go staggering about in the throes of primitive religious ecstasy. When recovered, Peong would yammer at them for hours while they sat around him in a circle; it was apparently a form of preaching, although I did not know enough of the language to understand. This went on for hours, while I grew cold and miserable and wished myself back on the *George Henry.* But there was no cure for it. Once in the midst of this *an-koo-ting,* as they called it, they were all deaf, and resented interference. In spite of this senseless performance, *an-ge-kos* did have some peculiar power, and knowledge too. A woman in a village near the *George Henry* had a dropsical condition, and Peong ran a knife into her stomach and let out the fluid. I was there, and I saw it, and the woman got well afterward, so that Peong became famous for a hundred miles about.

It was inevitable also, I suppose, that I should have trouble with Patrick Coleman. Some men are so constituted that they live on grudges and are not happy unless they cherish a hatred, existing on it as others do meat and drink. Coleman was this kind of man. Under other circumstances, I might have liked him. He was an old-time whaler, and his skill with the blubber spade I had seen and admired. But in the enforced idleness of the Arctic winter, he nursed his grudges. He disliked Mr. Hall since the time Captain Budington had taken him down for being careless with Mr. Hall's deckload of supplies. Now, seeing I was intimate with Mr. Hall, Coleman transferred his dislike to me.

"Think you're quite a case, don't you?" he growled at me one day. Having run low on coal, we were reduced to burning some of our whalebone in the stove. It was porous and filled with oil, making a fine fuel, but had first to be sawed and split into logs. "God, if there's anything I hate, it's a greenhorn know-all!" He straightened up from his labors, leaning on his ax.

I don't think I was afraid of him, but his words were so obviously an attempt to start trouble that I did not reply, only going ahead with my sawing of the bone slabs on the buck. My silence infuriated him and he went on, savoring his words with obvious malice.

"Captain's pet, that's what you are, Burritt! Too highfalutin to mix with us common seamen, ain't that it? Might contaminate you!"

This was unfair, of course. I liked Sterry and Keeney and Vess and the rest of the forecastle hands, and had great respect for them as fine men and hard workers. But I bit my tongue and said nothing. Nothing, that is, until he turned his vile tongue on Mr. Hall.

"Buddies to that crazy Hall, too, ain't you? I seen you going to his cabin all the time." He laughed coarsely and wiped his lips with the back of his hand. "Don't think you're fooling anyone, boy. I been on ships too long to mistake it." Leering at me, waving the ax to keep time, he began to sing a dirty song.

"Stop it," I said.

"You make me."

"All right, then, I'll make you!"

I flew at him, and the shock of my coming was enough to drive him against the deckhouse, the ax flying from his hands. For a moment we slipped and teetered on the greasy deck, then fell among the scraps of bone.

"Take it back!" I shouted, driving my fists into his midriff. "You damned liar! Take it back!"

I wish I could say I beat Coleman into senselessness and later, my knee on his chest, forced him to apologize, both to me and to Mr. Hall. But it was hardly so. Coleman had been a long time in the whalers. He knew every trick, every subtle advantage, every way to maim and injure and kill. He twisted under me like an eel and wound his muscular arms around my chest, squeezing me in a hug like an iron vise. His chin was dug into the nape of my neck, and the pressure made my eyes swim and dark spots dance in my vision.

The captain was gone on a visit to one of the villages and Mr. Rogers was in charge. Close in many ways, he and the captain saw differently in this kind of a situation. Old Bud would not have violence on his ship, but Mr. Rogers demanded only that it be a fair violence, conducted according to rules. Almost at once we were surrounded by spectators. I saw Mr. Rogers there also, his face grave, but making no attempt to stop the fight, nor did I want him to. I had struck the first blow; very well, I would finish it myself.

I bent, thrusting out a leg. Coleman lost his bear squeeze and tripped over my outspread leg. I jumped on top of him and got his throat in my hands. "Take it back!" I said again. "Every last word of it, you lying rascal!"

Again he skittered away beneath me, and at the same time

caught me on the side of the head with his knotted fist. Lights flashed; my head rang with the sound of far-off bells; I rolled blindly over in the scraps of bone and struggled to my knees. I saw Coleman's boot coming at my head and I rolled away from it, managing somehow to twine my arms around his leg and pull him down again. But this time he fell heavily and expertly on me, driving his knee into my chest, and all the air whooshed out of me in one great sobbing breath. I lay there, beaten and helpless. Almost as in a dream I saw Coleman snatch up the bone ax and swing it over his head. In the nick of time, someone jumped forward—I think it was Sterry—and said, "That's enough of that!"

Coleman struggled with the ax, still trying to split me like a salmon. But others came forward and pinioned his arms, and finally he tossed the ax aside, eyes glazed in a kind of stupor.

"Go below, Adam," Mr. Rogers said mildly. He turned to Vess. "Give Coleman a hand with the bone."

I went below and sat on my bunk. Sterry brought a wet slab of meat and held it over my eye, which was rapidly closing. "Beef's usually prescribed," he said, "but maybe seal will do."

My shirt was torn from my back, my mouth was cut, my knuckles were barked and bleeding. But I hadn't done too badly.

"Next time," I said, "I'll kill him." It was an idle and vapid statement, but when you are young you do not recognize defeat.

It was not long after that when Mr. Hall got his great chance at the Dreaded Land. It came about in a peculiar way. There was among the Esquimaux, both of Greenland and of Baffin Island, a dreadful custom, making sense to them, I suppose, but cruel and inhuman to my way of looking at it. Whenever a person was very sick and his life was despaired of, it was the custom to build a new and fresh igloo in which the sufferer was put, walled in with only a small opening to hand in occasional food and water. So far as I could find from Blind George and Jennie and Annawha and the rest, this placed the whole matter in the hands of some Great Being. If this Being decided the sufferer would live, very well; if he decided the sufferer should die, then he would have died anyhow. Since he was already in his tomb, it was a neat and practicable system. Moreover, there was fear among the Innuits of contamination by the death spirit; a person was required to die thus alone, out of contact with his fellows, lest he somehow contaminate them. Now Hannah, or Tookoolito, had been pregnant when we last saw her in Oolootong village. Mr. Hall found out through Blind George, who was a walking newspaper, that Hannah was dying. Because of trouble with her baby she had been put, as custom required, in an isolated igloo to await the end.

Mr. Hall was like a madman when he heard of it, intending to go at once to Oolootong village and rescue her. But Captain Budington would not hear of it.

"I say ye shall not! This is an Innuit custom, and what they do in that respect is their own business. We depend in the whaling on their good will, and I will not have anyone meddling in their customs and practices!"

"I don't care what you say!" Mr. Hall was vehement, and with his uncut beard and wild eyes he looked like a Biblical prophet. "It is a cruel and barbarous custom! I wonder that you, Captain, being a good Presbyterian, can countenance such a business!"

"I do not countenance it or otherwise. I simply say that it is none of your business, nor mine either."

"The Lord looks on all of us as his children. When one suffers, all suffer. Because this woman's skin is brown, is that any reason to close our eyes to her suffering?"

There was a curious difference between these two men. To old Bud, his religion was a familiar and everyday sort of thing, as common and useful as his boots or hat, but not, I fear, going very deep below the surface. To Mr. Hall, on the other hand, the Christian religion was a mystical thing, tied up somehow

71]

with his search. In its influence he was transformed, seeing visions, elevated into starry realms which were often impracticable, however Christian otherwise.

"If ye go, then," shouted the captain, "don't mind to come back, sir! Ye have caused me enough trouble, and Williams and Haven, too! Take your sledge and dogs and your damned traps and be gone!"

I felt desolate at this new outbreak between them. They were both good men, God-fearing and sincere. It is a pity that often some ingredient in one man will break out in a rash on the other. But that was the way it had to be. Mr. Hall got together Barbekark and his dogs and sledge, and I helped him load his supplies aboard for the trip to Oolootong village again, where he had once gone unwillingly by his boat.

"Good luck," I said.

He was still not well, but I had no doubt he would reach the village. On nothing but sheer will, disregarding the limitations of his body, he would do it.

"Thank you, Adam." He wrapped the plaid scarf about his neck, and with a wave to me trudged off behind the heavily loaded sledge.

I watched him until he had disappeared into the dark, although for a long time I could hear the creaking of harness, the barking of his dogs, and the occasional crack of his whip. In spite of his high purpose, I was inclined to agree with old Bud. No good could come of this. I did not know, however, that the whole business had in it the key to the Dreaded Land. And if I *had* known, I wonder if I would have given Mr. Hall credit for a Christian act of love, or seen in it only a very shrewd maneuver to serve his own purposes. He was a dedicated man, but I was not yet too sure to what, or whom, he was dedicated.

Chapter 5

WE ARE creatures of the sun and cannot live for long without it. The Arctic night, the winds, the desolation of ice and snow—all seemed to bear heavily on the *George Henry*, pressing her crew down and ever down into apathy, then boredom, and finally an uneasiness not far from panic. It was a disease well known among the whalers, and could be fought only by activity. Captain Budington knew the signs, and knew also the treatment. He worked harder than any of us simply in keeping jobs laid out; anything to keep his crew busy and out of mischief. Gear was painted, metalwork polished till it shone. The tools of whaling were gotten out; blubber spades were honed to razor sharpness, line gone over inch after endless inch, doubtful sections cut out and new pieces rove in. Oil and bone was moved here and there, out of this place and into another, trying, I suppose, to find an arrangement which would make more room for the coming summer's haul, yet I suspected that old Bud was simply at his wit's end to keep us busy. But after the long winter, even made jobs became scarce. Restless and edgy, we sat in the forecastle, for the most part silent and grouchy, playing San Pedro. Some of the men darned and sewed clothing; others lay in bunks staring at the overhead, thinking long thoughts. Occasionally there would be a sporadic outburst of activity. Sterry and the older hands would get up a football game, played on the ice in the moonlight with a walrus bladder as ball. One night, almost in desperation, I made a drum out of a cheesebox, and Vess contrived a banjo from a tin pan and scraps of bone. We had a concert that turned into a rough-and-ready dance, the men linking arms and stamping and shouting, reeling back and forth, forgetting the Arctic night. But soon that wore out, also, and we sat down again, looking covertly at each other. Would the sun never come? Were we in some strange Hades, shut off forever from light and heat and growing things? I thought of grass, how green and delightful it was, and had dreams of lying in a lush bed of it, soft and velvety and fresh-smelling. I thought also of Mr. Hall and envied him his activity. Better die in a howling storm, eaten by one's own dogs, than lie in my bunk on the *George Henry* withering in boredom!

But at last the sun came back. Once I had seen it rising red over the southern horizon, I wondered how I ever doubted the laws of physics. It shone like a red coal, a glowing ember balanced on the mountain peaks. Shadows threw the frozen land into sharp relief. How blessed a thing was a shadow! The upper works of the *George Henry* were tipped with gold, and a grotesque ghost ship lay alongside us for a moment, the image of the *George Henry*. Because of the low elevation of the sun, the shadow stretched a mile or more across the bay. As we watched, the sun wheeled and the shadow went around, reminding me of a sundial.

Men cheered at the sight and swore, pounding each other on the back. Tin pans were beat on, a charge of black powder set off, and the captain ran up the flag. Before we had a proper chance to celebrate, the sun was gone again, dipping below the horizon, leaving only a flush in the sky to mark its passing. But it was enough; we had seen it, we knew it was there and had not abandoned us. A new life poured into our veins. Men who had not spoken to others for weeks became cheerful and co-operative. Others who had lain for weeks in filthy bunks, wearing foul and tattered clothing, became suddenly sanitary, washing shirts and drawers. Cookie, surly no matter the time of year, brought out a hidden store of raisins and pickles and made a duff from the last of the dried apples. The alchemy of the sun was unbelievable.

Day by day it visited us for a longer period. In its growing light and warmth we chopped the *George Henry* free of her winter prison. From successive snows and storms she had been frozen into a gigantic ice palace, her contour lost, only spars and upper rigging showing above the great white mound. Axes and saws were passed out and all hands fell to, hacking and shoveling. Once we uncovered her to the water line, then the ice saws were brought out. Twenty-odd feet long, they were passed through holes chopped in the bay ice. Two and three men to the handle, we sawed out great chunks of the bay ice, making a narrow channel out to the already weak and rotting ice at the mouth of Kowtukjua Bay. As the spring wore on, we worked stripped to the waist, herding the blocks of ice with pike poles, pushing them down the channel and out to the open ocean. The time was not far off when the *George Henry* would fill her sails and move down the narrow corridor to the sea.

One sunny day, with fleecy clouds moving windily in the sky, Mr. Hall came back to us, his sledge moving around the edge of Kowtukjua Bay on thin and dangerous ice. I saw him first, recognizing him with the aid of Mr. Rogers' spyglass, and ran to tell Captain Budington.

"Back, is he?" Old Bud's face was a study.

"There are some people with him."

"God help us!" The captain closed the log, in which he had been writing, and came topside with me, buttoning his black coat. "Aye, it's him, all right!"

The sledge halted below us on the ice. Mr. Hall came up the ladder hand over hand, with a speed and agility that surprised me. Where last he had been gaunt and hollow-eyed, he was now vigorous and healthy; even his nut-brown beard seemed to sparkle glossily and his tattered muffler whipped in the wind like a banner.

"Adam! And Captain Budington!"

He shook hands warmly, as if there had never been any problems among us. After him two Innuits came up the ladder. One, I saw, was Joe, the Esquimaux. The other was Joe's wife, Hannah, the handsome and gracious woman who had nursed Mr. Hall through his sickness at Oolootong village. On her back, strapped in a fur sack, was a baby, a black-eyed, healthy butter-ball.

"I'm glad ye're back," old Bud admitted, somewhat grudgingly. "To tell the truth, I worried somewhat."

"I too," I said.

Mr. Hall chuckled. "A bad penny always turns up." He turned to Hannah and tickled the baby under the chin with a big finger. "Meet Tuk-e-lik-e-ta, Hannah's child. You might say I am his godfather. Aye, and midwife, too! It was a near thing, Adam."

"I am glad it turned out so well," I said.

Old Bud cleared his throat and tugged at his whiskers. He was, I think, wondering as I was, and perhaps embarrassed. But Hannah was not at all embarrassed. She looked at Mr. Hall with love and devotion in her dark eyes. "Father Hall saved me and my baby," she said. She took his hand in hers and kissed it while Joe nodded with approval.

"Everything," said Mr. Hall, "is in books. In my studies, I neglected nothing to prepare for my explorations." He threw back the hood of his *koo-lee-tang* in a vigorous gesture, and his

[76

deep-set eyes sparkled as he looked about him. "Lord, what a land! Smell that air! Look at the way the sun sparkles on the snow! God must love this land as I do."

I knew he had not come back to the *George Henry* to smell the air, it being no different here than it was at Oolootong village. Captain Budington knew this also, and was uneasy. Finally he blurted out, "And what are your plans now?"

Mr. Hall was serious.

"Captain, I need a boat."

"I can spare none. They will be needed for the summer's whaling."

Mr. Hall raised his hand. "Now hear me out, first!" He nodded at Joe and Hannah. "These good people are grateful to me for saving their baby. Not that it was I who did it, really; the Lord guided my hand. But nevertheless they want to thank me for it. To do so properly, they have agreed to go with me to the Dreaded Land!"

"But—"

"Think of it, Captain! These simple, uneducated people, frightened as they are to go into such a place—nevertheless they will go, simply to show their gratitude. Can you, a God-fearing and knowledgeable Presbyterian, do any less than they are willing to do for me?"

I think old Bud swore under his breath, but the words were not intelligible.

"Think of the Franklin people!" Mr. Hall said. "Think of those unlucky men—Europeans, white men—lost somewhere up there—" He waved his hand northward. "They are waiting up there in the wilderness, praying for deliverance. One small boat, Captain; that is all those lost souls ask from you! One small boat to take me and my company into the Dreaded Land and rescue them from imprisonment."

Hannah stepped forward, eyes downcast. The gilt band in her black hair shone in the sun, and around her neck was looped a barbarous necklace of bear claws and colored beads. Even in her odd rig of sealskins, ornamented with dozens of federal copper cents traded for with the whalers, she was ladylike and impressive.

"Captain, sir, I beg you to give Father Hall what he needs to find these unfortunate people." She pulled the child around under her arm and touched him on the head. "Father Hall has given me this small life. Maybe he can find the Franklin people in the Dreaded Land, and give life to them also." Saying "The Dreaded Land" in her Innuit tongue, she paled noticeably but her voice was steady and composed. "Please do this, sir."

Old Bud blew out a long breath. "God damn it, what kind of a choice do ye give me?"

"Then you'll do it?"

"Number four whaleboat has got some rotten planks. I intended keeping her by for a spare. But I'll warn ye, I take no responsibility for anything. She's leaky, and cranky in the water, and with a sail up she goes sideways like a crab."

Mr. Hall shouted with delight. He capered about the deck, hand in hand with Joe and Hannah.

"I'll have Mr. Rogers break her out," said Captain Budington. "For the most part, the ice is gone from the bay. Ye can leave whenever ye're a mind to."

Convinced against his better judgment, he went below, shaking his head and muttering again under his breath. I followed, intending to lose no time. Knocking at his cabin door, I asked to talk to him.

"I know what's on your mind," he said, sitting down at his table, the log spread before him and his inkstand to hand. "The idiot's infected ye too, Adam! Isn't that true?"

"He's no idiot. He's a remarkable man!"

Old Bud shook his head. "They make the best idiots." He put his chin on his hand, staring at the pages of the log. I realized with a shock that it was the first time I had ever seen him without his black hat. His skull was bare and pink, fringed with a grass of white hair. "If Williams and Haven ever ask me again to take an amateur explorer north, I'll put sinkers in my breeches and jump over the side. It's easier that way."

"But may I go?"

"Ye signed on for the whaling!"

"I did," I admitted. "But I'm willing to give up my lay right now. Only let me go with him!"

"But why?"

"I don't know. Maybe it's just that I believe in him. Maybe it's just that I like him. Maybe he's a great man, in spite of all, and I want to go with him and do the things he's bound to do."

The captain picked up his pen and examined the nib. "Aye, I guess that's it! Maybe that's why I haven't thrown him off my ship and bade him go whistle for a boat." He threw the pen from him and leaned back in his chair, chin on his chest. "I knew Doctor Hayes, and Doctor Kane, and the other men who once came here to explore. They're all of a stripe. There's something in them that drives them on, and on, and on. A touch of spirit that's denied to the rest of us."

"I can go, then?"

He looked at me with exasperation. "I didn't say ye couldn't, did I?"

Grabbing his hand, I pumped it wildly, and ran to find Mr. Hall.

In the heavily laden whaleboat it took us almost a month to round the southern tip of Baffin Island and make our way northward into Frobisher Strait. Although this was the long way around to our destination, it was the only way to get there, now that the snow was leaving the land and sledging was no longer possible. So we set our tiny sail, all hands pulled at the oars, and we crept northward through Frobisher Strait—Mr. Hall, Hannah and her baby, Joe, and me. For a time, the Innuits being so sociable, we had the company of other native boats, friends of Hannah and Joe. But as we bore northward into this forbidding country, our friends left us. One by one they turned back, for fear of the Dreaded Land.

Mr. Hall was in the bows, spyglass to his eye, examining the shore line. From time to time he wrote in his journal, entering measurements made with his thermometer, or the angle to a certain headland. "Adam," he said, "what do you think of this country?"

I rested for a moment on my oar, sweat running down my neck. "It's well named."

All round us were forbidding, precipitate peaks, wreathed with gray storm clouds. In spite of the advanced season, the air was cold and metallic-smelling. The waters of the strait were laced with whitecaps, and where we would ever put in for a landing I didn't know. The shore line seemed one long rocky escarpment, ready to pick a small boat to pieces and spit the wreckage about for miles. Since we had come into the strait, we had seen no living thing—no birds, no seals, nothing. It was as if some Power had put a stamp on this land—FORBIDDEN. I shivered and looked at Joe, who was pulling the other oar. He blinked back at me and spat over the side, his brown face pale. Behind him, in the stern, sat Hannah, clutching the Bible Mr. Hall had given her, little Tuk-e on her lap. When time permitted, Mr. Hall was teaching her to read from the Bible. She wet her lips and called out to him, pointing. "Over there, sir. In that break in the rocks. There is a small harbor where we can put in for the night."

In civilized life there are risks, of course, but a man is not apt to be much in danger. Protective barriers are put around dangerous machines, horsecars have bells to warn encroachers on the rails, police are at hand if a footpad accosts a man. Living in the society he has organized, man is at least partially insulated from the consequences of his indiscretions. But here, in this barren and sterile country, we were directly in the hand of nature, and nature did not care whether we survived or not.

We found that out as we tacked in through the narrow inlet to the bay that Hannah had indicated. One moment, we were working hard with sail and oar, trying to point up into the wind and struggle within the rocky gap. The next, we were caught in a great sucking tide that bore us high and fast, like a cork in a sewer drain. The wind was offshore, that was true; but pouring through the entrance to fill the bay was a tidal bore that roared and spat foam high into the air, driving us with the speed of a bullet.

"Pull!" Mr. Hall shouted. "Adam—Joe—pull!" He stumbled across the thwarts reaching for the sheet, but before he could slack it off the wind ripped our patched sail into ribbons. Seizing a spare oar for a sweep, he stood in the stern and tried to turn us away from the maelstrom. "Pull!" he shouted again, pointing northward to the course that would set us at right angles to the current and perhaps take us out of danger.

We slewed sidewise. Joe and I dug deep with our oars, and stood on the thwarts with the exertion of our efforts. But our strokes were not together and the only result seemed to be to lay us broadside to the current. We heeled dangerously over and were in danger of broaching. Indeed, our rail dipped once, and a flood of foamy water came over the side. When the boat righted, it lay a foot deep.

Hannah, brave but pale, clutched her baby in one arm and attempted to bail with a tin bucket. But we were deep in the water. The battered whaleboat rolled sluggishly, as if contemplating going under for sure.

"We've got to go in whether we want to or not!" Mr. Hall shouted. "Hang on tight, everyone! Joe, you and Adam stop rowing! Just hold your oars out, and fend us off from the rocks if we come too close!"

Traveling at terrible speed, we were now only within a hundred yards of the rocky gap. Faster and ever faster we hurtled, the hull actually making a singing noise as we drove on. The dun rocks loomed up fast, larger and larger. The noise was deafening as the bore flung itself through the gap. Spray leaped high in the air and the noise was like some great rapids, which indeed it was. *To have come so far,* I thought to myself, *to die.* I was not frightened; only perplexed, and a little sad.

"Our Father," shouted Mr. Hall, "which art in Heaven—"

Standing in the waist, hanging on to the small mast, he put one hand down and touched Hannah on the shoulder.

"Hallowed be Thy name!"

We soared up, and up, borne on the wall of water. Blindly I poked out my oar, trying to fend us off the rocks. A jar ran up my arm, and the oar splintered and was flung back into the boat.

"Thy Kingdom come, Thy will be done—"

The gap was filled with spray as thick as driven snow, and we could see nothing. A swerve of the boat toppled me from my seat and I fell over backward, hitting my head. The ribs shivered and grated, and more water poured in through the seams. Stunned, I lay on my back in six inches of water, staring up at the evening sky. I blinked, suddenly realizing that the spray was gone, the roar of the gap was now only a dull murmur, the whaleboat now floated placidly, although low.

"On earth," said Mr. Hall, "as it is in Heaven."

He still clung to the mast, looking down at me. "If you and Joe will take up your oars and row, very carefully so as not to swamp us, we can reach that gravelly beach over there, and boil some coffee."

We were low in provisions, not having started with much, and having taken longer to pass through the straits than we intended. The *George Henry* was also short of provisions, being already almost a year in the Arctic, and could not spare a great deal. Captain Budington, with the interests of Williams and Haven at heart, had sold Mr. Hall ship's biscuit and coffee and molasses, taking a note for supplies. Mr. Hall was penniless but had promised to pay off the note with money from friends, once he was back in the States. Now we huddled on the beach, drinking coffee and gnawing biscuit, watching Joe stalk an undersized duck in a shallow backwater. It was a peculiar chase, and I did not hold much hope for a duck dinner. But Joe knew what he was doing. Endlessly, and with great patience, he slipped up on the duck. The duck, annoyed, would dive and swim underwater a few yards away, bobbing up with a ruffle of his tail. Again Joe would make for him, and the duck would dive. Being forced to stay so much underwater, the duck eventually tired. With a shout of triumph, Joe flung himself on the bird and wrung its neck.

"How much farther to where the *kod-lu-na* house is?" Mr. Hall asked Hannah, gnawing on a drumstick only half-cooked. Blood oozed down his chin, and he wiped it away with a corner of his muffler.

"Two days," said Hannah. Squatting in the firelight, she nursed her child. "Maybe three. We go to where water stops." Her voice trembled a little as she spoke of going farther into the Dreaded Land. Beyond her, Joe's dark eyes flickered in the firelight, and he said nothing. He spoke little, preferring to leave talk to Hannah.

"Where the water stops?" Mr. Hall was puzzled. "But the water doesn't stop." He got his map, printed on oiled silk, and spread it out in the firelight. "We are in Frobisher Straits, Hannah. The maps show the straits going north to the Great Arctic Sea."

Hannah shook her head. "Stops up there." She pointed. "A two-day sail. Maybe three. No more."

Mr. Hall scratched his head. He knew, as I had found out, that the Innuits were great geographers. Almost any one of them could make a sledge journey for a thousand miles and come back with an accurate and neatly done map. Hannah was not likely to make a mistake on such a matter as this. Mr. Hall grinned and threw away the drumstick, licked and sucked clean of marrow.

"Adam, just so are great discoveries made!" He pointed to

his map. "Frobisher Straits is not a strait at all. It is a bay. The Hall expedition has already made a contribution to science."

It was true. Two days later, having patched up our whaleboat and mended the sail, we came to the end of the so-called "straits," now renamed by Mr. Hall Frobisher Bay. Here we drew our boat up on a sandbar and looked about us.

"Someplace around here," said Hannah. "Ookijoxy-Ninoo is never wrong." Sniffing the air like an animal, she walked the length of the bar, little Tuk-e in his sling on her back. Back and forth she walked, pale but determined, pausing only to crane her neck stiffly, stare about at the shoreline, and move on. "I will find the place."

Joe, I believe, was too terrified to leave the boat. He sat dejectedly in the stern, looking from one of us to the other in turn, as if waiting to hear the suspension of a death sentence. In a way, I did not blame him. The country at the head of Frobisher Bay was unreal, almost unearthly. Clouds hung near the peaks of the low mountains and beyond the narrow perimeter of sand and gravel the earth was boggy and black. Trying to walk in it, I sank to my knees in the ooze. A sulphurous odor rose up and almost strangled me. No birds were here, no animals, no sign of life. All about was only silence.

"Think of it!" Mr. Hall whispered. "We are here, in the Dreaded Land at last! This is a moment for history, Adam! Maybe there are Franklin survivors within a mile or two of this spot. Perhaps they are within sound of our voices." He took a deep breath and let out a bellow at the top of his voice.

"Hallo-oo-oo-oo!"

The sound spread round us in the mists, reflecting back from the rain-shrouded peaks in gentle echoes, growing softer and ever softer until at last completely gone. The only sound was the lapping of water on the bar.

"Halloo-oo-oo!"

Echoes, again, and when they were gone it started to rain;

a rustling rain that was not far from a mist, although it wet us through at once.

At this time of the year the sun stayed above the horizon until late in the evening. We could not see it, of course, because of the rain clouds that wreathed the mountains, but it must have been almost seven in the evening. "It will be getting dark soon," said Mr. Hall. "Hannah, do you have any idea of which way we must go to find the hut and the coal and the anvil Ookijoxy-Ninoo said was there?"

I think that Hannah knew. She looked at Mr. Hall, however, with expressionless eyes, eyes that were wooden and empty. "I don't know where," she said. "I am not sure this is the place. It is very late, too. Maybe we better get in the boat and go back."

"But you told me it was here!"

"I cannot tell. It looks like the place, but I am not sure."

Mr. Hall looked at Joe, but Joe only looked away.

"Come now, Hannah." Mr. Hall was very gentle. "There is nothing here that can hurt you. I have depended on you and Joe to help me. I know you are good people, and I can trust you."

Hannah began to cry, torn between her love for Father Hall and dread of this silent place. Joe, troubled too, came and stood beside her, shifting from one foot to the other, not meeting Mr. Hall's eye.

"Very well," said Mr. Hall. "Adam and I will go, then. We are not frightened of ghosts or spirits." He threw the plaid muffler about his neck with a flourish. Picking up his musket he motioned me to follow. "I think it is this way, near that pile of gray rocks that looks like an elephant." He looked at Hannah and she nodded her head dumbly, but made no move to join us. "Very well, then. Joe, see if you can find some dry twigs and brush and start a fire. Hot coffee will taste good when we get back."

We started up the gradual slope that led to the mountains,

85]

floundering about in the ooze, making our tortuous way from one rock to the other. Fortunately, after we had gone a hundred yards or so, the earth became less boggy. "It can't be far from here," Mr. Hall said. "They would have built it near the water, perhaps to be able to launch a boat or to catch fish."

In the misty twilight there was no sound but the scrape of our boots on the rocks, and the sighing of the wind in the rocks high over our heads. Looking back, we saw the orange wink of a fire on the beach below. "Moments like this," said Mr. Hall, "are worth a lifetime of pedestrian effort, Adam." His eyes searched the barren hillside. "Perhaps someone is still there, even now, waiting for the sound of a human voice!"

I could hardly keep up with him. Twice my age, and encumbered with the musket, he scrambled ahead like a goat, pausing only to shout and listen to the echoes that came back. Sweat ran off me in rivulets and my heart hammered in my chest. *Let him find it,* I thought. *It means so much to him.*

We found it. We found it by falling headlong into a long shallow pit someone had dug on the hillside, a long time ago. Mr. Hall disappeared from view. When I had crept up to the edge of the pit, I found him sitting in the bottom holding a lump of coal in his hand.

"Coal, Adam! The coal!"

From my perch at the edge of the pit I saw something else in the twilight, a few yards beyond the long trench. It was the ruins of a house, a stone house covered with moss to the extent that it had lost its sharp outlines. I ran to it, and Mr. Hall followed me, clutching the lump of coal in his hand. Pulling aside the blanket of moss, he ran his fingers over the joints between the stones. "Cemented," he said. "Very expertly, with lime and sand."

Standing beside the house, we could now see the length of the mysterious trench. It had apparently been dug out of the stone with pickaxes and crowbars. About a hundred and fifty

feet in length, it was oddly constructed, representing an inclined plane starting at the surface of the earth beside us and
sloping to a depth of twenty feet or more at the far end, near
the water's edge.

"This must be it!" I cried. Stooping, I picked up something
that shone dully in the faint light. It was a metal button, cor-
roded and greenish, with the outline of a kind of upright
rearing animal on it. "Look at this, sir!"

Mr. Hall seemed dazed. Instead of sharing my excitement, he
looked down at the lump of coal in his hand, weighing it
with a kind of repetitious gesture.

"You've found the place!" I cried. "They were here, some
time ago. Maybe they have left a note, something to guide us!"

"Aye," he said. "Some time ago."

"But what's the matter? I don't understand."

He tossed the coal away, looking at me with an expression
that pierced me to the heart. "Look over there, Adam. Do you
see the other stone houses? That pile of rocks near the largest
stone house is probably the remains of a blacksmith's forge.
And these—" He dug the toe of his boot into a moss-grown
mound. "Pyrites of iron. There was a mine here, a long time
ago. Ah, what a joke on me, to waste a whole year in coming at
last to—to *this!*" Shaking his head, he sat down on the mound,
supporting himself with the musket as if very tired.

"What do you mean?"

"Just this; there has been no one here for three hundred
years. These ruins have nothing at all to do with the Franklin
people. I should have known from what the old woman said!
The stone houses, Adam, are all that is left of the Frobisher
party, which left England in the year 1577 and came here to dig
for gold."

"But how do you know?"

"I have read Sir John Barrow's book on Frobisher."

"What, then, is the long trench?"

"They built a ship here, Barrow says. Look; in the bottom of the trench you can see the remains of the wooden trestles they used."

"And we are the first white men here since?"

"I suppose so," Mr. Hall said wearily.

Seeking to cheer him, I said, "Well, that is not a half-bad record! A new bay discovered, and the three-hundred-year-old remnants of the Frobisher expedition."

"That is not what I came here for." An aura of despair surrounded Mr. Hall. His frame seemed bent and defeated, losing its outline and form much as the stone houses had done under their covering of moss. "Oh Lord, to trick Thy servant so! What have I done? Adam, I wasted a year in this wild-goose chase! A year out of my life, and out of *theirs,* also!"

He meant the Franklin people, of course.

"No man can blame you," I said. "Look at what you have done! With no experience, you have come into this land, lived like one of the Innuits, learned their language, explored hundreds of miles on sledge journeys and by boat, determined that this strait is not a strait at all, found the Frobisher site—"

"No," he said. "I have failed, and that is all it can be called."

When we got back to the *George Henry,* it was late in the season. As a matter of fact, we were lucky to catch the vessel as she was getting ready to depart. Mr. Hall was desolate, keeping to his cabin, talking only to Joe and Hannah, whom he had prevailed on to accompany him to the States in an attempt to raise funds for a new expedition, this time to King William Land where he believed he should have gone before. As well as I had known him, he seemed to avoid me. I believe he was ashamed of his debacle, as he called it, although he had no reason to be so.

We reached St. John's, in Newfoundland, late in August of 1862. That was when I first learned the South had gone to war against the North, and also that Mr. Lincoln had been elected President in such a terrible time. At New Bedford I left the ship. Captain Budington insisted on paying me my lay, and I had six hundred and eighty dollars in my valise. Saying good-by to Vess and Sterry and Mr. Rogers and Joe and Hannah and the rest, I went over the rail. Piqued at Mr. Hall's coolness, I determined to leave without farewell. But as I walked away up Merrill's wharf he called to me.

"Adam?"

He leaned over the stern rail, gaunt and haggard in appearance, the old plaid muffler whipping in the wind. "Thank you, boy. Thank you for everything you have done for me! And good luck."

I waved back, and trudged toward the railway station.

THE SECOND VOYAGE

1864–1869

Chapter 6

THAT winter I worked in a New Haven boatyard, not making much money but gaining a great deal of experience. When spring came, I felt restless and so I quit my job and went home to see my father. Cincinnati looked dingy and overcrowded after the limitless vistas of the Arctic. I tried to find some of my boyhood friends, but the war had uprooted most of them. Charlie Baylor was dead at Bull Run, and Oren Fickas too. Billy Knox—the one we used to call Tootie because he ran around chuffing like a steam engine—was a colonel in Tennessee someplace. "No," I was told, at door after door, "John isn't here. He's in the army." Or it was Henry, or Jimmy Digges, or whoever. I wandered around Cincinnati, feeling lonely. I'd end up in the army, that was sure, if I wanted to see anyone I knew. They were raising volunteer regiments in Cincinnati, but I didn't take to them. A sheriff or a county judge would talk a bunch of courthouse loafers into going down to the Federal Building to sign up with him, and then they'd make him colonel. No, that wasn't for me. I'd been to Harvard College for a year, and I'd had experience as a whaler, too. I talked it over with my father and decided I'd go to Washington, D.C., to try for a commission.

Before I left on the steamcars, I remembered Mr. Hall had lived in Cincinnati, on Celestial Street. I got out a dog-eared note from my wallet. The number was 1051.

A quiet, soft-spoken woman answered the door, two small children peeking from behind her skirts.

"Mrs. Hall?" I asked. "I'm Adam Burritt. I was with your husband last year when he went to the Arctic."

She looked at me uncertainly. "He—he isn't here."

"Where is he then, ma'am?"

"I—I think in Washington." A woman who does not know the whereabouts of her husband is apt to be at a conversational disadvantage, and she fussed at her apron and pushed the children farther behind her.

"Well," I said, "I had hoped to see him."

I turned to go, thanking her, but she took me by the arm and pulled me back. "Won't you have a cup of coffee, Mr.— Mr.—"

"Burritt," I said. "Adam Burritt."

The house was well kept, but small and drab, with a minimum of furnishings and an odor of boiling cabbage. On a carved stand near a window was a framed water color of a bride, and a bearded groom which must have been Mr. Hall, although the resemblance was poor. His wife put a lump of coal in the stove and measured coffee into a pot.

"I didn't mean to be short with you, but we're all alone here, just me and the babies, and my land, you *did* look so rough with that beard and stocking cap!"

Over coffee and oatmeal cookies she made me tell her the story of the voyage, interrupting every now and then to hush the children or to say nervously, sitting on the edge of her chair, "Yes, that's so. That's exactly what he said."

It became quite late. Mrs. Hall invited me for supper, saying, "It's not much. Just boiled cabbage and potatoes." But I was talked out. She had kept me gabbing for three hours or more, and I had to refuse. Disappointed, she wrapped up some cookies for me to take on the train. "If you should run into him," she said, wrapping the cookies in paper, "tell him—will you tell him we miss him, and think of him always?"

Suddenly she burst into tears, clinging to me and weeping.

"Why doesn't he come home, Mr. Burritt? Why? Tell me why! I've been a good wife all these years. I've put up with everything because I love him. I've borne his children, I've scrubbed floors and cooked and done sewing to buy books and maps for him. Doesn't he love me any more? Has he forgotten me and the children?"

I was embarrassed at the sudden outburst and did not know quite what to do. "Well," I said, "I don't know, ma'am. He's awful busy, you know. He's probably planning a new expedition. There's a lot of work that's got to be done, you see. I mean —well—"

I broke off, angry with myself at being forced to make excuses for Mr. Hall again. It was not the first time it had happened, and it would probably not be the last. To compound the confusion, the children started to weep also, in sympathy with their mother. Being tenderhearted, I felt tears well into my own eyes, and considered fleeing the scene. But Mrs. Hall hushed them and held out the packet of cookies, drying her eyes on the hem of her apron.

"I didn't mean to cry." She seemed angry and put out. "They're my troubles, and I'll deal with them myself somehow. But you'll look him up, perhaps, and tell him you saw us and we were well?"

"I'll do my best," I said. "And thank you for the cookies, ma'am."

I went away feeling puzzled and perplexed, and more than a little unhappy.

Washington was quite a place. Carrying my valise, I walked up Pennsylvania Avenue looking for the War Department building. Promenaders sauntered in the hot sun. Loaded hacks rumbled among the horses of officers, and elegant ladies drove in barouches, with black coachmen and footmen. At sidewalk stands pitchmen hawked patent soaps and elixirs. I stopped at a stand under a canvas awning and bought an orange to suck. Across the street a man with a lung-testing machine bawled for customers. Eating my orange, I went up to a policeman in a blue flannel coat and a straw hat, and asked him where to find the War Department.

"Up there." Grinning at me in a sly way, he pointed up the street. "Corner of Seventeenth and F. They're waiting for you, I suppose."

"I don't know," I said, "but I doubt it."

I found the place all right, but it didn't do me much good. A man in a flowered waistcoat, damp with sweat, sat at a desk in the foyer. When I told him what I wanted, he scribbled something on a piece of paper and told me to wait. I waited all that day, finally going to sleep on the wooden bench. When I woke up the clerk was gone for the day, and I went down the street and found a room at a brick house—number 1740, it was. To-morrow, perhaps, I would go back and try again, just to satisfy my father. But it didn't look as if they needed officers there.

In the morning it was hot again. It had rained during the night, just enough to make the air steamy and oppressive. I went back to the War Department. Another clerk listened to my story, promising a Colonel Halliday would see me if he had time. Thanking him, I went out and sat down on a bench in a little park nearby.

It is a small world, made every day smaller by the telegraph and steamships and railway engines. Sitting on my bench, I became aware of a familiar figure sitting across the park, writing in a ledger. My eyes popped in disbelief. It was Mr. Charles Francis Hall. If I had any doubt, the tattered plaid muffler hung limply from his neck. Why any man would wear a wool muffler in Washington in August, I didn't know.

"Adam!" He stared unbelievingly at me and then jumped up, the journal and his notes falling to the grass. "Adam Burritt!" He pumped my hand. "Of all people! What are you doing here in Washington?"

I told him. "And you?"

"Trying to raise money for my next expedition. Writing a book. Seeing congressmen and senators—the Army, the Navy —anyone who might give me a hand." Motioning me to sit beside him on the bench, he carefully rearranged the notes in his journal. "I am glad to see you again. When you left the *George Henry,* you went in such a hurry."

"I guess I did. But you didn't seem to want to see me."

He nodded and stroked his beard. "It was foolish of me, I know. I am often childish, and easily hurt. I was desolate, really. To have gone north, and then to fail so! I didn't want to talk to anyone; even—" He put his hand on mine. "Even a good friend."

I told him I had been in Cincinnati, and had visited his family.

"You did?" He seemed pleased, but not overly concerned. "That was nice of you."

"Where are Joe and Hannah?"

"We are living in a boardinghouse on H Street, near here. They will be pleased to see you, Adam! They are part of my traveling circus, you might say. Barbekark is here too, tied up in the back yard and suffering in this terrible heat. We have been giving talks wherever we could find an audience, asking for contributions to the expedition."

"I have some money. If you need it—"

"You will need money when you go to war."

"I'm not sure I'm going," I said. "At least not right now."
I told him about my experience at the War Department.

"But what do you plan to do?"

"I don't know."

He looked at me for a long moment, pulling at his beard.
"Then come with us, Adam! Be part of Professor Hall's magnificent Tent Circus and Arctic Display." He laughed and
banged me on the knee. "You can sell tickets! With that scraggly pink beard and stocking cap, you'll set the right tone for
my talk."

"You're joking," I said.

"No, I'm not." He slumped on the bench, looking at the
scuffed toes of his boots. "I will make no apologies for my little
company, Adam. It is a sorry thing when a man must sink to
being a clown to get money for a worthy purpose. But I still
believe there are Franklin people alive, somewhere, and they
must be rescued. I will solve the riddle of the Franklin expedition if I have to black boots to do it."

Impressed as always by his sincerity and determination, I
said, "If you really want me—"

"If I want you?" He sat bolt upright. "Adam, will you do it?
It will be like old times again—all of us together. You and me
and Hannah and Joe and little Tuk-e and Barbekark!"

I had not really wanted a sash and shoulder straps. And I
had tried. I picked up my valise and said, "Of course I'll do it.
I'll do whatever you want me to. Now, where is this rooming
house? H Street, did you say?"

From that chance encounter, I stayed two years with Mr. Hall
and his Tent Show, as he ruefully called it. How we lived I
don't quite know. My lay from the *George Henry* went the first
year, paying for an endless succession of dingy rooms, cheap
sausages and bread and coffee, with an occasional nickel left
over to buy a cake of ice to give Barbekark a bath. Born in the
Arctic, the poor dog suffered in the unaccustomed heat, and the

ice bath was all that saved him. Hannah and Joe, too, suffered from the heat. Sometimes I wondered why they were so loyal to Father Hall, and endured so much without complaint. They were stared at, treated rudely, and several times refused rooms because the proprietor thought they were "colored." But through it all Hannah remained ladylike and composed, and Joe was always gentlemanly, much more so than many of the people they performed before. "If it help him," Hannah told me one day, "I do anything for him. It is up to Father Hall to say when we don't try any more."

Our little troupe performed in many cities. Providence, Norwich, Hartford, New Haven, Hudson, Elmira—in these and many more we set up our show and tried to make money for the expedition. Hannah and Joe would sing Innuit songs, and dance; I acted as barker, ticket taker, and what might be called sergeant-at-arms when someone got unruly. Barbekark pulled a crude sledge across the stage, and Mr. Hall, at the end of all this, mounted the rostrum and spoke for an hour and a half about his latest expedition, and showed some of the Frobisher relics. But our financial condition remained poor. The reviews were not bad; one critic commented, "The lecturer could not claim polish or ease of oratory, but secured close attention by the tact and enthusiasm of these conversational discussions." It took a lot of money just to keep us all living and breathing and— need I add?—eating. The war was going badly too; people were worrying about places like Vicksburg and Lookout Mountain and Chancellorsville, and had little interest in us.

The situation was not helped by Mr. Hall's health. Ever since his illness from the abscessed shoulder at Oolootong village, he had been subject to spells of weakness; indeed, often fainting. A doctor in Boston diagnosed it as thickness of the blood and prescribed two pounds of raw beef each day by way of thinning it out. But prime beef was expensive, and this took our exchequer down even further. Besides, Mr. Hall was working on his book; having some trouble with it, he had to hire an Englishman, a Captain Snow, to help him. Harper Brothers had already made all the advances they cared to. Until the manuscript was finished, they would advance no more. So we struggled on, making a few dollars here, receiving a few contributions there, but dismayed to see it all eaten up by living expenses.

I don't know how Mr. Hall took care of his family. I didn't ask, and he didn't mention them, although he did sometimes write to his wife. Perhaps he sent some small sums, but that was his business. He had friends who might have helped—Mr. Henry Grinnell was one, but Mr. Hall still owed Grinnell quite a sum of money for financing his first expedition and hesitated to turn to him. We might have gone on this way for a long time, getting nowhere, if it had not been for the fresh disaster that struck our party. In New York City, on a windy February day, Hannah's little boy Tuk-e died.

For some time the child had been ill, coughing and having trouble with his breathing. Mr. Hall brought in a doctor, with the last money we had. "Something wrong with the lungs," the doctor said. "Consumption, I'm afraid."

"Consumption, in such a child?"

The doctor nodded gravely. "It's common among aboriginal peoples such as these."

Hannah cradled Tuk-e in her arms, singing softly. After a while she said something to Joe in Innuit which I didn't catch.

"But what can be done?"

"A change of climate, perhaps. Rest—good milk and fresh vegetables. A trained nurse would be helpful."

He might as well have recommended green cheese from the moon. Hannah appeared to have forgotten her English. She spoke sadly to Mr. Hall in Innuit again, pressing her lips against Tuk-e's feverish cheek.

"What does she say?" I asked.

"She wants an *an-ge-ko*. She thinks an *an-ge-ko* could help Tuk-e." Mr. Hall sighed. "I don't know where a man could find an *an-ge-ko* in New York City. But the worst of it is, it is all my fault. I talked Joe and Hannah into coming to the States with me. And look what I have done to them! Poverty, sickness—now even death, perhaps. And for what?"

A few days later Tuk-e died, very quietly. Hannah did not realize the boy was gone until Mr. Hall, tiptoeing into the room, saw the staring dead eyes and felt the cold body. Hannah fought us, not wanting to give up the small form. But Father Hall prevailed on her, and we buried Tuk-e. We were penniless. Even Hannah, that good and gracious lady, had given up. Desolate at the loss of Tuk-e, she sat for hours in a rocker at the window, staring out at the street.

"Don't grieve so," I said, trying to comfort her. "Little Tuk-e is in a far better world by now than we are in, you and I and Father Hall."

Used to her gentleness and unfailing courtesy, I was taken aback by her sudden anger.

"What do you know about it, Adam Burritt? How can you tell me this? It doesn't cost anything to talk, that is right." She flung herself to her feet, wrapping her arms about her as if to keep from flying apart in sorrow and grief. "My baby is dead, here in this cold bare land. Tuk-e is dead, sir. I have tried to be a good woman, to go with Father Hall wherever he wanted to walk, to help him, to cook for him, to do whatever he said. But now look at me!" Her dark eyes shone like jewels, hard and glittering. "The God that Father Hall tells me about is not good, or why would He have taken my baby away from me? What good is Tuk-e to Him? That God is great and powerful. He does not need a small baby!" Walking quickly about the room, she forgot her English and lapsed into Innuit, raving and almost incoherent. From time to time I heard whalers' words— strings of profanity that shocked and saddened me. In her grief poor Hannah was irrational.

"Hannah!" I begged. "Please! Don't carry on this way. I am very sorry for you, but this will do no good."

In the midst of her railing she stopped, hands still clasped about her, her brown tattooed face frozen in lineaments of grief and despair. "No." Her voice was hoarse, almost a whisper. "You are right, sir. It does not do any good. Tuk-e is dead. That is all." Coming to me, she took my hand in hers, patting it, holding it to her cheek. "You must not bother yourself with me," she said, tears in her eyes. "I am a bad woman, Adam. The devil just got into me, that is all."

"No," I said. "You are a good woman, Hannah. One of the best. It is just that times are bad with us."

"I think this is the end for Father Hall."

"Yes," I said. "This is the end."

But I reckoned without Mr. Hall. One day, coming into his room in search of him, I could not help but note the latest entry written in his journal. "Our greatest glory consists not in falling, but in rising every time we fall." Entering shortly behind me, he greeted me. I was somewhat embarrassed, but he did not notice and sat heavily in a chair.

"Adam, we are going to Washington."

"Washington? But how?"

"I have talked Harper Brothers into giving me a little more money for the chapters I have just finished."

"But what good will it do us to go back to Washington?"

"Washington is the center of the universe now, with the war going on, foreign military missions there, representatives of European newspapers. I am going to put everything I have— all my strength, what funds I have been able to beg, borrow, or steal—into one great assault on the problem. I will rent a hall, advertise in the papers, plan one last show. If that does not do it, then I will give up." He looked up at me, eyes burning in their sockets. He was sick, I knew, but undaunted. "I do not ask you to come with me if you do not want to. The Lord knows a young man like you, in the prime of life, has many opportunities denied to me. Go, if you want to!"

"I won't go, if you need me!"

He sighed and put his head in his hands. "God knows I need you, and Hannah and Joe, and any good friend I can get. Friends are hard to come by when a man is thought to be a crackpot. Even at Harper Brothers they are beginning to think that—" He broke off, shrugging. "Well, what does it matter?"

Unity Hall was a drafty brick building near the river, damp and ill kept, soon to be torn down to make room for an addition to the Observatory. Gaslights flickered on peeling walls, and a day-long airing by an indifferent custodian had removed much of the musty smell, if only to replace it with the dank atmosphere of the Potomac. It cost us twenty dollars out of our scanty funds, but it was the only hall available in the crowded city. Because of some clause in the deed to the hall, it was not permitted to sell tickets, as we had wanted. Instead, Mr. Hall intended to ask for contributions at the end of the lecture. We placed a small advertisement in the *Evening Star,* and hoped for a good house.

People started to arrive early, and I peered out through the dank curtains. The hall resounded with the clack and banging of chairs, the hum of voices, the rustle of feminine finery. Mr. Hall had sent invitations to several scientific men and professors who were interested in the Arctic. In the main, they had heretofore been unimpressed by his efforts, taking especial pains to point out his lack of education and training, but he hoped tonight to convince them. I saw one of them in the front row, pointed out to me by Mr. Hall. "Professor Thorne, the one with the gray beard and pince-nez! Beside him, that's Dr. Beckett, of the Geographical Society."

He was flushed, and I do not doubt he had a fever. Feeling that the daily ration of beefsteak was too much for our purse, he had given up this prescription, insisting he felt better.

After our little show, which was received with curiosity but not much enthusiasm, Mr. Hall stepped up the lectern and poured himself a glass of water; nervously, I thought. He had no notes. He never used notes. The whole case was in his head. I, too, had heard his talk so many times I could almost repeat it by rote.

"Fellow citizens," he said, clearing his throat.

His was a good voice and he knew how to use it. Against the hiss of the gas jets and the rustle of people and their breathing, his words came hard and sharp, with great conviction.

"I wish to deal tonight with the sad and lamentable case of the last voyage of Sir John Franklin and his ships *Erebus* and *Terror* to the far north."

The hall was silent. They were listening well.

"I see among you many scientific men, men who have visited the Arctic, as I have, and explored there. I know they are acquainted with the facts. But for you others whose support I seek, I will restate the facts. In May of 1845, some eighteen years past, Sir John Franklin set sail from England on a voyage of exploration, with a total of a hundred and twenty-nine men aboard his two ships. In the latter part of July of that year, the ships were seen in the vicinity of Lancaster Sound, north of Baffin Island, at a north latitude of almost 74 degrees. Never more were they seen by civilized man."

It was a dramatic and impressive start. He went on, telling about the relief expeditions that had been organized to search for the vanished ships—Sir James Ross, McClintock, and the rest—and explained why he thought they had failed. Warming to his task he demanded, "And what of the hundred or so men of the Franklin party? Can they be yet alive, some of them, living in hardship and peril in the frozen North?"

This was his chief point, of course. He went on to tell them about himself, his studies, his correspondence, his obsession with the Arctic, and his recent expedition there. "For the past ten years I have studied this riddle. I have read everything that has been published on the subject. I have corresponded with Lady Franklin herself, who is as anxious as I am to find the answer. I believe I am now on the right track."

[104

Now was the time to ask for funds, to press home on the note of American enterprise and intelligence now taking over where other nations had failed. But a disturbance arose in the audience. A voice called out, a voice casual but authoritative.

"Mr. Hall!"

It was Professor Thorne. He dangled his pince-nez from its ribbon, and it swung ominously in the gas flare, giving off sparks of light.

"Mr. Hall, you have been kind enough to invite me to attend your talk this evening. I thank you for this courtesy." He smiled and looked down at the swinging spectacles. "But for this courtesy I am bound to extend to you a similar one—my opinion of your theories."

"Sir," said Mr. Hall, "I am not quite finished. If you will bear with me—"

"No matter," said Thorne. "There is little more to be said anyway. The whole subject has been exhausted."

Someone tittered, and the audience rustled in anticipation of a diversion. Thorne was well known as an extemporaneous speaker and a wit.

Mr. Hall held up his hand to silence the growing buzz of comment. "Only a moment—"

"Mr. Hall," said Thorne, his voice rising, "you have wasted my time, sir, and the time of these good people. I think this is a calculated fraud, trading on the good will of our citizens. The puzzle of the Franklin expedition is no longer a puzzle, and has not been for some years. It is well established that all those unfortunate men have perished. What good will it do to suggest further risk of life and financial expense? What can be done now that has not already been done by well-qualified Arctic experts?"

Mr. Hall became angry.

"I will tell you, sir! So far what has been deduced? A meager theory, from scant evidence! So long as there is a possibility that one of those unfortunate men is still alive, why should not attempts be made again and again until all the facts are known? Are there not Esquimaux now living in those frozen lands? Why is it not possible for some of the Franklin survivors to be living there also, eating Esquimaux food, the raw flesh of seal and deer, dressed in furs, sustaining life day by day and waiting for delivery?"

"It is hardly possible," Thorne said. "A white man could not live on such fare. He would die. His stomach is not used to it."

"But I *have* done it!" Mr. Hall fairly roared the words. "To one educated otherwise, as we whites are, feasting on uncooked meats is repulsive, but I say eating meats raw or cooked is entirely a matter of education!"

Uproar fed on uproar, and several troublemakers began to catcall and stamp their feet. Others, wishing to avoid trouble, rose and started to leave the hall. "Only a moment!" Mr. Hall begged. "Wait! There is a box at the door for your contributions!"

"Mr. Hall!" Professor Thorne shouted. "I cannot allow you to appeal for funds for such a project without it being understood what your qualifications are. You are not a scientist, nor ever have been! You are not educated or trained in this field, and have made one short trip north, that due only to the kindness and generosity of Williams and Haven, the whaling firm. Now you propose to discount the body of scientific opinion, you propose to ignore the experts in this field, you propose another wild-goose chase to the Arctic, wasting the money of well-meaning citizens to satisfy your own morbid curiosities! No, sir, I can not countenance this, nor will I. Sir, you are a humbug, and an impostor!"

"Wait a minute!" Mr. Hall held his hands high in supplication, but the damage had been done. "Wait a minute! Please. All of you. Listen to what I have to say!"

Tittering started, a cruel tittering that grew into guffaws and jeers.

"Sir," said Professor Thorne with finality, "I am very sorry for you." He turned and walked out, followed by Dr. Beckett. Others joined in the exodus.

"Please, listen to me—"

Hurrying down from the stage, Mr. Hall took an arm here and a sleeve there, begging to be heard. "There is a box in the doorway there! Any contribution will be appreciated. Please, listen to me—"

They brushed past him, some sorry for him, some delighted, some frankly hostile, but none of them giving the contribution box anything but amused smiles. A man in a plug hat overturned the box with his cane, and someone else kicked it into a corner. "Fake!" a raucous voice called. A young lady who looked gentle and demure otherwise slapped at Mr. Hall with her reticule. Outside, a summer rain had begun to fall.

"Wait!" Mr. Hall called, but there was no one to speak to now. The hall had emptied and the spectators were all gone, some hailing hansom cabs, others turning up their coat collars, still others waiting under the trees for the rain to stop. "Wait," he murmured. "Please wait."

We had decked the foyer in bunting and wrapped yards of it about the contribution box, hoping to appeal to some patriotic motive. Mr. Hall picked up the box with its bedraggled bunting and held it in his hand. The colored man who was custodian of Unity Hall came up and said, "It ain't but a few minutes past nine, Cap'n. You got almost another hour before your twenty dollars is up."

Mr. Hall looked at the box and plucked off a bit of torn bunting. The bunting was wet from the rain, and the red and blue dye ran off onto his hand.

"I shan't need the rest of the time," he said.

Chapter 7

MR. HALL, as I have said, owed money to his friend Mr. Henry Grinnell. Grinnell, I later found, was a good and great man who had contributed from his private fortune over a hundred and fifty thousand dollars to various Arctic expeditions, that being a field in which he was greatly interested. But Mr. Hall, proud and obstinate, refused to accept any more aid from Grinnell. Indeed, he hesitated even to communicate with him. "I owe him so much," he told me, "that I can never repay him. Not only in dollars—that is considerable, also—but in his warm support and encouragement." Now, in the depths of our despair, came a telegraph message from Mr. Grinnell.

CAN YOU MEET ME WILLIAMS AND HAVEN NEW LONDON 17 MARCH DISCUSS POSSIBILITY NEW EXPEDITION?

Mr. Hall showed me the message. When I finished reading it he took it from me, crumpled it into a ball and flung it from him. "It isn't fair, to tempt a man so."

"What do you mean?"

He went to the window of our lodgings and stared into the street below, hands locked behind him. "Why, I mean just this! I am discredited from one end of the country to the other. No responsible authority believes me capable of anything. I am a fool, a mountebank, a subject for jest." He pointed to Hannah, rocking silently in her chair, and Joe, who was whittling at a stick of firewood—our last. "I have done myself no good, and as for these poor people, I have brought them to the brink of poverty. You also, Adam—you have wasted two years of your young life following me about. And now this!" He kicked savagely at the crumpled paper. "If I were half a man, I would thank you all, and then cut my throat with a razor. That would be the humane, the sensible thing to do."

I had not often crossed him, but now I conceived it to be the right thing to do.

"Fiddlesticks," I said.

"Eh?" He looked at me over his shoulder, startled.

"You are feeling sorry for yourself. I have not complained. Hannah and Joe can speak for themselves, but I am convinced they are ready to go north with you whenever you say the word —north or to Hades, if that is where you propose to go."

Hannah stopped rocking. "Sir," she said to Mr. Hall, "Adam says the truth. We owe very much to you. We do what you say, always." Sitting on the bed, Joe nodded and went on whittling.

Mr. Hall ran a hand through his hair. "No one owes me anything."

"But you owe *us* something," I said.

"Eh?"

"Why, just this! We have our own lives, you know. We have linked them with yours, for better or for worse. If we are not to count all this wasted, all of our struggles and doing without, then we are bound to try again, are we not? And again, and again—whatever it takes."

Mr. Hall was a man who lived for the most part within

himself and did not often show strong emotion. But at my words his face betrayed the inner struggle tormenting him. Looking from one of us to the other, he clawed at his beard and scowled ferociously.

"Do you think so, Adam?"

I nodded.

"Hannah—you and Joe—"

Hannah smiled her sweet smile, and Joe nodded vigorously. With a muttered word that might have been thanks, although I do not know, Mr. Hall swept us all into his embrace. "This time we'll do it!" he shouted. "With such friends, I'd try the Pole itself."

From our straitened circumstances we were swept up on a tide of rich good fortune. Mr. Henry Grinnell was a fatherly man out of whom shone the light of a good, an almost saintly, soul. Although wealthy, he was now in difficult circumstances himself because of his unremitting support of Arctic exploration. But wealthy or not, he had a tremendous amount of influence in New England. A word from him was enough to cause Williams and Haven, his good friends, to set about finding a way to put a whaling vessel at Mr. Hall's disposal.

"Not only that," he explained, sitting back in his carved chair, eyes twinkling through steel-rimmed spectacles, "but I have arranged for you, Charles, to speak before the American Geographical Society in New York." He consulted a memorandum pad before him. "Let me see—ah, here it is—next week, on Tuesday. I am to introduce you."

Mr. Hall was disturbed. He tugged at his beard trying, I think, not to scowl, which was such a habit with him. "I don't know how it will come out. My lecturing has not been going too well." He told Mr. Grinnell about his experience in Washington.

"I would not worry about that, Charles." Mr. Grinnell

smiled and took him by the arm. "I have been doing missionary work for you. It will go well, you will see."

Mr. Williams, of Williams and Haven, was a spry and elderly gentleman with a quick and curt way of talking, all the time capering about like an ancient stork. "Yes, yes! I remember Mr. Hall! Of course I do. Don't forget a man; no, I don't. Sit down, man, sit down. You too, boy—sit over there. What was your name, now? Adam, that was it. I'll never forget it, make your mind up to that. Adam Burritt. A and then a B, just as in the alphabet. I have little tricks to jog my brains." Good-natured and indefatigable, he dug me in the ribs, winking, and went on springing about the room.

Mr. Grinnell told him about Mr. Hall's plans, old Williams nodding and scratching his nose. Mr. Hall showed him some of the Frobisher relics, and made a very good and detailed presentation of his plans to explore King William Land.

"I am not a finished speaker," said Mr. Hall in conclusion. "Perhaps I have convinced you, sir, and perhaps not. But I will finish by saying this. Whatever it is humanly possible for a man to do in the way of finding the Franklin people, I will do. I would give my life, if necessary, to aid them. I cannot promise success in such a venture, but be sure of this: Williams and Haven can someday be proud of having assisted in a worthy venture."

Old Mr. Williams whipped out a handkerchief and blew his nose, looking brightly from one of us to the other. "Remarkable! Very remarkable, indeed, sir." He wheeled around and stared at me. "What's your opinion, Adam Burritt?"

Mindful of courtesy to elders, I got to my feet and stood at attention. "Sir, I know Mr. Hall, and have traveled with him in the Far North. There is no one I respect and honor more. I count it a privilege to be associated with him, and I know you will never regret helping him."

"Good," said Mr. Williams. "Very, very good, boy. Well, we will see what can be done."

The upshot of it all was this: Williams and Haven decided to put at Mr. Hall's disposal the whaler *Thomas Yates*, and worked out with us a deal whereby a kind of co-operative project could be carried on. The *Thomas Yates* would carry on whaling operations whenever time and circumstances permitted, hoping that the take of oil and bone would pay for the voyage. But Mr. Hall's Arctic operations were to take precedence, and the search for the lost Franklin people was to be first order of importance. Mr. Grinnell would talk to some of his friends and get what funds he could from them to assist, but in any case the *Thomas Yates* was going north, with Mr. Hall in general charge. A sailing master, of course, was to be furnished, accountable to Williams and Haven for the safety of the vessel.

Before Mr. Hall left with Mr. Grinnell to fill his speaking engagement in New York, we had a champagne supper in the Gibbs House in New London. Mr. Williams was there, and his partner, Mr. Haven; also Mr. Hall and me, along with Joe and Hannah, the mayor of the town, newspapermen, and local whalers and sea captains. Mr. Williams paid the bill, and all had a gay time, toasting Mr. Hall and wishing success to his venture. Afterward, Mr. Hall and I sat in our room, I a little giddy from the champagne. Joe and Hannah, who did not drink, were sleeping in their room down the hall. They had been a sensation. One of the newsmen was writing up a story on them for the New London paper. With luck, the Boston papers might print it also.

Mr. Hall was thoughtful. He paced the room and finally said, "Up and down, eh, Adam? A few weeks ago I was in the depths of despair. Now—a vessel, an invitation to address the learned do-nothings of the Society, even financial support. All or nothing—it seems there can be no middle ground for me." He lay down on the bed, legs crossed, hands locked behind his head. "I was made to plumb the depths, or reach the heights."

He sighed, and then added in an amused tone, "Even champagne! We now drink champagne."

The champagne must have loosened his tongue. I never knew him so loquacious.

"It would be nice if my wife were here to see me address the Society. But it would be very expensive. We need all our money for my expedition." He chuckled. "My wife is very moral, and strait-laced. She would not like champagne. But she is a good woman, and has always stood by me."

I wondered if he had written her of late, or sent money, but I did not say anything.

"Well, she is entitled to her ways. We are different, all of us. I am different, you are different—" He broke off and rolled over and sat up, looking at me. "You are indeed different, Adam. I suppose that is why I like you."

"Different? How?"

A change came over his face, a shadow that might have been regret, or sadness, or mere thoughtfulness; I did not know.

"Why, Adam, you are so—so—" He stammered and seemed embarrassed. "Look at me! I am so unfamiliar with the characteristic I seek to describe that I can't find the proper word for it!" His journal lay on the writing desk, and he picked it up thoughtfully, holding it in his hand. "I can write things down —I am never at a loss there!"

Such a feeling of bonhomie between us was rare, and I enjoyed it. Mr. Hall was silent for a moment. Then he said, choosing his words, "You are—congenial, Adam. Yes, that is it. Congenial." He tossed the ledger back on the desk. "People like you. You have a knack for making friends readily. With Mr. Henry Grinnell, for instance. And old Mr. Williams was quite delighted with you. There was an electrical spark that flashed between you."

"I don't know of any sparks," I said.

"That's just it, of course!" Mr. Hall got up, agitated. "Those that have it are just those who are not aware of it. And those poor devils who do not have it are only too aware of it! Some, for instance, are thought thorny and difficult, but this is unfair. It is only that they do not know how to handle friendship. They mean well, but they have a way of grasping at a sentiment too hard, and perhaps breaking it—through unfamiliarity, I say, and not because of any lack of appreciation!"

Uneasy at his vehemence, I said, "Sir, this is a little thing. I would trade all this electrical fluid you say I possess for one small part of your own ambition, your drive, your conviction and abilities—"

"A little thing?" He shook his head, smiling ruefully. "Because I have not this little thing, Adam, I have become what I am. Lacking this human and wonderful rapport, I buried myself in books at an early age—Lord, how early! But then, books are not too bad, really. They have been my only true friends, though the bookish man longs sometimes for people, for human friends."

"But you *have* friends! Mr. Grinnell, Mr. Williams—Hannah and Joe and myself—"

As if feeling he had said too much, Mr. Hall sat down at the desk and opened his ledger. "You know," he said, "that I have never let a day go by without writing in my ledger. This day is almost gone."

"Well," I said, somewhat piqued, "I do not wish to disturb you. I will go down and take a little walk before I go to bed."

He did not answer and I left the room. As I closed the door he was hunched over the desk, pen scratching in the candlelight, his bulky figure cast in shadow on the ceiling.

There was, however, a worm in our apple of good fortune. I suppose there always is. I found out about it when Mr. Hall returned from his trip to New York City with Mr. Henry Grinnell. I had been kept busy with building a boat and a sledge in the Williams and Haven yard, and did not know that Mr. Hall had returned until he entered the shed where Joe and I were steaming runners into shape.

"Well, sir," I said, "you have returned to us safe!"

He nodded and took off his hat. There was something so dispirited in the gesture that I was concerned. Something must have gone wrong at the Society.

"But what is wrong? Was not your speech a success?"

He sat down on a keg, unknotting his muffler. "I suppose so. Oh, they do not take me very seriously, I fear! If it were not for Henry Grinnell's sponsorship, I do not think they would want to listen to me. I told them as much, some of them. But then, I am used to rebuffs of that nature."

"But why are you so solemn?"

He looked down at the tattered plaid and picked at a worn thread. "I have had bad news since I returned. Williams and Haven have withdrawn their offer of a vessel. They have had reverses, news of which just came. One of their whalers was lost near Disko, when fire broke out aboard. Another, bound for England with a cargo of oil, was sunk by a Confederate gunboat. All in all, things have gone very badly for them—and for me."

Catastrophe again! I laid down the sledge runner I had been working on. How many times had the story been the same!

"But what will we do?"

"I don't know." Mr. Hall went to a window obscured by steam and wiped a clear place with the corner of his muffler. "There appears to be nothing we can do this season. They are putting the *Thomas Yates* into the European trade, hoping to recoup some of their losses. The chances are risky, but the return can be tremendous. Well, by next year the circumstances may have changed in our favor again."

"Next year!"

He nodded, staring out the window. His hair was becoming noticeably gray; more so, it seemed, since the trip to New York

City. His beard was flecked with it, and his usually erect figure drooped.

"Next year," he murmured.

"A year is a long time!"

"To you, Adam, perhaps. And to the poor Franklin people, if any are still left alive. But for me the years go too fast. Ah, they race by! My vital juices dry up, and the body stiffens. My joints ache, Adam, and I feel very old."

It was the first time I had ever heard him express doubt that he would someday find at least a few of the Franklin survivors. Joe, too, was disturbed, and whistled between his teeth.

"One more year?"

"Long time." Joe laid down the clamp he had been using and looked at it as if it were a new and strange instrument. "Don't know if Hannah and Joe live one more year in this place." He shook his head. "Need snow and ice. Need seal, need *took-too*. Need everything, bad."

He had never complained before, and it was a measure of the gravity of our situation.

"The whalers have all gone for the season," Mr. Hall said. "I am afraid it's too late to work anything out. But next year—"

"There may be no next year!" I protested. "Joe and Hannah want to go home, and the Army will be after me, I am afraid. Already I have been asked several times why I was not in uniform."

"You are free to go, both of you," Mr. Hall said. "This is my fight. While I have been grateful for any help, I have not liked the idea of dragging others into my struggles." His eyes, under their jutting brows, were filled with despair. When I was young and roamed the green hills along the Ohio River, I saw that look in the eyes of trapped animals. "No, Crazy Hall is not so crazy, or so heartless, as to attempt to keep you with him, Adam. You are a young man, as I have said. Go find your fortune."

He turned away, but I was so bitter and upset that I called

after him, saying some obscene thing, something I had picked up on the whalers.

"Eh?" He turned, looking at me with mixed amusement and incredulity. "What was that, Adam?"

Embarrassed, I dropped my eyes. "I only meant—well, I will go with you next year; if you still want me, that is."

He was not often gentle with anyone, except with Joe and Hannah, for whom he had a parent's fondness and indulgence, as he did for all the Innuit people. But his eyes, so weary and harried, softened as he looked at me, biting his lip and pondering. Then he turned away. Joe and I went back to our work on the sledge, not knowing now where our efforts might lead.

Several times during the next year I wondered whether I had been rash in promising Mr. Hall to stay. The New London winter was harsh and miserable; not the clear blue cold of the Arctic, but a bone-chilling frigidity that struck through any number of coats and sweaters. The dampness was everywhere. When I got out of bed in my furnished room of a morning, the windows would be coated with a rime of ice. Our landlady was penurious, and a scuttle of coal was as hard to come by as diamonds. We lived together again; Mr. Hall and I in one room, Hannah and Joe in another, Barbekark tethered in the back yard next the privy.

How we got by I do not clearly recall. Joe and I did odd jobs for Mr. Williams in his shipyard, for which we were paid, not handsomely, but the rates were fair enough. Hannah did needlework for the New London ladies, at which she was very good, and it distracted her thoughts from the loss of her baby. Mr. Hall worked on the proofs of his new book, to be called *Arctic Researches*, and managed to get some few more dollars from Harper Brothers, although most of that had to go to Snow, the Englishman, who had sent a large bill for services in connection with editing and smoothing Mr. Hall's rough draft of the manuscript.

In the spring, Mr. Hall went on the cars to Cincinnati for a brief visit with his wife and family. I did not leave New London except for a short trip to New Haven to see the girl I knew there when I was in college. The visit was not, I think, too successful. With my scraggly beard and rough ways, I did not resemble the callow and pomaded young gentleman Emily had remembered. I did not even stay to supper, although both hungry and invited. Well, Emily was not a patch on a woman like Hannah! I supposed I was cut out for an Esquimaux wife, although it appeared it might be some considerable time before I had the opportunity to court one.

Although I had doubted it, the spring came on. The trees put on a mist of green, New London's streets were a quagmire from melting snow, the winter-sick sun began to get a little body to it. Williams and Haven were still in financial troubles, but they were planning to send out the *Monticello* this season to the Hudson Bay whaling grounds. It was a far cry from our original lofty plan, but the *Monticello* would set Mr. Hall and his party ashore near Repulse Bay in the latter part of the summer. The distance from King William Land where Mr. Hall planned to explore was still extreme, some six or seven hundred hard miles. It would take a long and carefully planned journey to reach there. But it was all that was offered us now, and Mr. Hall accepted.

On July 1, 1864, we sailed from New London on the *Monticello*, accompanied by the tender *Helen F.* Again Mr. Hall's sledge and boat and supplies were stowed on the foredeck of an Arctic-bound vessel. Poor Barbekark, suspecting some great venture, went nearly mad, barking at every gull that lighted on the rigging, finally to collapse exhausted, tongue hanging out. Joe and Hannah were so excited they wept, looking ahead to a long-delayed reunion with friends and kin of their own tongue.

Mr. Henry Grinnell was at the dock to see us off. While Mr. Hall was busy seeing to the lashings of his deckload of pemmican and instruments, Mr. Grinnell took me by the arm and led me aside.

"It is a thrilling prospect, eh, Adam? The departure of a ship makes my pulse race."

"It is indeed thrilling," I said.

He sighed. "I wish I were young again. But no—I must stay here and cheer on those who are better qualified."

"If it were not for you," I said, "those who are better qualified, as you call them, would remain at home, and nothing would be done in this great Arctic business."

Adjusting his spectacles on his long nose, he peered at me. "Adam, I have only one request to make. In all else I leave judgment to you."

"What is that?"

He nodded toward the foredeck where Mr. Hall, no longer seeming weary, nor gray either, ran among the seamen calling out orders and assisting.

"Charles Hall is a worth-while man, Adam, else I would not have bothered my old brains with him. He is stubborn, not too grateful, and very opinionated. But he is a great man, for all that, and someday the world will listen to him. Have you heard his theories about the use of balloons in the Arctic?"

"Aerial balloons?" I said. "No, sir."

"No matter." His eyes twinkled. "Well, at any rate, Adam, keep an eye on him for me. Watch out for him. These last years he has been so busy he has not had the opportunity to develop as gracefully as he might. Talk back to him, Adam; question him, force him to think things out, encourage him. Be his conscience and his friend. Will you do that—for me, and for him?"

I was taken aback at how neatly Mr. Henry Grinnell put it. He knew Mr. Hall as well as I did.

"It is a big order."

"It is, but no one else can do it."

I took a deep breath.

"I'll try, Mr. Grinnell."

Bad luck dogged us, it seemed. Late in August the *Monticello* put us ashore at Whale Point, which the captain believed to be on the Wager River. Due to a mistake in navigation, however, our party actually landed some forty miles south of where we intended. Mr. Hall had planned to sail up the Wager River in our small boat, reaching Repulse Bay itself before the winter season set in. In this way, we could make preparations for a spring journey to King William Land. But the mistake in navigation cost us dear. With the winter storms already setting in, it was too difficult and dangerous to reach Repulse Bay at this season. Instead, we were forced to sit out the winter in this unfavorable location and wait for spring.

"Destiny," said Mr. Hall, "is a black dog, about the size of Barbekark, which pads along in my footsteps, pausing only to sniff at my marks and put a foul spell on me and my plans. Well, Adam, there is no cure for it."

I did not particularly like the country south of the Wager. It was bleak and forbidding. Game was scarce, and the few natives who lived in the sorry villages were inclined to be surly; deficient in spirit and wholesomeness, as they were in worldly goods. Now that the *Monticello* was gone, we were alone with them, however, except for an occasional whaler that passed by, running down Roe's Welcome. Even the whalers, it seemed to me, were different in this country from the vessels that fished for the great whales in Davis Strait. There, off Baffin Island, there seemed to be an easy, almost co-operative relationship among the vessels. The skippers, though stern and Godfearing, were in the main just men and fair in their treatment of the crew and the running of the ship. For the most part, those vessels were owned by Williams and Haven or the Knox brothers or one of the other great whaling firms. Standard practices and business customs had been set up which provided a fair degree of control of the whaling business. But here, in the Hudson Bay country, the situation was different. Most of the whaling vessels were small and mean, owned and captained by the same man, who was apt to be a villainous and cheeseparing blackguard, exploiting his crew, the natives, and anyone else who got in his way. No, I did not like this country, and often wished we were back at Kowtukjua Bay again.

Hannah and Joe were delighted, however. The storms, the steady dropping of the mercury thermometer, the cold dry air —all these seemed to revivify them. Barbekark, too; after long imprisonment in our New London back yard, he showed only too plainly he was glad to be home, wagging his tail until I was afraid it would fall off from overuse.

Though chafing at our forced stay in the Wager River country, we kept busy enough. Joe and I caught fish and soon had a mountainous pile, all glassy-eyed and frozen hard, for dog food. Hannah sat daily and most of the night in her *tupik,* working skins to make them soft for our needed winter clothing. Mr. Hall unboxed some of his scientific instruments—a pendulum, an alidade, and an equatorial telescope on a tripod, occupying himself with scientific observations. The pendulum, by means of which the attraction of gravity was to be determined at that northern latitude, was swung on steel knife edges and suspended in a box of strong board with a glass door. It had been loaned by the Society, through an arrangement by Mr. Grinnell. Mr. Hall was very particular about it, allowing no one else to go near. There was little chance of any of us harming it, because its workings were incomprehensible to me and Joe and Hannah shunned it because they believed it some kind of evil spirit.

The winter wore on; we labored to make ready for our spring journey to Repulse Bay, and beyond. One day, when the ice had pretty well gone out, I saw a whaler creeping down the sound; a poor-appearing vessel, with yards askew and needing paint. She was sounding for an anchorage, and a while later she dropped her hook. A small boat put out for shore, having seen our tiny settlement and the national flag Mr. Hall kept flying from a staff.

In the bow of the boat was a bearded man in a nautical cap. He fended off with a long boat hook, and then sprang nimbly ashore, driving the hook into the snow.

"You, there!" He came up to me, hitching his pants and looking at me from an eye with a cast in it. "What're you up to, eh?"

I had been drying a net, and took my time in replying.

"What does it look like?"

He swore at me and stuck out his unshaven chin. "Don't get gay with me, laddie, or I'll take a stick to your breeches!"

"I'm Adam Burritt," I said, "of the Hall Expedition to Boothia and King William Land. You'll find Mr. Hall over there, in that little shelter."

The whaler looked at me and rubbed his nose, finally spitting out a mouthful of tobacco juice near my foot. His brow had such a slant to it that if a decent idea ever thought to strike there, it would glance off and go elsewhere to seek lodgment. "All right," he said. "Fair enough, laddie." Thumbs hooked in his belt, he swaggered away.

The men in the boat pulled it up on the gravelly bank and lit pipes, watching me askance. They were a rough and a foul lot, and being to leeward of them was not pleasant. One put a mouth harp to his lips and played a jig. Another, a lean man in a striped shirt under a dirty sealskin jacket, strolled toward me. Thin-lipped, pale in the face, a kind of a soft-footed way of walking—why, it was—yes, it must be! Patrick Coleman, off the old *George Henry*!

"Well," he said, "if it ain't Holy Boy Burritt! Yes, that's right. Adam Burritt himself. Still with Crazy Hall?"

I remembered the time I had seen Patrick Coleman on the business end of a blubber spade, trying to divide me in two equal parts. But there seemed to be no rancor in him now, beyond that which was natural to his way, as familiar and un-premeditated as breathing. Besides, I was now some twenty pounds heavier and a great deal broader in the shoulders and chest.

"Yes," I said, "I'm still with Mr. Hall. Have you any objections?"

He grinned, tongue flicking out to skim his lips; that odd gesture he had that reminded me of a snake's forked tongue darting this way and that. "No need to be unfriendly. It might cost you dear, for I've got something your Mr. Hall might be interested in."

"What could you have that he would want?"

Slyly he took a chamois bag from an inner pocket. "Carried this around with me for better'n a year. Never knew when I might run into that feller Hall." Opening the bag, he held it high and shook it. A teaspoon fell into his hand, a heavy silver spoon with florid engraving. "Here, take it. Look at it. Tell me what you think."

I held it close and examined it. On the stem was some kind of a queer animal, looking like a sea monster done by a man who had never seen one. Around the animal was a fringe of raised tiny bosses. The handle was bent and twisted straight again. The bowl was worn and scratched as if it had seen long service.

"Well," I said, "I don't see what—"

I broke off, suddenly knowing what the sea monster was. It was an eel. The eel was always prominent in Sir John Franklin's life. His crest bore the eel—the flag on the *Erebus*, the lost *Erebus*, had been the eel flag. Now here was a piece of Sir John Franklin's silver; battered and scratched, and hardly service-able. But there was no doubt about it; the sign of the eel!

"Where did you get this?"

Coleman, who had been uncomfortable and worried while I scanned the piece, suddenly looked happier, more sure of himself. "Now wouldn't you like to know!"

"Of course I would! You know what this is, or you wouldn't have brought it to me. This spoon is one of Sir John Franklin's! Where did you find it?"

"I didn't find it myself. I traded one of these gecks a cloth coat and a pound of tobacco for it. But he told me where he found it, and that's what's important, ain't it?"

"All right," I said. "We'll make it up to you. But tell me—"

He snatched the spoon away and put it back in the chamois bag. "I knew it was valuable. But I ain't dealing with a common seaman. I'll talk to your precious Mr. Hall about this, see what he's willing to pay for the story that goes with it."

"We haven't got much money."

He leered at me and winked. "There's always money for something a man needs bad enough."

The whaling skipper came out of Mr. Hall's hut, followed by Mr. Hall. They were deep in conversation as they walked toward us, and some acrimony seemed to be involved, because I could hear anger in their voices. Patrick Coleman seemed apprehensive, also, because he took me by the sleeve and whispered into my ear.

"He's a tough one, Captain Burden. As soon cut your throat as look at you. Don't say nothing to him about the spoon, Adam, or he'll want in on the deal himself."

"All right."

"Good." Coleman heaved a sigh of relief. "They're planning on laying to for a few days and careening the *Jessie*. She's got a sprung plank forward and's been shipping water. Just sit tight, mate, and I'll drop in soon and see your shipmate Hall."

"All right," I said. "But take care of yourself. Don't get your throat cut before you tell Mr. Hall your story."

Chapter 8

WE watched the unpleasant Captain Burden and his men row away in their boat. When they were well out from the beach, Mr. Hall snorted. "Alcohol, that is what they wanted! Strong drink, rum, anything of that nature! They were out of liquor, and seeing our camp, decided we could supply their wants!"

Except for a little port for the stomach's sake, and champagne on such occasions as our party in the Gibbs House, Mr. Hall eschewed liquor; not on any moral base, but simply because he felt it fogged the mind and affected the judgment.

"At first," he said, "not knowing exactly what they were after, I made the mistake of telling them we had a bottle of alcohol in reserve for some of our scientific instruments. That, I see now, was a mistake. Captain Burden, or whatever his name is, became angry at my withholding it."

"They may be back," I said. "I understand they are going to

be in the vicinity for a while, careening ship to repair some damaged planking."

"Did you learn anything else from them? As we came toward the beach I saw you talking to one of the scoundrels."

"That was Patrick Coleman," I explained. "You remember Coleman, off the *George Henry*. He was the one who beat poor Kudlago and was probably the cause of his death."

Mr. Hall's eyes became somber at the mention of Kudlago. "Aye, I remember, well enough. And you and Coleman had an altercation with a blubber spade one day."

I told him about the eel-pattern spoon, and Coleman's offer to sell it and information concerning its finding, for a price.

Mr. Hall was delighted. "The eel, of course! Adam, do you know what this means? Perhaps I am on the verge of a solution to the Franklin mystery!" He grew suddenly sober and calculating. "How much does he want for it?"

"I don't know," I said, "but from the way he talked about it, he thinks it's very valuable, and will want a great deal."

He tugged at his beard, looking at me. "You know our financial position as well as I do. We have few dollars, a very few. I could not afford much."

"Sir," I said, "I have known Patrick Coleman for a long time. Longer, perhaps, and under more intimate circumstances, than have you. Coleman is a liar and a cheat. I would not trust him very far. He has this spoon, as he says. The important thing is where it was picked up. I am not sure Coleman even knows where it first came from. Knowing your great interest in the Franklin matter, I would not put it past him to make up some unlikely story, lacking one otherwise, simply to convince you he had valuable information."

Mr. Hall sat down on a rock, looking at the *Jessie*. "I doubt it, Adam. After all—why, I mean—in a matter of this kind how could any man so far forget his humanity as to lie? Even the vilest blackguard would, I think, hesitate to hinder our search!"

Sometimes I despaired of him. With all his great abilities, he was often naive and guileless.

"Besides," I insisted, "you have made your plans. King William Land is where you are bound for. From examining all the data available, you told the gentlemen of the Society that King William Land is where the fate of the Franklin party could be settled for once and for all." I remembered what Mr. Grinnell had said to me on Merrill's wharf that last day, so many months ago. *Speak up to him, be his conscience and his friend. Will you do that, for him—and for me?* I had said I would try. "Is it wise," I asked, "to turn aside so soon, and go looking in a different direction?"

We had never quarreled before, and there had always been a good and friendly relationship between us. Now, in the rising pitch of his voice and the well-remembered scowl, I detected signs of anger.

"Yes, that is right! I said so, and that was my position at the time, the best position that the facts supported. But the spoon is new and important evidence!"

"I do not trust Patrick Coleman." I tried hard to keep my manner objective, not wanting to anger him, but in duty bound to point out the facts as they were known to me. "He is a liar and a cheat. Sir, your purpose is too high to be turned aside by a rascal only out to line his pockets."

Mr. Hall's weathered face reddened. "I was not born yesterday, Adam. What I do, I do only after full consideration. I will see that spoon! I myself, and none other, will decide if the story of the spoon is a reliable and reasonable one. If a promising clue should be presented, I care not who presents it. Liar and cheat he may be, but I have traveled this Arctic country for some years in my search, and I will go wherever the spoon points, if I think it a good idea."

There was no point in arguing with him. I saw the familiar set of his chin, the tugging at the beard—besides, what did I know about the matter? Perhaps he was right; Coleman might be in a position to shed light on our quest.

"Yes, sir." I turned away, and went to mending a tear in our net.

For a while Mr. Hall paced up and down the shingle of the beach, pausing once only to stare at me and ponder, though I was too angry and too proud to do anything but be very intent on the net. Presently he stamped away, hands clasped behind his back. I was sorry and thought of calling after him to make amends, but the Burritts were never known as diplomats. I let him go, and finished my mending of the net. Afterwards, dispirited, I went into Joe's *tupik* to talk with Hannah, the always-understanding Hannah.

"Why are you angry, Adam?" was the first thing she asked, biting at a thread.

In my distraught condition, sitting on the sharp edge of my emotions, the question, directly phrased in her clipped British syllables, struck me as funny. I looked around me at the welter of articles in the tiny tent. A proper lady, so demure and feminine, in a gingham pinafore over the *koo-lee-tang*; yet all about were uncleanliness and confusion. The skin floor of the *tupik* was littered with uneatable flesh, skins, blood and bones. Hanging over a low flame the customary stone kettle, black with soot and oil, bubbled with black meat, swimming in a smoking fluid as if made by boiling down the scrapings of a butcher's stall. Yet Hannah sewed with a steel needle, and near her lay a copy of *Leslie's Illustrated Weekly*, which she used to practice her English reading.

"I am not angry," I said.

"But you are." Now pregnant with another child, Hannah was sweetly radiant. "What has happened, Adam?"

"Mr. Hall and I have disagreed, that is all."

Her fingers flashed as she sewed in and out, bending over her work. "That is too bad. But these things happen. I am sometimes angry at my Joe, whom I love more than me. It is all right. Do not feel bad."

Squatting beside her, I envied her unfailing good humor.

"There is *took-too* in the kettle," she said. "Eat. It is good."

There was indeed reindeer meat in the pot; a *pot-au-feu* of heads and necks, boiled in the blood. I snatched out a fat chunk of neck, in my haste dropping it on the floor. Shaking off the debris I started to gnaw on it. What strange chance had brought me to eat such unlikely provender? The Lord, if He took any real account of Adam Burritt, moved in *very* mysterious ways.

"I am happy," Hannah said. Still squatting in the way they did, she wriggled over beside me and touched my cheek. "Poor Adam, are you not happy too to be away from those big cities down there?" She pointed, taking in New York and Boston and New London and all those rabbit warrens in a scornful gesture. "Too many people! They are crowded up and you cannot get your breath."

"Well," I said, gnawing on a neck bone, "it is not bad if you are used to it."

"But who would want to get used to it?" She laughed, shaking her head. "Who would want to get used to it, except a silly *kod-lu-na?*" She bit again at a trailing thread and spat out the end. "You know the story about the *kod-lu-na;* how the Great Being tried to make a man one day?"

I had heard it many times. It was an old story, common to many civilizations.

"He tried very hard, but could not make a good one. Finally, when he had done the best he could, he called it *kod-lu-na.* But the next day, when he felt better and had the knack of it, he tried again and made a better one."

"I know," I grumbled. "That was your people."

She stared at me, puzzled. A tear started in her eye. Throwing the sewing from her, she bent her head and wept.

"I didn't mean to offend you," I said. "That is a very funny story, I think, and maybe it is right. Really, Hannah, I—"

Now she was laughing; unaccountably laughing, giggles mixed with tears. "Oh, Adam, it is so funny!"

"What is funny?" I demanded, completely confused.

"I did not think about you being a *kod-lu-na!*"

My dignity was injured. "I don't think it very funny."

"Adam," said this remarkable lady, patting me on the knee, "I am truly sorry. But it is really a nice thing I said to you; one of the best things I could say to anyone. You, Adam Burritt, are one of us. I am proud to say it. There, now—is that so bad?"

"Hannah," I said, "thank you. Thank you very much."

Outside, the long day was dying. Saffron streamers veiled high in the sky, lit from below by the waning sun. Birds called; in the sound a fish jumped, and the circles grew and grew from that point in the water. Mosquitoes hung in the air, and the careened *Jessie* was a ghost ship trapped in the mud flats, spars pointing like blackened fingers. Aboard her a yellow lamp went on, an eye in the dusk.

I wonder, I said to myself, *why you are here, Adam Burritt!* A filthy skin *tupik,* no money—Mr. Hall did not pay me, except for my keep, had never spoken of repaying the money from my lay which he borrowed—supper of boiled reindeer heads, bitten by mosquitoes, newly at odds with my mentor; it was too much to understand, my being here.

Then suddenly I knew. I was in love with the Arctic. I was here because I wanted to be. I would never want to be anyplace else. I went to bed feeling very good, and comforted. Perhaps my love for this land was not so grand and ecstatic as Mr. Hall's, but it was no less strong.

One day Patrick Coleman came to us, as I knew he would. Captain Burden had sent ashore a party to fill casks with water from a pool near us. Through his glass Mr. Hall watched them land, not saying anything. After a while there was a crashing in the underbrush. Coleman burst out, panting for breath, hands and face scratched and bleeding.

"Where's Hall?" I pointed, and Coleman hurried toward him. "Ain't got much time," he called over his shoulder. "They'll miss me before long."

When I came up on them Coleman was arguing and gesticulating. I squatted nearby, not too near, but at hand if there was any need. I still did not trust him.

"But it's worth a hundred dollars or more!"

Mr. Hall's eyes shone as he examined the teaspoon. He held it up and said, "Look, Adam! The eel spoon!"

"I know. I have seen it."

"I haven't got a hundred dollars," Mr. Hall explained. "I am almost penniless. I don't know where you got the idea, Coleman, that I am made of money and filigreed with gold coins. But I must know where you got this! I cannot impress on you how important the facts are. They may mean life to some hundred or so poor souls!"

"All I know," said Coleman sulkily, snatching away the spoon, "is it's worth money to you. If you want the story that goes with it, you must pay the piper." He looked over his shoulder into the brushy growth. "There now—I hear the whistle! I'll have to be going back. It's your last chance! The *Jessie's* most fixed up. The cap'n 'll be taking her out again in a few days."

"I must have it," Mr. Hall said stubbornly, reaching into his pocket.

"Don't try no monkey business!" Coleman drew the knife from his sleeve and looked from one of us to the other.

"I wasn't thinking of that." Mr. Hall brought out a scrap of paper; one of the many he was always writing on, to enter later in his bound journal. "Look, man, will you take a note?"

Coleman laughed a shrill laugh. "A note, is it? Payable on the Bank of the Wager River?"

"Payable by me, when we get back to the States! Adam here shall be my witness."

Coleman blinked, and wiped his nose with the back of his hand. "No tricks?"

"You have my word of honor. And Adam's too."

I didn't see how this involved me, but I said, "That's right."

"I don't know you very well," Coleman said to Mr. Hall, "but I know Adam here, and I trust him. I don't like him, but I trust him. But a note's different from cash on the drumhead! It'll cost you more. Two hundred dollars."

Mr. Hall was dumfounded. "Two hundred dollars!"

"Sir," I said to Mr. Hall, "this is extortion. Don't—"

"Two hundred ain't much, considering all those people involved," Coleman whined. "I give a pound of tobacco for the information, and I'm running short on smokes already!"

"You're a damned scoundrel, but I have no choice," Mr. Hall said fiercely. He grabbed the chamois sack from Coleman and scribbled out a note. "Here, Adam." He handed me the paper and a stub of pencil. "Sign there, as witness."

I was not sure I ought, but I did.

"Now," said Mr. Hall, "where did the spoon come from?"

"From Igloolik," said Coleman. "I sneaked a look at one of Captain Burden's charts. It's up by what they call the Straits of Fury and Hecla. This geck said they was more stuff there, too; pots and pans, and the old men in Igloolik remembered a boat captain, a long time ago. Eshemutta, they called him—a big man with gray hair and spectacles."

"Sir John!" Mr. Hall burst out. "Franklin himself!"

"There was a pile of rocks," Coleman said, "and some papers."

The shrill bleat of the whistle sounded again, nearer this time.

"That's all I know!" Coleman said in sudden panic. Before either of us could raise a hand, he bounded away like a hare and disappeared in the thicket.

"Igloolik," said Mr. Hall. He put the spoon back in the sack. "I think the story hangs together." Talking almost to himself, he walked away to his tent. "There is not much time. I must prepare for a journey at once."

"Yes, sir," I said, following in his footsteps. I do not think he heard me at all.

We went to Igloolik. At least, we started for there. Igloolik, near the Straits of Fury and Hecla (named after the ships of Sir William Edward Parry, the explorer), was three hundred miles north of our camp. The season was too late for sledge travel. Our only route appeared to be northward by boat via the ice-choked Foxe Basin. It would be a rough trip.

"Adam," said Mr. Hall, "do you trust our party to voyage so far in the boat you and Joe have built?"

In the excitement of the forthcoming voyage he was in good spirits again, forgetting our angry words.

"Yes, sir," I said. "The *Lady Franklin* is a good boat. I will trust her anyplace."

The *Lady Franklin* (which is what Mr. Hall had named her) was stoutly fashioned of white oak; twenty-eight feet long, a five foot, ten inch beam, and drawing about twenty-six inches, fully loaded with our supplies. The supplies were considerable, and our party even more so. Although the *Lady Franklin* had a sail stepped on a short mast, we would often be put to rowing. A heavy boat, low in the water, required a considerable crew. As a corollary, the crew required considerable supplies. When we left, we looked like a queer kind of ark departing Mount Ararat. Some hundredweight of dried meat and biscuit, Mr. Hall's scientific instruments, our guns and powder and ball, bladders of fresh water, a fishing net, maps and charts; in addition to all this were Joe and Hannah, their friend, fat Pikeula, and his wife Artoona, their son-in-law Koklee and his cousin, whose Esquimaux name I do not recall but who was known as Casey, after a whaler he had once befriended. Then there was Nartuk, the *an-ge-ko*, a withered little man with a face like a dried-up plum whom neither Mr. Hall nor I trusted, but

whom Artoona and Pikeula revered. Mr. Hall and I completed
the party—nine souls in this frail cockleshell, loaded to the gunwales with our freight!

We would have been satisfied to travel with a lesser company,
but that was one of the disadvantages of exploring these northern latitudes. One was forced to depend on the Esquimaux for
so many things; to row the boat when the wind failed, to serve
as guides and hunters, to interpret when meeting other Esquimaux who did not speak the lingua franca of the North, the
Innuit tongue. In addition, the Esquimaux were expert map
makers, and Mr. Hall depended much on them in his surveying.
Also, in these far northern latitudes about which so little was
known, there was the chance of encountering unfriendly natives. In our numbers there was strength against such a possibility. So off we bowled, practically a convention, into Foxe Basin
against a stiff northerly.

Mr. Hall was at the rudder. He said to me, beard fluttering in
the wind, "Northward again, eh, Adam? Always northward! It
is a fine and familiar direction, one of the best. When I am
bound in that direction all cares drop away from me."

Already we had been forced to bail a little. Pikeula and Koklee dipped out water with an old bucket, laughing and joking
with Artoona, who sat in the waist on a sack of our dried *tood-
noo*. Joe handled the sheet and Hannah squatted next him,
reading from the Bible Mr. Hall had given her.

"Give me a northerly course any time. There is something
lackadaisical about steering south. East and west—what are
they? Merely points on the compass card. But north is the prime
direction, I think."

"Northward, then, we go!" I said.

"Atee!" called Joe. "Good!"

There was a chorus of *atee* all around, and it was plain we
were in agreement.

The Foxe Basin was filled with great bergs. We tacked in
and out among them, moving handsomely, Mr. Hall handling

[134

the rudder and calling instructions to Joe. He was very good at
small boats; another skill he had learned for the most part from
books, and from secondhand information received from others
in preparation for his Arctic journeys. Squatting in the bow I
watched the awesome bergs loom up, tower over us, and then
slide away aft. One seemed like the ruins of a lofty dome about
to fall, a portion of its arched roof already tumbling down. As
I watched, a great ledge came undone and slid slowly into the
water, raising a cloud of spray and ice. The cold breath of the
dying berg rolled over us and we all shivered, hanging on the
gunwales as the waves occasioned by the fall rocked our boat.
Another great berg, around which Mr. Hall expertly maneu-
vered us, looked like a monstrous elephant with two large cir-
cular towers on its back, Corinthian spires springing out from
the rubble of alabaster in which it stood. As we left it astern and
saw it from another angle, it resembled a lighthouse atop high-
piled rocks, all whiter than drifted snow. I was giddy at this
great spectacle and clutched the gunwale, having a momentary
vertigo. The Esquimaux, too, were impressed. In their small
ki-as, knowing the treacherous nature of these mountains of ice,
they did not often venture thus near them. Old Nartuk, the
an-ge-ko, started a chant, and the rest broke into flutelike whis-
tlings, which was their custom. The sound was weird and other-
worldly against the background of high-flung spray and the
sighing of the winds through the lonely ice castles. I was glad
when the late dusk came and we went ashore for the night.

We pitched our *tupiks* on the gravelly beach. Hannah and
Artoona soon had tea going and cooked a stew of dried meat.
The evening sky was filled with high-piled clouds, ripped with
gold and red, underlaid with a long gray bank, like mother-of-
pearl in the way it caught and held the rays of the sun. Ducks
fed offshore, bobbing and diving for fish among the floating
bergs. It was a scene of pastoral simplicity and peace, but it was
not to remain so. Almost immediately after supper, old Nartuk
decided to start his *an-koo-ting*. For the rest of the night he and

the Esquimaux kept at it, hooting and whistling and caterwauling around the fire.

Mr. Hall came out of his tent, where he had been working on his surveying tables and maps by the light of an oil lamp.

"I ought to stop them," he said. "We will have a hard day of it tomorrow, with the ice as thick as it is. They will need their strength at the oars."

I nodded, watching the figures capering in the firelight.

"Hannah is soon to have her baby. It cannot be good for her to be dancing so."

I knew them well, the Esquimaux, and liked them, understanding if not approving many of their customs. But this business of the *an-koo-ting* was one I had never been able to stomach. It was too wild, too animal-like. Old Nartuk, jealous of Father Hall's influence on his people, stood in the firelight gesturing, speaking in a hoarse and strenuous voice. Surrounding him, arms linked, the rest swayed back and forth in a shuffling dance. Some whistled in the way they had, others simply moaned, eyes shut tight and sweat rolling down their faces. From time to time Joe or Koklee or one of the men would shout, "*Atee! Atee!* Good! Go on!"

I never knew what the *an-ge-ko* was saying. Although both Mr. Hall and I spoke Innuit and some of its variations, he better than I, neither of us was ever able to make much out of an *an-ge-ko*'s harangue. Perhaps it was a special dialect, saved for these occasions. At any rate, it had a powerful effect on his hearers. They were mesmerized, seeming almost to sleep and yet high-strung and trembling, in a kind of spell. It would have been dangerous to cross them during these fits; even Joe and Hannah, who were devoted to Mr. Hall. Now, I think, the shrunk-faced Nartuk had them in even a nastier mood. I do not doubt he was working them up against Mr. Hall.

"This will not do!" Mr. Hall laid down his notebook and started toward them. "Casey!" he called. "You and Koklee— Joe—Hannah—"

[136

Nartuk rushed toward him screaming some malediction. He had been thumping on the *key-low-tik*, a bone hoop over which was stretched a piece of deerskin. He shook it in the air, his fingers thrumming it, and called out in the strange tongue. The dancers broke their circle and looked at each other and at us in a dazed way.

"Stop this!" Mr. Hall said sternly. He looked at Joe and at Hannah particularly. "I forbid this—this excess, or whatever it is! We have a busy day ahead of us tomorrow, and it is time for you all to go to bed and sleep. Do you hear me?"

I am a Christian, or try to be, and so do not believe in evil spirits or spells. But there was such an atmosphere of evil in the firelight that I drew back. Not conscious evil, perhaps; Joe and Hannah and Casey and the rest were good people, fundamentally decent, and a credit to any civilization, however different from our own. But on this summer night they were in the grasp of something inexplicable and sad. Against their own wishes, against their own decencies, they had been caught up by the expert Nartuk in a weird revel, black and bitter and permeated with evil.

"We just dance," Hannah said in a forlorn voice. "We do not do any harm."

Mr. Hall was patient. "I did not say you were doing harm, any of you. It is just that it is very late, and I shall need all of you in the morning! Go to sleep, all of you, and rest."

They went away in ones and twos, straggling and slow as if to express defiance, looking back over their shoulders and whispering among themselves. Old Nartuk remained by the fire, thumping softly on the *key-low-tik*, eyes closed, oblivious to us. But I knew enough about Nartuk to know that he thought himself mightily insulted.

"I suppose," Mr. Hall said, "that it was foolish of me to interfere. But one man must have the say. And I say it is better for them to go to bed and leave off this heathenish shouting and dancing."

He turned and went back to his tent, leaving Nartuk still shuffling his feet and strumming the *key-low-tik*. I did not like the feeling of being alone on the grassy hummock with the *an-ge-ko*. I went into the *tupik* also, and rolled myself in my blankets. The last thing I remembered was the shadow of Mr. Hall, magnified on the wall of the *tupik*, as he worked at his figures.

That was only the beginning of our misfortunes that summer. We struggled on and on; the perverse ice became ever thicker as we tacked northward. This late in the summer we had every right to expect Foxe Basin to be free of ice, but it stretched before us, blinking a dazzle into our eyes, blinding white in the sun, only too ready to crush and grind the *Lady Franklin* into matchwood. Strong head winds buffeted us, each hour's sailing meant another hour in patching ripped sails. While to Mr. Hall the difficulties tolled a knell for his hopes to reach the Straits of Fury and Hecla that summer, to our Esquimaux companions the whole affair was a glorious lark. Spurred on by the jealous Nartuk, they became wild and irresponsible. Seeing a seal lying on a floating ice cake, they would disregard Mr. Hall completely in their eagerness for the hunt. Letting the sail drop they would all seize an oar, paddling as they did their *ki-as*, laughing and shouting in excitement. It did not matter if bellies were full of seal meat from the noonday meal; no matter, they paddled away on a silly hunt for a seal we did not need, and became vicious and unco-operative if balked. Even Hannah, the mild and ladylike Hannah, was infected with this queer fever. I think it was the tonic effect the summer had on them, as I have heard it has its way on the Scandinavians, releasing spirits (both good and bad) pent up by the snows of winter.

"I do not understand you," I said sulkily to Hannah. "For a while I thought you were a perfect lady, and a very civilized person. Now I do not know what to think."

"Why do you bother to think at all?" she exclaimed. "It is not good to think so much, Adam. Do not be so eternally stuffy!

There is not always a right and a wrong. Do what the heart says, always; that is the only good way."

Perhaps it was not so bad for her to be happy because a grief was soon to come on her. Near Point Elizabeth Hannah's baby was born, and it was almost immediately apparent that it was not to live long. Not deformed, that is, but somehow listless and never crying, the way a healthy baby does. For a week or more Hannah sat in the stern with the blanket-wrapped bundle on her lap, trying to coax the baby to nurse, while the rest of us fought the perverse northerly winds and saw the unseasonable ice grow thicker and ever thicker. In only a short time, I knew, we would be forced to turn back. We would not reach the Straits this year.

One night the baby became worse, growing dark and flushed in the face, while the body writhed and the eyes turned up in the sockets. We put ashore none too soon. A blinding snow-storm whirled down from the north, lashing the open water into foam, shrieking around the bergs. Mr. Hall and I huddled in the *tupik* we shared, while Hannah and Joe and the baby shared the one next.

Mr. Hall sipped his tea and wrote in his journal. After a while he read back what he had written. "How cheerless is our *tupik!* The moss wick of our lamp, which (when we have our full supply of blubber) gives a continuity of flame of two feet six inches, is narrowed down to a simple wick point, and makes the gloom more dismal than total darkness. Long and cast-down faces are now faintly seen, that otherwise would be veiled from us. Our huts are sad, our voices almost hushed. But away, away, thou Fiend of Despair! This is no home for you. We are the children of Hope, Prayer, and Work. God is our Father, and better times will come."

He had medicines which he tried to get Hannah to give the baby, but she stubbornly would not have them, putting her faith instead in Nartuk. Pleased at her trust and relishing his victory over Father Hall, the *an-ge-ko* went through a long ceremony (for which Joe paid an ax) to determine whether the baby would live or die. I did not blame poor Hannah. Being presented to Queen Victoria did not make a Christian out of a poor Innuit woman, nor did her gingham pinafore. She put her faith in the greatest influence she knew, as we all do in time of trouble. No one could blame her for that.

Old Nartuk was glad for an audience as we all squeezed into the small tent to watch. First, he made Joe lie down on a bed of skins and put a leather strap around Joe's brow, all the time whistling and humming to himself. When all was set, Nartuk pulled up on the leather strap. This, he explained, told him the answers to the questions he was about to ask. If Joe's head came up readily, the answer was "yes." If Joe's head remained firmly down, the answer was "no."

For almost a week we remained at Point Elizabeth going through this mumbo-jumbo, Nartuk enjoying the center of the stage. After exhausting the baby's father with his head lifting and dropping, and amassing a great quantity of "yes" and "no" answers that did not seem to prove anything, he started on Pikeula. After Pikeula came Casey, and then Koklee, and then he started on the women; Artoona and Hannah herself. Would not the child be poisoned by taking Mr. Hall's medicines? Had Hannah somehow put a curse on the child by adopting too many of the *kod-lu-na*'s customs? If Hannah were to give up tea, would this help? Was it not dangerous to the child to keep on going north, the way Mr. Hall wanted to do? The Esquimaux lay respectfully on the ground in the *tupik,* all of them puzzled but trying to help, bobbing their heads up and down while Nartuk giggled and put his finger in his mouth and stared at Mr. Hall with malevolence in his gaze. It was only too plain; the *an-ge-ko* was using the situation for his own ends. I was ready to thrash him, evil spirits or no.

"The devil!" muttered Mr. Hall. "If he does not come to some conclusion by tomorrow, I will force some of my calomel on the baby. It can do no harm, and may save the child!"

Fortunately, or perhaps not, the end came suddenly. There was no need for the open break Mr. Hall contemplated. The baby died, and that was an end to it. Hannah rushed out of the *tupik*, the lifeless body clasped to her bosom. Leaving the *tupik* so quickly was, I remembered, Innuit custom. If this is not done when anyone dies in it, everything becomes worthless. In this case, it was felt that the bereaved mother went out soon enough so the bedding and everything else did not have to be thrown away.

"Poor woman," Mr. Hall said. "I have failed her, I think."

In ten minutes she returned and took her seat on the bed platform, very pale and composed. She allowed Artoona to take the dead baby from her bosom to be wrapped in a small furry *took-too* skin. Nartuk, very officious, insisted that the child be buried at once, but in response to Hannah's piteous wailing, Mr. Hall faced down the old man. The child was not buried until the next day, after we had sat with it through the night.

The next day we buried the infant who had not lived long enough to have a name. At one in the afternoon the tiny corpse was bound with a leathern thong, making a loop that fitted over Hannah's neck, for it was part of the rites that the mother carry the body to the burial place. Although it seemed like an unnecessary mutilation of a good *tupik,* a hole had to be cut in the back of the tent and the burial procession crawled out that way. To leave by the front flap was unlucky.

We buried the baby in a rock cairn some distance from the beach. I stood on one side of Hannah, holding her hand, and Joe on the other. Mr. Hall, at her request, read from the Bible over the small body. "If I listen to Father Hall," she sobbed, "my baby not dead. Adam, I have been bad, very bad, and I am punished now."

After the services were over we wended our way down the hill and got the boat ready for the trip back to the Wager River. The sky was leaden and gray, and a chill was in the north wind. Winter storms were not far away. When we had knocked down our *tupik* and stored our supplies again in the *Lady Franklin,* Mr. Hall took the eel-crest spoon out of his pocket and looked at it.

"Not this time," he said. "Ah well, there is no cure for it, I am afraid."

He wrapped it up in the cloth that he always carried around it, and put it back in an inner pocket.

"Next year," he said. "For sure, eh, Adam?"

Chapter 9

WHEN I came back to the Arctic on the *Monticello,*
I had not reckoned on being in that icy country for so many
years. But it was so. Delay after delay, trouble after trouble;
they plagued us in unending succession. Mr. Hall's old trouble
(the thickening of the blood) came back on him, and he was
ill through most of that winter. When he had somewhat recovered, and was in hopes of mounting a sledge expedition to
the Straits (although it was a dangerous time of the year for a
sledge journey), sickness struck the Esquimaux dogs of the area,
wiping out three-quarters of them, including our own noble
Barbekark. It was a queer and vicious disease that ran like
wildfire. First, there was a telltale restlessness and a slavering. If
not chained, the dog ran wildly about barking and whining, unable to understand the nature of its feelings. In the final stages
the dog fell on its side, unable to rise, coughing and pawing at
mouth and jaws. Too weak to move, the poor beast died in the

snow. Around about us, and in the villages, were dozens of the unfortunate animals, frozen into grotesque positions, dead of the mysterious blight. There was nothing to do with them but let them lie until the spring thaws and the heat of the sun should destroy them.

Croton oil and solution of morphia did some little good, and Mr. Hall ministered to poor Barbekark as intently and faithfully as ever a physician did a mortal patient. The treatment did not help. Barby stiffened and died, and Hannah and Mr. Hall were in tears as the gallant beast breathed his last.

"Poor fellow," said Mr. Hall. "He was like one of us, really."

That winter the ice in the bay "sang" with the pressure of the storm-driven waters beneath it. Word reached us that people at Ningook village, fifty miles west of us, had died of starvation, not being able to hunt for the bad weather, and not having put by the dried *took-too* meat which they should have done. The Esquimaux were a curious and improvident people, never foreseeing trouble, only too ready to live off the charity of the whalers; the old fable of the ant and the grasshopper. Hannah and Joe, although somewhat civilized, still exhibited this same improvidence. That winter, when it was drawing on toward spring, the goodhearted Joe decided that Hannah needed a party to cheer her up. Though we were in short supplies, living off dried meat which we had laid by in preparation for the sledge journey, they nevertheless planned a party, inviting the neighbors for miles around, including old Nartuk.

The big igloo Joe had built for the occasion was crowded with guests; forty or fifty people were crowded within its icy walls. Joe was there, and Hannah, Mr. Hall and I, Nartuk, Pikeula, Artoona, Armou, Nukerzou, Ouela, Neitchi, and dozens of others whom I didn't know. A one-eyed small girl whom Mr. Hall gladdened by giving her a comb for her unkempt hair; a distant relative of fat Pikeula with a nose eaten away by some disease, but merry and joking withal; two silent and bony uncles of Artoona who sat glumly in a corner and ate our ship's biscuit

with alarming speed. Food was the principal attraction at an
Esquimaux party. As standards went in that country, our bill of
fare was not bad. Pemmican soup, a dish of boiled reindeer
heads, stew of dried meats, isinglass jelly, sea bread with coffee
from our meager supply. The men ate first, as was the custom.
The women cleaned up the scraps and licked the pot, meantime
stuffing the children to suffocation. To secure the maximum
benefit, everyone scraped the grease from his mouth and cheeks
and licked his fingers, belching contentedly.

Afterwards there was dancing, and playing on the *key-low-tik*.
The women took an active part, and many of them were quite
attractive, or so began to seem. They were gaily dressed, wearing
on each side of the face an enormous pigtail constructed by
wrapping the black hair on a wooden pin a foot or so in length,
strips of reindeer fur being wrapped with the hair. Shining
ornaments were worn on the head, and the picture in the flickering lamplight was a pleasing one.

Mr. Hall threw away a gnawed bone and got to his knees.
" 'Twa drifted heaps, sae fair to see . . .' " he murmured.
"Burns, I think, Adam. Undoubtedly Burns. Well, it is late and
I am going to bed. In this howling mob I will not be missed."
He signed to Joe and Hannah, and before they could remon-
strate, slipped out into the night.

I stayed for a while longer, enjoying the rough horseplay and
the singing and dancing, but when they all fell again to *an-koo-
ting*, with Nartuk ascending the pulpit, I decided to go to
bed also. Outside, I breathed deep of the frozen night air,
only then realizing that I had been half-suffocated in the igloo,
taking into my lungs that foul atmosphere of seal oil, smoke,
and human sweat.

Mr. Hall was standing near, lost in an attitude of thought,
gazing into the moonlit waste. I did not know how long he had
been there, but by my estimate he had left the igloo an hour before.

"Sir!" I said. "You will be ill, standing here this way! Go inside, I beg you, and get into your blankets!"

For a moment he did not seem to hear me, and stood motionless. Then he threw off the hood of his *koo-lee-tang* and said in an astonished voice, "Eh? Who is there?"

"It's me. Adam."

He raised a hand to his brow and rubbed it. "I had lost track of time, I think." Pointing toward the low-dipping Pole Star he said, "Think of it, Adam; up there, in its lonely grandeur! The Holy Grail, almost, in isolation and unattainability."

"What do you mean?"

"Why, the Pole, of course!" He took a deep breath, and clouds of frost exhaled from his lips. "The North Pole itself! Such a small space from us—only lying beneath that star—and here am I, balked from it. But someday I will stand on it, Adam. *On* it, do you hear? I can not be stopped. I *will* not be stopped!"

His voice trembled. I wondered if he were feeling ill again and thought it best to change the subject.

"When we left New London, Mr. Grinnell spoke to me of a theory you had on the use of balloons in the Arctic. I have been meaning to ask you—"

"Balloons?" He pondered. "Yes, perhaps. You read in the newspapers of Professor Lowe and his balloon ascents over the Union lines in the war. Well, that is one reason this great white land is so important. Until now I have not said much about it, but listen!" He seized my arm. "Up there, directly over the Pole, is the shortest route from New York to India! We already have the steam engine, we have the aerial balloon—why not, someday, a fleet of aerial vessels sailing over the Pole itself, bound on errands of commerce? Eh?" In his enthusiasm he shook me, forgetting my own slightness of stature compared to his bearlike dimensions.

"I suppose so," I said. Anxious to get him back to the *tupik,* I took his hand and pulled him along the path after me. "But for now—"

[146

"Eh?" He peered at me. "Or do you also think me a fool?"

"I think," I said, "you have eaten something that did not agree very well with you. Remember, you have been ill."

He seemed disappointed and scowled, but went along with me. Balloons! I thought. *Good Lord, what next?*

As spring came again, our chances faded for a voyage to the Straits. A boat journey was impracticable through the ice-choked Foxe Basin, and it was too late for a sledge trip. Besides, Mr. Hall vowed he would never again attempt such a trip with an Esquimaux crew. Perhaps when whalers came into our bay again in the summer, we might find some malcontents who would risk a trip. But the castoffs from the whalers were not apt to be fit travelers or fellow adventurers, and Mr. Hall brooded much about the topsy-turviness of his plans and the sorry end they had come to. He would sit for hours looking at the battered silver of the Franklin spoon, his only sign of life an occasional sigh. Exploring was his life; now that he was limited to local surveying and the keeping of his daily journal and the entering into it of weather data and the barometric pressure, he was dispirited.

With the advent of summer many whalers came into our bay. There was the *True Love,* which I remembered from Kowtukjua, long ago; also the *George Kimberly* and the *Hand of Friendship* and the *John P. Casey.* Joe and I kept busy netting and drying fish, making pemmican, mashing the berry the Esquimaux called *tin-noot* into a paste that dried in the sun, making a palatable tart stuff that was good for the scurvy. In addition, we undertook some whaling with the *Lady Franklin,* the boat I had built in New London. The whalers paid us fifty dollars each for whales towed to their "stages." It was not money, exactly; only an order of credit against them for molasses, flour, meal, matches, or other staples. We had forgot the color of money, having had so little of it for so long. Besides, it was not of much use in this land. Everything was bartered for, even children. Most of the Esquimaux families had extra children. Girl babies, particularly, were in excess and were often even given away, if not left to perish in an isolated igloo. The Esquimaux character was always a puzzle to me. Happy people, affectionate, appearing to love their offspring, a man might suddenly fall in a mood and trade off two or three of them for an old shotgun and a can of powder.

The homely routine of summer went on without incident. Joe and I worked hard, Hannah sewed winter garments, Mr. Hall wrote endlessly in his journal and took long walks into the mountains. And one day, beaching the *Lady Franklin* in a cove some distance from our camp, I stepped into a corpse. My boot plunged through the rib cage of a flesh-stripped skeleton, making a splintering and crushing sound. For an instant I stared down at the eyeless sockets of the skull, still plastered with a few strands of dead hair. Shreds of clothing clung to the bony structure, and the boots were whole and sound.

"Joe!" I called.

Disturbed at something in my voice, Joe came running. He stood beside me looking down at the remnants of the man. Then soundlessly he pointed at a hole in the skull. It was a big hole, perhaps the size made by a bullet, and a network of small radial cracks surrounded it.

"Shoot him," Joe said in a trembling voice. Dead people were ritually unclean to the Esquimaux. "Someone shoot him! There, in head."

I did not feel much better about it than Joe, but I knelt and examined the bones. It was not too bad. Stripped of its flesh, a man's body is more like a jointed wooden toy than anything else. It is the flesh that carries the significance; the life, the pulsation of the blood, the look of the face, the spirit, perhaps even the soul itself.

"An old woolen coat, and sea boots." I touched the leathern belt and examined the buckle, covered with verdigris but otherwise sound. Patrick Coleman? He had been in fear of his life when last I saw him. "Who do you suppose it is—was?"

[148

"Dead, him." Joe shuddered. "We go away, you and me, eh, Adam?"

"Wait a minute." I fingered a shred of what had been a shirt. Striped, it looked like; maybe red and white, though the reddish cast might have been blood. "Do you remember Patrick Coleman?"

Joe's brown face was pale.

"You leave 'lone, Adam. Him dead."

"I know he's dead. But I'm trying to recollect whether it might be Patrick Coleman. Do you remember whether Coleman was wearing a red and white shirt that day he rowed in from the *Jessie*, the day he brought the spoon?"

"Could be Coleman. Same size, all right, you bet. Now come away, Adam. No good, no good!" Entreatingly Joe pulled at my arm.

Coleman? It could be. I seemed to remember that shirt. But there was no way to be sure. And in this uncharted country, a life more or less was of little consequence; *lost overboard,* with a scribbled entry in the ship's log for a headboard. Or perhaps *died of scurvy,* which was frequent enough.

"You come 'long me!" Joe begged, his face such an exercise in panic that I threw stones and handfuls of earth over the remains and followed him back to the *Lady Franklin.* Coleman? I thought it was. Coleman the villain, come to a villainous end.

A man may live all his life in a great city, and still not know himself for what he is. In the Arctic no such deception is possible. Alone much of the time, enduring hardship, starvation, and great natural forces, what a man *is* comes out. Then *he* knows, and others know, too. After five years in the high latitudes, I was beginning to know myself, as well as Mr. Charles Hall. My knowledge of him, as well as that of myself, burst out one day in a way that separated us for a short span of time, only to reunite us more firmly than ever.

Hannah, that admirable lady, was visibly pining away before

our eyes. She grieved for her lost baby, which she had given birth to on that unfortunate attempt to reach Fury and Hecla. Too conscientious to complain, the poor woman drove herself on, furtively wiping away a tear when she thought no one watched. Her fresh gingham pinafore hung on her in loose folds, and her usually merry face became distraught and sallow. We all knew her grief and sought to share it, but she insisted on shouldering her burden alone. Finally Mr. Hall, despairing of any other solution, traded one of our two precious sledges for a girl-child; a sweet-faced little thing of two or three years.

"Pun-na, they called her," Mr. Hall said. He closed his ledger with a bang and got up, rubbing his hands together in a satisfied way. "Ah, Adam, it warmed my heart to see them together! Hannah was transported with joy." Not noticing my discomfiture, he walked to the flap of our summer *tupik* and threw it open. I could hear Hannah's voice from the tent she and Joe shared, and little Pun-na's shrieks of joy as her new father and mother played with her. "I suppose it is an un-Christian thing to do—buying a child, I mean—but surely there can be no wrong in it. The parents might have gotten rid of the child in the winter, when food is scarce. In this way I have made Hannah happy and given the child a good home, all at the price of a sledge."

When I was silent, he turned and stared at me.

"Is something wrong, Adam?"

"But our sledge!" I protested.

In this country a sledge was worth a great deal. The Esquimaux prized a good sledge and dogs more than anything else. Since a sledge was the only way to make any extended trip, a man put more value on his sledge than he did his wife. The Esquimaux artisans would work for months shaping runners, cunningly fashioning rawhide lashings and bone pins, ornamenting the whole with carved figures. The sledge Mr. Hall had bartered for Pun-na was an unusually fine one. Now, with only the one sledge that I had made in New London, we were seriously handicapped for any long trips.

"What is a sledge," demanded Mr. Hall, "to that poor woman's happiness?"

A picture had long been in my mind; indeed, it was seldom absent. I remembered a modest house in Cincinnati, the smell of boiling cabbage and potatoes, a patient woman with tear-streaked face who wrapped up cookies for me to take on the train. *Doesn't he love me any more? Will you tell him we love him, and think of him always?*

Piqued by the loss of the sledge, I burst out with what was on my mind.

"That poor woman's happiness? I wonder that you can speak so of Hannah, and give away one of our only two sledges, when you have so far forgotten your own wife and family, sir!"

He stiffened, and dropped the flap of the *tupik*. In the light of the oil lamp, his face became ashen. Clenching his fist, he came a step toward me, and I believe he would have struck me. A horrible change came over his face; it seemed almost to writhe in anger, or perhaps it was a kind of personal agony.

"Forgotten?" His voice was strained. "Ah, Adam, to say such a thing to me! Forgotten?"

Reckless, I plunged on.

"It is all very well to speak of love and happiness when you have abandoned your own family, I suppose, but it sticks in my craw. Sir, I admire you, and what you have done with so little, and in spite of opposition. But I would a damned sight rather you were more human and loving in your character! A sledge for an Esquimaux baby! Better some affection for your own flesh and blood, that is what I say!"

His face became suffused with a sudden inrush of blood. With an oath which I had never before heard from his lips, he seized me by the shoulder and pushed me down on the skin coverings of the floor. In his violence the net was torn from its customary place over the smoking lamp. It fell to the ground, spilling out the load of damp socks and underpants that was drying there.

"Listen to the boy!" He towered over me, biting at a corner of his lip. "To talk of familial love and affection—words that roll off the tongue glib and cheap! Damn you, Adam; oh, damn you!" Beating one fist into the palm of the other, he threw his head from side to side like some great bear caught in a trap. "Adam, do you then know me so little? After all these years, so great a mystery?"

"I don't know," I said sulkily. "All I know is—"

"Listen!" He knelt beside me. "I need not explain my life to any man. I made my decision a long time ago, and it is too late to have it any other way. But let me tell you some things, Adam." Tugging at a corner of his beard, he stared down at me, his eyes unfathomable; filled with hurt perhaps, or anger, or pride—I did not know the emotion that made them so hard and unseeing. "Do you know what it is to have made a great decision? To risk all, to turn your back on the homely life, to renounce love and affection for the darts and arrows of mean and jealous men?"

"I made a decision when I decided to come back to the Arctic with you," I pointed out.

"True! True!" Mr. Hall nodded violently. "But you are only a boy, Adam, or at best a young man, with no family to speak of! It has always been natural for young men to leave the fireside and go into the world looking for fortune. Observe Mr. Charles Hall, however! Some forty-odd years old with a wife and family, and a not especially successful printing business! Can you not understand how much more it means to such a man, settled in his ways and encumbered with family and obligations, to throw off the traces?" He ground one fist into the other in that gesture that showed how much he was distraught and concerned. "Adam, I tell you it was not done without great soul-searching! Many is the night I got out of my bed on Celestial Street and walked the paths about our house for hours on end, asking myself if this was the right, the proper thing to do!

I would go back, and by candlelight examine the sleeping faces of my children, and ponder. I would sit on the edge of the bed and listen to my wife's light quick breathing, asking myself what to do. Oh, God, what to do! I knew the Franklin people were alive; I felt it in my bones, and felt obliged to go and look for them. No one was making such an attempt, and these poor people called to me and cried out for help. Adam, could I do less? Could I let my own comfort and ease keep me from the hard and dedicated life? Could I do this, and call myself a fit father and husband?"

"I remember," I said, "that when you were in Oolootong village, and very sick, Captain Budington and I came after you. Then you talked to me about your plans, about what drove you, about why you felt obliged to do what you have done, and continue to do." I was thinking about the way he had talked of the descending mathematical curve he felt himself rushing down; of the fact that he was forty years old, and undistinguished. He had spoken then of his urge to make something of himself, and I found this to be at odds with his presently stated concern over having left his family and friends to roam the Arctic.

"I do not wonder that you should bring this up," he said. "But I can convince you it is not inconsistent. No man acts ever, Adam, from completely unmixed motives. We are all such an obstinate bundle of impulse and will and desire that we are never quite sure of our own motives, let alone those of others." He picked up a shard of bone; squatting beside me, he traced a complex pattern on the earth floor of the *tupik*. "I am only human, Adam. I will not deny that I have thought of fame and glory, and desired to have my name someday inscribed on a medal. All men desire fame; it is a way of seizing the immortality they might doubt on a heavenly basis. But all I can say is this. Franklin people or no, fame or not, here I am and here I stand on this Arctic continent. I will succeed here, or perish. And that is all I have to say."

He was a persuasive talker. How else would he have done so much with so little? Even with my nagging doubt, and the picture in my mind of that small Cincinnati home, I was swept along with his eloquence.

"I am sorry I said what I did," I told him.

He did not look up. Instead, with a single-minded intentness, he went on scribing in the dirt with the fragment of bone, pausing only to sigh heavily and shake his head. I finally turned on my side and pulled my furs about me, deciding to sleep. For a long time I lay there listening to the night sounds: the rustle of a small animal near our tent, the grinding of distant ice, the lap of water in a wind-stirred pool. Who was I to question his motives? In such a great undertaking as his, was it not carping and unfair to bring up the matters I had struck on?

I went to sleep, and awoke only once during the night, hearing Mr. Hall groan and twist in his sleep. I think he spoke the name of his wife, though his voice was heavy and muffled and I was not sure. At any rate, I felt somehow pleased as I rolled myself again in my skins. This was a queer and complex man, and I was beginning to understand the mainspring that drove him. Proud and stubborn and of great ability, I think he resented the circumstance that forced him into the printer and engraver's trade, with its inkstains and stone plates and cutting chisels. Seizing on the Franklin matter, by sheer force of will he had made it his own, by way of pulling himself from obscurity. Uncertain and disappointed, he called out now for the wife and children he had not seen for many years. Of course he had not abandoned them; he wrote when he could and sent small sums of money when he had it, which was not often. But he loved them, I do not doubt it. His tenderness with Joe and Hannah and little Pun-na was a natural outpouring of love for the familial life denied him.

He must often have questioned, as he said, the decision that took him north. Ill, discouraged, penniless; was he then not a better man than I for hewing to the decision in spite of such odds? Rushing down the descending curve he had mentioned, fighting the elements and men and fate and public indifference, he somehow managed to stumble on in a way that was magnificent. When Adam Burritt moldered in his winding sheet, Charles Hall would still be remembered. Such determination could not die with man's physical body. It was too bright, too blinding, too hot. The ashes would at least warm others. I went to sleep.

The Franklin survivors! It was a will-of-the-wisp that danced ever before us. Now, after five years of searching on Baffin Island and the Melville Peninsula, we were still unsuccessful, with only a worn silver spoon for all our hardship and toil. I, an ordinary man, saw the futility of our efforts, but Mr. Hall was made of different stuff. Though from time to time discouraged, he came back like a tenacious bulldog to the purpose of our Arctic sojourn. Not that he any longer entertained any real hopes of finding the Franklin people alive; the last that had been heard of them was now twenty years before. But a hundred-odd people do not vanish without leaving a trace. He was determined to settle for once and for all what had happened to them, and lay the mystery at rest. He was fond of quoting his findings of the Frobisher relics to me, pointing out, "If I have found these leavings of Frobisher from three hundred years ago, how much more likely that I can find well-preserved traces of a party which vanished only some twenty years ago!"

Old Nartuk, as I have said, had been a thorn in our side. Jealous of Mr. Hall's influence, seeing him as a rival *an-ge-ko,* Nartuk had been instrumental in our failure to reach the Straits of Fury and Hecla. Even now, he went on with his endless *an-koo-ting* in his big igloo at Noonoolik, some miles west of us, and encouraged the Esquimaux to rise against us and throw us out, claiming that the disease that had taken away so many dogs was of our doing.

"This situation," Mr. Hall said, "is becoming serious. Only yesterday, when I went out to take a sight, a little band gathered to mock me and call out evil things. It is not like these people to do such things without being incited and urged on."

"Nartuk," I said.

"I suppose so." He sighed. "Well, so long as there is no open break between us, I do not intend to do anything."

Things might have gone on this way for some time, and eventually actual bloodshed might have occurred. We were well armed and could take care of ourselves, but that was hardly the point. We knew and respected these people. I think the letting of blood, even in necessity, would have so affected Mr. Hall that he would have given up his Arctic hopes and gone back to the States. Blood was shed eventually, although it was not of our doing. The event led, also, to a new journey to the Straits.

It happened in this way. One day old Nartuk himself came to our igloo. We had not seen or heard from him for some time; in fact, our relations with the Esquimaux had been somewhat better. Even though we bore no love for the *an-ge-ko,* we were shocked to see him very weak, covered with blood and sores, bearing the evidence of having been treated badly.

"*Ki-e-te,*" said Mr. Hall. "Come in."

Old Nartuk knelt for a moment in the low tunnel, his face a study in fear and uncertainty. Then, reassured by the kindness in Mr. Hall's voice, he got stiffly up and tottered toward us.

"*Pe-ong-too!*" he croaked. "Bad. Very bad." He helped himself to a chunk of boiled seal meat from the pot that bubbled over the lamp, and squatted between us. "Oh, very bad! I am in bad condition."

This was certainly evident, but in view of Nartuk's hold on the Esquimaux, we were both curious as to how he had sustained such a beating.

"*Kod-lu-na,*" he explained. Famished, he plucked out a seal eye, and after juggling it for a moment in his withered fingers, popped it into his mouth and licked his hands and wrists.

"White men from whalers." He gestured west, toward Noonoo-lik. "They beat me. They drive me away from my own igloo! They are very bad men, all of them. They will kill me if I come back." He looked pleadingly from one of us to the other. "You help me. You good men. You go back with me, help kill those bad *kod-lu-na*."

"White men?" Mr. Hall tugged at his beard. "From whalers, eh?"

It was not uncommon, in view of the brutal treatment of men on the Hudson Bay whalers, for some to desert and set up housekeeping at a native village, hoping to beg passage back to the States on another vessel.

"Why," asked Mr. Hall with some acerbity, "did you not put a spell on them? You are a great *an-ge-ko,* Nartuk—greater than I, to hear you tell it."

Nartuk looked embarrassed as well as he could. His face was such a mass of wrinkles, scars, and wounds that it did not come off very well. "I tried," he said. "It did not work. I think there were too many of them for me."

"On one *kod-lu-na* your magic works, eh?" Mr. Hall glowered. "But not on many. Is that it?"

Nartuk nodded.

"Well," said Mr. Hall, "I would be well advised to let you stew in your own juices, but I cannot. These evil men may harm or injure other Esquimaux—people we know and love—so I think Adam and I had better go along with you, Nartuk, and look into this matter." He turned to me. "Adam, load our sledge. Get our little shotgun from its flannel wrappings, and take plenty of powder and ball and caps for our pistols. We will go to Noonoolik village and see what can be done."

We went to Noonoolik, not knowing what we would find.

Chapter 10

IT took us three days of hard sledging to get to Noonoo-lik village. The sun was just beginning its annual trip above the horizon and most of the trip was made in darkness, Nartuk pointing the way by landmarks which we could often not see even when he called our attention to them. A slight hummock here, a pile of low rocks there, a stand of shrubs stark and bare in the snow. Mr. Hall took star sights and referred often to his compass, but no one had ever established the latitude and longitude of Noonoolik village. We were forced to rely entirely on the *an-ge-ko*.

"Not far now," Nartuk said. He pointed to a flickering light in the dusk, at the base of a range of rocky hills. "That Noonoo-lik." His toothless gums gaped in a grin, he being convinced that death and destruction was imminent for the *kod-lu-na* who had misused him. "You kill them all, eh?" He patted the stock of Mr. Hall's shotgun. "Shoot them in belly, eh? Long time to die. Very bad. *Pe-ong-too!*"

I do not know why I was surprised to find Patrick Coleman at Noonoolik village. Like a bad penny, he had turned up again to plague us. Somehow or other, Coleman and his thin-lipped smile seemed to follow us like a spirit. Now here he was at Noonoolik, living like a lord in the igloo from which he and his companions had evicted Nartuk, levying tribute from the poor Esquimaux by force of arms.

"Well!" Coleman stood up in the gloom of the snowhouse, a pistol in one hand and a half-gnawed bone in the other. "If it ain't Adam Burritt! And old Hall!" He gestured to a frightened Esquimaux man who cowered in the shadows. "Mukko here said you was on the way. Figured it wouldn't be long till you showed up."

Coleman's four companions were an evil lot. There was a shrunken spidery little man named Nellis; a giant and slow-witted hulk who answered to Parkes; a fat man with face so porcine his eyes were only slits in the rich flesh of his cheeks, and his name was Hobey something-or-other. The fourth was a Negro; a silent man who sat in a corner and looked from one of us to the other, all the time fingering a knife in a sheath at his waist. Sam, he was called. A prime lot.

Mr. Hall sat down, shotgun across his knees. Nartuk, from fear, had stayed outside. I beat the snow from my furs and sat beside Mr. Hall, one hand on the butt of the pistol inside my waistband.

"No need to be hostile!" Coleman said grinning, his tongue licking in and out in the way he had. "Put your scatter-gun away. Ain't no one going to harm you."

Mr. Hall kept the gun across his knees. "I am not worried about myself. I understood you beat poor old Nartuk, the *ange-ko*. He is outside, expecting some redress."

Coleman guffawed. Parkes, the giant, laughed in an imitative way, without real humor. The fat man grinned, a facial contortion almost lost in the folds of his flesh. Nellis shot a sharp glance at the Negro, who only went on fondling his sheath knife.

"Sam did it." Coleman pointed to the Negro. "Deef and dumb, he is. Hard to get through to him. He was only having a little fun, though. No harm meant, I'm sure, mates."

Mr. Hall looked around him. "Isn't this Nartuk's igloo?"

"Sure it is." Coleman chuckled. "He went away, didn't he? No use such a nice place going to waste." He looked around him and patted his stomach. "Real comfortable. The old man left a nice stock of meat. Living like kings, we are."

"Nevertheless," Mr. Hall said, "what you have done is wrong. You have no right to mistreat these people and move in on them this way. By so doing, you only cause trouble for the rest of us who are up here on a legitimate purpose."

"I ain't taking orders from you!"

"I do not ask you to take orders from me," Mr. Hall said steadily. "I only ask you to live among these people as friends, instead of giving all *kod-lu-na* a black name." He shifted the shotgun on his knee. "I will ask you to start off by moving out of here and giving Nartuk back his house."

Coleman stared at Mr. Hall in complete unbelief.

"Now," said Mr. Hall firmly.

Under other circumstances, or at least without that shotgun muzzle pointing at his belly, Coleman would have laughed, secure in the knowledge of his strength. After all, there were five of them and only two of us. But the shotgun muzzle stayed dead-center on Coleman's belt buckle. When Parkes came to his knees like a faithful dog, big hands working at his sides, I pulled out my pistol and waved him back.

"I am only doing this for your own good," Mr. Hall said. "These Esquimaux can be very warlike and cruel. They will put up with so much of your kind of mistreatment; then they will strike, and you will be the sorrier for it."

Coleman squatted beside the lamp, lean legs folded under him like a crane. "I ain't saying we will, and I ain't saying we won't. But it don't do no harm to talk things over a little first."

"All right," said Mr. Hall. "But no tricks, sir. Someone will get killed, and it may be you."

Coleman waved his hand. "Hell, we're all white men, ain't we? Except Sam here, but he's a good man. We got to stick together in a country like this with all these gecks around. Ain't that so?"

There was a general chorus of approval. Parkes looked at Coleman and nodded his big head slowly and massively. The fat man Hobey said, "We're all friends, ain't we, mates?" Nellis only grunted, and Sam the Negro picked his nails with the sheath knife, watching our lips with an intentness that made me uneasy.

"We can come to some agreement," said Coleman. He pointed to the simmering kettle. "Eat up, mates. There's tea in the pot there." Turning to Mr. Hall he said, "I still got that note you signed for the eel spoon. Anything ever come of it?"

Mr. Hall scratched his chin. He seemed suddenly thoughtful. "No. At least, not yet. I took a party of natives on a journey to the Straits, but we never reached Igloolik. Bad weather turned us back. Bad weather, among other things."

I remembered the body Joe and I had found in the cove. "A while back I found a man lying on the beach near our camp. He had been murdered. There was a bullet hole in his head."

Coleman spat. "Aye. That was poor Bender, Solomon Bender." He swore horribly and said, "Burden did it, that damned Burden, of the *Jessie*. I tell you, that was a hellship! Burden strung Solomon up and had him whipped, account of a bottle of wine missing from the lazaret. Bender was cookie, see? He couldn't stand it no more. He nipped over the side one night, and Captain Burden went after him himself. I dunno rightly what happened, except we heard the shot, and after a while Burden come back with his pistol stuck in his belt and a look on his face like a cat with a saucer of cream. 'Won't trouble us no more,' he said. 'Won't steal no more of my wine, 'e won't.'

That's what he said, and offered the same to any man that didn't like what he done." Coleman shook his head, and for a moment I felt almost sorry for him. "Right after that was when my mates and I jumped ship. We was in fear for our lives. Ever since, we been here at Noonoolik, waitin' for old bloody Burden and his *Jessie* to leave Hudson Bay. Next fall, when he's gone, we'll pop out and beg passage on some other whaler if we can."

"And if not?" Mr. Hall asked.

Coleman laughed. "If not, we'll stay on. Hell, we're good Arctic hands, all of us! We know our way around. Live like the gecks, that's what we'll do. We ain't scared; no, not a bit of it. If a man's got to die, he might as well do it here as in some foul rooming house in Nantucket. The devil ain't choosy. He'll come for us at Noonoolik soon as anyplace!"

"I suppose so," Mr. Hall said. He was thinking about something, thinking very hard.

"Help yourself to the stew." Coleman took a bottle from a knapsack hanging from a peg in the ice wall and handed it around, Mr. Hall and I refusing. "It's a shame old Burden scragged Solomon Bender," Coleman sniggered, "when it was me run off with the port, eh, boys?" He dug Parkes in the ribs, and the giant chuckled.

We talked for a while, even with some amicability, though I was thinking of poor Nartuk huddled outside and wondering when Mr. Hall was going to enforce his edict about evicting these scoundrels from Nartuk's igloo. But the conversation took an unexpected turn that made me gasp. Mr. Hall started it off.

"You are, as you say, good Arctic hands. And we *kod-lu-na* must stick together, for safety and success. Now I have a proposition to make to you all."

Coleman put down the bottle. "A proposition?"

"Aye, a proposition. I need men to go with me to search for the lost Franklin expedition. We were, as you know, turned back by bad weather and unwillingness of the natives to go farther. I am convinced that a party made up of white men can succeed in a sledge journey this time of year—if we start immediately, that is. What do you say?"

Coleman was astonished, as I think the rest of us were also.

"Us, mate? You mean you want—*us* to go with you?"

His surprise was almost ludicrous.

"Yes," said Mr. Hall. "That is what I mean."

Coleman looked from one of his cronies to the next. Some were eager and interested, others apathetic. Sam went on picking his nails with the knife.

"What's in it for us?" Coleman asked. "Hell, we're doing right well in this little cove here! Sit out the rest of the winter, walk over to Repulse Bay when the weather lifts, work our way home on a whaler." He looked crafty and cunning, which was not a great effort.

"I'll pay you," Mr. Hall said. "A hundred dollars for the lot of you, to be split however you decide best!"

Coleman spat. "A hundred dollars? You still owe me two hundred on that note you give me." From an inner pocket he took the folded bit of notebook paper. "Don't think I forgot it, either." He waved it aloft.

"I have not forgotten it." Mr. Hall got out his small notebook and a stub of pencil. "What do you say, eh? A hundred dollars for the lot of you, secured by my further note."

Coleman rubbed his stubbly chin. He and Nellis and Hobey withdrew outside for a while to confer. The giant Parkes and Sam remained inside; Parkes muttering to himself and rolling his eyeballs, Sam tossing the knife in a game of mumblety-peg on the frozen ground.

"I don't understand you," I whispered to Mr. Hall. "These men are villains, all of them! What business should we have of them?"

"Of course they are villains!" In the light of the lamp I could see that he was perspiring; hardly from fear, for he was indomitable. Nervousness perhaps, or a return of his sickness. "They are villains all, but rough and capable men, knowing where their own self-interest lies. I will make it to the Straits with them, or never! We cannot be choosers, Adam; therefore we must be beggars, and buy their services with whatever we can offer."

"There will be trouble."

"I do not doubt it. But I will meet it when it comes, as I have always."

Villains all, they came back into the igloo. Hobey conversed with Sam in sign language, and the giant Parkes watched with a kind of childlike awe. "All right, then," Coleman said. "We'll go. But that makes three hundred you owe me."

"I know."

Mr. Hall handed Coleman the scribbled note, again witnessed and attested to by me, for what good that did.

"We'll be back by summer?" Coleman asked.

"Yes."

Coleman kicked aside a litter of bones and squatted on the floor examining the note. "Looks good enough to me."

"Let me see it." Hobey scrabbled near him, but Coleman snatched away the note and stuck it in his pocket. "Who's boss here?" he growled.

"You, I guess," said Hobey. He pulled his forelock and sat down again, beaming.

"When can we go?" asked Mr. Hall. "We'll have to sledge back to our camp first and make ready for the journey."

Coleman laughed, licking his lips. "Why, *we* ain't got much baggage, Cap. We travel light, we do!" He got up, grinning. "On your feet, all of you. Nellis, Sam—" He gestured. "Hobey, Parkes, you idjit!"

Outside, Nartuk was waiting in the snowy dusk. When he saw Coleman he ran away and cowered behind a snow-laden thicket. I had to go after him and convince him he would not be harmed.

"You kill them?" Nartuk asked Mr. Hall, his teeth chattering.

[164

"No," said Mr. Hall, "I do not kill them, Nartuk. But they are sorry they mistreated you, and your igloo is yours again. These men are going away with me now, and will not bother you."

Coleman sniggered. "That's right. We're awful sorry we bashed you, old man."

We drove away, Mr. Hall riding the runners of the sledge and the rest of us walking behind. The moon rose, a blood-red orb winking across the snowy waste.

The Straits of Fury and Hecla were, as I have said, more than three hundred miles north of us. After our long trip back to our base camp, we took over a week in resting, getting together our supplies, repairing our sledge, and borrowing another through the good offices of Joe and Hannah. These latter were desolated by Mr. Hall's refusal to let them accompany him.

"But we *want* to go!" Hannah insisted. "Father Hall, you will need us. Who will hunt for you, sew for you, keep your lamp going and dry your clothes?"

"We will manage," said Mr. Hall.

Remembering the shambles that had been our last trip with them and the rest of the natives, they did not press the point too much, though Hannah especially was grief-stricken.

"Pun-na will miss you," she said, holding up the baby.

"And I will miss Pun-na." He pinched the baby on the cheek. "But we will be back soon."

Altogether we had twenty-two dogs, two sledges, a folding skin boat, Mr. Hall's scientific and surveying instruments, two *tupiks,* five gallons of prime seal oil, a hundred and fifty pounds of pemmican, three pounds of tea, two rifles, three revolvers, and Mr. Hall's shotgun, with an abundance of ammunition. It made a heavy load for the dogs.

The Melville Peninsula was rocky and mountainous, difficult to traverse by sledge, whereas the Foxe Basin was at this time of year only a great jumble of frozen ice, forbidding all passage.

But wherever there is land there is what is called an "ice foot" —a narrow strip of level ice along the coast over which sledge travel can be easily carried on. The fringe of ice along our route followed an irregular line, more or less distant from shore; depending on the depth of the water, the level stretch was from three to five miles in width, and made easy going. The first day we made good almost twenty miles, and anticipated even better going after we had all become hardened again to the trail. The temperature was not extreme, being only forty to fifty degrees below the freezing point on the Fahrenheit scale.

Actually, we did not get on too badly as a party. These rough men were accustomed to the Arctic and knew its dangers. At the moment, at least, they made common cause with us, and we had good progress toward Igloolik, our goal near the Straits. Mr. Hall organized us into parties; some to drive the dogs, some to hunt seal, others to assist him in his surveying and astronomical observations, which he carried on constantly. Like most sailors, Coleman and his cronies were impressed by Mr. Hall's ability at navigation.

"I don't like him, understand," Coleman said during one of our brief tea pauses, breaking crusted ice and snow from his beard, "but I'll say this for him. He knows what he's doing, that he does."

It was a good thing Mr. Hall *did* know what he was doing. In this trackless waste, the jumbled frozen sea on one side and the mountains on the other, bereft of landmarks, he and his sextant and charts were all that could point the way to Igloolik—or find the way back, once we had reached there.

As we went on, the country seemed to become more desolate and abandoned. The heavens above and the earth below revealed only an endless and fathomless quiet. Nowhere was there evidence of life or motion. No footfall of living thing reached us, wild beast howling in the solitude, no tree in whose branches the wind could moan and speak to us. We seemed almost to hear and see the silence, broken only by the murmuring of the frozen sea under our feet.

"I don't like it," fat Hobey said. Even in the bitter cold he perspired; droplets that turned into icy pendants in his beard. "Does it have to be so everlasting quiet?" He stopped in his tracks and put down the sack of bread he had been carrying. "Hark! What's that? Sounds like someone whispering!"

It was only the fitful complaining of the trapped water; half sound, and the other half a slight vibration under our boots. Although to the eye the expanse of ice seemed as stable as the solid land, it nevertheless moved, and Mr. Hall's instruments would demonstrate the fact. The pressure increases and decreases alternately, currents set in, a kind of slow, groaning noise, in which silvery tinklings mingle with the low undertone of the great natural forces. The effect was weird and solemn.

In less than two weeks we reached Igloolik, a very good record. There was a small village there, almost hidden in the recent snows of a great blizzard which we only touched on, it moving for the most part to the west of us. I committed folly on the journey, neglecting to change my socks when my feet had become wet from melted snow. In the tail end of the storm, I froze most of the toes on my right foot. On reaching Igloolik I was fairly hobbling, but otherwise the trip was without incident.

The *an-ge-ko* of the village came to meet us, a small and surly man with a sinuous drooping mustache and a scraggly beard.

"No," he said, in response to Mr. Hall's questioning. "No *kod-lu-na* here. Never!" He was very firm, assuring us that this was too distant from their country for the *kod-lu-na* to come.

We were disappointed. Patrick Coleman had the good grace to appear embarrassed at the collapse of his story about the eel spoon. "But that's what this geck told me," he insisted. "Maybe we better look around a little before we decide it ain't true!"

Mr. Hall agreed. We sledged to the top of Cape Inglefield, but not a sign indicated that white men had been there, nor could we find the cairn and the papers that Coleman's informant had spoken of. Coleman and his gang labored for many hours cutting with their iron snow knives into various spots, without the least sign of a cairn. We did, however, find a tenting place, which the unpleasant *an-ge-ko* admitted must have been built by white men. It was traced by four stones weighing each from twenty to thirty pounds, which had doubtless been used to hold down tent corners, and by rows of smaller stones to secure the sides.

"Well," said Mr. Hall, unwrapping the plaid muffler from about his nose and mouth, "I am convinced this was a tenting place made by white men, at least." He unrolled his map and pointed out our present location. "I believe the Franklin people came by this way." He traced what he believed to be their route. "Here, through the great Foxe Basin, through these very straits, and into the Gulf of Boothia. It is plain to me that they were looking for a northwest passage. My original estimate of King William Land is not so very far off, you see. That would be on their route, and there we will find further evidence, I think."

We had squatted in the lee of a rocky ledge and were boiling water for tea. Coleman, listening to us, stood up suddenly. Hobey stopped chewing on his chunk of dried *took-too*, and Sam aware of the quick tension, folded his case knife and looked from one of us to the other.

"King William Land?" Coleman demanded. He took another sip of tea, staring at Mr. Hall over the rim of his tin cup. "Why, that's a good—my Lord, it's a thousand mile from here!"

"That's right," said Mr. Hall.

"We didn't bargain on nothing like that."

"I did not specify any particular distance," said Mr. Hall.

Coleman turned red in the face. "By God, we ain't going to stand for it." He turned to Hobey and the rest. "Are we?"

"No, we ain't!" they chorused. There was an immediate babble of protest.

"I need you all," said Mr. Hall, "but you need me more. Does any of you know how to navigate?"

There was silence. Coleman stood motionless, holding his tin cup. "So that's it," he said after a moment. "Blast you, that's your dirty game!"

"No game at all," Mr. Hall said. "You will recall I asked you simply to go with me to search for the lost Franklin expedition. I did say we were going to the Straits, but did not state that Igloolik was to be the limit of our search. I also paid you all—liberally, I think."

"A piece of paper!" Coleman said bitterly.

Mr. Hall wrapped the muffler again about his neck and rolled up the map, sticking it into the leather case. "Nevertheless, I consider my obligation binding. And you all had better do the same, because if you do not, Adam and I will go to King William Land and leave you here to perish!"

It was not correct to call it an impasse. There could be only one conclusion. Coleman flung the tin cup from him with an oath.

"You've got us now!" he raged. "All right! We'll go. But I ain't forgetting what you done us."

"That's the sensible way to look at it," said Mr. Hall calmly.

It bordered on sharp practice, I suppose, but in Mr. Hall's shoes I do not know that I would have done differently. Time was running out on us—and on the Franklin people, if they still survived. On we went toward King William Land, traveling in a great arc across the icy curve of the world. Some days we made better than fifty miles, the ice foot stretching long and straight before us. On other days we were lucky to make as much as ten miles, being forced to unleash the dogs and carry our sledges by hand across great jumbles of twisted and broken ice, some of the chunks as large as a house. My foot continued to pain me, in spite of Mr. Hall's salves and powders, and some of the skin started to slough from the frozen toes.

169]

"I do not like the looks of that foot," Mr. Hall said.

"Nor do I."

In our snow-blanketed *tupik* he examined it by the light of the lamp. "Does it pain you much?"

"Not much."

"Perhaps we should dig in here for a while, and let it heal."

Knowing his eagerness to reach King William Land, and knowing also the growing mutinous nature of Patrick Coleman and his cohorts, I shook my head. "It will get better. I think walking on it keeps the blood in circulation and promotes healing."

He looked at me for a long moment, bearded face half in shadow. Then he re-dressed the toes with a scrap of rag and some more salve, clapping me on the back.

"Another three or four hundred miles will do it."

"Let us hope so," I said.

Somewhere near Pelly Bay the long-continued friction broke into open heat. Taking refuge from a long-continued storm that sent the thermometer plunging to the bottom and put three to four feet of fresh powder-dry snow across our path, we were forced to build snowhouses and stay indoors for better than a week. The period of enforced idleness was probably what brought the open break. When the weather cleared and it was time to go on, Coleman and his associates refused to move.

"It's comfortable here," Coleman said. "We got food for a long time. We been on the trail better'n a month, and a man's got to rest."

"We must move on," Mr. Hall said. "If we are to reach King William Land before the ice goes out, we must—"

"To hell with King William Land!" said Coleman. "We don't move from this spot till you give us your solemn word you're facing about and taking us back to Repulse Bay, where we can get passage home!"

Mr. Hall smiled thinly. "We are several hundred miles from Repulse Bay, and I am the only one knows how to get there."

"That's what I mean," said Coleman. Behind him Hobey scrambled to his knees and looked at us with bright eyes. Sam stopped his eternal playing with his knife, and Nellis and Parkes got up and stood between us and the low entrance to their igloo. "That's exactly what I mean." Coleman licked his lips and took a deep breath. "And you're going to take us there!" Suddenly, at a gesture from him, the fat man Hobey burrowed in a pile of furs and brought out one of our rifles which they had there. Coleman took it from him, pointing it at Mr. Hall. "See what I mean?"

"I see," said Mr. Hall. "I see also that Adam and I should have taken better care of our firearms."

"We've got you dead to rights," cried Coleman triumphantly. "Now what do you say?"

"I say to hell with you," Mr. Hall shouted. Profanity never crossed his lips, and it was a measure of his exasperation. "Put that gun down, you rascal, or I will take it from you!"

I hobbled erect, as ready as I could be for trouble, which was not very ready. Parkes and Sam fell on me, and bore me down kicking and fighting.

"Put that gun down, I said!" Mr. Hall called to Coleman.

"I'll shoot you first, and worry later about getting out of this snow desert!" Coleman said. Seeing Mr. Hall reach into his pocket he said, "Here, now; stop that, or I shoot!"

Indecision in such an undertaking was fatal. While Coleman vacillated, calling out threats and brandishing the gun, Mr. Hall drew a pistol from beneath his furs and pulled the trigger. The blast caught Coleman as a wind catches a leaf and bears it away. He tottered back, gouts of blood spurting from his chest. For a moment the rifle waved uncertainly and then went off, blasting down a shower of snow and ice from our roof. Coleman dropped the weapon and fell heavily backward, moaning in pain and feeling his wound with frantic hands.

"Help me!" he called out. "Hobey, Parkes! **Damn** you, all of you! Look what he's done to me!"

"Don't move, any of you," said Mr. Hall sternly, "or I'll give you a dose of the same medicine!" He drew another loaded pistol from his furs and looked around him. "Are there any more mutineers?"

"Not me," said Hobey.

"Nor me," muttered Nellis. Parkes and Sam only looked on the scene with gaping mouths and offered no threat. "Criminey," said Hobey, "look at him bleed, will you?"

Mr. Hall handed me the loaded pistol and bade me keep it ready. Kneeling on the floor, he pulled away the tattered furs and examined Coleman's wound. Used as I was to the bloody whaling, I turned sick and almost dropped the pistol. The sight reminded me of a butcher's shop; the bucket of offal kept under the counter.

"Am I hurt bad?" Coleman whimpered.

Now that the violence was over, the relation between him and Mr. Hall was curiously restrained; more like doctor and patient than enemies. I suppose it was only reasonable. None of us but Mr. Hall had the skill or knowledge to cure such a horrible wound, although I did not know that he himself could accomplish much under these primitive conditions. Calomel was no specific for such a mangling.

"Yes," said Mr. Hall. "You are in bad shape, Coleman. Now lie quiet and let me take a look at where you are hurt."

While Mr. Hall probed for the bullet with a pair of surgical forceps, I held an oil lamp over the wound. Hobey and the rest of them stayed away and would not come near, even to bring a basin of warm water. "Can't stand the sight of blood," Hobey said earnestly. Parkes, the giant, buried his face in his hands and cowered in a corner. Nellis puffed his pipe and Sam squatted in shadow beyond the rim of light, his eyeballs rolling.

Coleman had fainted.

"There!" said Mr. Hall. He held up the battered bit of lead in his tongs. "Now to sew up the wound as best I can."

With gut and a bone needle he stitched the gaping lips of the wound together and put a bandage over the whole. Standing up, he rolled down his sleeves and wiped his bloody hands with a handful of dried grass. "I am no surgeon," he said, "but I think I have done a good job. The rest is in the hands of the Lord."

For the next two weeks we stayed in our ice huts, Mr. Hall nursing the wounded Coleman with the gentleness of a woman and the dedication of a saint. No task was too mean or unpleasant for him to perform. When the wound began to suppurate and generate a pus, he opened it again, cleaned the wound, and sewed Coleman up. I think Coleman might have recovered if it had not been for the fever. Delirious, he wandered into the frozen night when none of us was watching, and came down with a high fever.

He moaned continually, not recognizing any of us. "Can't anyone help me?"

He grew so violent that we were forced to bind him. On the morning of the seventeenth day after Mr. Hall had shot him, Patrick Coleman died, a green froth on his lips and terror in his eyes.

"Well," Mr. Hall said, dropping the lifeless hand, "he is gone."

"And you killed him, too," fat Hobey said. "Ain't that so, mates?"

"I did what I had to do," Mr. Hall said.

"It's murder, that's what it is!" snarled Nellis.

"You know it's not," I said. "He would have killed Mr. Hall otherwise."

Mr. Hall seemed dazed. He got carefully to his feet, looking down at the dead face of Patrick Coleman. "I did what I had to do," he said again. "Only what I had to do. That is all."

Hobey beamed his false smile. "Well, now what, mates?"

I do not know why I was so angry. I turned on him, though, and almost drove him back with my ire. "What now?" I shouted. "Why, on to King William Land, of course!"

Chapter 11

THE memory of that last few hundred miles is dull in my mind; dulled by backbreaking labor, semistarvation, sickness, bad luck. Now that the ringleader, Coleman, was dead, entombed forever in the igloo where we left him, the rest of our recruits worked hard and soberly, knowing that only the maximum effort would get them to Hudson Bay, and a whaler again. But the weather turned against us. Raging storms beat and buffeted our party, and food ran low. Perversely, not a seal was to be had. We ate boiled rawhide and were glad for it. After a while we ate some of the dogs. I never thought to be able to kill a dog, always having had one for a pet when I was a child.

On we staggered, our few animals pulling one sledge while men pulled the other. My foot was healing, but the heavy toil broke the skin on it. Frequently I was forced to come to a stop, the caravan waiting while I dried my foot from the blood and bodily juices that had wet it. Then on we would reel, pulling

the odd sledge and falling down and then painfully getting up
to pull some more.

Mr. Hall was ever before us, calling us on, or behind, pushing on a stalled sledge. He butchered another of our dogs and
made a kind of purée for fat Hobey, who was ill and had already
lost twenty pounds. Mr. Hall was here, there, everywhere;
beckoning us on, telling jokes, always taking his sights and making notes in his journal. I do not doubt that without him we
would all have perished. But with him, we came at last to King
William Land and the end of our search. On the 10th of April,
1869, our few remaining dogs scented new igloos and broke into
a run, overturning the sledge in their anxiety. Poor beasts—they
were as starved as we!

Apprehensive of a hostile meeting, being among new and
strange people, Mr. Hall and Sam went cautiously forward.
It was well that they did, because their appearance caused an
uproar in the Esquimaux camp. People ran about shouting,
some of them came forward menacingly, carrying their seal
spears, but fortunately being without firearms.

Mr. Hall and Sam fell back to us, and for a moment our two
hostile groups faced each other across a jumble of ice.

While we waited and pondered, one of the Esquimaux men
ran forward shouting insults and threw his spear. It hurtled
through the air and narrowly missed Hobey. With an oath the
fat man raised his gun, but Mr. Hall dissuaded him.

"There is something more here than we know," he said.
Handing me his shotgun he added, "Adam, take this. I am going
forward again to try to talk."

He talked to them a long time, giving them presents of needles and cloth. But they still retained their fear of us, and did
not want us to approach their village.

"I do not understand this," Mr. Hall said. "What can they
have to hide?"

When he showed them the eel spoon, this brought a fresh uproar. Fearing some violence to him, I came up with one of our

rifles. "They want us to go away," Mr. Hall said to me. Pointing to one old man, very aged and wrinkled, he said, "This is Eshong, the chief of the village. He says they want us to go away. They do not know anything of Eshemutta and the white men. They say we will bring sickness and bad luck to them, and they want us to go away."

"Well," I said, "perhaps we had better go. I would not like to risk a fight in our present condition."

Squatting in the snow opposite the belligerent Eshong, Mr. Hall shook his head. "No. This is the area where I believe the Franklin party may have come. We must search this area thoroughly, Eshong or no." Turning to the chief he said, "We will stay here for a while. We are looking for Eshemutta—" He held up the eel spoon. "We will stay here until we find out something about him, and what happened to him."

Old Eshong was indignant, shouting, "*Pe-ong-too—pe-ong-too*—bad, bad!" Esquimaux sweat only on the nose, and Eshong's nose glistened with sweat, showing his excitement. But Mr. Hall was adamant, and although I feared violence would break out at any moment, the Esquimaux sullenly permitted us to camp near their igloos.

"I am puzzled," said Mr. Hall as we took out our snow knives and started to build our own icehouses. "These people are backward and poor, that is true, and isolated. But it is not like them to treat strangers so—even *kod-lu-na*."

We set up housekeeping in the village, and managed to barter some looking glasses and tobacco for enough meat to sustain us until hunting should prove more profitable. Mr. Hall organized us into groups and we combed the snowy hillsides above the camp, looking for evidence of the Franklin party. There was nothing; no cairn, no huts, no evidence that the Franklin people ever got thus far. As days went on, Mr. Hall seemed visibly to wilt, to lose stature, to become smaller and drawn and haggard.

"Nothing."

"Ah, well—tomorrow, then."

We searched the ice foot, the beach, the foothills beyond, and the mountains. We hacked endlessly at snowy mounds that might contain a secret, we dug up hillocks with our snow knives, we burrowed and grubbed like animals, all the time knowing the season was passing. To make a safe return to Repulse Bay meant that we must soon leave. And yet there was no evidence of the Franklin people.

"To have come so far," Mr. Hall said, "for nothing. Well, I am an idiot. That is all there is to it."

And then one day, so perverse is destiny, we stumbled on the key to the whole thing. We understood suddenly why the villagers were so reticent, and things came suddenly aright from their skewness. It was Mr. Hall himself who made the discovery.

Going to the village in another fruitless attempt to talk with the old men, to gain from them some shred of information to guide us in our search, he and I were walking along, heads bent against the wind. An urchin of the village stormed by us on a homemade sled, coming down a snowy slope with a great hallooing. As the boy bolted past us, coming to a stop a few yards away, Mr. Hall stopped, eyes wide.

"Adam," he said, "did you see that?"

"That what?"

"Why—why—" In his excitement he stammered. "Why, that sledge!"

"I did," I said, "but—"

He ran toward the boy. Frightened at the bearlike creature pursuing him, the boy dropped the sledge and ran away crying. Mr. Hall picked the thing up in his hands and stared at it.

"This is a piece of a boat!" he said. "Look—clinker-built and copper-fastened!"

Sure enough; it was a bit of a white man's boat, and how it ever got to this remote village I did not know! The people of the village had said they knew of no white men in this area. They had denied any knowledge of *kod-lu-na*.

"But where—"

Mr. Hall gestured toward the village. "We will soon have an opportunity to find out." The boy's parents, and from the size of the crowd I think most of his relatives, came menacingly toward us from the village.

Mr. Hall seized the initiative and spoke the first word. Holding the sled aloft, he said, "You have not told me the truth! You said there were never any *kod-lu-na* here, but what is this?"

I have never seen such a remarkable effect on an angry crowd. It was as if someone suddenly doused them with a stream of ice water from a fire hose. From heat and anger they were plunged into uneasiness and quiet, a stillness that developed further into fright and near panic.

"What is this?" Mr. Hall demanded again, holding up the makeshift sledge. "This is made from the boat of a *kod-lu-na*, and yet you, Eshong, and the rest of the old men told me that never in your history were there *kod-lu-na* here, in this country! But you people have told lies to me!"

There was an instant chattering. It was as if a dam had burst and let out all the words these people had wanted to say, but had been somehow prevented from saying. They all spoke at once, shrieking and demanding attention and seeming to accuse each other of some crime.

"Listen!" old Eshong screeched. He held up both hands. "Listen, all you people. Don't talk. Let me talk now. I am the chief, and I will explain."

"I am waiting," said Mr. Hall sternly.

Old Eshong scraped his feet and did not look at us. He was obviously embarrassed and ashamed. Finally he blurted out, "Yes, there were *kod-lu-na* here, a long time ago."

"How long ago?" Mr. Hall asked.

Eshong screwed up his face in thought. He spread out his fingers several times, looking at them thoughtfully. Finally he said, "Many winters ago. Maybe ten, maybe fifteen, I do not know." He scratched his head and went on. "Aglooka and his men—they came. Aglooka had a telescope hung around on his neck on a string. He was a brave man, that Aglooka. With him were many men—oh, maybe a hundred. They had boats with them, boats they dragged like a sledge. They did not have any dogs. They were all very sick, and Aglooka said they had come a long way."

"Aglooka?" asked Mr. Hall. "Who was Aglooka?"

"Their chief," said Eshong. "A tall man with a dark beard and a big nose."

"Was Eshemutta with them?" asked Mr. Hall. He described Sir John Franklin as best he could.

"No Eshemutta." Eshong shook his head. "Only Aglooka. Aglooka was the chief."

"Then Franklin was dead," muttered Mr. Hall. "Aglooka must have been Crozier, Franklin's second in command."

"Ice broke up their ships," Eshong said. Beginning in a way to enjoy his important role, his voice took on the singsong of the minstrel, the storyteller. He gestured largely with his arms and looked about him for confirmation from the old men. "Aglooka said many of their men had died, and these were all that were left. He said they were going to Iwillik."

"Iwillik," I said. "That is Repulse Bay."

"Well," Mr. Hall asked, "what happened then?"

Old Eshong looked pained. He glanced about at his fellow elders and they all groaned ludicrously, as if remembering some unpleasant incident. It reminded me of the chorus in a Greek drama. "There were many of them," Eshong said. "They were all very hungry. We did not have much food." He avoided our eyes. "We went away," he said. "What else could we do, sir? Our small village—we left our igloos and went away to find another camp. These men, sir—they wanted to eat all our food, and we did not have very much." He looked around him, and the Greek chorus howled.

"You mean," demanded Mr. Hall, "that you abandoned these poor men? You went away, and did not help them? You took your food and went away from them?"

Eshong did not answer. A wail escaped from the chorus.

"So that is it!" Mr. Hall was very angry. "So that is why you would not tell me about the *kod-lu-na!* You were ashamed, and thought you would be punished. Is that it?"

Eshong essayed a smile, a weak and vacuous grimace. "Yes, sir," he said. "We are all very sorry. It was a bad thing to do. But there were so many of them, sir. We—"

"Damnation!" blurted Mr. Hall. "You abandoned these men, these poor starved souls? What kind of an act is that?" He turned to me in exasperation. "I have never known Esquimaux to act so. By the very devil, it was a cruel and heartless thing to do."

Some of the women began to weep, and the old men raised their hands and wailed, calling down punishment on their heads for such inhuman conduct. They were all very sorry, but the act was done. Aglooka and his hundred men or so had perished, it appeared.

"What happened then?" demanded Mr. Hall.

Eshong sniffled and put out his hands in a supplicating gesture. "Sir, do not punish us! We did wrong. We did not think. It was a bad thing to do, that is right, and we were bad people. Please, sir—"

"What happened then?" thundered Mr. Hall.

"We came back," said Eshong, very meek. "Many moons later, we came back. The men were all dead. Every one. Some dead here—" He pointed to a snowy hillock near the camp. "Some dead there—" He pointed to the beach. "Others on that island there." He pointed to what was known as Todd Island, a few hundred yards off the barren shore.

We had searched the area, doing the best we could, but it was not surprising, in that snowy waste, that we might have missed some sign.

"Take me to them," cried Mr. Hall. "Quickly—now!"

"Yes, sir," said Eshong. "We will show you where they died, sir. But please do not be angry with us. We did not know what else to do!"

Eshong and the old men shuffled off through the snow. It was a gray, leaden day, with the Fahrenheit thermometer forty to fifty degrees below the freezing mark, and the cold bit at the bones. A half mile or so beyond the camp, not far from the shoreline, Eshong paused, his ancient head raised, sniffing the air as if to locate by scent the grave of the Franklin people.

"Over here," he said.

I do not know how we had missed it, but in a snowy copse of shrubs, half buried in the snow, was the remains of a boat—a large boat, clinker-built and copper-fastened like the bit of one that had served us as clue. An attempt had been made to rig a kind of canvas shelter over it, and the shreds of canvas still flapped in the wind, hanging dismally from the poles.

"Good God!" breathed Mr. Hall. "Adam, this is it!"

In the bottom of the boat were bones—many bones, in disarray. To some of them still clung rags of flesh and bits of cloth and buttons. A withered hand still clutched a rusted musket barrel, the wood of the stock long disintegrated. The door of a locker hung open, and within was an ancient chronometer box inscribed with the Queen's broad arrow. Bones, bones, bones— they were everywhere.

"Our search is ended, Adam," said Mr. Hall.

He knelt among the sad remnants of the Franklin party. "Our Father," he said, "which art in Heaven—"

Eshong and his people drew back, knowing that some magic was going on. Around us the wind howled through the copse, powdery snow blew like dust; there was a solemnity and grandeur about the scene that made me think of a cathedral, and Mr. Hall the bishop saying some great religious service. All about lay the dead bones, the silent congregation.

"And forgive us our trespasses—" whispered Mr. Hall.

He said the rest in a tone that was almost inaudible, his voice dropping in pitch until I could barely hear the last words. "For Thine is the Kingdom, and the Power, and the Glory, forever and forever—"

"Amen," I said.

"Amen," he repeated.

For a long time he was silent, kneeling among the bones. Then he pulled up the hood of his *koo-lee-tang* and said, "Ah, it has come to this, eh? Well, so are all great undertakings brought low."

"Sir," I said, "I have counted the skulls in the boat. These poor souls come to some forty or thereabouts. Eshong said there were more in the neighborhood."

He tugged at his beard, lost in thought. I am sure I saw tears in his eyes.

"More," said Eshong respectfully. "Down along the beach. That way."

Mr. Hall sighed. "Well," he said, "let us go and look."

In the next few days we seldom had an opportunity to eat or sleep, such was Mr. Hall's passion for searching the area. On Todd's Island we found the remains of five men, on the seashore two more, on the west of Point Richardson the wreck of another boat (from which the boy's sled had come) with thirty more. A little distance inland from Terror Bay we found the shreds of a large tent with its floor covered with bones, adding up to thirty or so.

We found also silver watches, a mahogany writing desk that must have belonged to Sir John himself, many pieces of the eelcrest silver—spoons and knives and forks—and bones, again— bones, bones, bones. I had grown so used to tallying bones that I thought no more of handling them than I did a stick of wood.

"Do you know what this means, Adam?" Mr. Hall asked me. "Here, at the end of our search? This is where they perished, those great men! Searching for the Northwest Passage, as I had suspected. They came thus far, and no farther. They died here, over a hundred of them, and we are the first white men here since!"

We were having tea in our snowhouse, and Nellis spat and said, "Nothing but a bunch of bones."

"Holy bones!" Mr. Hall flared. "Consecrated bones! I hope that when I die my bones may have done as much."

Nellis shrugged and sipped his tea.

Finally, having exhausted ourselves, we ended our search. Even Mr. Hall was finally forced to agree that we had done all we could. We had accounted for well over a hundred members of the lost Franklin expedition, and had determined what had been their sorry end.

That night, in our igloo, I said to him half-jokingly (for he was not a humorous man, and did not appreciate a joke), "Well, I've been and seen and done everything now. I suppose I'd better think about going home and marrying some nice little girl and raising a family." I skinned my sock off and looked at my toes. They were healing handsomely now. Once I got back to Cincinnati I did not think I would ever want to see snow again. Perhaps I would emigrate to California.

"You have been and seen and done everything, eh?" Mr. Hall had been examining the remains of Sir John's writing desk— a brass-cornered mahogany box with a hinged lid. "Well, not *quite* everything, Adam."

"Enough to hold me for a while!"

"There is something left," he said. "The Pole. Remember? The Pole sits there—" He pointed northward. "In melancholy grandeur she sits up there, and waits."

"She'll wait a long time for me," I said.

The journey back to Repulse Bay was a long and arduous one, but it was improved by the fact that now we were on our way home. I would hesitate to bore anyone with the details. After all, one snowy hummock looks like another; this whitened plain is no different from the next; the pangs of hunger on Monday are little different from those on Friday. At any rate, not much more than two months saw us at Repulse Bay again. It was now the latter part of August, and the year was 1869.

Joe and Hannah were overjoyed to see us back. Old Nartuk had burned some bones and deduced from the shape of the smoke that Mr. Hall and Adam were dead, slain in a battle with people of a fierce and far-off tribe.

"But you are here!" Hannah protested. She took Joe's hand and together they capered about, singing and chanting. "Father Hall is here! Everyone come look! He is here again." Not forgetting me, she rushed forward and clasped me to her breast. "And Adam! You are both here!"

"I am, indeed," said Mr. Hall gravely. "And thanks to God, we have found the remains of the *kod-lu-na* we were searching for."

"Then your work is done?" Hannah's lip quivered. "You go away now—back to—to—"

"Yes," he said. "I must go back now. And you and Joe must return with me."

Hannah's good-natured face was an exercise in mixed emotion. Surprise, pleasure, disappointment, uncertainty—all were mirrored there. "Me? And Joe?" She did not want Father Hall to leave them, that was sure; yet she did not relish the idea of returning to the country where she had lost her baby. "Pun-na too?" One hand touched the brown vee at her neck, rubbing in an anxious gesture. "All of us go?"

"Yes," said Mr. Hall. "Of course, Hannah! I need you and Joe to help me. We must get ready for another expedition; this time to the Pole itself!" He pointed northward, and his dark eyes sparkled. "As far as a man *can* go, without coming back again! Yes, this time it will be the Pole itself."

On our trip to King William Land, I thought I was beginning to know him a little better, to understand the strange demon that possessed him. But now I was puzzled again. Poor Hannah, caught up in a dilemma, was almost in tears. She wanted to be with Father Hall and thought herself and Joe obliged to him, yet the prospect of returning to the land of great stone buildings and smoke and rushing dray wagons terrified her, that was plain. Mr. Hall was quite cheerful and careless about it all, seeming not even to notice the poor woman's anguish. "We will leave as soon as we can," he said. "Get your things together, all of you! The *Ansell Gibbs* is anchored off Reindeer Point. I will see to begging passage on her for us all."

It was not until the *Ansell Gibbs* was nearing St. Johns that I found the opportunity to speak privately to Mr. Hall, so busy was he with his journals and private papers, his scientific monographs, the logs of his journeys. Wanting to speak with him, I finally knocked on the door of his cabin.

"Come in!"

Mr. Hall was in his shirt sleeves, dipping a pen into an inkwell. All about him lay scraps of paper, some crumpled into balls, others stained and blotted.

"Ah, Adam!" He shook his head ruefully, indicating the litter. "Today is not a good day for me, I fear."

"Well," I said, "we all have our good days, and our bad ones." In response to his wave I sat on the edge of a chair near his writing table. "We are almost to St. Johns now, sir, and I—well, I want to talk to you."

He laid down the pen and sat back in his chair, hands pressed together before him in a kind of steeple. "Well, lad, what is it?"

I swallowed. "What I wanted to say—I mean—sir, I have had enough of the Arctic. I hope that you were not counting on me to go on with you to the Pole."

"What's this?" He got up, agitated, and started to pace the floor. "Mutiny, Adam? Is that it?" Half joking, half serious, he pulled at his beard and scowled, and then smiled and rubbed his nose vigorously, and paced up and down, all the time looking at me from the corner of his eye. "Whatever can have put such an idea in your mind? You are joking, surely." He swung around and stared at me hard, eyes as hard and unfathomable as obsidian. "Yes, that is it! This is a little joke Hannah put you up to."

"No, sir," I said miserably. "It is no joke."

"But Adam, you know how I depend on you!"

My frozen toes ached, and reminded me of the hardships of the North. "I am flattered," I said, "but I do not think it is a good idea to count on me." I thought of my father in his cobbler's shop in Cincinnati, and how long it had been since I had seen him. "No," I repeated. "Sir, I have made up my mind. When we reach the States, I am bound to go on my own way. I will regret leaving your company, for you have taught me a great many things, including perseverance. But I am not a child any longer, and must take up a trade to support myself."

He sat down, fists on his knees, and stared at me as if I were a creature from the moon. "Leave me? You cannot."

"Sir, you make this very difficult for me—"

He waved a hand, growling. "I did not put it too well! What I meant is this; you cannot leave the Arctic, no more than can I, Adam Burritt. You are in love with that icy land. You will wither and waste away if you do not return. There is no sustenance in city streets, no fresh air in a brick and stone dwelling, no slaking of the thirst in a ridiculous rabbit warren like Cincinnati!" He said the name with a rolling and derisive touch that damned it forever. "No, Adam, we are forced to come back to the States once in a while for money and supplies, but we cannot stay there!" He pointed northward, and his eyes sparkled like polished agates in the murky light of the cabin. "Up there, in that pure and clear air at the top of the world—why, that is the only place where a man can breathe and live—and die, if need be!"

"Before," I protested, "we were engaged in a humanitarian search. We were looking for the Franklin people, and I am not sorry to have been a party to such a great effort. But now—simply to go there again, to reach the Pole—for what? It is there, we know that. If we go there, and stand on it, and come home again—then what? What boots all this?"

He chuckled. "You were not serious, of course. Very well, joke with me then. I will not be angry. Deprecate the Pole; it can well stand it, and I do not mind."

"Sir," I said, almost desperate, "I must make you see that—"

"Here." He shoved into my hand a scrap of paper. "This is the telegraph message I am composing to Henry Grinnell. I will send it off as soon as we reach St. Johns. See what you think of it. Does it have the right touch, do you think? The flair, the majesty, the style?"

I read it.

> SUCCESS HAS CROWNED MY EFFORTS. FATE OF FRANKLIN
> PARTY HAS BEEN ESTABLISHED. I AM NOW EN ROUTE TO
> THE STATES TO MOUNT A GREAT FINAL ASSAULT ON THE
> POLE ITSELF GOD WILLING.

"It sounds very well," I said.

I went back to my bunk and lay for a long time staring at the overhead, watching the smoky oil lamp swing back and forth as the ship rolled. A madman? No, certainly not. If he were, there were methods for handling madmen, and everything would be easier. But he was a man of genius, which is ever so much more difficult than a madman.

THE THIRD VOYAGE
1870-1873

Chapter 12

IN SPITE of Mr. Hall's protests, this time I went
home to Cincinnati for good. I had spent ten years of my life at
this Arctic adventuring, and what did I have for it? A frostbit-
ten foot that pained me whenever the weather got cold, and an
empty pocket. No, it was time for me to marry a nice girl and
settle down. I would learn a trade of some sort—I was a fair
enough hand with a lathe, or with a saw and hammer, or at any
one of a thousand odd jobs. The Arctic had taught me that
much; somehow to make do and get the job done.

My father's cobbler shop looked the same; the narrow
spider-webbed panes, the door with H. BURRITT—BOOTS AND RE-
PAIRS in faded and peeling gold leaf; inside, the familiar
smell of leather dust and hides and dyes. A bell tinkled as I
opened the door, and my father came to meet me, fussing
with his steel-rimmed spectacles.

"Yes, sir? What can I do for you?"

He always looked at a man's boots first, for he said that you could tell about a man from the condition of his boots. It was a long minute before he let his eyes come up and fix on mine, puzzled perhaps at this customer who wore Innuit *muk-luks* and said no word, silently grinning at him in the dusk of the shop.

"Adam?" His voice quavered. "Not—Adam?"

I threw my arms around him. He had not changed, being still the same wispy small man in a stained apron. I had changed, but he was a dear and venerable object to me; the one thing on earth that was of my blood, and of my flesh, and that cared whether I lived or died.

"It is indeed Adam," I said. "And look!" I fumbled in my pocket. "Here is a bit of scrimshaw I brought for you all the way from the Hudson Bay country—a carved Innuit god of some kind, made from a walrus tusk!"

He took it, examining it carefully, turning it in trembling hands, first one way and then the other. "But you were dead, it was thought! They printed it in the *Enquirer*, that you and your Mr. Hall had not been heard of, and must be considered to be lost!" His blue-veined hand trembled; he put the ivory trinket in a pocket of his drill apron and took off his spectacles, wiping his eyes with his sleeve. "Adam, Adam, is it really you?"

"It is," I said, "come home to be with you like a dutiful son."

"If you only knew the nights I have lain awake, thinking of you, wondering, hoping—" He turned away, blowing his nose. "I am not a religious man, as you know, not having even brought up my son in Christian ways. But I learned to pray, Adam. We all do, sooner or later. And now here you are back home, and I guess there is something to prayer after all."

It was almost suppertime. Against my protests he sent out for a tray of food for me from a tavern across the way, contenting himself with a glass of beer. "For," he said, "I do not eat much any more. You will remember that I was never much of an eater. Now I find that work is my chief sustenance." He placed the carved ivory piece on a shelf over his bench, and went back to sew on a pair of boots while I ate a fried chop and applesauce and home-baked bread, washed down with a pot of coffee.

"Here," he said, "is my own little world. I seldom venture out. But you must tell me where you have been, and the sights you have seen."

For the better part of an hour I told him about Mr. Hall's second voyage; about our trip out on the *Monticello*, and how we found the eel spoon, and of our long and dreadful trip to King William Land; of how we had fought our way inch by inch through howling blizzards, and of how Mr. Hall had been obliged to shoot Patrick Coleman; how we made our way back to the *Ansell Gibbs* and home after five perilous years. As I talked the room darkened; an autumn night came on; the wind rose outside. My father lit a stub of candle.

"Surely," he said, "you are not cold, Adam, accustomed as you are to the Far North. And it does not take much to warm my bones. After a while, perhaps, I will start a small fire."

In spite of his cheerfulness, I do not think the business of cobbling made him much money. He had taken the last piece of change from his pocketbook to buy my supper, and as for all that talk about my being accustomed to Arctic cold, he sounded apologetic when he said it. I doubt there was any coal in the scuttle.

"Well," I said, "the Arctic is all behind me now. I have had a bellyful of ice and snow and walrus and the Innuit tongue that sounds like a turkey gobbling. Tomorrow I'll start early and make the rounds of the shops and foundries. I'll get me a job, that's what. Nothing like work to keep a man's mind off his troubles!"

My father gave a nail a final tap and held up the boot, peering at the sole. "Aye," he said. "God bless a man's work." He went with me to the door of the small lean-to behind the shop where he had his narrow cot and the old walnut bureau I remembered from our home, when my mother was alive. It still shone rich in the light from the candle, and I knew he polished it often. "You take my bed, Adam," he said. When I objected, he raised a hand and was very stern with me, as he used to be when I was a small child. "No, no! I insist! I don't sleep much any more. I'll just put a few coals on the fire and doze in the rocker by the stove with a shawl around me. It's all I need."

He would not have it any other way, seeming to be pleased to do things for me, so I went to bed and pulled the ragged comforter up under my chin. After a while, when he must have thought me to be sound asleep, he came to the doorway with the guttering candle and looked in, very quietly. When I stirred and called out to him, he seemed embarrassed.

"Just wondered if you were all right. Thought maybe you might want something—a glass of water, perhaps."

"No," I said, "and thank you."

It didn't take me long to get a job. Now that the war was over, Cincinnati was booming. A foundry on Commercial Street hired me right off. It was my job to dump ladles of molten iron into sand patterns. I often wondered what perverse fate brought me to this—broiling in the glare of the furnaces, blistering from the heat of the molds, spattered and singed by droplets of flying metal—me, Adam Burritt, come straight from King William Land where the mercury froze in the bottom of the thermometer and the winds howled at fifty miles to the hour. But the pay was good—eight dollars a week. Now I had money of my own, and could pay some small amount each week to my father, too.

I do not mean I had forgotten the Arctic. I would find myself leaning on the bar we used to tip the melt buckets with, staring into the hot eye of the bubbling metal, seeing only the iridescent banners of the aurora. My eyes dazzled by the heat of the blast furnaces, I would close them against the shock of the flames and bathe them in remembered snowy vistas—Oolootong village, perhaps, with its great sweep of white broken only by the small mounds of the igloos. That was where old Bud and I found Mr. Hall so ill and discouraged. I heard again the dogs yapping as they smelled our coming, and saw the blink of sun on snow, smelled the rich odors of rotting fish and long-dead seal meat as we approached the village. Well, it did no harm. It made my work easier, to think so. It did not mean I missed Oolootong. What sane man could miss a circle of snow-houses and brown-faced fish-stinking men, and dogs so vicious they would take your leg off for a snack while waiting on supper?

I did go, once, to the house on Celestial Street. I do not know why, particularly; that part of my life was done now—finished, over with. But Mr. Hall had been my good friend, and taught me much. Surely it was only the friendly thing to do—to stop by and inquire from Mr. Hall where he was and what he was doing.

On the pavement a slatternly woman was carrying out a hod of ashes, her thin nose red with the cold. When she saw me going up the porch stairs she called to me, voice piercing the February wind.

"Ain't no one there, mister."

"I'm looking for a Mrs. Hall," I said.

She wrapped her arms about her against the cold and sniffled once or twice. "Moved away from here better'n a year ago. Ain't no one lived at 1051 since then. Hall, did you say her name was?"

I nodded. "Mrs. Charles Hall."

"Yes, I remember. Poor woman—sick, and a widow to boot." She tucked a stringy lock of hair back under her boudoir cap. "Near as I recollect, she went to live with relatives in Columbus."

"Did she leave any address?"

The slatternly woman shook her head. "Never said boo. Just took her children and left. A dray wagon pulled up and took a few sticks of furniture after she left. Maybe she sold 'em—I don't know."

"Thank you," I said.

I stood for a moment on the sagging rotten porch. A scrap of curtain whipped out through a hole in a broken pane, and I thought I smelled boiling cabbage and wet wash. I remembered a red-eyed woman wrapping cookies for me to take to Washington on the steamcars. *Why doesn't he come home, Mr. Burritt? Has he forgotten me and the children? If you see him, tell him we miss him, and think of him always.* A ghost voice, thin and querulous from almost ten years ago. Ten years? Good Lord! It was indeed.

"Ain't nothing I can do for you?" the red-nosed woman asked as I passed. I shook my head, and she went back to dusting ashes on the brick walk.

I wish I could say this sad happening soured me on further Arctic adventuring, seeing what unhappy consequences may come to the family and loved ones of an explorer. But to say so would not be true. Day by day the foundry palled on me. I found myself daydreaming, no longer from choice but from necessity. In the rear room of my father's shop I would sit staring into space, silent and uncommunicative, while he read his *Enquirer* by the light of the Argand lamp we could now afford.

"Tired, Adam?" he would ask, rattling the paper and peering over it at me.

"Yes, Father."

"Better go to bed, then."

"All right."

I went to bed, only to dream again, and toss and turn, and occasionally to mutter something in what must have been Innuit, according to my father's astonished report. It had been a second tongue to me once, almost as familiar as English.

"It sounded like a turkey gobbling," he said.

I might have fooled myself, or tried to, but I did not fool my father. One night he pushed up his spectacles and leaned across to tap me on the knee. "Why don't you go back, Adam?"

Startled, I blurted, "Back where?"

"Let's not skirmish about it, lad. Why, back to the Arctic again, where you're longing to go so bad that you're making yourself sick over it!"

I shook my head. "That's all behind me now. I've had a good chance in the foundry to work up to foreman."

"Pish!" It was the strongest word I ever heard him say, and he said it so forcefully and angrily that it took on a kind of borrowed grandeur. "If you dream at the foundry the way you do here, they're ready to sack you by now!" He fumbled in his pocket and took out a folded clipping. "I cut this out of the *Enquirer* the other night, before you could see it. I'm sorry, Adam, for the deceit. I shouldn't have. But I—" His voice trailed off, and he handed me the clipping.

Washington, D.C., was the dateline, and the date February 3, 1870:

> Mr. Charles Francis Hall, formerly of this city, has called on President Grant to report on his recent expedition to King William Land, where he determined the lamentable fate of the lost expedition of Sir John Franklin. Mr. Hall brought with him a plan for a proposed new expedition to the North Pole, and has asked the President for aid in introducing legislation to make Government funds available for the undertaking.

"Another expedition!" I cried. "And to the Pole itself, this time!"

My father stared at me, half rueful, half amused. "See, then! Did I not call the turn? You are not interested in the foundry, nor in Cincinnati either, for that matter. All that matters to you is the Far North, Adam. I have known for these several weeks."

"Well," I stammered, "I—I—"

He put his hand on my shoulder. "Go, boy, if you must! You will never be happy here."

"But what of you?"

With more enthusiasm than I think he felt, he swept his arm around the shop. "A man always has his work. And I would not be happy at that if I thought you were not happy, Adam. Go, now; as quickly as ever you can buy a ticket on the cars and travel to Washington to see your Mr. Hall."

The upshot of it was that I packed my other shirt and collar in a valise, bought my ticket, and went to Washington. My father was at the station to see me off, and I had a queer and prickly feeling that I would never see him again. All the way to Washington I sat moodily in my seat, lost in thought. I had long condemned Mr. Hall for what I thought was his neglect of his family to go exploring; now here was I, Adam Burritt, guilty of the same fault. All I needed to remember was my father's quick good-by, his touching my hand and turning away as if not trusting his composure. Yet I, aware of his grief, was callously turning my back on him and huzzaing off to a life of adventure. I could rationalize it, I supposed; I considered myself caught up in the sweep of something which it was useless to fight—the great campaign for the Pole. But even then, muttering high-sounding phrases to myself, I could not forget the small figure of my father standing on the platform, waving a handkerchief until lost in a cloud of steam and smoke and cinders. At the very least, I was now barred from ever criticizing Mr. Hall for dereliction to his family. He and I were tarred with the same brush.

In Washington, I found Mr. Hall at Thibeault's boarding-house in H Street, the one where we had stayed that hot summer of 1863, along with little Tuk-e, Joe and Hannah, and the faithful Barbekark. But it was not hot now. Rain—steady and dismal sheets of winter rain—slanted down on the avenue, and the streets were channels of icy liquid mud. Bootblacks abandoned their trade and stood at intersections, offering for a penny to wash the boots of pedestrians with the pails and sponges they carried. Most of the ladies I saw had their dresses pulled up over their petticoats by a patent arrangement of loops and hooks. Drays splattered by, drivers hunched miserably, wheels sucking in the gumbo. It was a far cry from the colorful summer I had remembered, when the streets swarmed with hawkers and soldiers and pretty ladies with parasols.

"Adam!" Mr. Hall hurried into the foyer to greet me, very grand in a stiff-bosomed shirt. "Adam, is it you?" He called up the stair well. "Joe! Hannah! Here is Adam! Come—bring Pun-na with you!"

He helped me out of my rain-drenched coat and boots, and I was caught up in a maelstrom of kisses and dancing and hugging from little Pun-na and Joe and Hannah. They threw their arms around me, cried and laughed at the same time, chattered like magpies in both Innuit and English, ran their hands over me as if to assure themselves I was real.

"We knew you would come to us," Hannah declared. "Didn't we, Joe?"

"Sure," said Joe.

Hannah took a handkerchief from a pocket of her starched gingham apron and dabbed at her eyes. "You are like my son."

"And mine, too," Mr. Hall said, pressing my hand. "Even more than a son, Adam. A younger and very dear brother."

"But what is this" I asked, pointing to his fashionable attire, anxious to allay the effusion of sentiment which was about to make me weep also. "You have never been concerned with clothes, beyond that they covered you and kept you warm. Now you look like a congressman!"

Mr. Hall smiled, stroking his gray-speckled beard. "In this city, they go a great deal by a man's appearance. When you associate with the political moguls it is necessary to resemble them, so that they do not squawk and peck at you and attempt to drive you away. Washington is one great barnyard these days!" Turning to Joe and Hannah he said, "Come now, off with you all! Adam and I have a great deal to talk about, and must be undisturbed for a while."

When they had left, he sat down on the velour sofa opposite me and crossed one leg over the other, knotting his big hands over his knee. "Adam, there is so much to tell; where shall I ever start?"

I showed him the clipping, already tattered from carrying it around in my wallet.

"Oh, by all means! That was where my good fortune started. The Honorable John Sherman of Ohio, my home state, arranged the interview with the President. A remarkable man, Mr. Grant. Very keen; not saying much until he has something to say, and looking you up and down constantly with those eyes like a pair of gimlets. Soft-spoken and diffident, but hard underneath; a sword sheathed in civilian black."

"Did he offer you any encouragement? About a new expedition, that is?"

Mr. Hall shrugged. "Oh, even the President cannot make such a decision without the consent and agreement of a few congressmen! But who else is there to lead such an expedition, Adam? Charles Hall, that is all."

I was not so sure, remembering some of our previous experiences in Washington, but I said nothing, only too pleased to see him so happy and well and confident.

"Mr. Stephenson of Ohio is introducing a resolution in the House to promote a polar voyage. My good friend John Sherman is introducing a similar resolution in the Senate. We have already picked out the vessel; a Navy tug, the *Periwinkle*, which can be refitted and provisioned for no more than a hundred thousand dollars."

My mouth fell open. "A hundred thousand dollars?"

He chuckled. "You see how I now handle these large sums. Yes, a hundred thousand. That is what we intend to seek in the Congress!"

Remembering our previous hat-in-hand wanderings, I was staggered.

"Mr. Hall, I hope that in all these grand prospects you have not forgotten Adam Burritt, and have made a place for him on the *Periwinkle*."

He raised an impressive finger. "*Polaris*, Adam, for that is what I intend to call her!"

"*Polaris*, then, for I am weary of this temperate country, and long for the North again. I have left my job in Cincinnati, left my father, left everything to seek you and join you, if you will have me."

"Have you?" He wrung my hand. "Adam, dear boy, I would not venture a foot nearer the Pole without you. Do you realize that between us we have shared ten years in the Far North, which is more than can be said for most gentlemen of the Arctic? Even Thorne, that mountebank, spent only two seasons there. No, you may make sure of it, we are in the vanguard of Arctic exploration now, you and I, for better or for worse." He frowned suddenly and dropped my hand. "And this brings up something else." He seemed uneasy, and paced the floor. "Strange, how I find it so difficult to discuss. I would rather make a hundred-mile sledge journey than talk about such things. But then I am a strange man, I suppose, and must lay it to my own queerness."

"I do not understand," I said.

He clapped me on the shoulder with an awkward gesture. "Adam, please do not call me Mr. Hall any more. Do not 'sir' me here and 'sir' me there. We are companions now, old friends, men united in one great bond. Can you not—" He shook his head like a wounded animal. "Can you not call me Charles, Adam?"

I was surprised at his hangdog look, his glowering at me from beneath the heavy brows; so surprised, as a matter of fact, that I laughed—a silly and absurd laugh, mostly of relief.

"If you want me to," I said. "I never thought—"

"To laugh at me," he blurted, "is not kind."

"But I only meant—"

"Hang what you meant!" He was like a man betrayed in an

indiscretion. "No," he added quickly, running a hand through his gray hair. "Strike that out, Adam. I did not mean it, but am only—well, embarrassed. It is that way whenever I attempt the gentler and more lofty emotions." Shaking his head he sat down, staring out the rain-streaked window at H Street. "I am a proud and lonely man, Adam, and lack for friends. It is not so difficult to understand, I suppose, when I come near to quarreling with my good Adam Burritt over such a trifling matter. It is only that I am in such strange territory, and feel uneasy and apprehensive, like the mountain cougar caught out on the grassy plain. Do you understand?"

"I understand. And I will call you Charles, and reckon myself privileged to do so."

Face working with emotion, he gripped my hand.

"We are friends for all time, eh, Adam? The best of friends."

"The best," I said.

During that spring of 1870 the bond of friendship was put to more than one considerable strain. Living together in our shabby rooms—Mr. Charles Hall, Joe, Hannah, Pun-na and I— we were on each other's nerves more often than not. I contributed my small savings to the cause again, and with this, some small advances from Mr. Henry Grinnell, and an advance against royalties on Mr. Hall's new book, we managed to exist. But the great matter of the new expedition dragged on and on in the Congress. Both Mr. Stephenson and Mr. Sherman worked hard and diligently, but there was a keg of molasses in the clockwork of our government. Endless drafts of resolutions —Mr. Hall worked on some of them himself, trying to find the felicitous phrase—referrals to committees, putting things on the calendar and then taking them off, backing and filling and maneuvering.

Spring came; the trees along the boulevard broke into a mint-haze of green. The dust of a new season rose under the wheels of

the heavy omnibuses plying between the capital and George-
town. Fishermen squatted along the banks of the Potomac, and
oyster peddlers cried their wares and tooted their horns. But
with all this activity—the going and coming, the noise, the
crowds, the traffic, the business of a city reborn in the spring—
there was no favorable word of our project. If we were to get
away this season, immediate action was necessary.

"I do not understand it," Mr. Hall said, gnawing his knuckles.
"Adam, there is more to this than meets the eye. I think there is
some complication somewhere—the Congress is a bartering
place, I have found, and I am beginning to believe there is a
quid pro quo being haggled over."

"I don't know what a *quid pro quo* is, Charles," I said, "but
there is certainly a great deal of haggling going on. They will
haggle away our chances to go north this summer, and I do not
like the thought of spending another season in Washington."

"Nor do Joe and Hannah and Pun-na. Already they are beginning to suffer from the heat."

I do not suppose we were entirely unprepared for the visit
of Mr. Sherman to our boardinghouse. A busy fat little man, an
enormous rope of gold chain across his middle, he nodded to
me and sat opposite Mr. Hall in the gloomy parlor, mopping
at his face with a handkerchief.

"Well, it's come."

"What's come?" Mr. Hall asked quickly.

"What I had feared. They have come out into the open now.
An appropriation is to go through—for only fifty thousand, and
not one hundred thousand, though that's not the rub."

"We can make do with fifty thousand," Mr. Hall said in a
quiet voice.

Mr. Sherman leaned forward, excited. "No, my friend—that's
not it. Our opposition has proposed Professor Edward Thorne to
lead the expedition."

Mr. Hall's voice was alarmed. "Thorne?"

"Yes, Thorne—and his adherents come close to having the votes to put it through. They'll tack it on as a rider to the money bill."

"Thorne!" Mr. Hall shook his head, unbelieving. His eyes were glazed, and he spoke in muffled tones. "Dear Lord, no—don't let them take this from me!"

"All is not yet lost," Mr. Sherman said. "They have not quite got the clear majority they need, and we can keep them from it for a while. But—" He shook his head. "Charles, I must tell you it does not look promising. Professor Thorne has an international reputation on the Arctic, and has written several books on the limnological geography of the area."

"And what am I?" Mr. Hall struck one big hand in the palm of the other. "John, what am I? A minstrel-show performer with bones and tambourine?"

Mr. Sherman's red face flushed even more. "It is not your record," he said testily. "It is a matter of politics! Professor Thorne is well known in the city, and has served on several important civic bodies. He comes from New York, too, and is well thought of by the legislators who are from that state. He has mustered a great deal of influence."

"Influence!" Mr. Hall shouted the word. "I am tired of influence and conniving and trading this for that—a principle for a bag of money!"

I remembered the time Professor Thorne had discredited Mr. Hall in Unity Hall. I remembered also the words of old Mr. Grinnell, standing on the dock at New London the day we sailed north on the *Monticello*. *Talk back to him, Adam; force him to think things out, encourage him. Be his conscience and his friend. He is a great man, and someday the world will listen to him.*

"Mr. Sherman," I said, "we are sorry to hear your news, yet if I understand you correctly there is nothing that can be done about it for the moment."

"That is true," said Mr. Sherman.

Mr. Hall only looked at me moodily, as if wondering what the devil I was entering into the discussion for.

"Then," I said, "we will bid you good day, sir, and go into a discussion among ourselves as to what plan of action to take."

Mr. Hall swiveled toward me, chin sunk on his chest. "Plan of action? What plan of action, indeed! We are beat, Adam; beat by political knavery!"

"Not yet," I said.

"What would you propose?"

"I think we had better sleep on this development, and let our cooler heads work something out in the morning."

Mr. Hall looked very queer at my interference but said nothing, only chewing at his lip. For my own part, I was in good conscience at what I had done. Given a little more time, Charles Hall would have made an enemy of the Honorable John Sherman, and we needed all the friends at court we could muster.

"I think that's very sensible." Mr. Sherman sounded to me somewhat relieved. "Gracious!" He took his watch out of his waistcoat pocket and looked at it in alarm. "Almost four! I had better be getting back to my office. Constituents waiting for me, you know." He shook Mr. Hall's hand, and mine too. "All is not yet lost. Remember that, gentlemen."

After Mr. Sherman had left, I went to my room and sat down with pen and paper, leaving Mr. Hall to brood in the parlor below. There was little to be gained in discussing the situation with him in his present mood; he was too upset by the news of Professor Thorne's candidacy for the great position he thought rightfully to be his own. *Plan A,* I wrote at the top of the sheet. There certainly must be a Plan A of some sort we could adopt. I would put down others, too; a Plan B and a Plan C and several others, and in the morning we would discuss them sensibly and amicably. But try as I would, I did not seem to come up with a Plan A, let alone the others. Next door I could hear Hannah giving a grammar lesson to little Pun-na, and up the stair well drifted the odor of boiling beef and coffee brew-

ing for our evening meal. I scratched my head, chewed at the
pen nib, and vainly considered one prospect after another.
What could we do?

Mr. Hall was silent and moody at supper, not eating much,
not saying a word even to little Pun-na, when it had formerly
been his habit to joke with her, tease her and pull her braids.
Joe and Hannah were troubled at his mood and looked fear-
fully at me for reassurance. After supper he rose silently, went
to his room, and closed the door.

"Father Hall is not well," Hannah said, shaking her head.

In the morning we had news from Mr. Sherman, sent by
messenger from his office at the Capitol. There was still no
agreement on the leader for the proposed expedition; however,
in view of the lateness of the season, it had been decided to
appropriate the fifty thousand dollars and let the fitting out of
the *Periwinkle* proceed at once. In the meantime, it was hoped
some agreement could be reached among the warring factions
on the choice of a leader.

Mr. Hall showed me the note. "Damned quibbling nincom-
poops! Oh, what folly—to fit out a ship and provision it with
no leader, no overseer, no one to point out the need for this and
the necessity of that!"

"Well," I said, "at least the work on the *Periwinkle* is going
forward. Delayed much longer, it might have put us over into
next season."

He crumpled the note into a ball and flung it from him.

"Now that it is morning again—what a succession of morn-
ings!—Adam, have you any advice for me?"

I do not think he meant it in the vicious way it came forth.
Knowing him as well as I did, I laid it to his agitated condition.
He had not slept the night; I had heard him pacing his room
until daylight.

"No, sir," I said lamely, "unless it be to wait, and hope that
Mr. Sherman—"

"Hope!" He laughed. "Hope is a meager ration." He went

to the window again, where he had stood for so many hours peering out into H Street, looking for some encouraging word from the Honorable Mr. Sherman. "No," he said, "hope must be supplemented by action. Adam, do you know what I propose to do this day?"

I shook my head.

"I will help those fools make up their mind." He looked at his watch. "At the stroke of noon I intend to march into the House and demand to be heard!"

"What?" I thought I had not heard aright.

"Exactly that. I will tell them they are fools! I will demand to be heard, and I *will* be heard." His voice was scornful. "All this tossing the matter from one committee to another, all this dickering and palavering—Adam, I tell you it is shameful to trifle so with such a great business!"

"You can't do that!" I burst out. "You will undo all you have done."

"I *can't?* Do you now tell me I can do this and can't do that?"

We had never really quarreled before, but now I began to smell brimstone. I had not written a book on the Arctic, I did not know the Latin names of all the plants and animals there, I never managed the trick of navigation with the sextant. But I was as good an Arctic hand as Mr. Charles Francis Hall in many other ways. I could sing to this tune as well as he could.

"I'll tell you who I am! I'm Adam Burritt, and I've sledged ten thousand miles with you and gone hungry and cold, and boiled tea over an oil lamp and frozen my damned toes and lent you money that you never paid back and given up every material thing in life to cast my lot with you! That's who I am, Charles Hall, and don't you forget it!"

It was a ridiculous situation. He stared at me as if I were the Great Nonesuch. His mouth fell open and he clawed anxiously at his beard, as if fearing it had been blown away in the blast.

"Furthermore," I shouted, "if you go down to the Capitol and set one foot where you shouldn't, I'll help the sergeant-at-arms drag you out, and certify that you are a lunatic and should be confined!"

He stared at me wide-eyed, puzzled, almost bemused. Then, when the tension between us had been drawn as taut as a sheet of India rubber, he dropped down on the couch, laughing so hard I began to fear that his reverses had driven him insane.

"Adam! Oh, Adam!"

He slapped his knee and sprawled out on the couch, arms and legs thrown wide, as if he could laugh better that way. "Adam Burritt!"

"What is it? Are you ill?"

Gradually his full-throated laughter slackened and he sat on the edge of the sofa, hands on knees, shaking his head from side to side and chuckling.

"I believe you would," he said.

"Would what?"

"Put me into a strait jacket, and certify me, if you thought that was what was best for me."

"I certainly would!"

"Adam, dear boy, thank you." Still chuckling, he wrung my hand. "And now I am quite restored. There is no immediate need to send me off to St. Elizabeth's, believe me. But what shall we do now, you and I? I cannot stand this inaction much longer."

Somehow, this happy incident had cleared my brains. When I had been so worried over him, I could not think clearly. But now that the tension had snapped, Plan A became clear to me.

"Stand on your record," I said. "There is no need to do anything else. Anyone who knows the Arctic must know that there is no question between you and Professor Thorne. There is only one man for the task—Charles Francis Hall."

"But how—"

"We will give another lecture," I said. "We can get Lincoln Hall through Mr. Sherman. We will invite the President, members of the Cabinet, the honorable gentlemen of the House and the Senate. There will be your forum. Joe and Hannah will be there, and Pun-na and I also. We lack only poor old Barbekark." I paced the room in my eagerness. "You need only *tell* them what you have done, trace your travels, describe your scientific findings, measure the thousands of miles by boat and by sledge, show them your Innuit dictionaries and notebooks. Before God, sir, I will swear that Professor Thorne can never stand such a cannonading! We will blow him off the face of the scientific world, politicians or no. Will you do it?"

When he looked at me this time, there was no laughter in his eyes; only a hope, and conviction.

"Adam," he said, "I could not do less. For you and Joe and Hannah, and certainly for myself."

Chapter 13

ON the 19th of April of that year, the Honorable Charles Sumner of Massachusetts, chairman of the Committee on Foreign Relations, reported back a bill to fit out the *Periwinkle,* but striking out all reference to a leader of the expedition, substituting the phrase "one or more persons." This was a prophetic phrase; I have often thought back to those times and pondered on that unhappy phrase "one or more persons." If the leadership of the polar expedition had been vested in Mr. Hall, and Mr. Hall only, then much difficulty and sadness might have been avoided. But at that time, of course, we knew nothing of what was to come. Wrapped up in our plans for the program at Lincoln Hall, we were happy only that the fitting out of the *Periwinkle* might now proceed, and confident that Mr. Hall would be chosen leader.

Added to our other concerns was trouble with Captain Snow, the Englishman who helped Mr. Hall with the manuscript of his first book, *Arctic Researches,* published by Harper Brothers. Though his labor had consisted only in some proofreading and a slight rearrangement of the chapters, Captain Snow now insisted that the entire book had been of his own composition, Mr. Hall having furnished only fragmentary notes.

"The devil!" Mr. Hall said. He showed me a court summons. "Snow is suing me for fifteen hundred dollars which he says I owe him."

"Ridiculous!"

"Nevertheless he has filed a suit for damages against me in the courts."

"What will you do?"

Mr. Hall laughed. In spite of the nature of the sound, it was an angry laugh. "Snow is a rascal, and may whistle for his money! I do not have fifteen hundred dollars; he might as well have said fifteen thousand. You have seen my notes, Adam. You know how complete they were. No, I do not have time to wrangle in the courts with this mountebank! They will have to send a bailiff after me and drag me away in chains before I leave my present business to haggle over such an absurdity."

It was only one of the pressing matters that weighed constantly on him that spring. How one man could handle so many matters amazed me. He carried on a voluminous correspondence with all who he thought might help his case, he prepared his talk for the affair at Lincoln Hall, he interviewed prospective crew members for the *Polaris* (never doubting the ultimate choice would be his), he worked on the manuscript of his new book covering our second voyage and the resolution of the Franklin tragedy. Night and day his pen scratched in the shabby third-floor room; he had a steady stream of callers, and as soon as they abated, he would walk down to the Capitol and buttonhole senators and congressmen. He investigated the merits of Texas corned beef and decided against it. He talked with millers about kiln-drying wheat before it was ground, theorizing that this operation would reduce spoilage. He spent hours waiting to see Secretary of the Navy Robeson, hoping to gain his favor, and walked back to the H Street boardinghouse for a meager supper, only to spend the evening coaching Joe and Hannah and little Pun-na in their parts for the Lincoln Hall program. To all who saw him, he appeared the embodiment of a single idea: the obtaining of aid for the projected polar expedition. He was driven by an obsession, and I do not think it is anywhere better described than in a letter he wrote to his old friend Henry Grinnell:

> Many who have written to me, or who have appeared to me personally, think that I am of an adventurous spirit and of bold heart to attempt to go to the North Pole. Not so. It does not require that heart which they suppose I have got. The Arctic region is my home. I love it dearly—its storms, its winds, its glaciers, its icebergs; and when I am among them, it seems as if I were in an earthly heaven, or a heavenly earth!

I was not so easy in the language, or so facile in expression. But I knew and recognized his feelings, for they were the same which motivated me in my own small and undistinguished way.

The great day came. Long before eight in the evening, Lincoln Hall was packed. Senators and representatives and their ladies, naval officers, distinguished scientists, government officials, even a sprinkling of oddly garbed visitors from the foreign embassies, in flowing caftans and tarbooshes. Senator Sumner of Massachusetts was there, the Honorable John Sherman of Ohio with his colleague the Honorable Mr. Stephenson, Senator Fenton of New York, and old Mr. Henry Grinnell. There was a great stir when the President came in, with Mrs. Grant on his arm. They made a striking couple; she very lovely in watered silk and a feather boa, the President small and slight and dark, chewing on a cigar and looking around him with sharp glances. Senator Sherman, from the President's own state, lead them to their box.

Mr. Hall, eying the house through a small hole in the curtain, watched them take their places. "I will speak to *him,* forgetting all the others," he whispered. "Adam, the President knows and understands this great project. These others—" He gestured. "Stiff-bosomed shirts and gold braid, paralyzed by their own indecision. No, I will strike out for the President. If I have won him, I have won the battle for the Pole itself!"

At precisely eight, the gaslights were dimmed and Mr. Hall came onto the stage. He always made an impressive appearance, but tonight he was magnificent. A phrenologist would have admired the ample development of the coronal and temporal regions, the broad ample reflective forehead. In the footlights his white shirt front shone like the Arctic snows, Hannah having spent hours laundering it and going back and forth with a smoothing iron.

"Your Excellency, and madam." He bowed toward the box in which sat the President and Mrs. Grant. "Ladies and gentlemen, members of the Congress, representatives of our great newspaper, honored guests. I will impose on you this evening to discuss a dream—a great and stirring vision—which has never ceased for the past thirty years to pursue me both sleeping and awake."

Joe and Hannah sat on the stage in their Innuit *koo-lee-tangs* and *muk-luks,* Hannah holding Pun-na on her lap. On the stage also were some of the Franklin relics, a sledge, and an exhibit of Innuit spears and knives and cooking lamps. Pun-na was very good; she clutched in her hand a tiny American flag and smiled pleasantly at the audience.

"Someday," said Mr. Hall, "I propose—to the greater glory of these, our United States, now whole once more, to stand at the top of the world and raise our national banner toward the heavens. My whole life has been dedicated to this vision. God willing, the next year may see it come to pass."

On a large map tacked to a board he traced out our travels in previous years. In painstaking detail he described our first sledge journey to the Meta Incognita in search of the Franklin people. With Mr. Hall's enthusiasm, the story was a sparkling and exciting account of hardship and adventure. No, it was more than that! Motivated by his great humanitarian purpose, it took on an additional luster, a high and starry purpose.

"And so," he said, "my party and I returned to the United States baffled and disappointed, but not without accomplishment. We now had accurate charts of the country, a knowledge of the Innuit natives and their customs, and an adaptation to the land and its ways that can be secured in no other manner. In addition, we had established beyond a doubt that Frobisher's Strait was not a strait but a bay, and had found evidences of Frobisher's visiting that country almost three hundred years before."

He went on to describe our second voyage—the five years we spent in searching the Melville Peninsula, Fury and Hecla Straits, the Boothia Peninsula and King William Land, always seeking to determine the fate of the Franklin people. It was a masterful performance; the dark winters, the searching cold, hunger and privation and hardship—all came alive. I shivered; whether from excitement or a re-experiencing of our travail I did not know. The audience was rapt, scarcely breathing. When he came to the successful culmination of our search in King William Land—the finding of the sledge made from one of the Franklin boats, the discovery of the skeletons and relics, the sad and pitiful remnants of the *Erebus* and *Terror,* there was a scattering of applause.

There was now a brief intermission, and the audience, its interest whetted, was allowed onto the stage to examine the exhibits, to talk with Joe and Hannah, and to look at the map (which I had drawn up myself and was very proud of).

"Charles," I said to Mr. Hall, who was standing in the wings, "it is going very well."

"Do you think so?" He peered out into the audience. "I don't see Thorne, though the footlights dazzled me so that I may have missed him. Do you think he is here?"

"No," I said, "for I believe he thinks himself at the advantage, and has no need to endanger his chances by an open debate with you such as he entered on that last time, in Unity Hall."

Mr. Hall smiled darkly. "I am almost sorry he is not here."

"Why?"

"Because," he said, "I would destroy him utterly and completely. Tonight, Adam, I feel at the top of my powers. There comes during a man's life a time—if he is lucky, one or more times—when all his powers combine in the right proportions and at the right instant to make him invincible. I feel it in my bones, I feel it circulating in my veins, I feel it all around me. I cannot fail—I will not fail."

"You will not fail," I said.

When the latter part of the program began, I left to take up my station in the wings but Mr. Hall called me back. "Have you watched the President, Adam? Does he follow me? Do I hold his attention?"

I had been so wrapped in the retelling of our story that I had not thought to watch the President's reaction, and I told him so.

"No matter," he muttered, waving me away.

The last portion of his talk was concerned with the proposed polar voyage. He spoke very briskly and confidently; although he did not mention himself by name as leader of the party, there could be little doubt of his intent. He described the necessary equipments, scientific and otherwise; the nature of the vessel that must withstand the rigors of the grinding Arctic ice; he sketched out a bold and comprehensive scientific program.

"Some astronomers," he said, "have made an issue of whether a man would ever truly know that he had reached the Pole itself.

Well, to these doubters I say this. On reaching that point called the North Pole, the North Star will be directly overhead. Without an instrument—with merely the eye—a man can define his position when there."

After a few concluding remarks, he paused for a moment. Then, very sober and with great feeling, he said, "The North Star is my beacon. It shines on me day and night, drawing me on with an irresistible magnetical impulse. Its rays illumine my life. I cannot help going northward—forever north—any more than the needle of a compass can help pointing in that direction. Someday, in the not too distant future, with God's help I will stand on the icy top of the world itself. In the dark of the polar winter's day I will turn my eyes upward, toward that God who knows all and forgives all and is the fount of all things good, and will see over my head, shining in the heavens, that spark of the infinite we call the North Star. Then, and only then, can I rest."

For a moment after he finished there was silence. For me it was an uneasy silence. A chair scraped, and someone coughed. Had he somehow lost them? At this moment of triumph had something gone wrong? Did some small miscalculation—some trick of timing or emphasis—betray us? I knew how slender and tenuous is the thread by which an audience can be held. I looked toward the President's box, remembering Mr. Hall's concern. The President sat there slumped in his chair, hands crossed over his breast. Beside him Mrs. Grant carefully folded her fan.

At that instant something entirely unforeseen happened. Little Pun-na, sitting on her mother's lap, slipped down and ran to Mr. Hall. Still holding the tiny flag, she scampered across the stage and sprang into his arms, kissing him on the cheek.

It was like the dislodgment of the keystone that holds the avalanche in check. People laughed delightedly at the simple gesture, but the laughter was almost immediately swamped in the great and general applause. The audience liked Mr. Hall, that was apparent. It liked his proposal, and it loved little Pun-na. Here and there men rose to their feet, still applauding, and there were some who stamped their feet and whistled. The President applauded also, nodding his head and speaking animatedly to his lady, who smiled and waved at Mr. Hall. Still holding Pun-na in his arms, Mr. Hall bowed to Mrs. Grant, and to the audience.

It was impossible to be heard in the din. Beside me Hannah was screeching something into my ear, but I could only grin and shrug like an idiot. It was something to see, to hear, to be a part of, and it made the frozen toes worth while.

Within the next week there came a communication to us at the H Street boardinghouse:

> Executive Mansion,
> Washington, D.C.
> July 20, 1870
>
> Captain C. F. Hall
> DEAR SIR,—You are hereby appointed to command the expedition toward the North Pole, to be organized and sent out pursuant to an Act of Congress approved July 12, 1870, and will report to the Secretary of the Navy and the Secretary of the Interior for detailed instructions.
>
> U. S. GRANT

We had done it.

Of course it was by now much too late in the season to get away. By the time we could have reached the Arctic, the winter season would have been well advanced. There was no recourse; we were doomed to remain in Washington for another nine months or more. But this time the situation was bearable. Charles was now Captain Hall, with a commission from the President himself; our ship *Polaris* was being fitted out, a crew was being hired, officers appointed, a Scientific Corps established, stores put aboard. In many of these operations I was a kind of major-domo, for, as Charles said, "You handle people much better than I, Adam." In the meantime he kept himself busy with the larger plans for the expedition; conferring with Professor Joseph Henry of the National Academy of Science which was to suggest fields of scientific investigation for us, picking the officers of the expedition, and discussing progress with Secretary Robeson of the Navy.

I do not know that I would have selected officers and scientific personnel any differently than Mr. Hall did. Yet I can say that had more time and attention been paid to investigating their backgrounds and previous experience, a great deal of trouble— even tragedy—might have been averted. Take our sailing master, for instance—Sidney Budington of the old *George Henry;* the same old Bud who had taken us north on our first journey to the Arctic, so many years ago. There was no more *yare* master than old Bud, for by that word New London used to mean skillful and daring. In most respects he looked no different from that day I first saw him when I shipped aboard the *George Henry,* ten years before. Small, sturdy—wearing, I think, the same flat-brimmed felt hat and rusty black coat he had worn then—he stepped aboard the *Polaris* and nodded to my greeting.

"Adam Burritt, isn't it? Never forget a man that's sailed with me. Well, that's a long time ago."

"It was, indeed," I said, shaking his hand.

I do not know exactly when I became aware of it, but there was a definite odor of strong drink about him, and his nose was red and heavily veined. Remembering his strict Presbyterian ways, I was shocked; especially when I saw that he was more than a little unsteady on his feet.

"I'll look about," he said.

The master of a vessel is the master, no matter how much he may drink, so I, mindful of courtesy, accompanied him about the vessel, very proud of her. She was on her ways at the Washington Navy Yard, where her wales, planking, clamps and ceiling had been removed and decks taken out in preparation to retimber her and increase her depth. At four hundred tons or so, and with new boilers, sails and rigging—her bottom double-planked and coppered—she was designed to meet any contingencies that would arise. But Captain Budington was not satisfied.

"There," he said, pointing. "That guard around the propeller well. That'll not last in the ice."

The Navy engineers had designed the guard, and I told him so. I put it as diplomatically as I could, knowing how quickly he could blow up a storm. But he had changed in more ways than one. There seemed to be something maudlin and indecisive about him, and he abandoned the subject of the guard with scarcely an argument, starting off instead on a long recital of his late misadventures, of how hard it was any more for a good skipper to get a berth. "For ye may know," he said, "that I would have not taken this command if there had been anything better offered. No, whaling—that's the ticket. This pottering about the Arctic on a scientific wild-goose chase—that's not a fit employment for a whaling skipper."

A little angry, I said, "Captain, when we reach the vicinity of the Pole, you'll find you need all the skill and daring you possess to get us safely through."

He took out a handkerchief and wiped his red-stitched nose. "The Pole, is it? And what is the Pole but more ice and snow, of which we have a sufficiency in Baffin Bay and other places which are easier to reach?"

"But the Pole is the object of our expedition!"

Again he abandoned his point, and started a kind of wool-gathering, telling me how hard the times were. The aroma of rum about him was so strong as almost to suffocate. His whole person—his rusty coat, his linen, even his woolly square-cut beard—reeked of it. I was sorry for him, to see how this tough sea dog had turned into a querulous old man. Not that there is anything wrong with age, as such; advancing in years myself, I began to think forty, for instance, only the threshold of maturity. But where old Bud of the *George Henry* had been an oaken block of a man, trustworthy and skilled, something in the last ten years had eaten him through like a canker. I did not know enough of his late career to speculate on the cause. Misfortune or disappointment of some kind, I suppose. Such experiences often turn men inward upon themselves, so that they feed on past glories, and do not have the stomach to excel again.

"Well," old Bud said finally, "I can do nothing more here. The work's well under way, and it's too late to change it, I suppose. I will hope for the best, and that's an end to it." He shook hands with me. At the rail he paused and put a hand on my shoulder. "I can trust ye, Adam, can't I?"

"For what?" I asked, puzzled.

"Why, for anything!" He gripped my shoulder and shook me. "Why, for anything at all, lad. Whatever arises!"

"Yes," I said. "Of course."

He waggled his head and made off down the gangplank, holding on with both hands as if fearing it would suddenly take flight and lift him into the heavens. At the foot of the gangplank he waved at me and walked heavily away, head bent and hands clasped behind his back.

Very puzzled and apprehensive, I spoke about old Bud's visit to Mr. Hall. "He has changed so. There is something queer about his manner. I think he had been drinking, also."

Mr. Hall laughed. Pleased with the progress he had been making on the writing up of our scientific program, he was not in a mood to deal harshly with anyone. He had been working all day with Professor Agassiz of the National Academy on the subject of Arctic glaciers, and the subject fascinated him to the exclusion of any critical faculty.

"I do not think we need worry, Adam. Old Bud has, I understand, met with reverses since we last saw him. He lost the *George Henry,* you know, off Cape Walsingham, and I think it has preyed on his mind. But I am still convinced that he is a good skipper. Besides, I owe him a debt of gratitude for his great kindness to me on our first trip north."

I hesitate to call it a failing in him, but one feature of Mr. Hall's character was his ever-abounding gratitude. His heart overflowed toward those who assisted him in any way, even the most trifling. Words seemed all too tame to express his obligation to those who had helped him in his Arctic travels, and he often allowed a natural and generous thanks to go to extremes. Thus, in the case of old Bud, I think he felt such a sentiment of gratitude that he allowed it to obscure his critical judgment.

"Well," I said, "he did not impress me very favorably. I hope no harm will come of it."

"Harm?" He smiled. "Whatever harm, dear boy? Old Bud is a yare skipper, and it is not fair to judge such a man on land. No, wait till you see him on the quarter-deck of the *Polaris,* searching ahead for our track to the Pole. Then speak so of him if you will, but I wager that the first cold breath of the Arctic will bring out the lion in him again."

"You are probably right," I admitted.

Bit by bit the fitting out of our good *Polaris* went forward. Washington is not famed for the salubrity of its climate. During that fall we seemed to have rain almost every day—a steely mistlike downpour that chilled to the bone. But in fair weather or foul, the necessary operations went on. Some days it was necessary to shovel the snow off her decks before work could be done, and on others her scuppers were awash with rain much as if she had shipped a green sea off Disko. The sun rarely shone, and even then it was a thin skimmed kind of sunlight that had no warmth in it, no cheer.

Our ship's hull was especially prepared by being planked all over with solid six-inch white-oak timber, which was then sheathed with sheet iron, the better to bore her way through the ice. Her boilers were arranged uniquely, one of them being fitted to use whale or seal oil as a steam generator. This was expected not only to be used for propulsion, but also to heat the vessel when in winter quarters. Another peculiarity of the vessel, due to Mr. Hall, was a new style of life preserver, in the shape of a buoy. This was slung over the stern on a davitlike arrangement. It could, when occasion required, be quickly detached and lowered to the water by means of a magnet, a galvanic battery, and a long wire which extended to the pilothouse. There was also a lamp in the buoy, rising above it two or three feet, the better to mark it in dark and stormy waters.

As the fitting out went on, so did the sailing list grow. There was Mr. Bryan, astronomer and chaplain to the expedition, a young man of very superior talents. Mr. Frederick Meyers was our meteorologist, a native of Prussia and a sergeant of the United States Signal Corps; a very thorough man, and one considered especially fitted for the position. Mr. Chester was first mate, from Noank, Connecticut. Mr. Schuman was our chief engineer, and a good draftsman. My meeting with Captain Budington I have already described, and Mr. William Morton was our second mate. Morton had made one memorable Arctic voyage with Dr. Kane, the explorer, having crossed the great Humboldt glacier in search of the Arctic sea. Mr. Tyson was our navigator, and I liked him very much with his quiet ways and his ready wit.

There were others, too: John Herron, steward; William Jackson, our cook; Mr. Campbell, the fireman. Seamen, too, to the number of ten: Anthing, Kruger, Lindermann, Mauch. When taken with Mr. Meyers and Mr. Schuman and the rest, our officers and crew had a heavily Germanic cast. It was foolish, but it made me uneasy to hear them together, *ja*-ing and laughing and saying things in the strange tongue. I had never had any knowledge of German, and it was completely incomprehensible to me. Like most things we do not understand, it took on a sinister shading that made me uncomfortable until I had the good sense to laugh at it.

I have left mention of Dr. Bessels to the last, and I do not quite know why, unless it was the quarrel he had with Mr. Hall before we had even left Washington in the *Polaris*. The doctor was chief of our Scientific Corps, and a native of Germany.

Though a comparatively young man, he had quite a reputation in international scientific circles. He had graduated from the famous University of Heidelberg and had done researches in zoology and entomology. In 1869 he had sailed north on the *Albert,* a walrus hunter, as surgeon and naturalist, and so already had some experience of the Far North.

One spring day he came aboard and asked for me.

"I am Dr. Bessels," he said. "I am to be chief scientific officer of the *Polaris* expedition."

In person he was slight, almost delicately built, and seemed of quick, ambitious temperament. The shape of the head showed great mentality, and his features were regular and pleasing. His eyes were bright and dark, and susceptible of a varied expression. All in all, I would have said a handsome man, though built on rather too small a scale.

"Captain Hall told me you were coming," I said. "He was very sorry to be called away. He had an appointment with Professor Baird to discuss the detection of something or other. I think it was ozone in the atmosphere."

"Indeed?" Dr. Bessels inclined his head.

I showed him round the vessel, taking considerable pride in the system of wooden lockers I was having a carpenter build in the main cabin, which was to be used as a laboratory. At Mr. Hall's request I had drawn up a sketch, which he approved and initialed, to direct the carpenter.

"But there are not enough cabinets," Dr. Bessels said. "For instance, I will require a great deal of space—almost as much as you have provided here—for my chemicals alone. Mr. Burritt, I need a great many chemicals for my work. Potash, the various sulphates, vitriol, niter, bluestone—"

"Well," I said, "this is something you will have to talk about to Captain Hall."

"Talk to Captain Hall?" He seemed astonished and distressed. "Why must I speak to Captain Hall?"

I was embarrassed, especially so since the carpenter looked at me and grinned in a sly way.

"Because," I said, "Captain Hall has given me my orders. I daresay it will be possible to change the arrangement of the cabinets if you want, but I cannot do it without Captain Hall's approval."

"But I am chief scientific officer of this expedition! It seems to me that if I need cabinets for my chemicals, then I should have them. Do you understand me? Do I make myself quite clear?"

I do not know how the matter would have gone had not Mr. Hall come aboard, back from his appointment with Professor Baird at the National Academy. He might have been standing in the companionway for some time listening to us; I do not know. The first I was aware of him was when he put a hand on my sleeve and said to me, "Adam, I will handle this."

Still perplexed, I said, "This is Dr. Bessels, Charles. He is to be the chief of the Scientific Corps of our expedition."

"I know. Dr. Bessels and I have already met."

"He wants some changes made in the arrangements of the cabinets in the deckhouse, and I have told him—"

"He had told me that I must come to you, Mr. Hall." Dr. Bessels' dark eyes were very intent, and I had the uncomfortable feeling that this small matter had turned into a *cause célèbre;* exactly how, I did not quite comprehend. "Is this not a strange arrangement, where the chief scientific officer must ask permission from—from—"

"From me, sir?" Mr. Hall demanded.

Dr. Bessels shrugged. In his excitement a guttural accent began to mar his carefully pronounced English. "I was giffen—given to understand by Secretary Robeson that in all scientific matters my decision was to govern. This matter of the cabinets I believe to be a scientific matter. *Nicht wahr?* Is it not so?"

It was not hard to see that he considered Captain Hall to be a kind of ferryboat captain who had been retained only to transport Dr. Bessels and his chemicals to the North Pole, and return. Even in this status he did not give him a great deal of credit, but scrupulously refrained from giving him his proper title of captain. Mr. Hall, too, noticed the omission, I am sure. His face reddened and he clawed at his beard; always a sign of great emotion with him.

"So," Dr. Bessels said, with great self-assurance, even smiling, "I will have my cabinets, eh?" He put his small hand on Mr. Hall's shoulder. "There is no need for any unpleasantness about this, surely?"

I had thought Charles Hall capable at that moment of striking Dr. Bessels dead with a thunderbolt of wrath. His face suffused with anger, his beard seemed to crackle with an electrical discharge, his big hands knotted and unknotted at his sides. For a long time he had been free of the symptoms of the disease that had plagued him our first winter in Washington—that thickness of the blood for which raw beef had been prescribed—and I feared to see him now so distraught, lest the sickness strike again.

"No," Mr. Hall said. His voice was thick and unsteady. "No, there is no need for any unpleasantness. Surely not." He turned to me. "Adam, do whatever the doctor wants in the way of cabinets for his supplies."

"But the sketch has been made, and most of the cabinets and lockers already laid in!"

He took out a neatly folded white handkerchief—Hannah kept all our linen sparkling—and touched it to his lips. "Nevertheless, make the changes." There was something queer and fixed about his sudden calm. It was not natural.

"Very well."

"Good," said Dr. Bessels. "Going on such a long journey together, it is very important that we understand each other, eh? There is never a need for unpleasantness when we understand each other."

No, I thought, *so long as Dr. Bessels gets what he wants there will be no unpleasantness.* I began to dislike the chief of our Scientific Corps, with his restless ferretlike way. Old Bud, too; a fleeting glimpse of him passed through my mind—his rheumy nose, the odor of rum, his maundering way of talking. Our two principal officers—one had already had a disagreement with Captain Hall, and in my opinion promised more; the other was a shell of the man I had once known, and I did not know that I would trust him as sailing master of such an expedition.

"Yes," said Mr. Hall, "we understand each other, Doctor."

Dr. Bessels looked at him sharply. Mr. Hall's face was grave and impassive. But if he had known the import of Dr. Bessels' chemical cabinets, he would have cried out.

Chapter 14

ON the 9th of June, 1871, Captain Hall sent a letter to Secretary Robeson:

> SIR—I have the honor to report that the steamer *Polaris,* selected by you for the expedition toward the North Pole, under my command, is now ready for sea, and will sail tomorrow. The officers and crew of the ship are all I could desire, and the provision made for the subsistence and protection of all on board is the best that could be devised.
>
> Your generous response to every legitimate request I have made in regard to the ship's outfit demands the warmest expression of my gratitude. The only return I can make now is the assurance of my determination, with God's blessing, that the expedition shall prove a success and rebound to the honor of our country, and to the credit of your administration. With an abiding faith that the results of the expedition will prove the wisdom of the Congress in providing for it, and justify the

generous manner in which you have performed the duty assigned you, I am,

Very respectfully, your obedient servant

C. F. HALL

Commanding

US North Polar Expedition

Sitting in his cabin on the *Polaris,* Captain Hall showed me the letter. The last few days, with the inevitable rush of final preparation, showed on him. His eyes had lost that sparkle they customarily possessed, and his face was etched with care and concern.

"There, Adam! What do you think of that?"

Overhead one carpenter cursed another, and a shower of shavings came down through an open hatch. Boots clumped on the deck, a donkey engine puffed and chuffed. A dray wagon with a load of salt beef came alongside and the wheels rumbled on the dock.

"What do I think of it?"

When I came to the passage where he said, "The officers and crew of the ship are all I could desire," I frowned, and read it over again. "Well, Charles," I said, "it's a fine letter, and should please the Secretary. But you have been less than truthful."

"What?" He sat erect. "Less than truthful? What do you mean?"

"You pay high praise to the officers and men. Yet I am not certain this is warranted. I do not like Dr. Bessels, for example, and if I am not mistaken, you do not either. He is high-handed and presumptuous, and there will be trouble with him before we reach St. Johns. Captain Budington has been more or less under the influence of liquor ever since he came aboard. In addition, he does not take too seriously our objective of reaching the Pole. As for the crew, too many are political appointees or ne'er-do-wells. I doubt they have much experience, or stomach for the Arctic winter either."

He snatched the letter from me. "I did not ask to be preached to."

"Nevertheless, it is something I must say. I have touched on it before, but you did not think it important. Now, at the very least, I do not think it wise to praise these men, and leave the impression with Secretary Robeson that everything is fine as frog hair."

He folded the letter and put it carefully in an envelope, sealing it with a stick of wax held in the flame of an alcohol lamp on his desk. The action was slow and deliberate; in spite of the fact that I had angered him, he was withdrawn, almost detached.

"You see trouble where there is none. Dr. Bessels is a competent and qualified scientist, and perfectly within his rights in insisting about the matter of the chemical cabinets. Captain Budington is an experienced and daring Arctic skipper, and I should not want a better one. As for our crew, some are inexperienced, but a few weeks at sea will blood them. Always, with any vessel, there is a shaking-down process that goes on. Do not be hasty in your judgments."

"I am not hasty," I said sulkily. "You know the truth of these statements as well as I do. There is no secret about them; I would repeat them to Secretary Robeson's face."

His detachment suddenly vanished. Springing to his feet, he took me by the arm. "You have not spoken your suspicions to anyone else?"

"To anyone else?"

"To any of the people from the Navy Department, or to Professor Agassiz or Baird or anyone from the National Academy?"

"No! Of course not!"

Relieved, he sat down. "Of course not. I am sorry I doubted you, Adam." With his fingers he pinched out the wick of the alcohol lamp and slumped in his chair, staring at the tiny curl of smoke. "Adam, do you trust me?"

"I would go through hell for you, and have nearly done so on several occasions. You should remember, Charles."

229]

"I remember." A ghost of a smile illumined his lips. Then, serious again, he said, "I know that circumstances will arise which you question. I want you always to question what seems to you wrong, or ill advised. We have been through much together, you and I, and I will never forget it. But if I have not the ready and facile explanation which you require, Adam, do not hold it against me. In this whole business there are many things that are strange and queerly gotten up. I know what they are, and how they came about, and I have my reasons for proceeding as I do." He reached for my hand. "Trust me, Adam. That is all I ask. Trust me!"

I had not thought it necessary to assure him of my trust, and I was a little piqued at the necessity of doing so to an old friend. But I shook his hand and said, "Of course I trust you. I would not be aboard now, making ready to sail, if I did not."

Hannah came in then, with a pot of coffee for him. On the way out I stood for a moment with her in an angle of the deckhouse. She did not like Dr. Bessels any more than I did, and old Bud's infirmity with alcohol distressed her. She and Joe kept well to themselves, not having much to do with the crew, though ordinarily they were jolly, and good companions. We looked at each other in wordless communion; one of those meetings of the eye where volumes are spoken, and thoughts pass from mind to mind with the swiftness of the electric telegraph.

To one who did not know of our troubles with officers and crew, our departure was a triumphal event, filled with good wishes and anticipating a speedy and successful assault on the Pole. On the 10th of June, 1871, we sailed from the nation's capital, steaming down the broad reaches of the Potomac toward Chesapeake Bay and the open ocean. Our sailing climaxed a week of fetes and entertainments; dining at Willard's with various legislative gentlemen, oyster suppers, parties, receptions and teas. We were sorry not to see the President again, since he was much occupied with official duties, but Secretary Robeson saw us off, also Professors Baird and Agassiz, and the Honorable Mr. Sherman and Mr. Stephenson, our good friends from the state of Ohio.

Our time to New York was sixty hours, the *Polaris* steaming along swiftly and efficiently. Though no great challenge was presented to her by the summer seas, she handled well and did a good eight knots, with great economy of fuel.

In New York Mr. Hall moved on to more triumphs. The American Geographical Society presented to him the flag which, in 1838, Lieutenant Wilkes of the United States Navy had borne nearer to the South Pole than any American flag had heretofore been. This flag had also been carried by Lieutenant DeHaven to a higher northern latitude than any flag had ever been; then Dr. Kane had carried it higher in latitude yet (well beyond 80° N.) and Dr. I. I. Hayes had transported it thirty-seven miles north of Dr. Kane's record. It was a historic banner. On accepting it, Mr. Hall said he believed that this flag, in the spring of the following year, "would float over a new world, in which the North Pole star is the crowning jewel." His remarks were well received.

On the 29th of June, 1871, we left the Navy Yard, steaming toward the Sound. Our old friend Mr. Henry Grinnell accompanied us, intending to return on the pilot boat. As we passed through the East River, with the great city of a million souls on our left, and a half million on the right, I could not help thinking how few of these took any interest in our peculiar mission. And most of those with any interest, no doubt, thought we were wild and reckless men, rushing heedlessly to our own destruction. But the Arctic can be come to terms with, and a man need be in no more danger there than on a crowded street in Cincinnati. No, man's chief danger is from man, and not a matter of geographical latitude and longitude.

231]

"Thinking, Adam?" Mr. Grinnell asked me. He stood with me a little apart from Mr. Hall, who was in conversation with Captain Budington.

"Yes, sir," I said.

"A penny for your thoughts."

"They are not worth a penny, save to me."

His eyes twinkled behind the panes of his steel-rimmed spectacles. "Come, lad—two old friends do not need to stand on ceremony!"

"I was just thinking how far Mr. Hall has come in this business. How far we *all* have come, though it is due in the main to his own efforts."

He nodded, instantly serious. "You remember, Adam, a little conversation I had with you on the dock at New London one day? July, it was—early one July, when the *Monticello* sailed north."

"I have never forgotten it."

"Then I have no need to repeat it. But it is no less true now than then. Charles stands on the threshold of the Pole. No one can defeat him but himself." Looking at me keenly, he repeated the words. "Do you understand what I mean, Adam?"

"I think I do."

"Help him. Help him from himself, if need be, but help him. He depends on you, Adam; you have made much of this possible by your own efforts in his behalf, and he is grateful."

At Hell Gate Mr. Grinnell left in the pilot boat after a round of affectionate farewells. We were now free of all connection with land, steaming smoothly on the waters of Long Island Sound.

"Good!" Mr. Hall said. "Now I will have a little time to myself to work on the manuscript of my new book." He had brought with him his notes of our last voyage, intending to work them into shape so as to have them ready for publication when we returned. "Captain," he said to old Bud, "the *Polaris* is entirely in your hands for the next few days. I shall be busy in my cabin."

The next day we were surrounded by fog, which continued for several days. On the evening of the fourth day, a great change came over the sky during the first watch; dark clouds were massed above the horizon, and the entire sky was covered as with a pall. Sudden rain squalls, with thunder and brilliant lightning, quickly succeeded each other. The lightning seemed almost continuous, and the very firmament was in a blaze from horizon to zenith. Thunder echoed and re-echoed across the sky like the rumble of artillery, but our good *Polaris* moved serenely on her way.

Soon after we sighted the coast of Newfoundland, we encountered loose floating ice as we approached St. Johns. And we encountered also the trouble I had predicted, although it did not come exactly in the way I expected.

Mr. Tyson, the assistant navigator, came to me one day wearing a worried look. "I see," he said in an embarrassed manner, "that there is not perfect harmony between Captain Hall and the Scientific Corps, nor with some others either. I am afraid things will not work out well, Mr. Burritt. It is not my business, but knowing you are Captain Hall's confidant, I thought I should mention it, if indeed you are not already aware."

I had not noticed any recent trouble, having been kept busy making up dog harness and assembling our sledges.

"What do you mean?"

Poor Tyson grimaced. "My cabin, as you know, adjoins that of Captain Hall. A man would have to be deaf not to hear the quarreling that goes on there."

"Quarreling? With whom? About what?"

He did not answer my question directly, but asked instead, "Who is commanding this expedition, Mr. Burritt? I should like to know. When a man receives conflicting orders, it is a deucedly hard job to carry out."

"Captain Hall is commanding," I said. "Does anyone doubt it?"

Mr. Tyson shook his head gravely. "Some do, I think."

Try as I would, I could not get him to say any more on the subject, he appearing to think that he had already gone too far. He did mention, however, that some of the crew were dissatisfied with their lot, and had broken up into little cliques that gave difficulty with setting the watches.

"All right," I said. "I am glad you came to me, Mr. Tyson. I will speak to Captain Hall, and see if we cannot settle this disagreement in an amicable manner."

I went to Charles' cabin to speak to him, knowing that at that time of the day he was usually working on the manuscript of his book, of which he was very proud, having done the whole thing by himself, with no assistance from anyone. I knocked several times; then, hearing no answer, I pushed the door ajar and went in. The swinging oil lamp cast its pale glow over the litter of neatly penned manuscript pages; an open porthole cover swung to and fro, clinking metallically. He was not there.

Captain Budington's cabin was across the passageway, around the huge column of the smokestack, and as I came out into the passageway again, I heard angry voices from old Bud's cabin.

"I will not have it on my ship!" Mr. Hall was saying.

"And I say ye shall!" old Bud roared. "It is my liquor, sir, bought and paid for with my own money. It is no part of your damned expedition stores!"

I pushed the door open, seeing a little tableau enacted before me. Mr. Hall, angry and distraught, held several bottles of London gin in his arms. Across the deal table old Bud confronted him, face red and suffused with passion. He leaned forward on the table, supporting his weight on his knotted fists, his woolly beard trembling with the violence of his emotion.

"You drink to excess," Mr. Hall cried. "Surely you cannot defend such a habit, when we are on our way to the Pole itself!

In these waters a man needs his wits about him at every moment! No, sir, I cannot allow intemperance on my vessel."

"*Your* vessel?" Old Bud's tone was ironic. "I will have ye know, sir, that I am sailing master here! In all matters relating to the safety of the vessel, I command!" With an angry gesture he reached for the gin, but Mr. Hall pulled it away from him.

"Give it to me!" old Bud howled. "Whoever set ye up as a judge over your betters?"

I was about to step between them, and wish to God I had. But I was too late. In sudden resolve Mr. Hall dashed the bottles down on the iron deck. Glass splintered, and bits flew into the air, flashing in the lamplight. Gin splashed in all directions, and the cork simply came undone from one bottle, so that it lay on its side, gurgling lazily as it lost its contents.

"There!" Mr. Hall cried. "You have forced me to do it, Captain. There is your precious gin!"

An awful silence pervaded the cabin, in which the only sound for a long time was the gurgling of the overturned bottle—the only one of the lot that was unbroken, but which was now almost as empty as the others.

"Charles!" I said. "What is going on here?"

He turned and looked at me, a queer light in his eye. Outside, in the darkness of the passageway, I could hear the shuffle of boots and whisperings, and I pulled the door to behind me and stepped into the cabin. Old Bud remained crouched over the table, staring down at the wreckage of his gin.

"Surely," I said, "there is a better way to settle matters of this sort!"

Mr. Hall took a deep breath. "I will not have liquor on this ship. We are a commissioned Navy vessel, engaged in serious work. I warned Captain Budington several times. This evening, when I came in to see him about our plans for docking at St. Johns, I found him in his cups."

"Ye did not," old Bud muttered. He remained rooted to the

spot, seeming not to look at either of us. "Ye found me having only a little drink, and where's the harm to that, eh?" He swung his head to and fro in a regretful gesture. "Ye shouldn't have broken up all my gin, Hall. Oh, ye never should have done that! I could kill a man for less than that, and have nearly done so at one time or another."

"Threats cannot move me," Mr. Hall said. His eyes burned with a fierce intensity, like coals in the dusk.

"Only a little drink," old Bud said. His voice was low-pitched and hoarse, and he continued to stare at some obscure recess of the small cabin. "That was all it was. A small drink."

"Come away," I said to Mr. Hall. "When heads are cooler, we can talk this over and smooth matters down. But for now, come with me." I took him by the arm, and he did not protest, being somehow gentle and very calm for his outburst of a moment before. As we left, I said to old Bud, "Captain, I'll send one of the deck crew down with a broom and a mop."

He looked at me from under his woolly white eyebrows. "All I did was have a little drink, Adam."

I could not help but think of him at that moment as a strong and ancient rock washed by the sea; a rock that has withstood decades of the batter and wash of the waves, and is at last eroded and worn so that the soft inner matter is exposed. I felt very sorry for him, and for Mr. Hall; for all of us, as a matter of fact.

"I am sorry, Captain," said Mr. Hall stiffly, "but I only did what I thought best."

I closed old Bud's door after us and went with Mr. Hall to his cabin. Inside, he sat heavily down at his desk, staring at the welter of manuscript papers. "Oh, Adam!" he murmured. "I am so tired, and there is so much to do!"

"If you ask me," I said, "you have done enough already. There was no call for an open break with Captain Budington."

He stacked the papers in a neat pile and picked up his pen. "I am going to write an order to the officers and crew, forbidding all liquor on board. I should have done it sooner, but I did not think it necessary. Adam, would you not suppose that men would have the common sense to know that in an undertaking such as this, we cannot afford to have our senses dulled by liquor?"

"I do not know what I would suppose," I said. "Men are men, and are bound to have their tot one way or the other. But with respect to Captain Budington, I told you my mistrust of him when he first came aboard. Now that you have chosen to disregard my advice, and that of others concerning him, I think you have made your bed and must lie in it. For better or for worse we are stuck with Captain Budington, and must work out a compromise of some sort."

At times there was a mulishness about Charles Hall that angered me. It was the same obstinacy that made it possible for him to win through to King William Land and the solution of the Franklin riddle, but in these circumstances it was endangering his drive for the Pole, and I wondered he could not see it.

"There will be no compromise," he said stubbornly. "I will order all liquor to be taken off the ship at St. Johns, and no more to be brought aboard!"

I shook my head. "This will only cause more trouble. The crew is already disaffected with some of their duties which they consider onerous. No, Charles, I should advise you to let this matter lie for a while, and see if it does not work itself out."

He lashed out at me in his blind way, not able to see that what I proposed was to his own advantage, and that what he proposed meant an aggravation of an already grave situation.

"Adam, I suggest you stop advising me. I have already had a gutful of advice! If I had taken all the advice that was offered me, we should never be this far along." He pounded his fist on the table so hard that some of the ink slopped out of the inkstand. "How do you think I got this crew together and fitted out the ship and sailed this far, eh? Not by taking advice, I tell you. No, sir, I held out for my principles, and did not give an inch. People, I have found, come to respect such an attitude!"

In spite of my sympathy for him for his dreadful responsibility, for the dark clouds of trouble that were beginning to gather around the *Polaris* expedition, I began to lose my temper also.

"It is all very well to prate about principles, but why did you not do so when Captain Budington came aboard, especially when you were warned by me and others of his drinking? And why did you not object to Dr. Bessels' assignment as chief scientist, when you and he were immediately at loggerheads? All this trouble could have been foreseen, Charles, and prevented!"

He got up, his eyes hard and cold.

"All this trouble could have been foreseen, you say, and prevented. Very well, Adam, you are welcome to your opinion. But let me tell you this. Some great undertakings are above even principle, and in my eyes the quest for the Pole is such. I would give my life to attain it, and count it a small thing. But giving my life would not have attained our object. No, what we needed was a ship and crew and funds. I accepted Captain Budington and Dr. Bessels and several others on the recommendation of influential men, men who had helped me get the *Polaris*, and saw to fitting her out and making the voyage possible. To have objected at that late date would have meant delay. I was forced, Adam, to cultivate a power of ignoring disagreeable facts when their recognition threatened to interfere with the progress of the expedition. Call me unwise, if you will—tell me I have made my bed, and must lie in it. But I have done what I have done, and I will now lay my trust in God, and see it through to the end!"

So this was at the bottom of his actions! He had not been as obtuse as I had thought, but I wondered if he had not been better advised to accept the delay and try for a more desirable complement of officers and crew and scientific men.

"Well," I said, "there is no cure for it."

"There is a cure for you," he said. "You have signed on for

the voyage, Adam, but I release you unconditionally at St. Johns. You are free to go back to the States if this final voyage is not to your liking."

I do not know when anything has stung me more, and my tongue got the better of me.

"You may go to hell in a hand basket, for all of me," I cried. "You do not know your real friends, Charles Hall, and I pity you, sir! Leave the *Polaris,* indeed! No, sir, I will not! I will stay aboard and see things through to the bitter end, for I do not doubt that the bitter end is approaching! As for advising you further, I would as soon think of giving advice to the wind, or the sea, or any of the great natural forces we must contend with. They will fling it back in my teeth as readily as you have done!"

I do not think he was paying any attention to me, being too busy counting the sheets of manuscript on his desk, as if to bring home the fact of his ignoring my outburst. Suddenly his face paled and he looked about the cabin.

"Some of these sheets are missing!"

"I do not give a damn," I said.

He searched the limited confines of the cabin, getting down on hands and knees to explore the floor, tearing aside the blankets on his berth, throwing open doors of cabinets and lockers. He went frantically through the brass-bound mahogany chest where he kept his papers and notebooks, throwing aside papers and journals as he searched. "They are not here! Some of the most important and significant pages have been taken!"

"Taken?"

"They are gone, and they were here."

"But who would have taken them?"

"God knows! They are of value to no one else!"

I remembered the shuffle of boots I heard in the passageway a few minutes before, the sound of whispers. I had thought it only a prying member of the crew, someone listening to the quarreling in old Bud's cabin. On a ship at sea there is no news, little to break the monotony of the ocean waste, and men search industriously for small titbits to exchange in gossip.

"They must be here," I said. "I see you have them numbered. Let me go through them."

Many of the numbered pages were missing—pages having to do with his scientific conclusions about the fauna and flora of King William Land, among others. My further search of the cabin did not reveal their whereabouts.

"You are right," I said. "They are gone. But where?"

Exhausted, he sat back in his chair. "They are of no value to anyone else. Unless—unless—"

"Unless what?"

Suddenly calm, he stroked his beard. In the yellow light from the swinging cabin lantern, his face was melancholy.

"Perhaps there is a theory. Yes, it is all of the same piece."

"Do you suspect someone? Is that it?"

He breathed a deep sigh. "From this moment on, I suspect everyone. It seems the only prudent thing to do."

"Do you suspect me, also?"

He shook his head back and forth, and in a way it was like the senseless motion of an animal in a cage at the Zoological Gardens.

"I will face this out myself. I do not need any help, nor do I want any. Have I made myself clear?"

"You have," I said.

I slammed the door and went out on deck. Mr. Meyers, the meteorologist, was standing at the rail in conversation with Dr. Bessels. They spoke in German and did not look toward me as I passed, going toward the vessel's head. I stood in the bows a long time, letting the icy wind cool my flushed face, and my passions. From somewhere belowdecks I could hear a concertina playing, a gay little sound, and from time to time our iron-sheathed bow ground briefly against floating chunks of sea ice.

He had invited me to leave the ship and go home! After all we had meant to each other, and to the ultimate success of the dash to the Pole! I counted angrily weeks and months and years of toil and danger and hardship, the short rations, the money of my own I had put into our ventures, with no thought or hope of repayment.

Mr. Chester, the first mate, came forward and stood beside me.

"A beautiful night."

"A night for demons," I said. "For ghosts and ghouls and harpies, crying in the rigging."

He laughed. "Whatever do you mean, Mr. Burritt?"

"Nothing," I said. "I am a little put down, that is all. When do we dock at St. Johns?"

"Shortly before noon."

I thanked him and went to my bunk, where I tossed and turned and did not sleep the rest of the night. Was ever a man so perplexed?

Chapter 15

ON the 10th of July we made Cape Race, and on the 12th anchored at St. Johns, Newfoundland. To me St. Johns was always the doorway of the Arctic, and I looked forward with a special pleasure to arriving there. But something had gone out of the Arctic for me. My tiff with Mr. Hall, the trouble aboard ship, the general atmosphere of tension and disagreement, took away much of my anticipation. If only I could have spoken to him, made him see how his stiff-necked attitude was endangering our plans! If I could have made him see that such a large party, with many divergent personalities and opinions and ways of working, must be led, not driven; that the peculiarities of people have to be taken into account, and compromises reached! But a wall of coolness had dropped between us and seemed unlikely to be breached, I being too hurt and vain, and Charles Hall being too wrapped in his great plans to concern himself about personal difficulties.

Even with Hannah and Joe he was somehow different, being more curt and businesslike. Joe was very stolid about it, saying nothing, but Hannah worried about Mr. Hall. I sat with her in her cabin where she was sewing winter furs for our party.

"Do you remember the old days?" she asked me, biting a thread in two with her strong white teeth. A pot of tea sat beside her over a small alcohol stove, and she was very neat and clean, as always, in a gingham pinafore over her *koo-lee-tang*. On another woman the combination would have looked barbaric, but good Hannah lent it a dignity that befitted royalty. "Do you remember, Adam, when there was only four of us? You and Father Hall and Joe and me?"

"I remember," I said, accepting a cup of tea.

"Things were better then." Her needle flashed in and out. "Not so many people, not so much trouble. Not this great ship and so much money and equipment and a man to do this, a man to do that, a man for everything. We did it all ourselves."

"That was because we had to," I said. "There was no one else."

"Is it better this way?"

"Why—why—of course!" I stammered. "We are ever so much better prepared now than we were then." As I said it I did not believe it, and reproached myself for lying to Hannah. But I think my face gave me away, because she reached over and patted my hand, giving me a sorrowful and understanding look.

"To be prepared," she said, "does not have to mean *things*, Adam." She struck her clenched fist on her breast. "In here— that is where a person should be prepared!"

"I know."

She jabbed viciously at her sewing. "That Dr. Bessels! Did you know he was *an-ge-ko?*"

The word, of course, meant medicine man, or shaman, or priest, or whatever you wanted to call it. There was also another implication. The Innuits respected their *an-ge-kos*, but it was for the most part a fearful respect, born of the *an-ge-ko* trafficking in the affairs of the other world, the spirit world; ghosts, spells, devils, all the unholy and unseen things which constantly surround the Innuit, and must ever be propitiated and avoided.

"He is a doctor," I said.

She shook her head firmly. "*An-ge-ko*, him! He is casting a spell on Father Hall." Reaching beneath her pinafore, she brought out a curiously carved bone. In a way, it resembled a cross. "It is not done yet. I am still working on it. I need a white dog's teeth, and walrus blood. It is very important, Adam. When I have finished it and said some words over it, it will break the spell."

I laughed. "Hannah, you disappoint me! A Christian lady like you, believing in charms."

She put the bone back inside her pinafore, very upset.

"I do not want you to laugh at me."

"I did not mean to laugh." I pointed to the Bible she always kept near her. "That is the proper charm, Hannah."

She rolled her eyes; for a moment she was no longer our sweet Hannah, but a fierce female savage who might have come from the hard and cruel country of Kik-i-Tuk—King William Land itself. "That book does not know about things like this! I have looked all through that book for a charm to protect Father Hall, but I could not find it. No, Adam, this is the only way. Joe and I love Father Hall, though a cloud has come between us. We protect him the best way we know how!"

At St. Johns, Mr. Hall was as good as his word. In spite of great grumbling from the crew and a stony indifference on the part of most of the officers and the Scientific Corps, he and Mr. Tyson conducted a thorough search of the vessel from one end to the other, looking for contraband liquor. I was afraid violence might break out, but after a few bottles of rum were discovered and broken Mr. Hall seemed satisfied, and went off to a reception given him and the officers by the governor of the island. Dr. Bessels put in only a minimum appearance at the reception, giving as the reason the series of photographic views he was starting to engage in, intending to keep a pictorial record of our Arctic journey. He did, however, spend considerable time in the town; there were rumors that he brought back aboard with him a considerable store of liquors, which he locked into his chemical cabinet so that Mr. Hall would not know of their presence. I hoped it was not true. But I knew also that a kind of alliance had developed between Captain Budington and Dr. Bessels, both of them having a very low opinion of Mr. Hall. If the rumor were true, I did not doubt that Dr. Bessels had done so at old Bud's instigation.

On the 19th we left St. Johns for Greenland. On the 27th we had our first sight of high snow-covered peaks, and welcoming natives in their *ki-as*. We stopped briefly at Holsteinsborg to take on coal. I remembered those old days on the *George Henry* when Sterry and Coleman and Keeney and the rest of us carried sacks of coal for three days. Now I was an officer of the expedition; I roamed the rocky tide pools while others worked, remembering my juvenile thrill at my first sight of an Innuit doing a full *ki-a* turn in the water for a plug of tobacco. I did not know the language then; now I knew Innuit well, but I found I had lost that other language, that language of the heart and of youth, when everything is high adventure and the soul has no limit to its capacity for delight and adventure. No, it was not the same. I turned and walked toward the dock again. Coaling was almost finished.

Mr. Hall was leaving the ship as I approached, a bundle in his arms. "Sir," I said.

He nodded curtly; then stopped.

"I have not seen you for some time, Adam. How are things going with you?"

"Well enough. I have been walking." Noticing that he held in his arms the manuscript of his book, tightly bound with string, I said, "Are you going to consult with the Governor about your book?"

245]

He shook his head. "I am going to leave it with the Governor for safekeeping."

"But I thought you had brought it along the better to work on during the Arctic night."

"I am afraid to leave it on board."

I remembered the incident of the missing pages and asked him about it.

"They were mysteriously restored. Now that I have the whole manuscript complete, I cannot afford to take further chances. Someone, I believe, is very jealous of me and my book."

He went ahead, then, up the gravel path toward the Governor's house. I stood for a long time on the dock, staring at the sea gulls dipping round our stern where William Jackson, our cook, was throwing the noon garbage over the rail. My words with Mr. Hall were the first we had spoken for almost two weeks, but there had been no satisfaction in them for me, nor for him either. They were casual words, devoid of warmth. I picked up a stone and shied it at a gull; he went shrieking and angry away, which matched my mood also.

I would not like to give the impression that our expedition was entirely girded around with dismay and unhappiness; there were from time to time some good news and pleasant happenings. While we were coaling in Holsteinsborg a Swedish scientific expedition, under the command of a Baron von Otter, sailed in from Upernavik. The Baron was a roly-poly little man with a shiny monocle and a breathless way of talking.

"A promising season, sir!" he said to Mr. Hall. "Very few bergs have been seen from Holsteinsborg and Disko, and none at all between Disko and Upernavik. It is likely to be an open season, well made for your great voyage."

The Baron was planning to stop at St. Johns, and Charles prevailed on him to take with him several dispatches to Secretary Robeson. I wondered what was in those dispatches. Was there any hint of trouble or dissatisfaction? No, I thought not.

For better or worse we were committed to the Pole, and there was little use in crying over spilled milk.

While he was waiting for Charles to seal his dispatches and put them into a waterproof pouch, the Baron drank tea with me and chatted animatedly.

"Such a great man!" His monocle blinked glassily as he nodded his close-cropped skull. "I had never thought to see him. Now here in Holsteinsborg we meet, and I have the great pleasure to carry dispatches for him. I am so proud." Little finger extended, he stirred more sugar into his tea. "In Göteborg and in Malmö, we follow his exploits, you know. We could not be more proud of him if he were a Swede himself. The Frobisher find, of course, and the solution of the Franklin mystery—his charts and maps and surveys, his Innuit dictionary, his book. Ah, if I had only brought my own copy along! Do you think he would have signed it for me, on the flyleaf?"

"Of course," I said. "He would have been proud to do so."

The Baron drained his cup and smacked his lips.

"He will make it to the Pole, you will see. Never have I seen such a well-equipped expedition, and with Charles Hall as leader success is a certainty. I wish my own government were so generous with its support." He nodded toward the scabby brigantine anchored nearby. "I do all this with my own money. It is expensive, but a man of wealth has a responsibility to mankind, you know."

He went off then to talk with Dr. Bessels, and they spoke together in German for a long time. When Charles had finished his dispatches he came on deck. He did not interrupt, but only waited patiently for them to finish. Seeing Mr. Hall, the Baron beckoned him to join the conversation, but Dr. Bessels begged off, saying he had some work to do in his laboratory. It was a deliberate and calculated affront, and the Baron's monocle fell out of his eye and dangled at the end of the ribbon. But he shrugged, recovering himself, and shook hands warmly with Charles and me, wishing us Godspeed.

Standing in the stern sheets of his small boat, he waved as it pulled away. "I shall read about it in the newspapers!" he called to us. "Good luck!"

I had, of course, made up my mind to stay with the *Polaris*. Being only human, I sulked for a while and minded my own business very severely. If Charles Hall did not want my advice and companionship, then I certainly did not want his. But I was not too obtuse to see that certain situations needed mending if the expedition were to be anything but a disaster, and I took it on my own, at last, to do some mending. Dr. Bessels was a physician, sworn to the alleviation of suffering. A man who has taken the vow of Aesculapius cannot be *all* bad, I reasoned. Perhaps I, and Charles, had misjudged him. On our way to Godhavn I found a time when Mr. Hall was busy at other things, and went to Dr. Bessels' laboratory to have a talk.

When I entered he was working on a long brass pendulum, by means of which he hoped to determine the exact attraction of gravity at the north geographical pole. It was several feet long, swung on steel knife edges, and suspended in a wooden box with a glass door.

"Ah!" he said. "Mr. Burritt, eh?"

"Yes."

"Come to the enemy camp, I see. And for what purpose?"

"I do not have enemies," I said, "except at *their* choosing. No, sir, I am interested in doing anything I can to ensure the success of our expedition, and to promote the safety and welfare of all."

He lifted out the pendulum, very carefully, and laid it on an oiled rag on the table. "It is not at *my* choosing, Mr. Burritt. I lay the whole affair at the feet of the stiff-necked and quarrelsome Mr. Hall. As for you, I do not dislike you. It is your association with that tyrant I do not fancy."

"He is my friend, and a great man."

Dr. Bessels shrugged. "I could not convince you otherwise."

"Try to do so," I said, putting my hand on his sleeve. "You

will find me of an open mind. Surely, Doctor, you must know
that we all imperil our chances of success—even our lives—
when we go on day after day as if we were an armed camp of
some sort."

"I know that as well as you do." He put down the wrench
with which he had been adjusting the steel knife edges, and
folded his arms. "I have been to the Arctic, you know, on the
old *Walrus*. I know as well as any man how unforgiving is the
Arctic."

"But can you not make a peace of some sort with Captain
Hall?"

He smiled, very thinly. "How does one temporize with a
madman? A poorly educated adventurer, intent only on self-
glorification—not a proper scientific man at all?"

"He has done great things, in spite of his lack of formal education. Even Baron von Otter spoke highly of him."

"Von Otter is a dilettante."

"Doctor," I said, "let us not fence with each other. I cannot
believe that you dislike Captain Hall only because of his lack of
education. I do not think, either, that you believe him only a
glory-seeking adventurer. You have some real, or perhaps only
fancied, grievance against him. Do you not have the courage
to tell me what it is?"

I had struck into a sensitive spot. He lost the composure he
had so far affected and his face became pale, setting into a determined and angry cast.

"Courage? Yes, I haf the courage! I tell you—you want to
know?"

"I do, indeed."

"This is not a proper scientific expedition! *Ach*, there is so
much that could be done, and that will not be done because of
your precious Mr. Hall! A great effort such as this, to end up in
little but standing on a square foot of lonely ice called the
North Pole! No, sir—if *I* had been asked about the scientific
plans, it would have been a very different business!"

"I do not think this is quite true," I said. "Furthermore, it is unfair."

He bristled at me. "It is all too true, and quite fair." Seizing a handwritten copy of the instructions which the National Academy had drawn up for us, he said, "Listen to me. I read. 'It is evident that the Expedition, except in its relation to geographical discovery, is not of a scientific character, either in the mind of Hall or of Congress.' There, it is well known!"

"You need not have come," I said, "if you were not satisfied."

"I have done the best I could, always. I got together the scientific instruments, with which we are richly supplied. I worked like a dog—*ach*, how I worked! But I was never taken into Mr. Hall's confidence. He, and he alone, worked out the details with the National Academy. When I tried to see him, to talk to him, to remonstrate, I was never able to see him. He was always too busy. Then I said to myself, 'Once we are under way, I can talk to him and convince him of the changes which the scientific program must have.' But that was no use, either. He does not listen to me, or anyone. He has made enemies of me, and the good Captain Budington, and of most of the members of the crew."

How to reason with him? He was as difficult as Charles Hall himself.

"It has been very difficult to get this party together," I said. "You must realize, sir, that Captain Hall has had to compromise a great deal just to get us this far along. Many of the things he has done—many of the solutions he has accepted—were brought about under duress. So far as the scientific program is concerned, it was well established when you came aboard, and changes would have delayed us well beyond our planned sailing date."

"Then," said Dr. Bessels tightly, "the delay should have been accepted. If *I* had been captain—" He broke off.

"But you are not captain."

"Perhaps I should have been! I am better prepared than he

to lead such a group into the Arctic. I am a scientist by training, and that is what this expedition needs—an accomplished scientist to give it significance and direction, not just a silly dash to the Pole, meaning nothing!"

In his own way, he was quite as single-minded as Charles Hall. He was also, I was beginning to be convinced, jealous of Charles and capable of any rash act to gain his own ends. In that slight, elegant frame there was a steely resolve and great determination. Dr. Eugene Bessels began to frighten me.

"I should hope," I said, without any real conviction, "that as we sail farther north, you will begin to appreciate Captain Hall more, and perhaps make up your quarrel with him."

He went to the chemical cabinet and unlocked it with a key from a chain around his neck. Taking out a small container of sperm oil, he closed and locked the door again, but not before I had seen what looked to me like several glass bottles of liquor —rum, perhaps.

"I intend to make up no quarrel, Mr. Burritt. The first move is up to him. I have tried, God knows—I have extended myself beyond what I would have done to any other man. No, sir, I am Chief of the Scientific Corps, and I know my duty. I will do it as I see it, and that is all I will say."

"Very well," I sighed, and turned to go.

"*Danke,*" Dr. Bessels said stiffly, and went back to oiling the bearings of the gravity pendulum.

Godhavn was the true Arctic at last. On the 4th of August we steamed into the harbor. Though it was almost midnight, the sky was filled with summer twilight; the sun was at that time only four degrees below the horizon and in another hour or so would rise again. We bought dogs here, and also took on board the Esquimaux Hans Hendrick and his wife and three children, with their luggage of bags, boxes, skins, cooking utensils, and three or four young puppies whose eyes could scarcely bear the light. For fifty dollars Danish per month Hans was signed on as dog driver and guide for the expedition. He had been on the expedition of Dr. Hayes some time before, as had Mr. Morton, our second mate. At first he did not recognize Mr. Morton, but when the latter pointed out some powder burns on Hendrick's hand which he had gotten from a powder explosion on the shore of Kennedy Channel, Hans remembered him, and they embraced joyfully.

At King-i-toke Island we bargained for more dogs, and finally got our complement. We also topped off our coal bunkers, and had plenty of wood and resin for emergencies. And now we were eight officers, three scientists, a steward and cook, two firemen, ten seamen, and eight Esquimaux ready for our dash into Baffin Bay and so north to the Pole.

Again the summer fog settled down over us like an icy blanket, seeming almost to have tangible substance as it was breathed into the lungs. It was dangerous going, we having little warning of any great bergs which might bar our path. But we headed due north, with a lookout calling out any dangers he might spy from the masthead. Crowds of walrus blackened the loose floe pieces which drifted and scraped along our iron-sheathed hull. Hans Hendrick and Joe fired at them in the hope of obtaining fresh meat, and wounded several. But Captain Hall was unwilling that the *Polaris* should stop to capture any, and on we forged, the engines throbbing as the vessel cut into the trailing mists.

"Be into the pack soon," said Mr. Tyson, coming up to stand beside me in the bows. "Wonder how far the old man will take her?"

"Captain Budington?"

"He's the sailing master."

"I don't know," I said.

On the morning of the 27th of August, we reached the pack itself, the solid and permanent pack south of Smith Sound. I went up on the hurricane deck where Captain Hall and Captain Budington were standing. From this vantage point, the fog having lifted, the entire Arctic vista could be seen: great floating blocks of pack ice, some the size of houses, others several hundred yards across, still others great steep-walled floating islands a half mile or more in extent. Their icy breath seemed to chill us like a malignant radiation. The wind having died, it was very quiet. The only sound was the occasional grind of ice on ice and on our hull, and the low-pitched throb of our engines as they turned over to keep steerageway on the *Polaris*.

"We have only reached the starting point of our journey," Mr. Hall said.

Old Bud had a woolen scarf bound round his ears and securing his old flat-brimmed hat. His nose was red, whether from cold or liquor I did not know, but I began to wonder whether Charles had judged him more correctly than I.

"Aye," he said, "there's the ice, right enough!" He went to the rail and looked over it at the pack, seeming to judge it as a soldier judges his enemy. For a long time he stood there, silent. Then he spoke to the quartermaster. "Take her through there, Mauch. That'll be a lead to the right of that big berg—the one that looks like a church with a steeple."

He rang up the engine room and the *Polaris* crept cautiously ahead, searching for the open lead that old Bud said was there. Sure enough it was—a meandering channel of black water, hemmed in by ice to a height halfway up our mast. I held my breath as we skimmed along the base of the sheer walls. Once, when a shower of ice came down on us from above, I almost cried out. But we negotiated the lead and came out again into an open lake. The way ahead was clear; at least for several hundred yards.

"Now," said old Bud, "we'll try again." Looking thoughtfully about him he said, "I'll have that one, Mauch. Around the big fellow that's undercut so at the water line."

Our decks were crowded with all hands that could be spared from their duties, for no one wanted to be caught below in case of accident. White-faced and apprehensive, they clung to the rigging or leaned over the rail, watching in silence. I saw more than one cross himself or mutter a prayer of some sort. It was indeed a formidable sight. Floes of three or four miles in extent, piled helter-skelter on each other in a great jumble; the strains they encountered in being so piled made them creak and groan and shudder as we steamed past. Sliding off their icy shoulders came great drafts of cold air, turning into mist as they encountered the warmer waters of Smith Sound. We should all have been frozen into mummies by those drafty vapors, but I know I was perspiring. As I looked around I saw old Bud take off the woolen scarf and wipe his red face. When he spoke to the helmsman his voice had turned hoarse.

"Well done, Mauch." He swallowed hard, as if his throat was paining him, and said, "Ring down the engines. I'll have a little breather now." So saying, he went belowdecks.

The strait through which we were working our way trended northeast; it was from twenty to twenty-five miles in width, and bordered by high mountainous land, broken in places by ravines but in general presenting a perpendicular line of cliffs, with a terraced debris at the base sloping toward the water's edge. The land was comparatively free from snow. Except for the great chunks of ice with which the sound was packed, there was no evidence that we were fifteen degrees beyond the Arctic Circle itself.

Mr. Bryan, the astronomer, came and stood beside me. A slight, pleasant man, he never gave offense to anyone.

"Well, Mr. Burritt, do you think we shall be able to go through any farther?"

"I hope so," I said. "The farther we can take the *Polaris*, the less distance a sledge journey to the Pole."

"The men are grumbling," he said. "I overheard several of them talking together, saying that we ought to put in to shore and not risk a further northern passage."

"All sailors grumble," I said. "It is a way of life with them."

There was a pronounced set of the current against us in the

narrow channel, and our vessel was beginning to drift south again. Mr. Hall went below and called Captain Budington on deck. The sailing master rang up the engines and we started churning north. The weather became colder and a breeze sprang up. From my own Arctic experience I predicted good weather from these signs, and hoped that we could yet make several degrees northing.

Mr. Hall stayed on the hurricane deck all that night, and the next day, and on into the next night. When he slept, if at all, I do not know. He was like a man made out of iron; indestructible, enduring, seeming not to need the creature comforts of food and drink and warmth and companionship. From time to time, unable to sleep because of the noise of ice grinding along our hull, I went up on the deck to watch the spectacle. Silvery white in the moonlight, the great bergs loomed over us, stark and forbidding. In the moonlit silence the chuffing of our little engine sounded loud and insistent, echoes reflecting off the icy walls and bouncing back and forth along the corridors like summer thunder in the mountains.

We steamed that morning through the entrance of Kennedy Channel and passed Cape Frazer, running along the land at a distance of five miles. On the 29th of August, Cape Lieger could be seen on the western coast, and at 1:00 P.M. the *Polaris* entered a strait some twenty-five miles in width and worked her way slowly through it. During the night and for several hours in the early part of the 30th we threaded our way through immense ice fields, the greatest I had ever seen, and were now, according to Mr. Bryan's estimation, at over eighty-two degrees north, the farthest north that any vessel had yet gone.

We had, for a time, been in somewhat more open waters, and Captain Budington turned the ice-piloting over to Mr. Morton, the second mate. Now, however, Morton expressed himself as being uneasy about going any farther north, and Captain Budington was roused from his sleep to attend a conference on the hurricane deck.

On coming up, he stood for a moment staring at the massive bergs that filled the channel. They were large, it is true, and forbidding, but the eye could still discern open-water leads between them.

"What do you think, Captain?" Mr. Hall asked.

The sailing master was unsteady on his feet, whether from loss of sleep I could not be sure. But one thing I was sure of; the strain of the continued ice-piloting had told on him. His face was haggard, and his ancient blue eyes shot with blood.

"We have reached our limit," Budington said. "There is no doubt of that."

"But there are still several promising leads to the north," Mr. Hall protested. He pointed to some, and to still others. "There, and there, and there!"

Old Bud shook his head, and seemed very tired. "No, sir, it is impossible to get any farther north! We must settle for this, Hall; some eighty-two degrees north."

Mr. Hall was very angry. "But we have been steaming through leads like these for days! Why stop now?"

Attracted by the controversy, some of the officers came up on the hurricane deck to listen, and many of the crew stopped their work and other interests, intent on the argument that was going on. I saw Dr. Bessels come to the door of his laboratory cabin and stand silent, a glass beaker of some kind in his hand.

"Why stop?" demanded old Bud. "I'll tell ye why stop, sir! For the last several days I have driven this vessel through chinks in the ice not fit for a walrus to go through! Every lead we have taken has had the possibility of smashing us like an eggshell. No, I say it is time to stop and tie up in some sheltered bay for the winter!"

Mr. Tyson was standing beside me, and he whispered in my ear, "It does not make a great deal of difference to me, but I should think the *Polaris* can make a few more miles to the north before we are stopped completely."

"I had hoped so," I said.

[256

Mr. Hall was completely alone, or at least unsupported, in his insistence that the *Polaris* steam farther north. Very angry, he continued to protest, again pointing out leads which he considered suitable to navigate. "I will take the vessel through myself!" he insisted. "I will be responsible."

Old Bud shook his head. "Ye cannot. I am sailing master, and accountable for the vessel. No one can relieve me of that responsibility."

"You are merely frightened," Mr. Hall said.

"And with good reason. I have lost one ship in ice not so bad as this."

Mr. Hall flung out his arms to the rest of us—Morton, Tyson, Mr. Meyer, Bryan, Mr. Chester, Mr. Schumann. "How do you all feel about this? Is it right to stop so short of our goal, and peril our whole undertaking?"

He had been very distant with most of them, and while some may have had a feeling that a few more miles northing could safely be made, none was willing to cross Captain Budington. They were sailors; old Bud was their captain. They shuffled their boots and looked from one to the other, and spat over the rail and said nothing. At the same moment, almost seeming as if to confirm the sailing master's stand, a cloud came over the weak and watery sun and a shower of fresh cold snowflakes came down. The wind rose, and the *Polaris* quivered in the dark waters of the channel.

"All right, then." Mr. Hall took a deep breath, staring at them, and at me, who had not supported him either. But then, he had not *wanted* my support, he told me. "I will agree, Captain, under duress. Put in to whatever shelter you require. But I say this. As soon as we tie up, I am going to make up a sledge team and go along the ice foot as far as I can, to spy out the country and determine if our path is truly blocked, as you say. And I will tell you this, sir; if I find a way farther north, I will return and insist on taking the *Polaris* through even farther. That is what I came to this country for and that is what I will do. I will not be stopped by a pusillanimous captain and a cowardly crew!"

These were strong words, and there was much muttering and stepping forward with clenched fists among the officers and crew. But Mr. Hall faced them down, staring back with a cool and calculating eye.

"Ye are a madman," Captain Budington said. "Go wherever ye will, but I intend to take the *Polaris* inshore and get her out of these great icy teeth that would mangle her, and us, at the least opportunity."

Mr. Hall stamped below and our little group broke up. Captain Budington went to the masthead with a spyglass and found a promising anchorage on the east bay of the channel, next to a gigantic berg to which we could anchor and which would give us some protection from the winter winds off the top of the world. Though it did not seem far—no more than ten miles— it took us over five hours to reach, having to follow a circuitous route through the jumbled ice.

During that final passage, Mr. Bryan was busy with his charts, his log, and his sextant. "It is impossible to be exact," he told me, "but I make our north latitude to be eighty-two degrees and sixteen minutes. Think of it, Mr. Burritt—we are farther north than any man-made vessel has yet gone!"

"Yes," I said, "and if I mistake not, we will go even farther north before the *Polaris* is frozen in for the winter."

"Do you think Captain Hall means it?"

"He has never been more serious," I said. "He will take the vessel to the Pole itself, if he has to drag it with a rope."

Mr. Bryan shook his head, his young face worried. "There will be trouble."

A light winked on in Dr. Bessels' cabin, a pleasant yellow glow.

"I do not doubt it," I said.

Chapter 16

THE harbor we found was no snug anchorage, but was at least out of the way of the swift main current of the strait, and sheltered somewhat by a bold cape some four miles west and north—a cape which Mr. Hall wanted to name after one of his Cincinnati benefactors, Colonel James Lupton, president of the Mercantile Library there. We anchored in the lee of the great berg; Mr. Chester measured it with a transit and some tables, and came to the conclusion that it was four hundred and fifty feet in length, three hundred feet in breadth, and almost a hundred feet high. Under the usual estimate for bergs, this meant a foundation of two hundred feet, promising stability. Mr. Hall named it Providence Berg.

Once we were tied up in the lee of Providence Berg, Charles made hurried preparations for his sledge journey north. He had decided on Mr. Chester, Hans Hendrick, and Joe to accompany him, and I do not know when I have ever felt so desolate. I had been with him always on his previous sledge journeys and looked forward to the crisp snow of the trail, the barking dogs, the exhilaration of new vistas revealed. But it was not to be. Almost, I think, I was on the verge of rushing to him, begging to go, taking on myself the whole burden of our quarrel as a fair exchange. But I restrained myself. He had not wanted my help. Very well; I had my pride, too. Let them go!

At one in the afternoon they left, Charles advising Captain Budington that they would be gone only a week or ten days and instructing him to make no permanent disposition of the *Polaris* until he returned with information on possible farther progress to the north that season. The sledge was heavily loaded; the twelve dogs barked and whined under Hans' long whip but could not budge it. Finally it took several of the *Polaris* crew to get it going. Away they dashed along the ice foot, making a fine appearance, as, to me, dog teams always make; ki-yiing, yipping, eager for the trail.

Captain Budington stood beside me as I leaned over the rail watching the party go. "I see Hall did not want your company, Adam, any more than he cherishes mine. Well, we are rid of him for a while, at any rate." He slapped me on the back. "Do not be sad, lad. Come, buckle to; there is plenty of work to be done! We must dig in for the winter."

"Dig in for the winter?" I remembered Captain Hall's explicit instruction. "But Charles will be back in a few days, with word as to whether we steam farther north this season!"

Old Bud spat over the side. "Here we are and here we stay, Hall or no Hall! I would as soon take my ship into the River Styx as try to make any further northing."

"But he said—"

"The devil with what he said! He is crazy, Adam, and ye know that to be a fact as well as I do! Clearer heads must prevail. Dr. Bessels and I have made our plans, and for the safety of the ship and party, we will do what we think best."

"There will be trouble," I warned.

"There is always trouble when Hall is about. There has been nothing but trouble since we left the Navy Yard." He shook his grizzled head and mopped his face with a corner of his shawl. "Ye remember how hotheaded he was that first trip out in my old *George Henry*, God bless her, and how he got angry and flung away from us to try to sail to King William Land all by himself?"

"I remember," I said.

"Look here now, Adam," the sailing master said, not unkindly. "We must join together to protect ourselves. Hall has treated ye very shabby of late, I must say, and I cannot think of what ye see in the man any longer. Come join with me and Bessels and the rest who see it our way. We welcome ye; I know ye of old, and consider Adam Burritt a fine Arctic hand and a good man. What do ye say?"

I did not like the sound of this at all, it seeming to border on mutiny. A man could, I suppose, make a fine point of it and say it was not mutiny, Captain Budington being the sailing master. But it still smelled of mutiny and I did not want any part of it.

"No," I said, "I join no parties. That is what the trouble has been all along; if there had not been so many different factions, we would not have had trouble."

This made the sailing master angry and he said, "If ye are not with us, then ye are against us!" and stamped away, muttering. I was sorry to have him angry with me, since it seemed of late I had made as many enemies as Charles Hall. But it went against my grain to plot and scheme, and I would have none of it.

Now that Charles Hall was gone, the opposition came into the open. A chain fall was rigged and the propeller and rudder unshipped. Dr. Bessels and old Bud did a great deal of conferring, very cheerful and polite to each other. Supplies were landed on shore, so that if the *Polaris* were destroyed by the winter ice, the crew could live comfortably. A small portable "recreation house" was set up, and Dr. Bessels erected a shelter for his instruments on what was called Observatory Bluff. Canvases were rigged over the decks of the *Polaris* to form a shelter and keep the heat from escaping. Once a heavy fall of snow had formed on the canvas, a kind of crust would build up so that by spring the vessel would be sheathed in a foot or more of ice. Yes, the opposition was digging in for the winter, and it was obvious there was no intent to move from that spot again until next summer.

The water began to freeze on the surface of our anchorage, first only a shallow rime disappearing each dawn, and then remaining to grow deeper and deeper; an inch one day, two or three the next. The Arctic day grew steadily shorter also, but as the day shrank, the spirits of the crew seemed to soar. Freed from their labors, they celebrated. Liquor—plenty of liquor—appeared from nowhere. Some of the men fell to making beer, and over the door of the galley appeared the sign NORTH POLE LAGER BEER SALOON. NO TRUST. ALL TRANSACTIONS CASH.

Card playing, especially gambling for money, became frequent, and the concertina played day and night. Discipline was very lax, Captain Budington seeming not to care, and Dr. Bessels being busy at his observatory ashore where he was making observations with the magnetometer. There was not the proper care taken of our rations. Someone should have been tallying them against our needs, husbanding them for emergency, seeing to it that the men did not overeat. But this was not done. Too much food, excellent food, was prepared: oyster soup, preserved meats, green pease, fruit pies, raisins, chocolate. The men feasted, and when they had filled their bellies the surplus was thrown over the side for the dogs. Also, the quarters were too warmly heated and we began to run low on coal. Somehow an essential section of our seal-oil boiler had been lost, and the plan for heating with seal oil had to be abandoned. All in all, our condition was rapidly deteriorating, and I was not sure we would last out the winter if some strong hand were not immediately to make itself felt. But there was no strong hand.

As time had passed and Mr. Hall did not return, the situation became to me a little more hopeful. By this I mean that the season was more advanced, the temperature was dropping and the light disappearing, and it became less and less probable that we should be able to take the *Polaris* any farther north. In such a case, Captain Budington's preparing the vessel for wintering would seem to be a sound decision, one to which Mr. Hall could not take exception. But when he did return, a week later, things were promptly in an uproar again.

The night he came back, I was on a long and solitary hike, enjoying the aurora. Luminous streamers extended in an arch through the zenith; fantastic forms of light came and went rapidly, and there were bands of yellow and white, which were not too common. Mr. Bryan, whom I visited at the observatory, told me that in spite of the brilliant display the magnetometer had not showed any marked deflection, and seemed disappointed. I had a cup of tea with him and started back to the ship.

On the way, I noted a spark of yellow to the north, along the ice foot. There being no moon, the only illumination the inconstant aurora, I could make out nothing more than the spark of light, and so paused, shivering, waiting until it should come closer. The wind had risen and the Fahrenheit thermometer was well below the zero mark. Under my feet I could hear the murmuring of the pent-up dark waters, sighing and moaning to be freed from their icy prison. Mr. Hall? It could be; he had long been awaited. But these will-o'-the-wisp lights were not too uncommon in the ice fields. It might only be some kind of phosphorescence, the thing the Innuits called *kis-i-tat* and which they attributed to devils.

I was not prepared for the speed with which the dancing pinprick of light advanced, and as a result it veered to the right of me, running out onto the frozen surface of the bay. It grew

larger and steadier by the minute, and I soon saw that it was
Charles and his party. Cutting directly across the ice, they were
at the ship before I could walk there.

"Hello, the *Polaris*!" Mr. Hall's voice boomed as they drew
up alongside. There was no watch; a result of the lax discipline
since he left. "Hello, the *Polaris*!"

I came up in my furs and said, "I am glad to see you all
back."

"A good trip," Mr. Chester said. Hans and Joe shook hands
with me, but Mr. Hall, very perturbed, went up the snow steps
that had been built to lead to the deck of the *Polaris*.

"Captain Budington!" he called. "Where are you?"

Someone roused the sailing master and he came on deck, very
grumpy at being waked. "Well," he asked, "what is it now?
What the devil is all the noise about?" Seeing Mr. Hall and the
rest back from their journey, he rubbed his eyes and grumbled.
"Oh, so it's ye, eh, Hall? Well, no need to make such a fuss."

Mr. Hall was angry at the appearance of the ship. "When I
left here," he said, "I gave explicit instructions to keep the
Polaris fitted for a further journey northward. Now I find her
prepared for wintering, the propeller and rudder unshipped,
supplies put ashore, our temporary buildings erected! What
does this mean?"

Captain Budington was instantly at crossed swords with him.
"What does it mean? Why, what should it mean but that we are
froze in for the winter, and intend to stay here? Man, how long
is it since ye have been gone? Do ye think we can tack up and
down the open water in the channel, putting off and on, waiting for ye to return? No, sir; I myself gave the orders to secure,
and I will stand by them, having sole responsibility for the
safety of the ship."

Mr. Hall looked from one of us to the other and took off his
fur mittens, slowly and deliberately. "Hans and Joe and I have
sledged almost to the edge of the great Arctic Sea, and we think
it possible to take the *Polaris* through the ice pack; not to the

Pole itself, perhaps, but at least several degrees of latitude
farther than the eighty-two degrees we have made thus far."

Old Bud's eyes popped. "But we are frozen fast in the bay!"

"The ice is not thick." Mr. Hall pointed to the Strait. "Out
there is still open water. As we go north, you will also find the
leads more numerous. No, I say we can break the vessel loose
with the use of ice saws and her engines, and get her into the
channel where we can again steam north!"

They clustered around him, protesting; Mr. Morton, Mr.
Schumann, Odell the assistant engineer, Mr. Coffin the carpenter, Mauch, some of the crew. Mr. Tyson, who had thought previously we could make more northing, said nothing, and Mr.
Chester and Hans and Joe became busy at unloading the sledge
and stayed out of it. Dr. Bessels came forward from his laboratory and stood at the edge of the group, watching everything
that happened.

"It is madness!" old Bud protested. "Whatever can ye be
thinking of, this late in the season?"

"The Pole!" said Mr. Hall stubbornly. "That is what I am
thinking of, and ever shall! Whatever else did we come north
for, sir?"

Dr. Bessels pushed his way through the group. "I do not think
it wise to attempt a further northward passage, at this late date,"
he said. "I advise you to think very carefully before risking
such an undertaking."

"Doctor," said Mr. Hall coolly, "I will remind you that you
have been hired only to head the Scientific Corps. When we
have arrived at our ultimate destination, you will have your
work cut out for you! In the meantime, I advise you to get a
crew together and start to dismantle your scientific hut on the
bluff. We must move fast!"

It was obvious that he had made up his mind. It was even
more obvious that there was to be an open break; the mutiny,
perhaps, that I had suspected in Captain Budington's proposal
to me. Dr. Bessels was livid with anger at Mr. Hall's dismissal

of him and his advice, and the sailing master almost speechless with rage. Dr. Bessels rushed off—where, I do not know—and Captain Budington said in a choked voice, "Mr. Hall, I say this change in plans calls for a consultation below, where the two of us can discuss the matter calmly, and out of earshot of the officers and men!"

There was something massive and obdurate in Mr. Hall's manner. I remember what he had said that night at Lincoln Hall, over a year ago. *I am at the top of my powers. There comes during man's life a time when all his powers combine in the right proportions and at the right time to make him invincible.* I think he felt himself so that night, standing on the deck of the *Polaris*, facing down his opposition. In spite of man, in spite of the elements, in spite of destiny herself, he was going to take the *Polaris* to the Great Arctic Sea, and farther. No man there doubted it. The wind howled about our ears and the fast-forming ice beneath us murmured and sang, but they were less the great natural force than he.

"I will not change my mind, Captain," Charles warned.

"Come below then for a cup of coffee to warm ye," old Bud said. There was something suddenly lifeless and resigned in the way he pronounced the words. He looked around him—perhaps in hopelessness, or for sympathy, I do not know—and in the yellow lantern glow his face was the color of old and mottled parchment. "Will ye do that?"

"For a moment," Charles said. "But we must begin our preparations this night."

"Aye," old Bud said. "Our preparations."

They went below, down the companionway. On deck a babble broke out. Everyone talked at once. Mr. Meyer had a group of the Germans about him and was haranguing them in that guttural tongue. One of them, I remember, still held a concertina, and as he raised his hand to say something the concertina sagged and let out a ludicrous squawk. Mr. Bryan was very upset about having to dismantle the observatory, and Mr. Chester stood to one side, sucking at his pipe and looking up at the stars, which were very bright and near.

"What do you think of all this?" I asked him.

He took the pipe out of his mouth and looked into the bowl. "I do not fear a little more northing as much as I do remaining here with this crew of malcontents and troublemakers."

"Will it be dangerous to steam ahead through the pack?"

He puffed on his pipe. "It is dangerous to be in the Arctic at all, especially in the winter season."

"You know what I mean."

"It can be done. I think Captain Budington became timid a little too soon. Yes, we can saw the vessel out of here and rock her free. It is only a few hundred yards to open water."

"Well," I said, "I—"

Someone pulled at my sleeve. I turned, and it was William Jackson, the cook. "Mr. Burritt, sir, please come quick! Captain Hall has been taken ill."

"Ill?" Only a moment before Charles had been in the best of health; contentious, stubborn, completely sure of himself and his destiny. "Ill?" I repeated. "What do you mean, Jackson?"

The cook shook his head. "I dunno, sir. He took a cup of coffee with Captain Budington, and of a sudden he started to vomit and retch. He was that ill his eyes rolled up into his head and I thought he was going to cash in his chips."

I looked at Chester, dumfounded.

"Better go below and see what's going on," he advised.

I hurried below. Charles had been carried to his cabin, and he lay on his berth, still dressed in his furs. Hannah had been before me, and quickly lit the lamp. Kneeling at his feet she pulled off his boots, her face pale.

"Charles!" I said. I bent over him and took his hand in mine. "Charles! What is it?"

He tried to speak but his words were hoarse and slurred, and I could not understand. His *koo-lee-tang* was smeared with sour-smelling vomit, and his face the grayish white of candle wax. Herron the steward stood in the passageway with Captain Budington, his eyes round and uncomprehending.

"Coffee?" I asked him. "Was that all he had? Just coffee?"

"That's all," Herron said. He looked down at the cup in his hands. "Drank it down, and in a minute complained his throat felt queer. Then he started to retch, and fell forward on the table."

I went up the ladder three rungs at a time to fetch Dr. Bessels. I had not seen him since the argument on deck, but a candle burned in his laboratory. He was sitting quietly on the edge of his bunk, hands clasped in his lap, staring at the candle flame. When I threw open the door he looked briefly up, then away.

"Doctor," I called, "come quickly! Captain Hall has been taken ill!"

He said nothing; I remember he only buttoned his shirt, very carefully and precisely, still sitting on the edge of the berth.

"Taken ill?"

"Yes," I said. "He is unconscious, or nearly so."

"Where is he?"

"I have seen that he was carried to his cabin."

"All right," said Dr. Bessel. "I am coming."

He followed me below. On our way we pushed through little knots of the crew standing aside and talking in hushed tones, looking askance at us. The news had passed electrically among them, and I heard one say to another, "Old Hall's dead; I heard it from Herron."

But it was not so, thank God. When we reached the cabin, Hannah had managed to get Charles out of his furs and into a nightshirt. He lay as if stunned, breathing with difficulty, taking the breath into his lungs in great rattling gasps. The small cabin was crowded with onlookers, and Dr. Bessel said, "Get them out. Everyone out."

I pushed them protesting into the passageway, all except

Hannah. Where Captain Budington had gone I did not know, but I did not see him then. His cabin was across the passageway, and he might have retired there.

"Apoplexy," Dr. Bessels said. He lifted a lantern over Charles' pale face and examined him closely. He pulled an eyelid down, forced the mouth open, put his head over the chest and listened to the heartbeat, took the pulse. "I am certain."

"What is to be done?"

Dr. Bessels did not speak for a moment. He only stood looking down at the heavy frame of Charles Hall, now so pitiably stricken. Then he said, "Quinine might help. Perhaps cold compresses to draw the blood from the brain."

"Let us go about it, then! We cannot let him suffer so!"

Dr. Bessels was usually very composed, but on this peculiar occasion he exhibited a calm that bordered on a hypnotic trance. A doctor, I supposed, was used to death and suffering. One of the chief benefits of the professional medical man is that he can manage to be unshaken and objective when those about him are apt to be excited and ineffective. But there was something peculiar to me in his behavior; he only continued to regard Charles Hall with a detached stare and finger his beard.

"Do you have quinine in your cabinet?" I demanded. "Quick, give me the keys! I'll run and fetch it."

He shook his head very sharply, seeming to recover. "No! I will go up and get it myself. In the meantime, you and Hannah take some cloths and make up cold sea-water compresses. Apply them to his feet and legs, *bitte*. I will return in a moment."

While he went in search of the quinine Hannah and I made and wrung out several compresses. Charles was still unconscious, breathing stertorously, and it took both of us to roll him into a more comfortable position and apply the compresses.

"He will not die," Hannah said between tight-pressed lips. "No matter what has happened, he will not die." She got out

269]

her carved bone idol and showed it to me. "Adam, it is all finished. I have got the dog's blood, and the teeth."

"No," I said. "He will not die."

While we were applying the compresses, Captain Budington came to the door. I do not know when I have ever seen a man so shaken. His hands shook, his lip trembled; when he spoke his voice quavered. It was not for fear, certainly. Death was a constant companion in the Arctic, and old Bud had seen his share of it. No, it was rather a great and powerful emotion that seemed to have him in its grasp.

"Does he live?"

"Yes," I said.

He nodded, saying nothing. At that moment Dr. Bessels pushed beside him through the narrow door, bringing the quinine in a small metal box.

"Hannah," he said, "get me a glass of water."

He mixed several of the powders in water, and while Hannah propped up Charles Hall in her arms, managed to get most of the medicine down his throat. "There now," he said. "Let him lie back."

The captain's head lolled drunkenly on the pillow and some of the bitter stuff ran out his mouth. Hannah dabbed it tenderly away with the hem of her pinafore. Dr. Bessels knelt beside him and listened to the sound of his heart.

"Will he live?" I asked.

"I do not know. An attack of this kind can often be fatal. The next twenty-four hours will tell the story. In the meantime, I am going back to my cabin. Have someone with him at all times to renew the compresses. Call me if there is any change."

I nodded, standing aside to let him pass. At the doorway he paused and looked for a moment at Captain Budington. They did not speak to each other, but I felt that something—some unspoken thought—passed between them. Captain Budington blinked, and one hand came up to touch his woolly beard. Then

Dr. Bessels passed out into the companionway. The sailing master's gaze followed him up the ladder and out into the Arctic dark.

All that night Hannah and I crouched beside the narrow berth, listening for any change in the heavy breathing, feeling the pulse with our inexpert fingers. Herron brought us cups of coffee and thick meat sandwiches. "Before God," he said to me in a shaken voice, "he just keeled over, Mr. Burritt! One minute he was strong as an ox, telling Captain Budington just what was to be done, and the next there he was on the floor, senseless!"

"It's all right," I said. "These things just happen, Herron; no need to worry now."

Toward morning the pulse seemed to become firmer and more regular. I was about to call Dr. Bessels when Charles opened his eyes, staring at the lantern. He tried to speak, but his words were thick and incomprehensible. Hannah caught at his hand and held it to her cheek. "There, Adam, do you see? He will be well!"

"Charles!" I said. I dropped on one knee beside him. "Thank God! We were all so worried!"

He tried to speak again, and this time made a better job of it.

"What—what happened to me?"

"You have been ill," I said. "You were suddenly taken ill in the sailing master's cabin last night. You were unconscious for several hours."

He tried to sit up, but Hannah forced him back with soothing words.

"You must be very quiet," I said. "Dr. Bessels believes you had an apoplectic stroke of some sort." I motioned to Hannah to call Dr. Bessels. "How do you feel?"

He frowned. "My arm. There does not seem to be any sensation there. Adam, what is wrong with my arm?"

Indeed, his left arm seemed to be in the grip of some paralysis. He rolled in the berth, trying to move it, but it was like a log, senseless and inert.

"There, now," I said. "Do not fret about it. It will pass in time."

Dr. Bessels came in then. He must have been awake all of the night because he was very pale and spent in appearance, and there were deep circles under his eyes. His hair was uncombed and his usually elegant beard in need of grooming. "Ah," he said. "Feeling better, eh?" He leaned over Charles and took the pulse. "Herron!" he called. "Fix a small dish of chicken broth and some arrowroot, if you please."

"My arm," Mr. Hall said thickly.

Dr. Bessels felt it, pinched it, raised it and let it fall. "It is common with a case of apoplexy."

"Apoplexy?" Charles asked.

"That is my diagnosis."

Mr. Hall said nothing, only looking at his lifeless arm.

"Now," said Dr. Bessels, "we must bleed him." He took a lancet out of a small leather case, and Herron brought him a basin. Mr. Hall was pale and weak, and closed his eyes while Dr. Bessels took a great deal of blood. I closed my eyes, being squeamish about such things. It seemed there was a gallon of blood in the basin, it being a large basin and nearly filled, to my eyes.

"He has fainted," Dr. Bessels announced.

I opened my eyes. Charles was pale as death and his eyes were still closed. I could not see any rise and fall of his chest under the nightshirt. When I rushed forward in alarm, Dr. Bessels restrained me.

"There is no danger," he said. "The loss of the blood will relieve the pressure on the brain and improve his condition." He rolled down his sleeves and told Herron to take away the basin. "As soon as he is recovered, give him a mustard bath. That will also aid the congestion, I think."

Herron came in then with the dish of food and looked from me to Mr. Hall and back again.

"He will recover shortly," said **Dr. Bessels.**

He did not recover shortly. Hannah and Joe and I stayed with him for the rest of that morning, and most of the afternoon. The infernal concertina played on and on, a shrill and unmusical sound to me, and I sent word for the men to be quiet. Charles lay as one dead, face still pale and pulse very weak and unsteady. But toward evening he recovered consciousness. I stood in the doorway, sipping a dish of soup the good Herron had brought me, when I was transfixed by a terrible groan.

"Help me!" Charles moaned. "Someone help me! Adam, where are you? Adam!"

Calling my name, he struggled upright in bed and stared around him, eyes wild and vacant. "Adam? Where are you?"

I dropped on my knees beside him, gently forcing him back. "Charles, I am here. There now, everything is going to be all right!"

"Where am I?" His big frame shuddered, and he seemed to be taken by a chill.

I pulled the coverlet around him. "You are all right. You are in your own berth, here on the *Polaris.* You have been very ill." I showed him the dish of chicken broth and arrowroot, now cold. "Here is some food for you. Can you not eat a little? After a while we will give you a mustard bath Dr. Bessels advised."

A sweat broke out on his forehead, and he closed his eyes, seeming a little more rational. "No, Adam—I cannot eat. I am sick at my stomach, and my throat aches and burns so." His fingers rubbed at his throat. "That coffee, Adam—ah, that coffee! I can still feel it in my gullet—warm and bitter and—"

"Don't talk," I said. "You will make yourself ill."

I was overcome with grief, seeing Charles Hall, formerly so robust and active, stricken low with this deadly illness. And yet—how pleasant it was to be with him again, to hear his voice call my name, to be of assistance to him! These last few weeks since our quarrel had been a bitter and lonely time for me, and I thought for him, too. Now, even under such sorry circumstances, we were at least reunited.

"The coffee!" His voice was weak and quiet, almost contemplative. "Ah, yes, Adam, that is it!"

I said nothing, not knowing what he was driving at.

"Do you remember, Adam?" he asked. "That descending mathematical curve I once told you about?"

"Yes."

"I fear someone has been trying to hurry me down it a little faster than I had calculated on going."

"What do you mean?"

"I mean—" He paused and rubbed his throat again. His eyes were still closed, and the little beads of sweat on his forehead grew larger, and merged, and joined, until they ran off and dampened his pillow. "I suspect I have been poisoned, Adam."

"Poisoned?"

I could not believe I had heard aright. Poisoned? There had been a great deal of unpleasantness aboard, that was true, and Charles had not been popular with many. But—poisoned?

"I am sure of it," he said. His voice was strained, whether from excitement or the pain of his throat I did not know. "Ah, Adam, it is a sorry end I am come to!"

"But Dr. Bessels attended you! He said that you had had a stroke of apoplexy! He has been very attentive, visiting you several times while you were unconscious."

He was very weak, and lay now for a long time, saying nothing.

"You had better try to sleep a little," I said. "Perhaps—"

"Book," he said, having trouble in forming the word. "The —book, Adam! The blue book on the shelf at the head of my bed." He pointed with an unsteady finger. "There. No, not that one! The—the other one. That—book."

It was titled *A Chemical Formulary and Compendium of*

Useful Herbs. I handed it to him but he waved it away. "Can't see—very well." With what seemed the faintest of smiles—a pleased expression—he murmured, "There, that is also part of the clinical picture! Difficulty in focusing the eyes. Ah, they have been so very clever, those people! But I will deceive them!"

I was worried at the turn things were taking. Was he delirious, or did his accusing words mean something? Were these the babblings of an affected mind? Had the apoplectic stroke softened his brain? Or was there a possibility this *was* the symptom of a fatal poison, slyly administered?

"There is an antidote in that book," he said. "I—I—you will have to look for me, Adam. I cannot see."

"But where?" I asked. "What is the poison you suspect? Charles, tell me, so I can do what I need to do!"

His voice failed him, and all he could do was clutch his throat and roll back and forth as in pain, fresh torrents of sweat rolling off his brow. He tried to reach the book; his fumbling hand knocked it from my grasp, so that it fell on the deck in a flutter of pages. Then, with a convulsive groan, he lay quiet.

I put my ear next his chest. He was still breathing. But what must I do? I picked up the blue book and riffled through it. Page after page of chemical formulae, meaning nothing to me. The antidote was there, he had said. But where?

From that moment on I do not think my thoughts were very clear, or my actions wise. Seeing Charles dying before my eyes, suspecting poison, requiring an antidote, I became frantic. Antidote? Chemicals? There was only one source of chemicals on the *Polaris*. As any poison must have come from there, so must the antidote come. I did not know how I would recognize the life-giving substance, but I could not listen to Charles Hall call on me in vain to save his life. I bounded up the ladder three rungs at a time and burst into Dr. Bessels' laboratory.

He was not there, probably being at dinner below. I stared at the chemical cabinet, thinking of the argument there had been over it when first installed. It was locked, as always. Heedless of consequence, driven only by a compelling urge to help poor Charles, I picked up a small iron bar, part of one of Dr. Bessels' scientific devices—a magnetometer, I think. I slipped it into a crack and prized at the door. It bent, cracked, and finally splintered free. There were the chemicals—row after row in neat labeled bottles! I fumbled among them, breathing hard. Latin? Was it the damned Latin they were written in, the Latin I was never good at? I searched feverishly among them, not knowing what I was looking for, hoping that by a miracle one of the handwritten labels would spring out to meet my eye.

I was too busy to see Dr. Bessels come in. One moment I was rummaging among the bottles, searching and praying, and the next he had my wrist in a steel grip and had pulled me around to face him.

"What is going on here? *Ach,* what are you doing?"

I jerked my wrist away and confronted him. "I—I am looking for a certain chemical."

"A certain chemical? What certain chemical?"

I did not know but I blurted out, "Captain Hall has been poisoned, and I am searching for an antidote."

"Poisoned? Who says poisoned?" His eyes glittered with anger, and his small, neatly trimmed beard stuck out furiously. "Such talk, you fool! There has been no poison! The man has had an attack of apoplexy! Who talks of poison?"

"Captain Hall does!" I said. "He believes he has been poisoned! He has told me so. He knows the antidote, but was stricken again before he could tell me. I beg of you, doctor, if you know the antidote—"

Attracted by the commotion, Captain Budington came in, followed by Mr. Chester and Mr. Tyson and several others.

"What is going on here?" the sailing master demanded. "What is this commotion?"

Dr. Bessels pointed a finger at me. "This fool has broken into my chemical stores with a cock-and-bull story about Mr. Hall being poisoned!"

Old Bud looked at me with a steady and unfriendly eye. "Is this true, Adam?"

"Yes," I said, "but—"

"Mr. Hall is out of his mind, talking about a poisoning," Dr. Bessels insisted. "Hall's symptoms are those of apoplexy, where the brain is often affected. Now this troublemaker Burritt has taken him seriously, and comes about accusing people of poisoning Mr. Hall. Captain, this is a serious charge!"

"What have you to say to this?" old Bud demanded.

What could I say? I had no proof of anything—only a sick man's babblings. I had done what I had with only a humanitarian purpose, and now I was being made to look like a lunatic.

"Well," I said, "I—"

I do not know what I was going to say, confronted by those hostile witnesses, because at that moment Joe threw open the door. "Adam? Is Adam here?"

"What is it, Joe?"

"You come quick, Hannah say! Father Hall, he die!"

As a climax to this weird occasion, we all hurried below. Hannah crouched beside Mr. Hall's bed, holding one lifeless hand in hers. No, not yet lifeless. The flicker of life was there, but fast guttering away. Already Charles' full face had a pinched and deathlike cast. His eyes were open, staring vacantly at the overhead. Even the rich chestnut beard, spread out on the nightshirt, seemed to have lost luster, and spread dank and lifeless.

"He is asking for you, Adam," Hannah sobbed.

I bent over, listening. "I am here, Charles."

His voice was so weak I had to strain to hear it, and the words were pronounced with difficulty. "Too—too late, Adam!"

"It is not too late. Hold on, Charles. We will win through, we always have."

"No. Too late." He said nothing for a long time. Then he called, "Adam?"

"I am here—and Captain Budington and the others."

"So—so much to do. And—I failed."

"You did not fail."

"I—perhaps I tried too hard. I—I made enemies. I—I could not see why others did not see things my way, always."

I thought he died then, but he struggled on for a few final words, delivered with great effort, seeming to come from very far away.

"Adam, take my hand."

I did so, and tears dripped from my cheeks onto his waxen face.

"I—I loved you, boy, and I was unfair to you. Can you forgive me?"

"There is nothing to forgive," I said.

"My wife—tell my wife—"

He died then, quickly and mercifully, merely ceasing to breathe. His head fell to one side, and a look of peace came over his troubled features. He died, with the name of his wife on his lips.

"He is gone," I said. I straightened up and looked about me at the tense faces. "That is the end to it. He is dead."

Hannah looked at me as if begging me to deny the fact of his passing. Then, when she realized it was so, she screamed—a shrill terrifying sound—and ran from the cabin, tearing her clothes.

"That is an end to it, whatever happened," I said. "Captain Hall is dead."

Chapter 17

AS we went to the grave that morning, the coffin hauled on a sledge and an American flag for a pall, we walked in procession. I went with my lantern in advance; then came Captain Budington and Dr. Bessels and Meyers, followed by the officers and seamen. After them came several of the crew, hauling the body by a rope attached to the sledge. Several of them also held lanterns, it being almost dark at that time of day, though there was a weird sort of luminosity in the air; partly boreal or electric, I suppose, but the stars shone brightly through it. Nearly all of us were dressed in skins; were there any other eyes to see us, we would not have looked like a funeral cortege, but rather a wandering tribe intent on some rude ceremony.

A party under Mr. Chester had spent the better part of two days in attempting to excavate a tomb in the frozen ground but had not managed to dig it deeper than about two feet, where they reached the permanent frost. It would not have been possible to go deeper without blasting powder. I had carved a headboard for the grave, with the assistance of Joe, which read:

To the memory of
C. F. HALL
Late Commander of the North Polar Expedition
Died 1871
Aged 50 years

The ship's bell tolled in the distance, a sad and mournful sound as we gathered round the grave. The ground was for the most part covered with snow, though a disagreeable wind had scoured some portions clear. The temperature was a few degrees below zero on the Fahrenheit scale, and the whole face of the earth seemed to me bleak and desolate in the last degree.

Mr. Bryan, the astronomer, pulled back the hood of his *koolee-tang* and read the service for the dead. Hannah and Joe stood beside me, and both of them wept, Hannah sobbing uncontrollably. I looked at Captain Budington. In the dim rays of the lantern his face was indistinct. It was only a trick of the light, but his craggy face seemed to me to have lost outline and form, being only a fleshy mask incapable of showing recognizable emotion. Beside him stood Dr. Bessels, saturnine and inscrutable.

After the service was read, the lid of the coffin was removed, and those who desired filed past to take a last look at Captain Hall. Hannah and I had bathed him, dressed him in fresh linen, and Hannah had combed and trimmed his beard and hair. I held my lantern high, and we looked down for the last time on the face of Father Hall, my dear friend and her idol. I had feared that the good woman might collapse completely at this point, but she drew on some inner reserves of strength to restrain herself.

"Good-by," she said simply. "Good-by, dear Father."

She bent over him and kissed him on the cold cheek, and Joe and I assisted her away. Behind us we could hear the scraping of shovels and mattocks as the grave was filled in. The little company separated to return to the ship, each one meditating on the event in his own way. I had my own thoughts, which were bleak enough, but I would not for all the money in the world have exchanged them for the innermost secrets of some of the other members of our expedition. The cold pure stars above looked down on us, I knew, and if there were bloody hands among us, it was known in celestial quarters.

Hannah showed me the bone charm.

"It was not very good. You were right. The Bible is the best, Adam. I was a wicked woman to think otherwise."

"You were not wicked," I said. "You did the best you could. We all did, I think. It was fate perhaps; destiny—whatever you want to call it." I remembered Mr. Grinnell's parting words to me. *No one can beat him but himself.* In the light of what had happened, the words took on new and tragic significance. "No," I said, "I believe there was some higher power at work here, something greater and more powerful than anything you or I might have done."

The time was noon, and we went up the snow steps into the *Polaris,* now without a commander, in my opinion.

During the weeks that followed, the weather was severe, dropping to thirty and forty degrees below the zero mark. In that climate it was all man could do to sustain himself and to maintain the body caloric. The crew were engaged in cleaning decks, keeping the fire hole open, and banking snow around the frozen-in *Polaris.* Hans and Joe, when the weather moderated, hunted for seal and caught some big ones—*Phoca barbata,* Charles once told me they were—which kept us free from the scurvy when our small supply of lime juice ran out.

The atmosphere aboard the vessel was poor. Lights burned all night. In one month more than two thousand pounds of coal were consumed in the berth deck, cabin, galley, and observatory. If the expenditure kept up at this rate, we would be out of coal before the winter was over and have none left for steaming purposes. Dr. Bessels, now that Charles was dead, had embarked on a new and extended scientific program, being anxious, I think, to make a reputation for himself. Captain Budington stayed in his cabin, where Dr. Bessels visited him occasionally to make further plans for the conduct of the expedition. But I had abandoned any hope for real progress. Charles was the mainspring, the guiding genius of the *Polaris* effort. With him taken from us, the whole effort seemed vitiated and without real intent to accomplish anything further than we had already done. Our eighty-two degrees and sixteen minutes must, it seemed, stand as a record, without hope of betterment.

Whether for good or bad I could not say, but the strange death of Charles Hall continued to prey on my mind. I, in common with others, believed it likely he had been poisoned; that someone, and I will not say who, had in desperation done away with him on his return, fearing his determination for more northing would be fatal to us all. I had no proof—nothing more than Charles' dying words. They, of course, might have resulted only from delirium.

I talked to John Herron, the steward, who had served Mr. Hall the coffee. I did not suspect him, he being an honest and obliging sort, but I had to start somewhere.

"That last night," I said, "Mr. Hall went below to have a cup of coffee with the sailing master. Did you prepare the coffee yourself?"

Herron's brow furrowed. "Aye, I did."

"Did anyone else drink of the pot?"

"Captain Budington. I had a cup myself after I carried some in to Mr. Hall and the captain."

"Was anyone else in the galley?"

"People went in and out all the time, like they do."

"You poured the coffee in two cups, did you not? One for Mr. Hall and one for Captain Budington?"

"A tin cup for Mr. Hall, and Captain Budington's old blue china one—the one with the broken handle that he favors."

"How long was it after you poured them that you took them in?"

Herron looked uncomfortable. "Mr. Burritt, are you trying to cause trouble for me?"

"No," I said, "not for you, Herron. But it is possible someone in the galley at the time put something in Mr. Hall's coffee to kill him."

He wiped his hands with a cloth. "I've heard all this talk of poison, some saying it was so and some saying it wasn't."

"If it was not so," I said, "then there is no harm done. If it *was* so, then the guilty person should be found, and punished."

"Well," Herron said, "I'm not saying it means anything, but I let the two cups set for a few minutes while I went and filled up the sugar bowl and put it on the tray."

"Were others in the galley at that time?"

"I guess so," Herron said. "Several passed through to have coffee or a bit of the cake that was baked the day before."

"Do you remember any of them?"

Herron shook his head. "Might have been any of a dozen or more. Mauch was there, I remember. Mr. Meyer, too. Might have been others—I don't know."

It appeared that someone *could* have had the opportunity to put something in the coffee. It would not have been too difficult to wait until Herron's back was turned while he filled the sugar bowl. Everyone knew old Bud's cracked blue coffee cup; the other—the tin one—was obviously for Mr. Hall. Many on deck had heard old Bud invite Charles to come below for coffee. The tray, laid out with two cups, and the steward busy at the sugar bin—it was surely possible.

I did not get much further with my detective work until I heard from Captain Budington. One day he called me to his cabin and showed me a document. "Here," he said. "Read this, Adam."

It was a paper dated November 13th, 1871, written in long-hand:

> First consultation held between Messrs. S. O. Budington and E. Bessels. Through the mournful death of our noble commander, we feel compelled to put into effect the orders given us by the Department, viz.
>
> "Mr. Budington shall, in case of your death or disability, continue as the sailing master and ice master, and control and direct the movements of the vessel; and Dr. Bessels shall, in such case, continue as the chief of the scientific department, directing all sledge journeys and scientific operations. In the possible contingency of their non-concurrence as to the course to be pursued, then Mr. Budington shall assume the sole charge and command, and return with the expedition to the United States with all possible dispatch."
>
> It is our honest intention to honor our dear flag and to hoist her on the most northern part of the earth, to complete the enterprise upon which the eyes of the whole civilized world are raised, and to do all in our power to reach our proposed goal.
>
> S. O. Budington
Emil Bessels

"Well," he asked, "what do ye think of that?"

"Think of it? What should I think of it?"

He folded the paper and pointed it at me. "I show it to ye, Adam, only to indicate that Dr. Bessels and I have every intention to do our best by the memory of poor Hall. Does not this sound as if we have every consideration for his goals, and will do all in our power to reach them? Can this document be written by men whose hands are stained with blood?"

I knew he had heard about my talk with Herron.

"I have not accused you," I said. "I have not accused any man —yet."

He put the folded paper in a breast pocket. "Forget the whole thing, lad; that is my advice to ye! Poor Hall is gone, and no one can be blamed for it. There has been enough trouble,

God knows, and no good can be done by the making of reckless charges." He seemed very distraught. "Adam, I have had a kind of fondness for ye over the years. Take my advice and let this matter drop."

I could not but feel pity for him; old, rheumy, a terrible concern and responsibility hanging over him. But I had a duty to Charles Hall, too.

"Thank you for the advice," I said, "but I must be governed by my own convictions."

About this time another horrible incident happened to unsettle the nerves of everyone on board. At midnight the ship's carpenter cried out in distress. Rushing in, we found him covered by his blankets and crouching in horror in a corner of his bunk, believing he had heard a voice calling to him from the adjacent storeroom, which proved to be closed and locked.

"A voice?" someone asked. "Whose voice?"

"Captain Hall's voice!" the poor fellow wailed.

To pacify him the storeroom was carefully searched, but notwithstanding the proof thus afforded of his having been deceived, the carpenter continued in the belief that Captain Hall had called out to him.

"Murdered, he was!" the carpenter cried. "Cried out he was being murdered, and thrashed about in the storeroom. Oh, can't one of you gentlemen stay with me the night?"

This was the first indication of what afterward proved to be a kind of mental instability on the part of the carpenter, and was apparently traceable to nothing but an unfortunate aberration. But it did its part in unsettling us all and making us uneasy.

On the 28th of February the sun returned after an absence of a hundred and thirty-two days. At 11:55 in the morning a small portion of the upper rime could be seen through a gorge in the surrounding mountains. At 12:15 the whole fiery orb appeared. Cheer after cheer went up from our company; cries of "Oh, how warm it is!" and "He has not forgotten us!" I could not help but think of poor Mr. Hall, now sleeping these many months in his icy bed. How he would have delighted in these first rays of the sun, knowing that they presaged the traveling season! But he was gone now, forever shut away from us, and from the Pole which he sought so. My thoughts of him were constant and unvarying. He had had a greater influence on me in my formative years than I at first thought. I found myself thinking like him, planning like him, keeping a detailed journal as he had, pulling at my beard when puzzled or angry in a way identical to his.

The advent of the sun was fortunate in another way. Most of the *Polaris* crew were not experienced ice hands; during the dark winter months there had been dissatisfaction and grumbling, not to mention a few fights and similar altercations. Mr. Hall's death, the mental instability of the carpenter, the rumors of murder and foul play, the constant living shut away from the sun's rays, all took their toll. Discipline was very poor, and the temper of the men even poorer. For a moment, at least, the return of the sun produced a kind of euphoria, and feuds and unpleasantness were forgotten.

Dr. Bessels and Captain Budington between them laid out a schedule of boat trips to begin a limited exploration as soon as the condition of the ice permitted. The dash to the Pole had, I think, been forgotten, but there remained the necessity for doing something to justify the expedition. As late as June, however, the straits were filled with pack ice. Mr. Chester, taking his crew out around Cape Lupton, had his boat crushed by the moving pack, and with it the box chronometer, the highly valued Casella theodolite, and other instruments. Another attempt, this time by Mr. Tyson, got only as far as the mouth of Newman's Bay before being forced back. It would be, it was plain, a poor season for exploring.

I was not asked to participate in any of these activities. The sailing master and Dr. Bessels ignored me, though I was anxious

[286

to do something—anything—to lay the groundwork for a sledge journey to the Pole. The season wore away with little being accomplished. To make it even less likely that any serious attempt would be made for the Pole, the vessel sprung a serious leak. Even before the close of June it was necessary to keep the pumps going twelve hours out of the twenty-four, and our scanty store of coal was almost exhausted.

At last, late in July, it became apparent that action would have to be taken to preserve the ship. There was left only coal for some six days' steaming—enough to see us to Disko, if all went favorably. After several days' hard work with the ice saws, the *Polaris* slid from the tongue of Providence Berg and was once more afloat.

"It will be a near thing," Mr. Tyson said to me. "All must go well if we are to reach Disko with only a pocketful of coal."

It was true. As for sail, it would be impossible to tack in and around the great bergs that now floated in the channel. We must reach Disko by steam or not at all. Failure would see us frozen in the pack for another winter, drifting God knows where, short on rations and fuel. It was a frightening prospect; when communicated to the crew, it resulted in something very near panic, and it took the best efforts of the officers to keep them at their work.

With great care the *Polaris* was piloted between heavy floes, laboring heavily and buffeted this way and that. From time to time she reached a position which seemed to be hopeless, and it was necessary to tie her up to a floe with ice anchors. Patient waiting usually resulted in a lead opening up, and away we would go again to make good another mile or so before tying up. This work required the greatest skill and judgment, and I could not say too much for the sailing master, Captain Budington, whatever I had thought of him personally. But this method of progress was also wasteful of fuel. At last, on the evening of October 15th, we came to the end of our tether.

I was in my cabin, writing in my journal, when I was thrown

off my stool and down upon the surface of the deck. The *Polaris* raised up, creaking and groaning, on her port side. I ran on deck, slipping and falling because of the angle to which the vessel had been raised. The ship's timbers were cracking with a loud noise, especially around the stern. A storm was blowing up and heavy snow began to fall, but through the drifting flakes I could see that the *Polaris* had been caught between two shifting bergs and was being relentlessly ground as with the jaws of a vise.

One of the firemen ran by me shouting, "She has been holed! Water is coming in the engine room!"

On the hurricane deck I could see Captain Budington, bareheaded, bellowing orders through his speaking trumpet. "Throw our supplies over the side onto the ice! She is holed, and sinking fast! Everyone onto the ice!"

One of the bergs lay immediately on our quarter, offering a flat icy surface some acres in extent, and it was on this that the men in panic began to throw over our supplies. Escape from destruction seemed impossible. The storm rose in violence, the ice ground relentlessly against our hull, timbers creaked and splintered. Mr. Tyson and I, working together, got one of the after hawsers onto an ice anchor on the surface of the berg, but the strain snapped off the cleat. We managed somehow to get the hawser secured temporarily to the mast.

"Onto the ice!" the sailing master shouted. "Everyone! Throw over all the supplies you can lay a hand to! Quick, she's shifting!"

Hannah ran by me, holding Pun-na by the hand, and Joe and I and Mr. Tyson helped them over the side to safety, or what we hoped was safety. Boxes, barrels, and cans were thrown over the side, and men performed feats of strength they did not know they were capable of. The balance of our small store of coal was put over in sacks, along with canned meats and tobacco, musk-ox skins and frozen seal meat. Cabins were emptied; bedding, clothes, even ornaments and souvenirs were thrown onto the surface of the floe. All the time a dusky saffron light prevailed, filtering through the scudding clouds.

I ran to Mr. Hall's cabin, hoping to preserve his papers; his journals, his notes, copies of correspondence and topographical surveys he kept in the brass-bound mahogany chest. It was gone; someone had been there before me. I only hoped that it had been put over the side for safekeeping. As I searched about the cabin a great beam over my head cracked with an ominous sound, and I ran out just as it splintered and dropped.

On deck the two lifeboats had been lowered, and along with a scow, had been placed on the floe. A little group huddled in the middle of the floe in the fast-failing light, surrounded by piles of boxes and sacks and cans. The wind, still strong, was trying to drive the *Polaris* away from the berg which had mortally wounded her. As I watched with horror, the ice anchor which Mr. Tyson and I had planted came free and let the stern of the vessel swing slowly around, away from the floe. I ran to the vessel's head and went over the side, sliding down the hawser which still held.

I was the last off the stricken vessel. With a report like an artillery piece the hawser parted, letting the vessel swing away from the floe. All were not off; in the gloom I could see heads lining the rail, and men shouted in fear and desperation. In a moment, free from any restraint and listing markedly, the *Polaris* was driven away into the darkness by the gale.

John Herron, the steward, was one of those who managed to reach the safety of the floe. I could hear him calling, his voice thin and strained against the howling of the wind. "Good-by, *Polaris!* Good-by!"

That night the gale roared down on us from the northeast, draining the warmth from our bodies and shrieking with the voices of banshees. In that storm it was impossible to do more than huddle together for warmth, waiting for daylight and hoping the storm would abate. The night seemed never to end. Mr.

Tyson occasionally looked at his watch by the light of a match, and I would have sworn each five minutes to have been a half hour's duration. But at last daylight came, enough weak and watery light for us to take stock of our party and provisions. Of the *Polaris*, nothing could be seen.

"We had better count noses first of all," I said, "and then make a tally of our provisions."

There were, the count revealed, twenty of us on the floe: Mr. Tyson, Mr. Meyer, John Herron, William Jackson, the seamen Kruger, Jamka, Nindemann, Aunting, Lindquist and Johnson, and the Esquimaux Joe, Hannah, Pun-na, Hans, Hans' wife, Tobias, Augustina, Succi, Hans' baby boy Charles, and myself. Our whole provision, when collected, proved to be fourteen cans of pemmican, twelve bags of bread, eleven dozen cans of meat and soups, one can of dried apples, fourteen hams, and a small bag of chocolate. Moreover, there were providentially the two lifeboats of the *Polaris*, the scow, two native *ki-as,* a canvas A-tent, and some instruments of navigation, which included a boat compass and a chronometer. With these we must make do.

I searched the floe for Captain Hall's mahogany writing box, finally finding it, broken open, on a far corner of the floe. But there were no more than one or two scraps of paper in it. His records had been removed, I felt, since nowhere else on the floe was there any piece of paper, as there would have been if the box had been broken open by the fall.

"I don't understand this," I said to Tyson, taking the can of improvised stew he handed me. "All Captain Hall's papers are missing. The box is in good condition, though the lid is broken open."

He had made a stove from a pemmican can with a canvas wick, and huddled over it, boiling coffee. Around him, in the lee of the boxes and sacks, over which we had drawn the canvas of the A-tent for shelter, the rest of our party ate their stew and ship's bread, scraping the empty cans that served as dishes and licking their fingers.

"I do not pretend to understand it," Tyson said. "We have too many other pressing problems to solve."

One of the first requirements was shelter. Due to the lateness of the season, daylight was very short. I do not know exactly how it happened, but I seemed to be chosen by common consent a kind of major-domo. I told off work parties; one to fetch the boats and arrange them in a quadrangle, another to stack up the boxes of provisions, Hans and Joe to take the *ki-as* and hunt for a seal or two, Hannah and Hans' wife to take care of the children, dry clothing over the improvised lamp, and prepare an evening meal. I showed the seamen how to use a snow knife to make an igloo, and in creditable time they had three of them built, which in addition to our shelter of boxes and the canvas tent should house us well.

"This floe," said Tyson, "is tolerably large and thick."

Neither of us said exactly what was in our minds. We were encamped on a floating block of ice which was drifting southward. No one knew how long it would hold together, or when it might start to crack and divide in the warmer waters to the south.

For supper we had stew again, made from canned meat and bread mixed with water and warmed over the lamp. It was apparent we must husband our rations closely, and I made a scale to weigh out the allowances. In one box I found a three-cornered scale and a broken aneroid lever balance. I attached to the ends of the scale two small cardboard boxes for pans and made up weights of shot which Hannah sewed into chamois skin. In this way we were able to measure out six ounces of bread, eight of canned meat, and two of ham for each ration, with one-half as much for the children.

The next day we saw the *Polaris* again! Having thought her sinking when she had been driven away from us, there was great joy and excitement on the floe. She was rounding a point some eight or ten miles distant from us, under steam and sail, and apparently in good condition. We screamed, we shouted (knowing this would do no good, but anxious to release our emotions); I had the men show a dark square of India-rubber cloth, flapping it like a banner, and we burned oil in a pan to give a high, dense plume of smoke. But all our efforts went for naught.

"She cannot help but see our signals!" Mr. Tyson protested.

"I would think so," I said gloomily.

"It is almost as if they were ignoring us!"

When in such straits, strange thoughts enter the heads of men. Thinking of Captain Budington's warning to me, I could not restrain myself from thinking that it might be convenient to him and others to abandon me here on this floe. But this could hardly be. I was only one of many, and the others included Tyson and Mr. Meyer and John Herron, the Esquimaux and little Pun-na, of whom the sailing master had been fond.

"No," I said. "This cannot be. Whatever else has happened, no heart can be so black."

On a tack away from us, she was soon gone in the pack, and that was an end to it. We settled down to an unhappy supper.

Day after day our floe drifted southward. Mr. Tyson, with his navigational instruments, made rough calculations of our position. Beyond knowing we were somewhere below Wolstenholme Sound, there could be little accuracy to our reckoning. Sometime during December the weather cleared a little, and we could see that our floe was now entirely surrounded by water. We were sailors on a great icy ship, sailing south through the middle of Davis Strait.

Christmas on an ice floe! Well, we were in tolerably good health and spirits, at least. We celebrated the festival by an extra meal, carefully weighed out on my improvised scales. Hans and Joe had caught an unwise seal who had stuck his head over the side of our floe, and we had a soup made of seal's blood, sausage meat, ham, and two ounces of bread apiece. For the occasion we opened the can of apples, and Herron told me it was the sweetest meal he had ever eaten. It was also, I told our party, the last of such magnitude until we should be rescued, because our rations were fast disappearing. Before long we should have to depend on what dovekies, seal, and walrus our Esquimaux hunters should manage to catch.

I found myself thinking often of Charles; what he would have done under our circumstances, how he would have handled this situation, and that. I spoke of him often to Tyson, who was sympathetic.

"Yes," he agreed. "He was a great man. Too much of a driver, perhaps, and not enough of a leader. But I respected him."

"When we get back," I said, "there are many things that must be explained."

He gave me a curious look and sucked for a long time on his pipe. "Aye," he said. "If we get back."

"I did not say if. I said when."

He knocked out the dottle from his pipe. All else were asleep, and over our head winked the Arctic stars, large and bright as gas lamps. The wind had died, and it was not uncomfortable, crouched in the lee of the overturned whaleboat.

"Do you know, Adam," he said, "there is a great deal of Charles Hall in you."

"I am happy if there is."

"And I, too. Perhaps we would not be thus far, still preserved, if Adam Burritt had not been with us."

On the last day of January our rations gave out completely, and we were forced to depend on dovekies which Joe and Hans shot. They were small, gentle birds, and a shotgun would bring down a cloud of them onto the floe, but it took twenty to thirty to make a mess for us. Added to our woes was the weather, for it turned bitterly cold again, dropping to thirty and forty degrees below zero on the Fahrenheit scale. Too, there were unmistakable signs of the scurvy: weakness, swelling of the limbs, a kind of dropsical condition.

"We must have help soon," Tyson said. "Once the scurvy starts, it will spread like wildfire."

Hunting was very poor and we had only a few ounces of seal meat each day. One day, I remember, I dined on two feet of seal intestine and found it tasty, though the amount left much to be desired. There was also, unfortunately, stealing going on. It became necessary to set a guard over the few bits of frozen seal meat left from a meal, in order to ensure that any would be left for the next. I sat up the first night myself, with a loaded shotgun across my knees.

"For you may know," I told them all, "that stealing is against the common good, and must be reckoned with. I will shoot the first man I catch stealing. It is harsh, I know, but we will win through. Trust me to see to that."

They grumbled, but the stealing stopped. The scurvy grew worse, however. Little Pun-na cried all night from hunger. The Esquimaux were not so affected by the scurvy, but they became very weak from the meager diet and were not able to hunt. Several of the seamen developed grotesquely swollen hands and feet, and their faces were puffy and too large for the rest of them.

We could see the west coast of Davis Strait now, some eight or ten miles away, and it was thought that we should make an attempt to reach it. But we had burned one of our boats and the scow for firewood, and it was doubtful if the one remaining boat would hold all twenty of us. In addition, in our weakened condition we were all poor seamen; were we to swamp, that would be the end of it. "No," I told them. "Our only chance is to stay on the floe as long as possible and hope to see a steamer. We are now, according to Mr. Tyson, at about 64 degrees north, and with luck should hail a sealer or whaler before long."

In spite of my feelings, it was soon necessary to abandon the floe. By the first of April, it had wasted to such an extent that it was no longer safe. At eight in the morning, we were forced to take to the boat, all twenty of us in that frail cockleshell. There was so little room it was difficult to handle the oars and yoke ropes. So deep did the laden boat sink that it was necessary to throw overboard almost a hundred pounds of seal meat we had laid by, and nearly all our clothing.

I called everyone together and said a short prayer. Then we embarked in the near-foundering boat. A gale blew from the eastward and a fearful sea was running. The boat was fast shipping water, but we bailed and prayed, and kept under way until almost two in the afternoon. After several narrow escapes we found another floe large enough to land on. When we dragged the boat onto the ice, we found that a hole had been punched in her below the water line, which was repaired with a piece of sealskin.

We stayed on our new ice-floe home for almost a week. Joe and Hans managed to catch a large polar bear, though it took most of our scanty store of ammunition to finally kill the enraged animal. I warned them all against eating the liver and counseled moderation in consuming the flesh. But such is the power of hunger that they ate the entire beast. Most of them were sick for a week, and some lost the skin of their faces, hands and chests. So crazy were the appetites of the men that they burrowed in the still-smoking body of the great white animal, digging with their hands at the vital organs, so that they were smeared and sticky with the blood.

After that, hunting became very meager. Our small floe began to break up still further, and it looked as if it would be necessary to take to the boat again.

"Well," said Tyson, "this is the end, I think."

"The end?"

"Food nearly gone, no ammunition, scurvy—" He rubbed at his cheeks, and I was distraught to see that his face was swollen also; not a great deal, but unmistakable. "We have fought a good fight, but there comes an end to everything."

"No," I said. "This is not the end. It cannot be."

That night the weather was calm and clear, for a change, and the sea smooth. In spite of weak protests that the small amount of seal blubber left should be portioned out with the scales, I took it aside and put it into two equal piles. When morning came, I set the piles on fire to serve as beacons, and told off two watches, of four hours each, to watch for relief. That done, I bowed my head and prayed. There was nothing left to do.

At daylight, a steamer was seen some eight miles off. The floating camp came alive with shouts and cheers. I had been asleep, and I jumped to my feet, fearing the dwindling floe had split. But we were rescued! We hoisted the colors, mounted the highest point of the floe, fired the last of our ammunition, yelled and screamed. Then, glory to God, the steamer fired three shots! She changed her course and headed for the floe. She was the barkentine *Tigress,* mastered by Captain Bartlett, of Conception Bay, Newfoundland.

The sure hand of God had saved us all—all twenty—after six and one-half months of drifting on an ice floe. Later, after we had been warmed and fed and recovered our wits, Captain Bartlett came below to talk to me.

"We saw your smoke," he said. "It was a narrow thing, Mr. Burritt. We had just changed course to drive south a ways when the masthead reported it." He rubbed his chin and looked at me. "I see you have now recovered your wits."

I sipped on a scalding cup of coffee, my feet wrapped in a blanket. "I did not know I had lost them."

He smiled. "You were talking to someone named Charles. That is all you would say. 'Charles this' and 'Charles that.' For the most part, 'Charles, we have won through!' "

"Yes," I said, "it was his doing. His—and the Lord's."

Chapter 18

ON our arrival at St. Johns the United States consul met us, and immediately sent a telegram to the Secretary of State, advising that we of the floe party were well and asking for instructions. Of those on board the *Polaris* there was no word; they were presumed to be lost. On the 15th of May the steamer *Frolic* was dispatched to St. Johns, arriving on the 27th to take aboard members of the floe party. Hans Hendrick and his little family, along with Hannah and Joe and Pun-na, elected to remain in St. Johns, hoping to get passage back to their homeland.

"For," as Hannah said simply, "that is where we belong, Adam. I lost little Tuk-e in a great city whose name I do not even remember. There is only unhappiness in those great places. Joe and I—we go back home, with our new daughter Pun-na. We live a long time there, and be happy."

"I hope you will be very happy," I said. "And I am sure that is what Father Hall would want you to do."

Her eyes brimmed with tears and she threw her arms about me. "Oh, Adam, to lose Father Hall—and now, you!"

Joe wiped at his eyes, and little Pun-na started to weep.

"Come now," I said. "This will never do." I pointed to the sky. "Father Hall is up there, watching us all, seeing what we do. He would not like us to be unhappy. No, we say good-by—that is all. We will miss each other—and him—very much, but someday we will all be together in the Lord's house, and have a very good time."

I hurried up the gangplank of the *Frolic*, unable to trust my own composure. To leave these good people, these stout friends, after all we had been through, was a great shock to my emotions.

"Good-by!" I called, waving at them as the *Frolic's* screws churned. "Good-by, Hannah! Good-by, Joe! Good-by, Pun-na!"

The last I saw of them were the three lonely figures on the end of the dock, coming out as far as they could. Hannah, starched and neat in her pinafore, Joe, hands in pockets and head downcast, little Pun-na still crying.

On the 5th of June we arrived at the Washington Navy Yard, which we had left with great hopes two years before.

"It looks much the same to me," Mr. Tyson said, leaning over the rail as we glided up the broad reaches of the Potomac.

"No," I said, "it does not look the same. Charles Hall is dead, and to me the landscape has changed. Nothing will ever be quite the same again."

Almost immediately after our arrival we were called before a hastily convened Board of Inquiry summoned by the Secretary of the Navy, Mr. Robeson. In addition to himself, the Board included Commodore Reynolds, senior officer of the Navy Department, Professor Baird of the National Academy, and Captain H. W. Howgate of the Army Signal Service.

One by one we were called to answer questions. Already

there had been reports of dissension and trouble among the personnel of the expedition, and the Board was anxious to secure individual accounts so they might be compared against each other, and the truth ascertained.

It was a steamy June afternoon, of the type in which Washington abounds. Walking to the Navy Department from Thibeault's (where I was staying at government expense) my clean starched shirt was soon sodden. The air taken into the lungs was so laden with moisture there seemed scarcely room for the life-giving oxygen man needs. Outside the door, a sailor in uniform motioned me to take a seat. The Board was still interrogating Mr. Tyson.

After a long wait, Tyson came out.

"How did it go?" I asked.

He shrugged. "I told them all I knew."

I didn't know quite how to put it, but I asked, "Did—did you go into the dissension aboard? The trouble between Mr. Hall and Dr. Bessels, and between Charles and Captain Budington?"

He seemed troubled. "I did not say a great deal, no. What is done is done. Adam, do you think there is any great advantage to raking over this sorry business?"

"I do," I said. "I do, indeed! I owe it to Charles Hall to see he is avenged."

"There has never been any proof of anything, you know."

"But perhaps proof can be adduced."

"Perhaps so." He sighed. "At any rate, it appears to the Board, from some of the testimony given, that there is a chance some of those on the *Polaris* survived. They are dispatching the *Juniata* at once, under Commander Braine, to look for her."

"Excellent!" I cried. "Then the culprits may be brought to justice."

Seeming sad and puzzled, he shook his head. "What is justice? I have seen so many things happen, seen men do this and

that under pressure of circumstance, seen honest error in judgment and devious ways also—I do not know, in this circumstance, what *is* justice, Adam."

"No man need fear justice," I said. "If no wrong has been
done, then it is only justice to bring out that fact. If wrong *has*
been done, then—"

"I am afraid you will have it no other way," Tyson said, shaking his head.

The sailor was motioning, and I opened the door and went
in.

"Good luck," Tyson called.

The Board was very kind. Motioning me to a comfortable
chair near the window, Secretary Robeson said, "You are nearly
the last of the witnesses to be called, Mr. Burritt. We are sorry
to keep you in Washington during this unseasonable weather,
but a full report must be made on the unfortunate *Polaris* expedition."

"I am happy to oblige," I said.

At first they asked many routine questions. Secretary Robeson acted as moderator, and left most of the questioning to
Professor Baird, Commodore Reynolds, and Captain Howgate.
I volunteered nothing, contenting myself with answering their
questions, waiting till I should see how the land lay. But it was
soon apparent they had surmised, or somehow learned, a
great deal about the situation aboard the *Polaris.*

"There is," said Commodore Reynolds, "some report of trouble between Captain Hall and the Scientific Department
aboard the vessel, Mr. Burritt. Can you give me your version of
it, if it was known to you?"

"It was known to all on board," I said. "Dr. Bessels did not
think Captain Hall fit for command of the expedition. He
stated in my presence that if he—that is to say, Dr. Bessels—
had been in charge, the expedition would have been in much
better hands."

I told them of Dr. Bessels bringing liquor aboard in strict

contradiction of Captain Hall's orders. I told them of the mysterious theft of part of the manuscript of Captain Hall's book, and that it was subsequently restored. I told them how Captain Hall was so worried about the theft that he left the manuscript for safekeeping with the Danish governor at Holsteinsborg. I told them also what was to me even more significant—that on the ice floe, after the separation, we found Captain Hall's mahogany writing box, burst open, with only one or two sheets of unimportant paper in it.

"He kept voluminous personal papers," I said, "including a journal in which, during his life, he never missed making some kind of daily entry. I am sure his personal journal, could it be found, would do much to confirm the things I tell you."

"Mr. Meyer," said Secretary Robeson, "testified that all Captain Hall's personal papers were put over the side onto the ice floe."

"Many things were put over the side," I said, "including several boxes of scientific notebooks, daily chronometer comparisons, magnetometer readings, and meteorological data. It was thought at the time of the ship's breaking up that the floe was the safest place for them. Captain Hall's mahogany box was one of those items. But, as I have said, it was empty when found. It is my opinion that someone, believing those personal papers to contain damaging evidence, broke open the chest, removed the papers, and threw the empty box over the side."

Commodore Reynolds cleared his throat. "Could not the wind have blown the items about the floe, so that they were lost?"

"Mr. Tyson and I searched the floe, thinking this might be the case. But they were not there; a long-continued search failed to reveal their whereabouts."

"We have heard also," Captain Howgate interjected, "of friction between Mr. Hall and Captain Budington, the sailing master."

"There was frequent disagreement between them. Captain

Budington liked his dram, and Captain Hall had forbidden liquor on the ship. I witnessed a quarrel between them when Captain Hall destroyed a quantity of gin which belonged to Captain Budington. At that time the sailing master threatened Captain Hall. Later, as I have said, Dr. Bessels brought liquor aboard at St. Johns, and there was frequent drinking among the crew in spite of Mr. Hall's best efforts to the contrary."

"Did you ever see Captain Budington under the influence of liquor?"

I tried hard to be fair. "I knew Captain Budington from our first voyage on the old *George Henry,* in 1861, ten or more years ago. At that time he was a yare skipper, as they say—a capable and trustworthy man. When I saw him again at the Navy Yard, just before we sailed in the *Polaris,* I was struck by his dissolution. He had, in my eyes, developed a taste for the bottle which weakened him and changed his constitution."

Captain Howgate was still not satisfied.

"But have you ever seen him under the influence of alcohol?"

I bit my lip. "It is hard to say. On several occasions he had been drinking. On several occasions he seemed to me to be unsure of himself, and to vacillate. I believe, in company with several others, including Mr. Tyson, that the sailing master was overly fearful in refusing to take the *Polaris* farther north than the eighty-two degrees and some minutes we reached. But whether this was the direct result of alcohol, or merely a weakening of character brought on by age and intemperance, I would not wish to say."

Secretary Robeson searched among some papers on his desk. Finding a particular one, he scanned it briefly.

"Captain Hall, according to reports, died of an apoplexy. You, Mr. Burritt, are not a medical man and cannot give us a capable medical opinion. But several others who testified stated there were rumors, at least, of foul play. I will warn you now, sir, that this is a very serious matter. The failure of the expedition is bad enough, though perhaps unavoidable in view of the

leader's death. But we are anxious to get at the bottom of these
rumors that Captain Hall was poisoned. What can you tell us,
sir, of this unfortunate event?"

I took a deep breath and then blurted out, "It is my opinion,
Mr. Secretary, that Captain Hall *was* poisoned, and so met
his death!"

This occasioned some excitement. The Secretary was very
perturbed, and Captain Howgate started to drum his fingers
on the table.

"No one, so far," said the Secretary, "has been willing to be
so forthright."

"I see no reason to be otherwise."

"What evidence have you to this effect?"

"No direct evidence," I said, but went on to tell them of the
quarrel that ensued when Charles had returned to the ship
after his sledge journey. "He was very excited and pleased. He
had discovered that Dr. Hayes and Dr. Kane, who had been
in Smith Sound in previous years, had not seen the Arctic Sea,
as they had thought, but only a further extension of Smith
Sound. Captain Hall had himself pushed through that extension of the Sound by sledge, almost to the actual Arctic Sea
itself, and according to his opinion it was feasible to drive the
Polaris even higher in latitude. But he met with dissension.
Captain Budington refused to take the vessel farther north at
that season."

"Would it have been wise to attempt more northing?" Commodore Reynolds asked.

"I think so. Others agreed with me. Charles Hall believed it
would be safe, and I trusted him."

"But was it not Captain Budington who was charged with
the safety of the vessel?"

"Safety in the Arctic is a relative word, sir. It is not safe
even to *be* in Smith Sound at that season."

"How was this quarrel resolved?"

"Captain Hall," I said, "went below at Captain Budington's

request to discuss the matter out of earshot of the crew, who were all listening to the argument and betting among themselves as to the outcome. I remained on deck with Mr. Tyson. A few minutes later, John Herron, the steward, called me to come below—that Captain Hall had been taken ill. I rushed below, and found him unconscious."

"What were the symptoms?"

"He had drunk a cup of coffee. Immediately afterward he complained of a burning in his throat, and he started to retch. He quickly became unconscious, and we carried him to his cabin. Dr. Bessels was called on to attend him, and delivered his opinion that Captain Hall had sustained an apoplectic seizure."

"What medication was prescribed?" Professor Baird asked.

"Quinine, and cold compresses. Later, a bleeding."

"Nothing unsound about that, from a medical viewpoint."

"Perhaps not, if it actually was an apoplexy."

"What do you mean?"

I told them how, when recovering consciousness, Charles insisted he had been poisoned. I told them how he had insisted on my looking up an antidote in the *Chemical Formulary and Compendium of Useful Herbs,* and how I had rushed to Dr. Bessels' laboratory for the antidote to save his life. I told them of the quarrel that ensued, terminated by poor Charles Hall's death.

They were all very shocked and took a grave view of the situation. "But surely," said Secretary Robeson, "you must take into account Captain Hall's mental state—his delirium, his sickness! Is it not possible that he was merely out of his mind, imagining a persecution?"

"It is surely possible," I agreed. "But I would not be doing my duty to this Board, and to the late Captain Hall, were I not to describe all the circumstances surrounding his death. I will only repeat that he was in the best of health on his return from his sledge journey, that he had a violent quarrel with two

men who disliked him intensely, and that he died soon afterward, having taken only a cup of coffee. Further, he himself
believed he had been poisoned. At the moment he told me his
suspicion, he seemed rational and clearheaded, although in
some pain. As a background to all this, you must remember the
troubles with discipline, the liquor business, the fear of many
of the officers and crew about going any farther north, and the
mysterious disappearance of Captain Hall's personal papers
after his death."

Secretary Robeson shook his head. "I do not know what to
say. Many of these statements, it is true, have been borne out
to some effect by other testimony. But the fate of Captain Budington and Dr. Bessels and the rest of the poor souls lost on the
Polaris remains to be determined. We can hardly make a rational approach to this situation in the absence of the chief
witnesses—men against whom, Mr. Burritt, you bring serious
charges."

I was too wily to be thus trapped. "I do not bring any
charges," I said. "I give it as my opinion, or feeling, that murder may have been done. All else is fact—the quarrels, the
liquor, the dissension, the threats. I believe it is up to this
Board to bring charges, if charges are warranted."

The Secretary bit the nib of his pen. "Perhaps you are right.
At any rate, there is nothing more to be accomplished for the
moment. If the cruise of the *Juniata* is successful, we may be
able to shed more light on this dreadful affair. In the meantime, Mr. Burritt, thank you for your co-operation, and your
recollections of how things were aboard the *Polaris*."

I bowed and turned to go, but at the door the Secretary called
to me.

"What are your plans now?"

"I have a father in Cincinnati whom I have not seen in many
years. I intend to go back there and visit. After that—I do not
know."

"Have you an address where you can be reached in case further testimony is necessary?"

I gave him my father's address.

"One more thing. I would be remiss, Mr. Burritt, if I did not take the opportunity to thank you, in the name of our Government, for your heroic performance of duty while on the ice floe, after having been separated from the *Polaris*. On one point there is complete agreement. If it had not been for Adam Burritt, there would probably have been no survivors of the *Polaris* tragedy."

"Hear, hear!" said Commodore Reynolds, and Captain Howgate and Professor Baird both smiled at me and nodded.

I went home to Cincinnati.

Home? Can any place be called home where there is no kin, no blood of one's blood, no family ties? My father had died almost a year before. The shop had been sold; all that remained to me was a small sum of money realized from the sale of his effects. An attorney counted out one hundred and thirty-eight dollars, and I signed a receipt.

"Where to now, Mr. Burritt?" Lawyer Prentice asked. "Cincinnati must seem dull after your adventures in the Arctic." He had read about our rescue in the newspapers, and also the account of our questioning by the Naval Board of Inquiry (in which there had been no mention of the troubles aboard the *Polaris* I had told them of).

"I don't know," I said. "I have had, at least for the moment, enough of the Arctic. It has cost me my best friend and ten years of my life, with this—" I looked at the money in my hand. "With this as my sole fortune."

"Things are booming here," Prentice said. "Cincinnati is by way of becoming the machinery capital of the world. Did you not once work for a while at a foundry on Commercial Street?"

"I did."

He opened a newspaper and showed me an advertisement. "They are looking for foundrymen again. I advise you to try for a situation there, if you are looking for work."

I did so, and had no trouble being taken on. Wages had gone up; I made twelve dollars a week now, instead of the eight previously, but prices were high also. They were so high, in fact, that I seldom had the price of a newspaper. It was only through Lawyer Prentice that I learned of the recovery of the rest of the *Polaris* crew: Captain Budington, Dr. Bessels, Mr. Chester, and the rest. On the 23rd of June the *Ravenscraig* of Kirkcaldy, Scotland, picked up two boats filled with survivors in latitude 75° 38' north and longitude 65° 35' west, about in the middle of Baffin Bay. They had, according to newspaper accounts, managed to keep the old *Polaris* afloat after abandoning us, though water was pouring in so rapidly they feared the fires would be put out before steam could be raised to work the pumps. By throwing into the fire every combustible material, including seal blubber, the engineers finally got the pumps going.

They had, they reported, never seen those of the floe party again, in spite of maintaining a frequent masthead lookout. A few days later, however, they managed to beach the damaged vessel, not far from Littleton Island. Breaking up the wrecked *Polaris*, they obtained materials to build a hut and also two boats, since the others had been thrown over the side onto the floe. On the 3rd of June, 1873 (only two days before I had testified at the Naval Board of Inquiry), Captain Budington and the others started a voyage southward in the manufactured boats, hoping to reach one of the Danish settlements of Greenland. They were shortly thereafter picked up by the *Ravenscraig*, but it was not until the month of October that enough of the survivors could be got together in Washington for another session of the Board of Inquiry. Some had been landed in Dundee by the *Ravenscraig*, some (because of crowding) had been transferred to other whalers with different home ports. Because the whalers had not finished their catch, a few of the survivors were forced to wait out the summer while the cruise was finished.

"Well!" Lawyer Prentice said, "it must be a considerable satisfaction that your shipmates are safe and sound, Mr. Burritt. Quite a record! In view of all the catastrophes encountered, not a man lost!"

"Saving," I said, "Captain Hall."

"Yes, of course. A remarkable man. One of Cincinnati's greatest sons."

He had not once been thought so. Now that he was dead, he was an historic figure.

On the 11th of October I returned to Washington at government expense to undergo further questioning by the Board of Inquiry. Although all fourteen of the *Polaris* survivors were not at that time available, Captain Budington was there, along with Mr. Chester, Mr. Morton, Dr. Bessels, Mr. Schumann the engineer, and Odell, his assistant.

Almost a year from that fateful day when the *Polaris* was wrecked and our crew split asunder, I met old Bud and Dr. Bessels again, in the hearing room at the Navy Department. I was kept waiting, and was in a sweat for some time. The uniformed sailor told me the Board was in session, and was now questioning the sailing master and Dr. Bessels.

I looked out the window. Autumn had come, and almost gone. The city looked sere and gray. Even though it was only a few days into October a light snow drifted down, through which wheels of passing carriages and dray wagons cut black traceries. The sailor put another chunk of coal on the stove and said, "They've been busy in there most of the day. Shouldn't be too much longer."

"Have they been talking to Dr. Bessels and Captain Budington all that time?"

"Yes." He clanged shut the door of the stove. "Too hot for you in here? You're sweating for fair."

"It is from nervousness," I told him.

In a conversational tone he went on. "Had a lot of shoulder straps and gold braid in there this morning. Surgeon-General of the Army, and Chief Surgeon Beale of the Navy."

"Are they still there?"

"No. Said their piece, whatever 'twas, and left."

Then the Board would have had medical commentary on Charles Hall's death. I wondered whether they had been satisfied, or (as in my mind) grave doubts were retained.

I was called in and told to take a chair. At the far end of the table were Captain Budington and Dr. Bessels, and between them and me Secretary Robeson, Commodore Reynolds, Professor Baird, and Captain Howgate, as previously. Captain Budington looked troubled as he gazed at me, but managed a nod. He looked old—incredibly old and worn—and had developed a slight nervous tic which consisted in blinking one eye rapidly and often. Dr. Bessels was neat and elegant as always, with an air of self-assurance which boded ill. He only stared at me briefly and then looked away.

"Mr. Burritt," said Secretary Robeson, "the Board has examined Captain Budington and Dr. Bessels, has interrogated them at length, and has called in expert medical witnesses to corroborate their testimony. I do not mind telling you that although there was bad feeling and perhaps some mismanagement aboard the *Polaris*, there has been adduced no evidence of foul play. Captain Hall, it appears, was a demanding taskmaster, and made many enemies. All the witnesses have attested to this. But we are satisfied that he died a natural death, and was well attended in his last hours. The Surgeon-General of the Army has confirmed Dr. Bessels' diagnosis, and treatment. Had it not been for the quantity of red wine which he took, contrary to Bessels' orders, Captain Hall might be alive today."

I was dumfounded. "Red wine?" I sprang to my feet. "He had no red wine! Dr. Bessels, is this your contention?"

Secretary Robeson banged his gavel for order.

"That is what I testified," Dr. Bessels said. "In view of the severe congestion of the brain, it was undoubtedly fatal. The wine heated the blood, and in such an excessive quantity, its effect—"

"But he had no wine to drink! I was with him, except for short periods, all the time! It is true Dr. Bessels did prescribe a small quantity of chicken broth and arrowroot, but Charles was too ill to eat even that."

Dr. Bessels only smiled and polished his eyeglasses. "Do you call me a liar, Burritt?"

"I do!"

He half-rose from his chair, face red, but old Bud pulled him back. Then Dr. Bessels turned to the sailing master. "I put the question to you, Captain. Did I not state the truth concerning the red wine?"

Old Bud's nervous tic returned. Looking down into the crown of his flat-brimmed hat which he carried in his lap, he said, "I have heard that this was so, though I did not myself see him drink the stuff. But Hall was a strong-willed man, very independent, and I believe he would have done so if only to aggravate Dr. Bessels, whom he did not like."

"But Captain Hall would not have liquor aboard! The prohibition of spirits was his chief quarrel with Captain Budington!" What kind of a cock-and-bull story were they telling, and for what purpose? A cover-up for the sinister plot I suspected? "Mr. Robeson," I said, "I must protest. The whole truth is not being told here."

Again Secretary Robeson was forced to gavel the session into order. If he had not, Dr. Bessels and I would have been at each other's throats. Everyone was talking at once.

"Sit down!" the Secretary implored. "Both of you! Let us have clear heads and civil tongues, if you please, gentlemen."

When we had subsided, the Secretary took up a sheaf of papers and selected one from the stack. "The matter of the red wine can be only hearsay to this Board, and I see no way to reconcile the conflicting accounts. I think we had better go on to another matter. Mr. Burritt," he went on in a not unkind voice, "your concern for your late captain does you credit, I am sure. But controversy often swirls about great figures, and it is often difficult to arrive at truth. I wonder if your regard and concern for him has not possibly closed your eyes to certain shortcomings in his character—some of the human weaknesses we all have."

"What do you mean?"

"From all reports, he was very impatient in his methods, and disinclined to take advice."

"That is true," I said. "Were it not for that, he would never have accomplished what he did. In the face of public apathy and indifference, he forged ahead. I do not consider it a shortcoming; I think it was magnificent!"

"I have information here concerning the killing of one Patrick Coleman, when Captain Hall was on his journey to King William Land. This informant, who has taken the trouble to write to the Board, hints that the act was murder."

"Murder?" I almost shouted the word. "Who, sir, was your informant?"

He hesitated a moment; then said, "He signs his name William Hobart."

Hobey! The porcine man; one of the mutinous whalers whom Mr. Hall had hired to accompany him to King William Land! William Hobart.

"He writes to claim from Captain Hall's estate a sum of money he says is due him and his shipmates for their services. Not only that; he claims that Captain Hall, unprovoked, shot and killed Patrick Coleman on that journey."

"It was mutiny, pure and simple! Hobart and Parkes and Nellis and the rest refused to go any farther, though to stop then would have meant death for us all. Hobey—Hobart— himself was the one who drew a gun and threatened us, at Coleman's command!"

Dr. Bessels smiled, and old Bud only shook his head, looking silently into his hat as if there to discover truth.

"I am pained to bring up these things," Secretary Robeson said. "I mention them only to show what a very different picture can be seen through other eyes." He took up another paper. "Is it not true, also, Mr. Burritt, that Captain Hall, during your acquaintance of him, was often ill with a thickening of the blood?"

I remembered the two pounds of raw beef daily that had once been prescribed for him. "At times," I admitted. "The sickness was not severe, however, and aboard the *Polaris* it did not plague him. I have never seen a man more vital and filled with the juices of life. I do not believe that this had anything to do with his death."

"It was a forerunner of the later congestion of the brain!" Dr. Bessels insisted. Once more he was composed and elegant; he managed even to give a deprecatory little smile. "Mr. Robeson, I do not doubt that much of Mr. Hall's rash behavior stemmed from this thickening of the blood; a progressive disease, familiar to medical science, and one which ultimately resulted in his death."

"And what did the red wine do?" I shouted. "Thicken it still further? You know this is all a damnable lie, Dr. Bessels!"

Again Secretary Robeson had to gavel us down. "Gentlemen, gentlemen! Nothing is to be gained by this unseemly conduct!"

When order had been restored, he went on.

"From all the testimony received and noted, it seems to be true that Captain Charles Hall was a single-minded and persistent man who was inclined to distrust all who did not agree with his own goals, and his own way of doing things."

"I do not deny this," I said. "It was this very single-mindedness that brought the *Polaris* to eighty-two degrees and some minutes north—a record, as you all know, and one which redounds to the credit of the Navy Department and the United States Government." Then, not content simply with answering questions, I determined to ask a few of my own. "In previous testimony," I said, "I developed the fact that Captain Hall's personal papers were missing, and never found. I ask Dr. Bessels, and Captain Budington, what they know of the mysterious disappearance of those papers."

Dr. Bessels looked for a fleeting instant at Secretary Robeson.

"I should advise you to answer," the Secretary said.

Dr. Bessels shrugged. "I had seen the mahogany box in his cabin. That is all I know of it."

Secretary Robeson looked at Captain Budington.

"I know nothing of such a box. Perhaps there was one, but it was no concern of mine."

Lies, all lies! What were not lies were half-truths. Yet there seemed to be nothing I could do about it. Charles Hall had made enemies; these same enemies, in my opinion, had caused the failure of the *Polaris* expedition, and then poisoned poor Charles Hall! I clenched my fists but said nothing. What else was there to say?

"This, then," said the Secretary, "must be our report. The late Charles Hall died of natural causes; we have no viable evidence to the contrary—nothing that would stand up in a court of law. I am sorry for you, Mr. Burritt; I know that you acted out of conscience and conviction. But—and do not take this too ill—I think your natural admiration for the man has overshadowed your critical faculties. It is something that happens to us all at times."

My emotions overpowered me. The United States Government had invested fifty thousand dollars in this catastrophe, and it appeared to me they were simply trying to get out of it as gracefully as possible, using poor Charles Hall as a scapegoat.

"Yes," I said soberly, "it is something that happens to all of us—this overshadowing of the critical faculty by other emotions. Today it has happened to this Board. You have condoned murder, gentlemen; I believe that with all my heart and soul. I have stood here amazed as I listened to lies and half-truths misrepresentations of fact and prejudiced testimony. I have even heard the proceedings turned into a kind of an attack on Captain Hall himself."

"We can only report the facts," the Secretary said, some sympathy in his voice. "All else is conjecture, or so it seems to the Board."

"Facts?" I cried. "Then take these down for facts! Charles Hall was a simple and trusting man who believed that others were like himself. If there was ever failure in a man, that was it; a trusting and ingenuous nature. He entered on a long and thankless career to explore the Far North, enduring gibes and disappointment and financial ruin. He starved and suffered, endured privation and hardship without a murmur, trusting always in the God he felt watches over us all. In the end he put his funds, his happiness—indeed, his life—into the scales, and only hoped they would buy the greater glory of the nation, and the advancement of science. Now he is dead, and his memory attacked by little men!"

I looked straight at Dr. Bessels and Captain Budington. Anticipating, Secretary Robeson raised his gavel, but no one spoke.

"I will say no more," I concluded, "except that I mourn him."

I opened the door and went out through the anteroom, out into the gray snow, the desolation that was Washington.

True enough, the report was a whitewash. Dated the 11th of October, 1873, it said in part the following:

> From personal examination of all the witnesses and from their testimony as given, we reach the unanimous conclusion that the death of Captain Hall resulted naturally from disease, without fault on the part of anyone.

Well, that was an end to it. Justice is often misserved, and perhaps the Naval Board of Inquiry could not be blamed too

much. Fact was hard to come by in that welter of criticism, re-
crimination, personal antagonism—the twisted web of human
frailties that caught the *Polaris* expedition and strangled it. At
last, when it was all over and the passions cleared from my own
mind, I could not blame even Captain Budington too much, or
Dr. Bessels. Some destiny greater than any of us had drawn us
all together, stirred the pot, and then laughed at the boiling
and bubbling that went on.

I stayed on at Thibeault's boardinghouse looking for work in
Washington. One night, not being able to get Charles Hall out
of my mind, I went for a walk. The streets were deep in snow,
and the gas lamps painted straggling ghosts on the high-piled
drifts. A damp wind—a Washington wind—blew across my
way, and I thought again of the Arctic. Charles Hall; he was
always there, in my mind. I saw him again the first day I met
him, seasick as a landlubber, leaning over the rail of the old
George Henry. I saw him kind and tender as a woman, nursing
poor Kudlago. I remembered him sailing angrily away in his
little cockleshell of a boat, trying absurdly to make his way to
King William Land, a grotesque picture of an Arctic amateur if
it had not been for his determination.

I remembered, too, the fiasco at Unity Hall, and poor Charles
standing bedraggled in the rain, a piece of rain-melted bunting in his hand, saying to the colored custodian, "I shan't need
the rest of the time." I saw him, in my mind's eye, facing
down Patrick Coleman and his ruffians, driving us on and
on to King William Land, drawing from a never-ending store
of courage and will to keep us going, ever going, pressing
on to the goal. I remembered his great kindness to the Esquimaux, especially Joe and Hannah, and how they called him
"Father Hall" with such a queer mixture of reverence and affection. A last picture sprang into my mind—this powerful, in-
exhaustible man lying mortally ill on the *Polaris*, crying out that
he had been poisoned; I, his friend, unable to help him, or indeed even to avenge him.

All these pictures came into my mind with the clarity of a stereopticon view. Some saddened me, some cheered me, all moved me with great emotion. But suddenly I stood stock-still —I remember it was under the gas lamp at the corner of Seventeenth and F streets—and an idea hit me with the force of a hammer.

I turned and looked north. There was the Pole Star—Polaris itself, hanging in the wintry sky. The Pole was still there, under that beacon light, waiting, beckoning. Charles had not gotten to stand under that magic torch, but perhaps—just perhaps—

I ran back to the boardinghouse. Once in my room, I counted out the money I had left. A little less than a hundred dollars, but call it that, in round figures. Charles had had less than that when he first started on his Arctic career! And I owned the advantage. I had had ten years in the Arctic. I was no tyro! My chest would hardly contain my thumping heart in the grandeur of the vision that was forming in my mind.

At one in the morning old Bill Thibeault knocked on my door, having seen the light under the crack.

"Ain't sick, are you, Mr. Burritt? Noticed your lamp burning."

"No," I said, "I am not sick. I am well—very well, indeed."

He nodded doubtfully, closing the door, and I went back to writing my letter to Mr. Henry Grinnell, Charles Hall's benefactor. It was to be a long letter, and an important one, and would have to be composed very carefully.

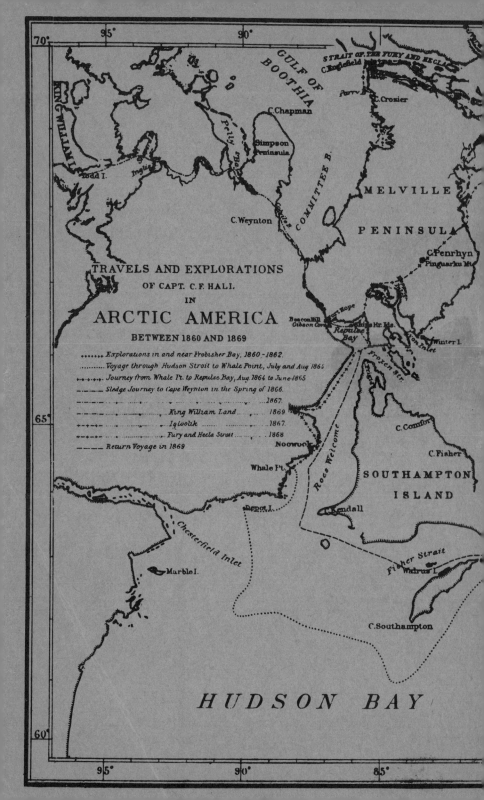

TRAVELS AND EXPLORATIONS

OF CAPT. C. F. HALL.

IN

ARCTIC AMERICA

BETWEEN 1860 AND 1869

...... Explorations in and near Frobisher Bay, 1860-1862.
.... Voyage through Hudson Strait to Whale Point, July and Aug 1864
-·-·-·- Journey from Whale Pt. to Repulse Bay, Aug. 1864 to June 1865
——— Sledge Journey to Cape Weynton in the Spring of 1866.
————————————————— 1867.
——————·——— King William Land 1869
—·—·—·—·— Igloolik 1867
—+—+—+— Fury and Hecla Strait 1868
———— Return Voyage in 1869